WHEN THE CHILDREN FIGHT BACK

Barry Kirwan

ISBN-13: 9798847361644
ISBN-10: 1477123456

Cover design by: Suman Chakraborty
Library of Congress Control Number: 2018675309
Printed in the United States of America

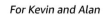

For Kevin and Alan

CONTENTS

BOOKS BY THE AUTHOR

Science Fiction

The Eden Paradox series
The Eden Paradox
Eden's Trial
Eden's Revenge
Eden's Endgame

Children of the Eye
When the Children Come
When the Children Return
When the Children Fight Back

Thrillers (J F Kirwan)

Nadia Laksheva series
66 Metres
37 Hours
88 North

The Dead Tell Lies

PROLOGUE

A rrive early, leave early. The Syrn's axiom for aeons. Macchain Shadiel IV wasn't about to moderate the winning formula for the most successful species in the galaxy. They already dominated an entire galactic spiral with their shock, shatter, subdue approach to colonization, their glorious warships held in fear and awe by dozens of conquered races. They would have spread to other spirals had the Axleth not intervened. But in the longer term, the Axleth turning, bending the mighty Syrn to their will, was nothing more than a setback, a footnote in the Syrn's illustrious history. And it had been a necessary wake-up call. The Eye was executing a scorched-planet business model that would leave the entire galaxy devoid of organic life. Worse, the latest intelligence suggested that the abominable AI had developed a new weapon, a game-changer that would render it invincible.

The Eye had to be stopped.

The Axleth approach of co-opting alien races into this quest was unorthodox but efficient. Yet in the three generations since the Syrn had been re-purposed by the Axleth, he and his brothers and sisters had begun to feel normal again, the genetic manipulation dampening as their own superior genes reasserted themselves. But the message had gotten through – literally to their DNA – and so here they were. And here he was, leading an armada of mega battlecruisers deep into Orion's Gate to obliterate the nemesis of all organic species.

Orion's Gate was a vast nebula, shaped like two boxes attached by a connecting tube, one box deep blue, the other scarlet, the connecting corridor a strident yellow. Gargantuan, even by usual astronomical standards, this nebula was different: it was a star nursery. Newly formed stars unleashed sporadic radiation spikes and tidal siroccos that could fry a vessel and tear it apart. These latest additions to the galaxy were like young Syrn children, oblivious to their raw power. Their tantrums would decimate his fleet if he ventured too close. Even black holes were predictable by comparison. The nebula was, of course, the perfect home to an inorganic species. Few ships had ever returned from this place.

Which begged the question of what *had* happened to the few ships that had dared to venture inside. No wreckage had ever been found. No comms made it through the violent stellar interference. Not even a single info-pod that most ships carried – jettisoned just prior to a ship's destruction – had been recovered. Given such uncertainty, Orion's Gate had become the stuff of legend.

He recalled the interrogation of a captured Ytrill pirate, shortly before the sad specimen's execution. He'd spoken of a ghost-like creature that appeared on their bridge, moments before his ship's demise. Macchain Shadiel IV had already heard the myth of the *Shrike*, a fable that had whispered its way even to the far reaches of the outward spiral hosting the Syrn's unparalleled, jewel-like homeworld. He'd presumed the stories apocryphal, tales told by all organic species to incline their young to listen to their elders, to behave, and to be careful. Yet he'd interrogated the pirate personally, witnessed the deranged fear in his eyes. The man had only escaped certain death because his loyal crew ejected him in a pod just in time. He'd drifted for months before being found. No doubt the isolation and slow starvation had rendered the inevitable hallucinations indistinguishable from actual memory. He would not have been the first. Macchain had almost waived execution. But pirates had killed his nephew decades before, and crimes against the Syrn could never, ever go unpunished.

He watched as translucent waves of turquoise washed past his bridge, and dismissed the Shrike myth. He'd have enough on his plate obliterating the Eye. No point worrying over childish stories.

Macchain's line of sight alighted on the ancient, almost fossilized Axleth pilot in front of him. Unable to move or speak, the sandy brown insectoid navigator knew how to thread a path through the white-hot plasma tornadoes and gravitic riptides. It would grant the Syrn fleet safe passage to the Eye's planetary system, nested just inside the nebula's yellow region. The pilot had initially resisted. The Axleth Masterplan all along had been for the twelve bastardized species to attack in unison in a precision-coordinated strike. But the Syrn had broken free of the Axleth yoke in the nine hundred years since the *culling*, hence the Axleth pilot's head was currently studded with opaque tubes feeding a chemical cocktail into its brain, assuring acquiescence.

The *culling*. The Axleth had arrived in deep orbit around Syrna Prime and affected the minds of all adults. All Syrn children slain. Every last one of them. By their parents, no less. Then the Axleth invaders, re-formed in the Syrn's own image, had mated with a crushed, bereft population to generate a new Syrn-Axleth breed.

Warm, slick venom leached into Macchain's fore-pincers at the mere thought of what had befallen them at the claws of the Axleth. *No forgiveness, no regret* – another Syrn axiom that he had every intention of enacting once this mission was over. Maybe before. His venom continued to pool.

The other eleven species were months away. They would be too late. The party would be over. Instead, they would find a victorious and invincible Syrn armada lying in wait.

Shock, shatter, subdue.

He closed all three eyes and immersed himself into the holo-net. He could see and feel the spearhead of thirty

Syrn planet-breaker warships, backed up by three hundred battlecruisers swarmed by hundreds of support vessels. They sliced through wispy blue gas curtains, his own ship a third of the way from the spearhead. Extending his mind forward via the sensor matrix, he watched from the lead vessel. The hazed starfield shimmered as deepening shades of blue gave way to the first glimmers of yellow.

They were close.

He injected a stim. This final stretch of the voyage could still take some hours. His fleet lengthened to steer a safe path, like a sky-snake writhing towards its prey. As time passed, the initial striking effect of the nebula interior with its raining sapphire sheets and dancing filaments of gold became mundane. He wondered why they'd encountered no resistance. No outposts, no surveillance of any kind. Was their enemy so arrogant, believing its hideout impervious to attack? He concentrated, increasing sensor power to peel away layers of detail in the charged ether around them. But there was no sign of organized electromagnetic activity of any kind.

No signals. No pings. Nothing.

He didn't like it.

He tuned in to the ship at the armada's tail and looked behind. No enemy ships. Nothing sneaking up behind them, or corralling them into some kind of trap. His venom sacs were full to bursting. He needed to lash out at something, the Axleth pilot topping his list. Could it be deceiving them? Leading them into danger, or a wild *Forell* chase, the horned beast he used to hunt with his father back on Syrna Prime? No, even if the pilot knew it was about to be killed, the Axleth desire to destroy the Eye was absolute, non-negotiable. They'd practically gone extinct putting their terrible plan into practice.

'How much longer?' he telegraphed to the pilot, knowing he'd like as not get no response, even with the creature's mind tethered and rendered pliable.

But he got an answer.

'One minute.'

Impossible! Raising the armada's vigilance level to maximum, he scoured the surroundings and stretched his mind along sensor vectors in all directions, a sphere stretching outwards, illuminating nothing but gases and space-dust.

Wait... There *was* something... A planet. Dark. Inert.

He slowed the armada, slamming on the brakes at the front while letting the mid-section fan outwards, keeping one-fifth at the rear, out of harm's way. The planet's readings were... strange. Gravity was fluctuating in the region. One of his generals queried him: *black hole?* But there was no event horizon. A message arrived from the scientific cohort: *black star.*

Was it possible? In theory, he knew it was. But no ship had ever encountered one. Yet it fit. A giant planetary mass collapsing in on itself, but the rate of collapse slowed... He flinched. The planet wasn't dark. It was simply that gravitational forces prevented most light from escaping the planet's surface.

For the first time, he felt a stab of regret that he had not waited for the other eleven species. Because if this was indeed a black star, and if, as he intuited, it had somehow been manufactured and was being controlled by the Eye, then he and the Syrn were in new battle territory, out of their depth.

He vid-called his ten generals. Each of their bold, battle-hardened faces arose in the ether before him.

'Callaris, you are the closest. Tell me what you see.'

But no sooner had the general opened his mouth than his face tumbled out of the frame, replaced by flames. His image vanished.

Macchain stood. 'What just happened?' he bellowed. Without waiting for an answer, he walked forward through the remaining nine holos, swiping through them as if they were cobwebs, and stood close to the viewscreen. With a twisting motion of his foreclaw, he zoomed in to see Callaris' mighty battlecruiser spiralling like a child's toy towards the black star. It wasn't alone. His entire vanguard – including two more of his generals – was being sucked in to the same fate, fifty ships sparking with short-lived fires snuffed out by hard vacuum, their hulls crushed as the ships and all their crews plunged to their doom.

He spun around, faced the seven remaining images, seeing fear and horror in men who'd never known such emotions.

'Retreat!' he shouted.

They tried.

Voice comms failed. Macchain returned to his chair and watched, his generals desperate to tell him what was happening and how they were trying to save their ships, before each image winked out. In one last vain attempt, he reached out to the ships at the rear, so they could escape. But he could no longer hear, see, or feel them. In fact, he no longer had contact with any ship in his entire armada. The holo-net had collapsed. He switched to a back-up multi-screen and witnessed his mighty armada disperse; at least they made a valiant attempt to do so. All frontline ships were already tumbling towards the black star, caught in its gravity well, which had ramped up a hundredfold. Not natural then, this black star, or more correctly, black planet. The Eye had plundered advanced scientific theory and butchered it to create a savage new weapon.

The planet reeled them in. Warships at the rear were attacked by blinding white-spiked Eyeships with shards that chopped through shields and super-dense ablative hulls as if they were paper. Where had they come from? It hardly mattered now. They were here. His helm no longer responded to his command. Aghast, he watched his entire armada, a thousand ships strong, dismantled, dissected, destroyed.

Macchain felt sick.

Four minutes. That was all it took. The might of the Syrn Empire's largest ever military force reduced to debris and corpses drifting in space, falling towards the Eye's homeworld.

Not a single ship had escaped. No one would even know

what had happened here today, and the other eleven species would remain unaware of this new weapon. The Axleth pilot had cautioned him countless times that it would take all twelve species to defeat the Eye.

He prayed it was wrong.

Only his ship remained intact. He waited. He'd already guessed what was coming.

The Shrike materialized on the bridge, almost within pincer-reach. A glistening silver being, with two legs, two arms leading to hands and long fingers ending in needle-like points. A sharp-ridged exo-spine ran all the way from its pyramid-shaped head to its thorny tail. No obvious orifices except a circular, lipless mouth and two bright holes for eyes. The stuff of nightmares.

No wonder the pirate captain had lost his mind.

Macchain Shadiel IV presumed it had saved him till last. He was the commander-in-chief. To what end, though? To exact surrender? No point. To crow over how easy it had been to defeat them? Not the Eye's style, he imagined. And how would it know *he* was the leader? The Shrike, which he assumed was an avatar, a physical presence representing the Eye, faced him, then turned towards the other bridge occupant.

Of course. Macchain was not the item of interest on board. The Shrike had come for the Axleth pilot.

Not on his watch.

Without hesitation, Macchain leapt towards the prone Axleth pilot, his left pincer poised high. The Shrike whirled, slicing off Macchain's entire left arm. But his momentum carried him forward, and the ship's gravity did the rest. He landed just short of the pilot and thrust his right pincer deep into its neck, unloading his venom.

Something colder than ice punched through Macchain's heart. His body stilled. He watched his reflection in the Axleth's myriad shiny black eyes, allowing himself a thin smile, as he and the Axleth pilot parted this life for oblivion.

PART ONE

WORMHOLE

CHAPTER 1

Awakening

Sally couldn't sleep. Not surprising, really. She stared at the blank ceiling, listening hard to pick up the distant thrum of the behemoth ship's engines, hundreds of levels below.

'You awake?' she whispered.

'No,' Michael replied, then turned over. 'Can I be big spoon for once?'

'You were last time,' she answered, but manoeuvred under his arm just the same.

'That was forty years ago.'

'You counting?' she asked.

'Someone has to. Happy birthday, by the way.'

'Never thought I'd make it past four hundred.'

'You're thirty-seven, Sal. Including stasis time is cheating.'

She inhaled his scent, nuzzled closer. 'You *are* counting.'

They stayed awhile, calm and close. Then he left, saying he had somewhere to be, and she showered, ate a nondescript soya muffin with a single candle stuck into it, and glugged down half a mug of disgusting coffee substitute. She headed up to the observation deck, which was where most others were going; those who weren't in deep sleep, which was 98 per cent of the crew.

That hadn't been in the brochure, she was sure of it, that most of the time *everyone* would be in stasis, a skeleton crew running the few ship functions that didn't run themselves, or just checking that everything was *still* okay.

She didn't rush; it wasn't recommended. Her limbs and muscle-memory needed to get reacquainted first. She needed time to think, to clear her head. She'd only been 'awake' a few days, and the post-stasis mind-fog and low-level nausea hadn't completely evaporated. *Four hundred years.* She almost had to pinch herself. The trip had been largely uneventful. They were still several months behind the other six ships in the Axel fleet, all of which had already passed through the wormhole, whose exit was a mere month's striking distance from the Eye's homeworld deep inside Orion's Gate.

Axels: human descendants born of a joining between a mutated Axleth and a human parent. They looked and acted like humans – a little colder, more *serious*, if that was the right word. Michael had reminded her a zillion times they were 99.9 per cent human, and she'd had few problems with any of them. They were humanity's future. And the Axel doctors themselves had pointed out that within a few generations, the genetic tampering inflicted by the Axleth to bring out the humans' *fight*, making them ready for the battle with the Eye – and making them more subservient to Axleth orders into the bargain – would diminish.

She hoped so. Sally got on okay with them, but had no Axel friends.

She brushed this all aside. She'd led a war against the Axleth, but the Eye was a bigger threat. And finally, after four centuries of travel, and after a total of seventeen conscious 'awake' years for her, it was almost time. She didn't need any genetic tampering to elevate *her* fight.

She recalled the trip so far. Two close calls with unanticipated comets, and a flyby near a black hole were the only postcards worth sending home. *Home.* Everyone she knew back on Earth – Nathan, Lara, Raphaela, all the rest – long dead by now. So many things she should have said to Lara, her erstwhile adopted mother, but somehow couldn't. At least with Nathan the parting had been as okay as never seeing someone close again could be. For that, she was grateful, given that they'd drifted apart for the last five years of their trip on the *Athena*. Michael said her relationship with Nathan had been like a comet, whose elliptical orbit had brought them back in sync just in time.

She blended in amongst others funnelling in the same direction, all hoping to gain a first glimpse of the wormhole from the observation deck, relishing the anonymity. She'd been president, briefly, but was now just Sally, not even leader of the hundred humans who'd hitched a ride. It was good to be just 'Sally'.

Ignoring the elevators, she took the long, curving ramp that ran around this level of their titanic bullet-shaped ark-cum-warship. Only a vertical quarter of a mile to the observation deck. This helical route took a lot longer, of course, so was deserted. Almost.

'Hello, Mom. Happy birthday!' Elodie said, catching her at the midpoint. She threw her arms around Sally.

Sally reciprocated as best she could. For some reason she couldn't fathom, she felt the same unease she'd had in her quasi-mother-daughter relationship with Lara. It didn't help that due to the way they organized stasis slots on the ship, she'd missed vast chunks of Elodie's childhood, of her growing up, much of which had happened in crèches and schools run by other adults awake at the time. It was the same for Elodie, of course; her personal experience of having a mother had been fragmentary. Yet that seemed to have affected Elodie less than her mother.

Michael, wise as ever, had counselled Sally never to fake emotions with their daughter, simply to be herself, and to be there for her. Thankfully, Elodie never seemed to mind, and had enough friends her own age, and, of course, a lot of responsibility, given that she had taken on her mother's mantle as de facto leader of the human contingent.

Elodie had close-cropped dark hair, the body of an athlete inside her black one-suit, and an unruffled, easy-going authority. She looked the part, and was every bit the leader they needed. She held out two closed fists towards her mother, a smile lighting up her twenty-year-old face. Funny, Elodie was the same age Sally had been when she'd boarded this ship, and gotten pregnant in the first six months of the voyage. They should have had twenty years together. In total, it had been more like five shared years.

Time on an interstellar voyage was a bitch.

'Choose,' Elodie said, grinning.

Sally felt her own facial muscles tighten, which was ridiculous. It was just a birthday present, probably some little bauble Elodie had picked up somewhere at one of the annual craft-days. Sally had never attended them. This was a warship, after all. Michael had quipped that occasionally people needed reminding of what they were fighting for. Maybe he was right. She tapped Elodie's left fist, which upturned and opened with a flourish. Sally stared at the small glistening object as if it was a poisonous spider. A platinum chip sprouting whiskers.

'Take it, Mom,' Elodie said. 'Medicine for your silver friend.'

Michael joined them. 'It took Abel five years straight, Sal. He's confident it'll do the trick.'

Sally stared at it. Her throat was dry. She'd had her hopes raised and dashed before.

She stalled. 'Five years in one stretch? That doesn't just break stasis regs, it tramples all over them.'

Neither of them spoke. She was cornered. She reached for it, gingerly. 'Did he test it?' she asked. A stupid question, given it was Abel who'd manufactured it. He treated engineering like it was a religion.

'As much as anyone could,' Michael answered. 'Countless simulations. You have to be the one to plug it in, though.'

Michael draped an arm around their daughter, who leaned into him. Sally envied their closeness.

'Thank you,' she said, a little stiffly, then bent forward and gave Elodie a peck on the cheek.

'Steady, Mom,' Elodie joked, 'You'll have me thinking it's *my* birthday. Now, let's go. First the wormhole, then Ares2. Oh, you'll need this,' she said, opening the other fist to reveal a small platinum tool not much bigger than a toothpick. Sally took it.

Elodie and Michael took off, then stopped and looked back. Sally hadn't budged.

'Told you,' Michael said to his pride and joy.

'Go, Mom,' Elodie said. 'We'll save you a seat. You have time. The wormhole's not going anywhere.'

Sally didn't notice them leave. She took the elevator and descended thirty levels deeper into the ship to the lab. An Axel armed with a pistol stood guard outside. His eyes narrowed at first, then relaxed as he recognized her. Few ventured here. She peered into a retinal scan device. A steel door slid open.

She stepped through, saw Ares2 sitting there, and immediately felt a pang. In fact two. First up was for her former mentor and guardian, the original Ares, who'd been lost in the battle for Earth, leaving behind a copy, Ares2, who was but a pale shadow of his former self. Second was on account of guilt, for her daughter, who'd be undone if she knew the emotions coursing through Sally's veins for this... machine. The door closed behind her. She felt safe again.

'Hello, Sally,' Ares2 said, in a flat metallic voice that was so *not* Ares. His platinum face and shiny bald pate were like the original Ares; concave depressions where eyes would normally be, a small nose, and a lipless mouth. 'It has been three hundred and forty-two days since–'

'Maintenance mode,' she instructed.

Ares2 stilled. She scouted around at the back of his neck. There was no obvious join in his platinum flow-metal skin, but at the touch of the toothpick-like tool, a gap widened like a small mouth on his skin. Ultra-dense complex alien circuitry glimmered inside. Many of the Axels wanted to cut Ares2 open for study, to understand him and make more like him. But Sally had repeatedly stated that would have to be over her corpse. She'd gone further, instructing Ares2 to defend himself while she was in stasis. The guard outside was mostly to prevent people getting *in*, not Ares2 getting out. Besides, Ares2 was Xaxoan tech; no one had a clue how it worked. Except Abel, and he would also defend Ares2 to the death.

Abel. The only other person besides her, Michael and Elodie, allowed access. Abel was one of the 'auged' humans. During their round trip after escaping Earth the first time, Ares had developed augmented biotech to upgrade certain human cognitive and physical functions, interconnecting the 'auged' individuals with each other, and with him. That latter connection had been severed in the battle against the Eye to save Earth.

Abel and the other augs missed Ares terribly, though they rarely spoke of it. They couldn't help it. Ares had been practically hard-wired into them. No wonder Abel had worked his ass off. She knew he'd been trying for decades. At first she'd been involved in the attempts, following them as best she could. But the relentless failures had taken their toll on her. Ares had been her mentor throughout her teens. There had been a closeness... But she'd considered him gone for a long time now, and Abel's increasingly desperate and wild theories had never matured into something practical.

Until now.

Elodie, though she wasn't auged herself, must have sanctioned the project, secured agreement and special dispensation from the Axel leadership.

Thank you, daughter.

Taking a deep breath, Sally focused on the task. She wasn't sure how to insert the reprogrammed tech. The augs originally linked to Ares had been analyzing Ares2 for years, trying to reverse engineer certain mental pathways, cognitive clusters, and – for want of a more scientifically nuanced word – memories. *Memory and history are not the same thing*, Ares himself had once told her in her adolescence, though he'd never elaborated. The idea was to reboot him, not from the factory issue he was now, but as he had been when he'd saved all Axels and humans alike by taking out the Eyeship attacking Earth and sacrificing himself in the process.

She pressed the piece of tech into a slot inside the gaping wound, which snapped shut with such speed it nearly pinched her fingers. Ares2 shot to his feet, knocking Sally backwards. She staggered a couple of paces and regained her balance. Ares2 stood tense. His fingers clawed the air, as if fighting something or someone only he could see, and then he walked towards the solid steel door. Without warning, his arms lifted high above him and his metal fists hammered against the barrier repeatedly, denting it, sending ear-crushing booms around the lab, noise that would not go unnoticed on adjacent decks.

Sally watched helplessly. This wasn't helping, but there was no way to stop him. He was too powerful. It continued for ten minutes.

Had Abel's work gone awry? Did Ares2 even register her presence? Would he kill her if he did? She glanced at the small handheld device on the other side of the lab, the one that would trigger immediate shutdown.

Ares2 was between her and the device.

The pounding ceased. The guard outside would have summoned reinforcements by now, tooled up with serious ordnance.

'Ares,' she said, knowing it was a risk. But she'd come here to save him, not engender his demise.

Ares2 turned his head a fraction, still facing the door. 'Sally,' he said.

Not flat. Not mechanical.

She took a step closer.

'They killed her,' Ares said, his voice unsure, more

human than she'd ever heard.

Killed her? Killed who? And then it struck her, and she shared the pain as well, as if it had been yesterday, when Jennifer had died. Ares had been connected to her via her aug implant. He'd known death for the first time.

Sally should have guessed. Abel had needed something to jolt Ares2, and so he'd used the most intense experience Ares had ever had, the closest he'd ever come to feeling an actual emotion. Funny, all Abel's prior attempts had been technological, because Ares was a machine. And now the approach that had finally worked was, at its core, so human.

Sally took another step. 'I miss her too.'

He turned. His eyes had reappeared, taking their rightful place on his face, in place of the usual concave troughs that Ares2 had worn. Sally witnessed something approaching sadness in those eyes.

'You are still alive?' he said. 'I remember now, but... It is as if my mind was small, seeing everything from afar, through a long tunnel, unable to think, to process, to... react. Four hundred years, Sally...' He punched the door one last time.

The door slid back. A dozen guards stood in two ranks, the front with shoulder-mounted cannons.

'It's okay!' she shouted to them. 'He's back. He's on our side. Remember, he's the one who saved you all!'

None of them looked convinced.

Sally heard running footfalls, sprinting, and shouting.

Not guards.

Augs.

Abel was at their head. They dodged around the Axels. Within seconds, a dozen augs surrounded Ares. A human shield. The guards yelled at them to stand aside. It wasn't until a high-ranking Axel arrived that they stood down, though several kept their fingers on the cannon triggers. The Axel lieutenant was talking on her comm, probably to the commander on the bridge, who would want to know of this development, because if Ares was really back they had another weapon with which to combat the Eye.

The human augs were an emotional mess, but she singled out one, and tapped him on the shoulder.

'You're a genius, Abel. I owe you, big time!'

'I know this means a lot to you, Sally, but trust me, for us augs, it means more.'

She didn't contradict him, didn't want to detract from the augs' profound joy that Ares was back. But in her heart she knew Abel was wrong.

This meant *everything* to her.

At the far end of the corridor, Elodie and Michael arrived. Sally stood apart from the crowd, facing her daughter, and placed her two palms over her heart. She mouthed *thank you*, as a single tear slid down her cheek.

CHAPTER 2

Dreadnought

Sally gripped the cool metal rail and gazed down the vertiginous central well of the bottom half of the Dreadnought, their Axel mega-warship. The name was fitting: dread nothing. Axels had less fear than original, unadulterated humans. Elodie, when five years old, upon seeing an external view of the ship that was her home, had said it was a silver bullet. Michael had laughed – to Elodie's joy – hoisting her in his arms, saying, 'I certainly hope so!'

Sally had prayed ever since that their daughter was right. If the *Dreadnought* was a bullet, the Axels and human crew were the gunpowder. A silver bullet to shoot the Eye dead. In under a month, they would join the other species and enter the nebula known as Orion's Gate, and attack the Eye's stronghold. Then they would see...

She focused. The circular well plunged half-a-mile straight down, a sheer vertical cylinder marked by alternate blue habitation and red stasis rings, two hundred of each, a splash of purple three quarters of the way down. The *Dreadnought* was a warship, but also a hybrid generational and sleeper ship. She'd opted for – and been lucky enough – to have slept most of the four-hundred-year journey. She'd elected for seventeen years of 'awake-time': four hundred years mostly asleep interspersed into eight planned and two unplanned 'awake' stages, the former with Michael to see their daughter Elodie grow up as far as they could, the latter due to her being on call for the two unscheduled crises during the otherwise uneventful voyage.

The first crisis had been the most dangerous – a ship-wide stasis failure near the end of the first century of travel. It had woken up everyone, all eight hundred and twelve thousand of them – of which all were Axels bar a hundred humans – at the same time. One of the four power generators deep in the bowels of the ship had suffered catastrophic failure. That put immediate stress on resources, and threatened the long-term viability of the mission, because no stops were planned en route to gather more materials to execute repairs, or to gather more food. Besides, given that space was largely empty, and that four hundred years of travel was still just one small step in galactic terms, there were no suitable planets in the 'Goldilocks zone' – hospitable to humans – en route, or asteroid belts to mine on the way. Re-routing and repairs on the scale required would have added ten years to their schedule. They'd have missed the battle at Orion's Gate.

It took months to engineer a fix. She recalled how vibrant and animated the ship had become during that time. And how crowded. Her grip on the rail tightened. When they all went back to sleep, the Axel mission controller made a startling and brutal decision. Resources had indeed been significantly compromised. Four thousand Axels who had returned to stasis were... switched off. It was that or jeopardize the mission.

Sally and several others of the human contingent railed against that decision when they found out, fifty years later, after their next big sleep cycle ended. Surely there could have been another solution? But the new mission controller wasn't receptive to their complaints, in part because her husband, the former mission controller, had elected to be one of those culled. The Axel command would not divulge the selection criteria either, saying it was an Axel-only matter. No humans had been selected.

She strained her eyes to see the bottom of the well. Four thousand ceramic pots – each one commemorative rather than containing actual ashes – lay there. As the *Dreadnought* neared the wormhole and Orion's Gate on the other side, she'd come to pay her respects; their sacrifice was every bit as important as those who would die in the forthcoming battle. She closed her eyes in silent prayer.

The second crisis, a century ago, had been more complex, and related to the generational contingent aboard the *Dreadnought*. Most crew – none considered themselves 'passengers', as all had a mission – opted for sleeper mode in stasis units. That meant gaining ten to twenty-five more years of physical aging during the four-hundred-year journey. You couldn't stay in stasis for more than fifty years at a stretch, and you needed to be awake for at least a year before going back to sleep, depending on how long the prior stasis period had been. Otherwise, incurable psychosis set in after five sleep cycles. Some stayed awake longer, according to their skill sets and the needs of the ship. Their awake 'shift' might be two or three years. Those who'd been infants at the time of departure from Earth – like Elodie – were left to age to at least twenty, to be ready for the upcoming war. The older contingent of Axels had reduced shift cycles. Michael called it 'demographic compression'. Sally had once seen the constantly updated shift cycle, a masterpiece of logistics to keep the ship going, train the young, and have a battle-force prepped and ready upon arrival at Orion's Gate.

However, heeding the wisdom of not placing all your eggs in one basket, there had been a tiny cross-section – less than 1 per cent of the Axel crew – who never entered stasis. They had children, raised them, grew old and died. Waves of successive generations followed, the number of children carefully allotted so as not to expand beyond a certain threshold.

Despite the Axels' cool temperament, or maybe because humanity's original genes gradually reasserted themselves in each generation, conflicts had arisen. It was only natural that these descendants had less and less memory of why they were on this interminable voyage, locked in a vast metal tube where they and their children's children would live and die. By the fifteenth generation, a rebellion broke out. For the first time in the Axels' brief history, Axels killed other Axels in the ensuing struggle. They almost lost the ship to the 'generationists', who would have headed off to find the nearest habitable planet. The Axel commander woke Sally up. Both sides considered her a neutral third party and asked her to broker a peace deal after seventy-three had lost their lives. The generationists were hopelessly outnumbered. They'd gained ground via surprise and stealth, but their gambit had failed, and they were at the mercy of the rest.

She stared down to the band of purple, where the generationists now lived in isolation. She'd offered stasis to them, or their children. None had accepted. One of the Axel commanders wanted to gas them, knock them out, force them into stasis. Sally won the day by arguing that the two-pronged strategy wasn't flawed; this was, with hindsight, a not-unexpected uprising. They just had to manage the situation better, or in this case, with a firmer hand. She recalled how her daughter Elodie, a teenager at the time, had watched her mother as if seeing her differently for the first time.

Now that she thought about it, Sally wondered why none of the generationists had been 'culled' during the first crisis. Despite their isolationism, and the occasional conflictual flare-ups, it was as if the other Axels held them in high regard. A rumour had circulated that the generationists had even developed a cult based around the Axleth, but that made no sense. Perhaps the Axels saw the generationists as their future. Maybe one day she'd knock on their door, see if they'd let her in. They had lush gardens in their enclosure. That alone would make it worth the trip. But alas, they were out of bounds for everyone except the highest-ranking Axel officers. No exceptions, for some unexplained reason.

After that unpleasant and traumatic episode, for the first time on the trip, Sally had welcomed her sticky, liquid gel-filled stasis chamber, and hadn't had that momentary pique of fear that she might never wake up.

Her head bowed a moment. She felt a pit inside her belly. So much death, so much tragedy. Most of her existence had been spent running for her life, fighting for her life, or preparing for battle. She longed for this endless war to be over. She thought of Nathan, long dead now. The very thought of him stopped her from tipping over into her personal chasm of despair. He'd saved her in so many ways.

No one knew, because the burial ground below was off-limits, but she and Michael had nested three more ceramic pots down there, for Nathan, Lara, and Raphaela. They'd had a private ritual when Elodie had been just ten years old. The same age as Sally when the Axleth had invaded Earth. Sally had said to her young daughter, 'Never forget those who died so that we could live.' A pretty heavy burden to lay on a ten-year-old, but that's how it was.

Like it or not, they were all soldiers now.

Ares pinged her via her wristcom. *Come now. I'm in the prow.*

It was good to hear from him. He'd been 'resurrected' less than a day, and she hadn't seen him all morning.

She pushed back from the railing and took the central elevator shaft that rose all the way to the highest point on the *Dreadnought*. The glass cocoon rose silently, passing five canteen levels, only two of which were operational at any one time, six levels of classrooms that catered for all educational needs from pre-school, to soldier, to pilot battle training simulators, and the single war council level with its smoked-glass windows. Next was the auditorium, a sweeping arena of concentric rows of seats. It couldn't hold everyone, of course, but they used it for major announcements and the bi-monthly sparring matches.

Sally's fingers curled of their own accord, recalling her time on the *Athena* and the almost daily training bouts of hand-to-hand combat. Less necessary this time around, given they'd be fighting an artificial enemy whose military tactics were on a far grander scale than fists or bayonets. In wars on Earth, Nathan had reminded her a lifetime ago, it usually came down to infantry: fighting where you stared your enemy in the eye and knew it was him or you, kill or be killed. Every soldier's perpetual nightmare-become-normality.

No more. This war would be about intelligence, ingenuity and agility in the thick of battle. And they had yet to meet the other eleven species assembling from different regions in the galaxy at Orion's Gate. She could only wonder what technology, weapons and skill-sets they would each bring to the war effort against the Eye. Yet Sally and everyone else were in the dark about their future brothers and sisters in arms. There were names and scant information, bequeathed by the Axleth and guarded by Axel historians. All the data focused on their capabilities, describing them as mission assets. Nothing about these species' values, their culture, who they really *were*. That was because the Axleth, God damn them, registered zero on the empathy scale.

Sally and a number of others hoped they might find true and lasting friends amongst the *Eleven*, as they were inevitably dubbed, rather than just temporary allies who would go their separate ways afterwards, or worse, turn on each other. That latter possibility had been granted precious little discussion time during war council meetings. *Same old, same old*, Nathan would have said. Generals only consider *winning,* and thinking stops there. They never consider the exit strategy, or post-war, assuming peace would happen naturally, and was someone else's problem.

We're not that good at learning.

The elevator doors opened at the last stop, the uppermost habitable point in the *Dreadnought*, a small observation area. Ares stood, platinum grey, looking distinctly human without the cloak and hood he'd 'worn' the first time she'd met him. He faced the oval portal showing the starfield ahead of them.

'Hello, Sally,' he said, without turning around.

She should have guessed he'd be here. Ares was *persona non grata* on the bridge. Then again, he – she could never call him an 'it' – was an AI, and his sensors went way beyond vision; he could have tapped into data-highways from his lab and garnered more information.

'I rather miss those times on *Athena* when you and I sat in the prow discussing battle tactics.'

'Me too,' she said, without really thinking. An old habit. She'd grown up with Ares, and never checked herself when talking to him.

She sat down on a small stool in the conical chamber that wasn't big enough to swing a rodent, let alone a cat. Not that there was one, or any other animals aboard. The entire ship was vegetarian, hydroponic gardens occupying a dozen levels.

'Can you see the wormhole yet?' she asked.

'Yes,' he said.

She peered outwards. It was still little more than a glistening blur the size of a small coin.

Ares' head turned to face her, his platinum eyes sharp and detailed, at the same time serene and penetrating. 'If only you were *auged*, Sally,' he said, the hint of a smile that caused splintering lines to appear at the edges of lips and eyes. His increased attention to human detail since his awakening was breathtaking. Even his eyebrows – since when had he had eyebrows, by the way? – were not just fine silver hairs of equal, sculpted length; a few curved randomly. So human...

'You've changed your look,' she said.

The smile faded. 'I need the Axels to trust me, if we are to win this.' He reached out and touched her shoulder. She didn't flinch, as she knew many others would have done. 'But I am not human, nor Axel, Sally. I am closer in nature to the enemy we seek to destroy. Never forget that.'

He faced forward again.

She digested what he'd just said, or rather, parked it for another time. Hopefully, never. After all, she'd only just got him back.

'Show me,' she said.

He reached forward and touched the portal, not glass but a highly sophisticated screen that gave a surreally realistic sense of depth. The scene rushed forward at her, causing her to gasp. Instinctively she leaned forward as well, as if she was Alice, about to topple through the looking-glass.

A sphere, a marble floating in the naked darkness. She couldn't help but think of it as a marauder, an anomaly that, although permissible by nature's laws, somehow violated them. Because it was not natural, that much she already knew.

But it was mesmerizing. She knew the *Dreadnought*, though decelerating, was still travelling at high speed, and as they approached at an oblique angle, an elliptical intercept in fact, the sphere appeared to rotate. As it did so, the distorted images inside its blinding white boundary moved, in the opposite direction to the ship's forward movement. She knew the patches of light and splashes of colour were the spatially-lensed view from the other side of the wormhole, almost two thousand light years distant. There wasn't as much distortion around the sphere as she'd expected, from the few classes on spatial phenomena she'd attended before the maths became too unfathomable. Some stars appeared to be moving in the opposite direction to the distortions inside the sphere.

Like shooting stars.

Ares was watching her. She knew he could see in far greater detail than a human, and could predict with great accuracy where she was looking. He could also read faces pretty well. Especially hers.

'The lensing is not so strong outside the wormhole's mouth, because its mass is low.'

She stared at the sphere's interior again, trying to make anything out, though she knew there was little point. Like everyone else – including Ares – she'd just have to wait and see.

She sat back. 'Is it safe?'

'More or less,' he said.

She couldn't suppress a smile. This was so much like the old Ares. In the early days, he'd been ultra-precise. But he'd learned the hard way that people rarely appreciated absolute accuracy.

'What's more, what's less?' she asked. Not the first time they'd played this game.

'The mouth and the throat are sufficiently large to accommodate our vessel, and there is no evidence of wreckage. The tidal forces appear to be tolerable. Whoever or whatever built this wormhole knew what they were doing.'

'The less?'

Ares' face tightened. 'I saw something,' he said. 'Twelve minutes ago. I called you straightaway. I would have called the bridge, but I do not think they will listen to me.'

She stared at him. 'What did you see?'

His face turned to her, the eyes no longer serene, but haunted.

'It was just there for a fraction of a second, at the limits of my sensory capabilities. I have been watching to see if it returns to the field of view.'

'What did you see, Ares?'

He didn't answer with words. Instead, he held up his palm, facing her, and upon it an image slowly etched itself into existence, then vanished.

Sally stared at the blank palm, then towards the sphere. She stood up and walked to the elevator.

'You're in touch with the augs on the bridge, aren't you?'

'Yes,' he replied.

'Have they seen this?'

He shook his head.

◆ ◆ ◆

Sally paced in the small elevator, oblivious to its movement until the doors opened. She strode onto the bridge, ignored various salutations, and walked straight over to Michael and Elodie. She guided them to a workstation away from prying eyes and ears. Her husband and daughter regarded her inquisitively.

Taking Elodie's tablet, she played with it a moment and then showed them.

'Ares saw this in the wormhole, just for a fraction of a second. Most likely it's at the other side of the wormhole rather than inside it.'

Their two faces mimicked Ares' haunted expression minutes earlier, except theirs paled into the bargain.

She looked again at the image she'd created.

A silver bullet, broken in two.

CHAPTER 3

Outside

Commander Stein looked every inch the man capable of leading the Dreadnought through the wormhole and onwards into battle. Average height but always seeming taller, he stood, feet splayed, in his all-black seamless uniform with a single diagonal orange stripe from left shoulder to right hip, signifying him as the top of the Axel command food chain. Surrounding him was a three-sixty-degree holo-field studded with stars, dripping with translucent figures that shifted and updated in real-time. He wore a thin silver headband that arced over his bald head, a grey earpiece in his left ear. But it was his left eye with its rotating golden iris implant that caught and demanded anyone's attention when facing him. It allowed him to zoom in and out at will, anywhere in the star-field, or to interrogate the patches of figures simply by focusing. His long fingers dabbled in the holo-ether, allowing him to interact with star systems, or, as he was doing now, with the glistening wormhole that appeared to rotate in the palm of his right hand.

'He's a mean poker player, too,' Michael said, noticing Sally's gaze. 'Go show him your hand.'

'Yeah, go Mom,' Elodie added with a wry smile, her hand on her dad's shoulder.

Sally surveyed the bridge, a walled-off enclosure the size of four basketball courts, shield emitters dotted around its circumference. It would probably be the last place to be destroyed in a battle. *Always protect the head*, Fisher had told her years earlier back on the *Athena*. She walked from the perimeter, past various workstations, single or multi-crewed islands dotted around the central commander's hub. She passed a station manned by Abel and Sasha, the only two human augs on the bridge. Abel looked up, his platinum aug eyebrow glinting in the overhead light, but only briefly to give her a nod of acknowledgement.

Sasha, a diminutive, unassuming woman with flaxen hair bound in a ponytail, could wipe the floor with most people in training combat sessions. She held the respect of many Axels as she was ultra-professional and said little. Right now, she was entranced in aug communication; eyes half-closed, body stiff, as if paralyzed. As Sally's gaze swept further, she realized everyone on the bridge was focused. No one else gave her a second look until she reached the inner ring.

'He's busy,' Anya said without raising her gaze from a screen reflecting red and blue lines onto her face. Anya was Stein's Number One, the gatekeeper for the invisible threshold between her workstation and Stein's. Nobody crossed it without her permission. Not even Sally.

'Any word?' Sally said, pausing in front of Anya's console.

Anya's brow rose slowly, as if out of immersion in another world. Which wasn't far off. She was using some kind of quantum tunnelling tech to try to reach anyone from the other side of the wormhole, namely someone from one of the other six Axel mega-ships. Abel had simply said *good luck with that.*

Anya's face held the answer, which she didn't bother to verbalize.

'What do you want?'

Sally showed her the image.

Anya's face froze. Not even a flicker of emotion,

given what the image could represent. Abel said that the Axleth meddling with the Axels' biology at the chromosome level had enhanced their *sangfroid*. No kidding. It made them consummate soldiers, that was for sure, but lousy at conversation, and as for humour...

Anya flicked a few fingers behind her, inviting Sally to cross the threshold to Stein's lair.

She did so, but Stein was clearly busy, murmuring into his microphone boom while Sally waited. She couldn't follow the words. Axels had developed a very rapid, clipped speech form for battle, a combination of single-syllable words, sounds and clicks. She didn't know it, though the augs did. Abel had told her it was 50 per cent more efficient than the usual mil-speak, though it wasn't as quick as aug-connectivity, which was instantaneous. She recalled Stein had been fascinated by aug tech. Not surprising, given his eye.

An elite Axel division *had* been auged, that much she knew, around 300 of them. The only one who knew how to aug safely was Ares, who'd been out of commission almost the entire trip. However, an auged human had suffered an accident during a training bout, decades earlier, and his external eyebrow unit had been damaged. Abel had just gone into deep sleep, so the Axel scientists worked on it and fixed it, reverse engineering whatever they could figure out. It had taken quite a few goes to get it right, and there had been casualties – not everyone took to auging, apparently. But eventually it had worked, though they remained networked to each other, and not to the human augs. Sally hadn't seen or met any of them, though Elodie, late one evening, had stumbled across a squadron of auged Axels training in secret. She'd said it had been pretty impressive. Presumably most were still in stasis. She hoped they'd fare as well in the upcoming battle as the human augs had back in the struggle to free Earth.

Thirty seconds slid past. She held the tablet up in front of him. He said something inaudible, then flicked the microphone boom up, away from his lips.

'You saw this?' he asked.

'Ares saw it.'

There was a pause. The Axels didn't trust Ares. They'd had hatred of AIs bred into them, given that the Eye, their sworn mortal enemy, was basically the AI motherlode.

'Did Ares propose a course of action?'

She recalled that Axels never assigned Ares a pronoun. At least they had the courtesy to avoid calling him 'it'. He hadn't suggested a course of action, and Sally had had no time to think of one either.

'Call a War Council meeting,' she said. 'We can–'

'We're weeks behind our schedule to rendezvous with the other ships. We're late.'

'No contact,' she countered. The intel Anya had just given her. They'd expected *something* to be sent back by the fleet from the other side of the wormhole. A message, such as *safe and sound*. Anything, really, would have been better than nothing at all.

'Point,' he said.

Sally realized there and then that during this trip she'd gradually relinquished her leadership. Why? She'd seen a lot of death on her watch during the attack to reclaim Earth. Lost people she cared about. She'd watched millions of others she didn't know slaughtered by the Eyeship and those damned, deadly shards. The nightmares, the cold sweats, had mostly passed. Mostly. Thank God you didn't dream in stasis. Half the crew on this behemoth had PTSD. She needed to reinsert herself into the decision-making chain.

She recalled Nathan having authority and responsibility thrust upon him by Colonel Matheson back on Earth. What had the colonel said? 'It's precisely because you don't want it that you're getting it.' Something like that. An idea stirred.

Stein raised the boom. Conversation over.

Not quite.

'Send a squad into the wormhole thirty seconds ahead of the ship,' she said. 'To give us an early warning, if we need it.'

He studied her.

Suddenly Anya was at her side. 'Not a bad idea, sir,' she said.

Sally said no more. it was Stein's call now.

'Very well,' he said. 'Augs.'

Sally pushed her luck. 'Human or Axel variety?'

True to Michael's assessment, Stein's poker face didn't so much as twitch. Anya turned away briefly, though, and when she faced forward again, her face was smoother, more relaxed. As if she'd had to wipe away a smile.

'Human,' Stein said, calling her bluff. 'Along with their non-auged leader.'

By the time Sally reached Michael and Elodie, the latter was staring down at her tablet. Abel and Sasha joined them. Word travelled lightning fast on this ship.

'Thanks, Mom,' Elodie said, beaming. 'I could really do with stretching my space legs.'

Sally felt a pang. Elodie didn't have to be one of the pilots placing herself in harm's way. Plus, Stein had said *augs*. Elodie didn't have one. Sally didn't really know why. But Elodie *was* the aug leader, their captain. Michael must have sensed what Sally was thinking. He shook his head, very slightly when only Sally was looking. She took the hint.

'Open comms,' Sally said.

'Of course,' Elodie replied. She kissed her mother on the cheek and left.

When they were out of earshot, Sally faced the wall, alone with Michael.

'Shit,' she said quietly.

'Tell me about it,' Michael said. 'Come on, I've got something to show you.'

'I should stay here,' she said.

'Trust me, there's somewhere better,' he said, grinning.

He took her hand, and they walked across the bridge to the elevator. Abel joined them. Inside, Ares was waiting. She felt like she was being ambushed.

Story of her life.

◆ ◆ ◆

Michael wasn't happy, his earlier grin a distant memory. Worse, this had all been his idea. He stared down at Sally's inert frame. Because right now, that's all it was. A broad metal band with wires trailing from it stretched across her forehead. Otherwise, she looked asleep. No rapid eye movements under her eyelids. Just asleep.

Except she wasn't.

'You're sure she's okay?' Not the first time he'd asked.

Abel sighed. 'How many times do you want me to say it? Her body is safe and sound in here, but her mind is outside, on the hull.'

She looked more than just in a deep sleep. Lights out. Nobody home. He eyed the holo showing her vitals, a pale spiderweb whose ghostly tendrils coiled outward from a central hub, all green so far. One was taller than the rest, its tip tinged orange.

Abel followed Michael's gaze. 'Relax, she's having fun out there.'

'Glad one of us is.'

Abel raised himself up to his full height, all wiry six-feet of him. He loomed over Michael like a ghoul. On anyone else it would have been intimidating, especially when his jet-black shoulder length hair fell forwards, shrouding his face. Yet Abel was basically a kitten, a pacifist to the core. Still, he made an attempt at exuding authority.

'Enough, Michael. I have a job to do in case you haven't noticed. Now sit the fuck down, enjoy the show, and take this.' He handed Michael an oblong white box with a small red button on top. It didn't really warrant a manual.

Abel could see he was having no effect on Michael. He shrugged. 'I'd rather you be the one to pull her back. I can tell you she won't like it when you do.'

Michael cradled the box in his palm. Sally was right next to him, but her mind was outside, slaved via neural link to Abel's computers via a maintenance bot with enhanced sensors, patrolling the hull, about to witness up close and personal what no human had ever seen. It had been sanctioned by Stein days ago, as no one knew how the wormhole would affect sensors. It was the equivalent of having a watchkeeper out on deck during a thunderstorm, except her external presence was virtual so there was zero risk.

In theory, nothing could go wrong.

As Michael watched a holo, the glistening wormhole approached fast. His grip tightened around the white box.

Sally was star-struck. No better word to describe it. She stood on the outer hull of the *Dreadnought* as it powered its way towards the wormhole. No spacesuit, no sense of heat or cold, just her, endless space and pinpricks of ice-white she felt she could reach out and grasp. All an illusion, she knew that, but, well, wow! Abel had excelled himself this time.

If she looked down at her feet and focused, she saw her legs fade and the drab, squat maintenance robot appear. A clunky, metal armadillo with thick treads instead of legs, with some kind of basic grav-tech so that it didn't peel off into space if struck by anything that got through the bow-wave deflector. She had an impulse to sprint around the circumference of the vast ship. But she could only move as fast as the drone she was tethered to.

The one thing that didn't work, for some reason, was speech. No way to tell Michael just how awesome this was. She began walking and ignored the mechanical whirring that accompanied her. Another odd effect, given that there was no air to transmit noise in space. She'd tell Abel when she returned, so he could iron out these anomalies.

She was on the cylindrical part of the ship. She

approached the front, the bullet-head. Her gaze drew to the dark, crystalline marble that spun slowly as they approached. She tried to recall the science that explained why a wormhole – a short-cut tunnel between two places in the galaxy – looked like a sphere. She knew the theory, that a wormhole travels through a fourth – or was it fifth? – dimension known as the 'bulk', held open by what physicists called 'exotic matter', a shorthand for particles that had theoretically possible properties... She ended up resorting to the less than satisfying rationale – itself a mental shortcut – that the mouth of a wormhole is round, and a circle in two dimensions is a sphere in three. She wiped her mental blackboard clean.

Right now, she just wanted to *see*.

Stars behind the wormhole moved in the opposite direction to the apparent 'spin' of the wormhole. She tried to untangle, as she'd done with Ares just a couple of hours ago, the images coming through the wormhole from the other side. Aside from a blue and red nebula that looked like a wrinkled Christmas cracker, it was just a shifting kaleidoscope of stars.

No broken Axel ships.

She walked faster.

The sphere grew large, and as she reached the edge of the cylinder where it bent towards a point, half a mile forwards, the surface of the sphere elongated, stretching away from her. She stopped, and just watched.

She'd asked Abel how the *Dreadnought* would enter the wormhole, and he'd replied 'Carefully.' In practice, that meant initially flying parallel to the surface – though there was technically no surface – and then turning on a vector directly into the 'mouth'. The scientific contingent aboard had spent years performing calculations and projections, concerned about shear stresses, especially as the *Dreadnought* was two-and-a-half miles long. If it approached 'head on' the front part would be subject to whatever wormhole stresses existed before the rear end did so, and one theory was that it might even stretch the *Dreadnought*, resulting in catastrophic stress that would rip it asunder and spill everyone into space.

A bullet split in two.

Was that what Ares had seen?

But then there would have been debris on this side, flushed out afterwards by the wormhole.

In the end, the scientists had decided the best approach was to skim the surface, and then to 'submerge' into the wormhole.

A flash of white and red caught her eye as a phalanx of nine single-pilot Stingers powered forward. Instinctively, Sally's virtual right hand rose to wave to Elodie, her daughter, in the lead fighter.

Godspeed.

They grouped around the nose of the gargantuan ship like small tugs leading a giant ship on a safe passage through a difficult channel. They would be the first into the wormhole, and the first to emerge out the other side, almost two thousand light years away, give or take. Stein was in contact with Elodie. Sally had to be content with watching silently. She'd almost refused this vista on that account alone, until Abel had reminded her she could exit at a moment's notice with a single thought command, and they would bring her back instantly if anything happened.

For the umpteenth time, she wondered why she could only feel anything for her daughter when they were apart. When they were close, it just didn't work. The psych – because she'd finally gone to see one – had said that Sally wasn't alone in this disconnection from her offspring. It was a side-effect of stasis-affected family evolution, with long, sleep-filled, contactless gaps in between her daughter's growth spurts. That wasn't good enough for Sally. Most other parents managed it. Why couldn't she? Part of her wondered if she was like Nathan, who'd never wanted children, and had seen them as a nuisance until he'd had his own kid, David. And anyway, Nathan had been a pretty good surrogate father to her in those early years on the *Athena*.

No, she couldn't – wouldn't – blame this on someone else, or stasis, or whatever. This was home-grown *Sally*. She'd just have to work it out. Still, she felt a tightness in her chest and breathed deeply several times to allay it, if for no other reason than Michael would see a small spike in her vitals and worry.

She turned back to the wormhole. They were so close now that it seemed flat, like a glistening lake, extending to the horizon in all directions. The detail from the other side was denser, but still distorted. She guessed she was seeing further now. More nebulae, more clusters of stars, a few so bright they made her squint before the wormhole's lensing effect washed them away.

Wait... what was that?

She stared, but it was gone. Something milky white. Just for a split-second. She closed her eyes, tried to catch the after-image on her retinas, but of course there was none since she was seeing only what the drone saw via its sensors. She thought about exiting, to see if they could find and replay the image, but then it would take another thirty minutes to recalibrate the neural interface, by which time they'd be on the other side. Besides, Stein, Anya, Abel and several thousand others were poring over every microsecond of image detail, trying to piece together a basic star map for when they reached the other side during this once-in-an-aeon opportunity to learn first-hand about wormholes.

It was just that it had reminded her of the tip of a shard from an Eyeship. But then stars often had a spiked visual effect and, again, she wasn't seeing with her own eyes but through the drone's digital optics and filters, which themselves had to be interpreted by the neural interface.

She made up her mind. If she saw it again, she'd exit.

The ice-white stars, the splashes of vibrantly coloured nebulae warping and coiling, accelerated before her, getting closer, larger, brighter. She reached out her hand as the *Dreadnought* slipped beneath the surface and plunged into the wormhole's mouth.

◆ ◆ ◆

'I'm telling you, she saw something,' Michael insisted.

'And I'm telling you I've got nothing, just stars and nebulae,' Abel shot back. 'The hike in her signals could have been a delayed reaction to seeing her daughter fly past.'

Michael wasn't buying it. 'Give me the feed.'

'There's a ton of data–'

'Just visual, just what she saw.'

'Okay... Done.'

'Thanks,' Michael said, trying to mean it. His frustration with this situation, heightened by what Ares had seen, dissipated as he pored through the digital recording. Having almost given up after fifteen uneventful minutes of going frame-by-frame through the thirty seconds when the emotional spike had occurred, during which he knew he was missing the show of a lifetime, he found something. It was blurred. It *could* have been the tip of a star. But there was too much riding on this trip to rely on '*could*'.

He glanced over to Sally, then stood up and handed the small box to Abel on his way out.

Abel looked surprised. 'Where are you going?'

'Tell Ares to meet me on the bridge.'

'Ares isn't allowed on the bridge,' Abel replied.

But Michael was already gone.

◆ ◆ ◆

Sally was captivated. In some senses, the throat of the wormhole was exactly that. The wormhole's blue, black and grey walls contained gelatinous mounds, gorges, valleys and crevasses that looked soft and fleshy, like blubber, as if the *Dreadnought* were barrelling down the gullet of a titanic space-dwelling whale. Shimmering particles like fireflies drifted forwards and backwards. She wondered if they were exotic matter. Up ahead and behind her, she watched the rotating, distorted discs of two different locations in the galaxy, the two mouths of the wormhole.

So, this was what the bulk looked like...

They were travelling at speed, the Stingers still in front. They were well past the halfway point now, the disc up ahead larger than the one behind, as if they were inside a telescope.

So far, so good.

Again, something caught her eye as it flashed past. Silver, metallic. This time, she knew what it was.

A charred and jagged airlock hatch, ripped from a ship's hull. Smaller fragments of metal accompanied it. Several hit the deck right in front of her, then ricocheted upwards. Pointlessly, she flinched and raised her arm to protect her face as one piece spun right through her.

Okay, enough was enough. She'd promised herself. Besides, she didn't know if Elodie and her crew had seen it. She concentrated on the mental exit command, a green diagonal cross she made flush red in her mind.

Nothing.

She tried again. A third time.

She looked down at her feet and focused. The robot wouldn't move when she tried to walk. Then she saw the damage, a sharp chunk of debris had embedded itself in the drone's central housing.

Shit.

Michael, Abel, get me out of here!

She heard and felt various clicks, and reckoned they were trying to do exactly that. Nothing worked. She tried various options for a full minute, then gazed forward to the exit mouth, looming large. The milky white star was back, lurking at the disc's edge, waxed and waned by the increased lensing effect. It didn't matter. Nothing could disguise it now.

An Eyeship, with a full pack of deadly shards. Waiting in ambush just outside the wormhole.

Sally wrapped her arms around herself, as if, finally, she could feel the unforgiving coldness of space, as she gazed towards the lead Stinger.

Elodie.

CHAPTER 4

Ambush

E lodie's fingers remained flexed, ready to tap in a command – literally at her fingertips – in a heartbeat. But despite being the wildest lightshow she'd ever seen, the past thirty minutes had proven uneventful, a slow chug down the oesophagus of a wormhole, swallowed at one end, about to be vomited out the other. She and her squadron of souped-up Stingers, with a new and as-yet-untested payload, were advance scouts, looking for trouble. Her dad had always told her that if you go looking for trouble, you find it.

So far, so good.

Yet it bothered her, like it did her mother, that the other six ships who'd made this trip months ago had sent nothing or no one back. No message, no electromagnetic handshake, no drone, no status report. One theory was that this wormhole was one-way. Being relatively new to space travel, it was possible, especially when no one had a fracking clue how exotic matter really worked. She imagined Abel poring over the data streaming in from sensors on that very subject, forgetting to steal a glance out the portal, and Mom looking over his shoulder, always focused on war.

She wondered why her mom had decided to have a kid. Probably Dad's idea, and her mom had never thought it through. Dad didn't miss a thing, and more than compensated, but still... She stepped over that rabbit-hole. She didn't get it; what the problem was. Her friends all saw it, too, but forgave Elodie's mom. *Well, she's Sally*, as Abel had once quipped while her parents had been in stasis, and she'd been introduced to home-brewed alcohol – Abel's talents covered a lot of space – as if her mother's very name explained everything, or else served as the perfect excuse for the chilled air between mother and daughter. She and Mom would have to have it out one day, get to the bottom of it all, though she got the distinct impression her mom – *Sally* no less – didn't understand it either. Maybe it was fine just as it was. Not broken, just imperfect.

Some things were better left alone.

She wondered if her mom realized that this mother-daughter tension was the main reason she'd never auged like the rest of her friends had done. If she 'took the platinum', as they jokingly referred to the augmentation process, then the others would see the inimitable Sally from Elodie's perspective. It would shatter the dream, the legend. Couldn't have that. Elodie was the human leader, but everyone knew Sally would play a big part in the upcoming battle. Elodie had no resentment about that. She was so proud of her mother.

She tensed. Spotted it ten seconds before Stein's call. The tip of a shard. Distorted, sure, but she'd seen plenty of images of the Eyeship that had attacked Earth, learned it was humanity's mortal enemy from the age of four. One of her classmates back then had nicknamed it 'Death Urchin', because it resembled an albino sea urchin, with a white spherical body whose surface simmered like a milky sea about to boil, and dazzling white spines that could spit out cutter beams capable of levelling a city in short order. As she approached the wormhole's exit, she realized just how large it must be, and why her mother called those spines 'shards'. She recalled the required educational viewing of several gigantic shards flattening Axleth mega-cities back on Earth, hard-headed nails driving into the Earth's crust, pulverizing millions.

Three of her squad, the first wave just behind her, pinged her. Good, they'd spotted it too. The Eyeship was waiting just outside the wormhole's mouth, its position given away by the extreme lensing effect this close to the exit, enabling her and her unit to see around the corner. She didn't know if that was an oversight on the Eyeship's part, or if it had wanted to see what was coming through, and judged it a reasonable risk to take. After all, Eyeships were close to invincible...

Stein's voice intruded.

'Eyeship to port on exit.'

She replied on the squadron broadcast.

'Ahead of you, Stein. Executing Plan Epsilon. UCO.'

She cut comms to the *Dreadnought*. UCO – urgent comms only. She and her squad were on their own. She glanced backwards over her delta wing, spying Ellie, formerly *Ellen*, one of the original second-wavers aboard the *Athena*. A deep-sleeper, only a year older than Elodie now. Yet somehow, having been *there* when barely nine years old, with the legendary Braxton, Nathan and Raphaela no less, Ellie was treated like a veteran. Through the slanted cockpit shield, she saw Ellie raise her left fingers from the armrest touch-pad in acknowledgment. Ellie was auged, the platinum arc above her right eyebrow reflecting the turbid swirl of fluorescent colour as they approached the exit. The single-pilot Stingers were fast and agile, but frighteningly small compared to an Eyeship that was easily five miles long from the tip of one shard to the opposing shard's pointy end. And a Stinger's firepower would be as noticeable as a mosquito bite to an elephant. But maybe not. Her gaze dipped to the outline of a torpedo slung under the belly of Ellie's craft. A new weapon, one they'd perfected en route. This time, the Stingers might live up to their name.

'Hold,' she said to her squad. Then, 'On my mark.'

She wanted to accelerate, to draw fire away from the *Dreadnought*. But normal physics was on a lunch break inside the throat of a wormhole, and she could no more push forward than Stein could slow the *Dreadnought* down. It was like being in a forest, seeing an open bear-trap right in front of you, but you couldn't stop your foot from falling into those steel jaws.

For a moment the lensing produced a weird effect, as if one of those shards reached across towards her prow to strike her. Then the warped image shifted as all the distortions snapped back into normal three-dimensional space.

'Break!' she shouted. She yawed her craft to port, using side-thrusters as the tight fist of Stingers burst apart like a firework. As she suspected, the ship didn't fire on any of them, at least not yet. It wasn't after them. It wanted the larger prize, thirty seconds behind.

Like hell.

Elodie hit what her dad called the after-burner, and shot straight towards the Eyeship.

'Epsilon,' she instructed the onboard computer, and her ship began zig-zagging and stuttering its course. Her eight fellow pilots were all auged, so they could coordinate their flight paths. Random was key. The Eye was a thinking machine, and the one thing a machine abhorred was chaos. The black of endless night lit up as a cutter beam lanced out from the closest spine. A star-hot lightning bolt, wider than her craft, chopped and sliced the vacuum.

They'd gained the Eyeship's attention.

Two pinpricks stabbed her back. She didn't have time to see which Stingers had just been vaporized, which of her lifelong friends had just been ashed.

'Spread!' she shouted, as two more cutter beams joined the fray, and she felt another stab.

A synthetic voice chimed in her ears, counting down the seconds to the *Dreadnought*'s exit, to when it would be in direct line of fire from the shards.

Ten, nine…

She knew the *Dreadnought* was pivoting on its axis, harnessing their tenuous grasp of multi-dimensional physics to make this single, critical manoeuvre, to present a less vulnerable target as the enormous ship exited the wormhole's mouth, and to have its heaviest weapons on a direct line of fire to the enemy. Over the past four hundred years, the Axel weapons scientists had been very busy.

...six, five...

She readied to get out of hellfire's path. Just a few seconds more.

A proximity alarm shrieked as one of her fellow Stingers, dodging a flailing cutter-beam, bumped into her craft, sending her careening to starboard. Before she could even see who it was, the other Stinger was caught in an intersecting downward cutter beam sweep. The craft luminesced skeletally for a fraction of a second, then was gone, the fourth pinprick telling Elodie what she already knew.

...two...

'Out!' she yelled and swung her joystick hard to port.

...one...

All around her blazed red as a succession of blinding pulses struck out from the *Dreadnought*. She was now parallel with the Eyeship, which ignored her and the remaining four Stingers. Ten of its spikes traded fire with the Axel mega-ship.

Big mistake.

'Release,' she said.

She and the other pilots unleashed their torpedoes, which broke into clusters of drones homing in on their target. Too late, the Eyeship turned its beams on the falling debris, but by now there were hundreds of drones spiralling towards it, like microbes attacking a sea urchin. Most drones boiled into vapour in the cutter-beam firestorm, but a handful made it through and splashed into the milky sea. Within seconds, grey spots appeared, extending tendrils that spread across the centre mass and up into the shards. It was a more aggressive version of Ares' original virus used to destroy the Eyeship that attacked Earth. A single, unaffected shard broke off and shot away from the fray, despite the *Dreadnought*'s attempts to disable it. Yellow tracer-like railgun pulses faded into the depths of space, unable to stop the escaping shard. It would no doubt take data all the way back to the Eye itself, so it could manufacture a defence.

As they'd feared. The virus trick would only work once.

But as the Eyeship's firing stuttered and ceased, Elodie saw something beyond the dying enemy, and her heart plummeted. A graveyard, a vast field of gutted ships and debris left by a fierce battle. She counted the shattered and burned carcasses of five Axel mega-ships.

She tapped comms. 'Well done. Return to base.' Then she called Stein, with the only intel he'd want.

'One of the Axel ships made it through.' She said it like it was good news. Like the glass was half full. More like almost empty. Five Axel battleships ships decimated. Close to four million dead. Snuffed out before they could even make it to the crucial battle. Most would have been in stasis when it happened.

Fuck!

She was glad she wasn't auged.

Her dad answered. 'Come home, Elodie, quick as you can. It's your mom. Something's happened.'

The stress in his voice told her all she needed to know.

'Ellie, you and the others do a sweep for any survivors, intact sleeper pods, any weapons and ordnance we can salvage... You know the drill.'

She didn't wait for the acknowledgment from her surviving colleagues. She swung her Stinger about to face the *Dreadnought* and hit the after-burner.

Abel looked wretched, his forty-year-old face wrinkled into the frown of an old man. He kept out of Michael's way. Elodie walked up to the latter, took his arm while they both stared at Sally's inert frame.

'It shouldn't have happened,' Abel began. 'I still don't understand–'

'You're safe,' her dad said to her as if Abel hadn't spoken. 'That's what matters.' Then he turned to Abel. 'My daughter just saved us all. Now it's your turn. Save Sally.'

Abel stared at Michael a moment, another wrinkle adding to the weight of the task as he nodded, and cocooned himself inside a cylinder of holos, schematics, and vitals.

She tugged her father out of the lab. 'Let him work, Dad.'

'I am. He's still standing, isn't he?' He shrugged. 'Just kidding.'

'I should hope so,' she said. 'Now, sit-rep time, please.'

He turned to face her, stared at her the way he did every time she'd woken from a sleeper cycle, going over her face in minute detail to see how she'd grown in the sleep tube, because for young ones, maturation still occurred, even if slowed down.

He traced the contour of her cheek with the back of a forefinger. 'How could a couple of broken kids like us produce something so perfect?' Suddenly, she was locked in a tight embrace. 'You scared the crap out of me, you know that, right?'

She squeezed him back. This made everything worthwhile.

He let her go.

'What happened, Dad? Why didn't she come back inside?'

Her dad's face began to age like Abel's. 'I was halfway to the bridge, because I'd seen what Sally had seen, what looked like a shard, when Abel called me back. The drone had malfunctioned, some of its internal mechanisms and sensors fused. Maybe something struck it inside the wormhole, maybe exotic matter interacted with it, maybe it was just plain dumb bad luck and shitty timing. Abel couldn't get her back. He was frantic, poor guy, especially when he realized what was out there lurking just beyond the rim of the wormhole. We tried to warn Stein, by the way, but they couldn't confirm the Eyeship's presence until they saw it for themselves.'

There was something in his eyes. 'What are you not

telling me, Dad?'

He swallowed. 'At one point we almost had her back. Abel remotely hotwired the drone somehow, and we had a five second window...'

Elodie stared past him into the lab behind, seeing her mother's face. She kept her voice level, with no small effort.

'She chose not to come back, didn't she?'

'You were under fire. Hell, I might have made the same choice. And how was she to know it was a closing door?'

She moved to his side, so she could see the data cylinder, her mother's vitals. More than half had breached the red zone.

The elevator door opened behind them, revealing Ares. He strode past them into the lab as if they weren't there. His hand reached forward, a finger morphing into some kind of jack plug. It entered Abel's computer stack.

'Hey!' Abel said, but Ares ignored him.

The finger retracted. Ares' hands closed into fists. Was that anger? He was an AI, incapable of emotion. He turned around, his implacable silver face serene as always.

'She does not have much time.'

'Her vitals are still out of the danger zone,' Abel protested.

Ares stayed where he was, facing Elodie and Michael, answering Abel but addressing them.

'It is not her body that is in danger. Her mind has been... cut loose. She is adrift. Each second in this condition can seem like an hour. Or a day. She is... lost. She will lose herself. Lose her mind.'

Elodie stared at Ares. What was going on with him? He never paused in speech.

'I... I could induce a medical coma,' Abel tried.

Ares' head turned a fraction towards Abel. 'Possibly the worst thing you could do.'

Abel slumped at his workstation.

'You can save her?' Michael asked, his voice edgier than Elodie had ever heard.

Ares nodded.

'Then what are you waiting for?' Elodie said, a sickly sense of panic rising in her chest.

Ares closed fists rotated, then opened. Nestling in the palm of each hand was a platinum eyebrow aug.

Elodie winced. Her mother disliked the very idea of being tethered in that way. So did her dad and, as if it ran in the family, so did she, because aside from maybe destroying 'the legend', she feared it would disconnect her from them, break the imperfect family relationship she clung to. It was all she had. Her mother might give her hell if she got through this, but that was better than the alternative.

'Why does she need two?' Michael said. 'All the other augs had just one.'

But Elodie already got it.

'I can open the door,' Ares replied. 'One of you must call her back. One of you must aug with her.'

Elodie and her dad stared at each other.

Ares turned back, facing Sally's inert form.

'Choose quickly,' he said.

Sally was adrift in space. The Eyeship was dark, lifeless. A death-urchin, as her daughter once called it, finally dead.

She shifted her gaze to the Axel battleship graveyard. Stingers patrolled and probed the carnage, seeking survivors, whether conscious or in sleeper chambers that hadn't been eviscerated by cutter-beams. Trouble was, once the power was off, sleeper beds, even if intact, would normally fail within a month, and this battle had almost certainly taken place far earlier; otherwise, they would have proceeded to the rendezvous point at Orion's Gate.

She glanced down at her feet. She focused, and tried to see the drone to which she'd been neurally tethered. All she saw were her feet. She'd blown it, she knew that now. The exit command had reappeared in her mind. But at the exact moment, her daughter had been in such danger. She'd watched one Stinger after another vaporized by cutter beams, knowing her daughter could be next, wiped out of existence at any second. She just *couldn't...*

Too bad. It was what it was. Elodie was safe. The *Dreadnought* had survived. They would proceed to the battle site and join the eleven other species, none of whom had needed to use this spatial short-cut, as they came from other parts of the galaxy, not the lonely outer spiral housing Earth. Together, they would destroy the Eye, once and for all. She'd done her part. Nothing else to do now, except...

She thought of Nathan, wondered what kind of life he must have had, and Lara, her mother-not-mother. It struck her that she'd been estranged with Lara the way she was now with her own flesh-and-blood daughter, unable to emote properly. Unable to connect. Wiring gone awry. Like the drone. Never mind. Michael would care for Elodie even more, if that was humanly possible.

She thought she heard something. Hallucinations starting early. Back on Earth when the Axleth had subjected her to a mental simulation they called 'Education', she'd been left adrift in sensory deprivation for what had seemed like days, though it had been only an hour. She hoped that experience would help her now. Not her first rodeo, Michael would have said.

The voice was ghostly, synthetic.

Sally.

She ignored that first tease of insanity. She didn't want to lose her mind, screaming her way into madness and oblivion. Instead she focused – because somehow, she could, meaning the drone wasn't completely dead – on one particular ship's metallic corpse, sliced open as if for an autopsy, yet slightly more intact than the others. A faint flash caught her attention. A reflection from the wormhole? She saw it again.

Sally.

Her mind drifted for a moment, then jerked as if waking from an unplanned nap. *Oh no you don't!* She focused again, watching, counting, forcing her mind into mental routines to prevent it unravelling. She focused on the ship. Once a minute, the glint. Not a glint. A pulse. She tried to see more, but was already at the drone's sensory limits. Instead, she tried to see where it would have been in the original ship before it had been carved up by shards and cutter beams.

SALLY!

Quit it, I'm busy here! Let me do this one last thing, then you can unravel all you like.

She created a whiteboard in her mind, dragging the pieces of charred, torn and twisted wreckage into a schematic. It took time. She was tiring, finding it harder to concentrate, to pull the pieces together, but she made it. Counted the rings in her mind. The pulse was coming from two-thirds down the shaft of the gutted ship, definitely from one of the habitat rings.

The Stingers were heading home. They'd missed it. *Wait,* she shouted voicelessly to them. *Go back. Somebody's still there! They might be alive!*

The puzzle in her mind broke apart. She felt an overwhelming need to sleep, knowing she'd never wake again, unless insane. She closed her eyes. Her part was over. Another name to add to the countless souls lost out here already.

The voice again. No longer synthetic. Female.

Mother!

Hah, that was a good one. Below the belt. So her mind was going to play dirty at the end.

Mom.

Sally mentally sat up, wide awake. Elodie? Was there a chance? She tried to turn toward the voice, but couldn't. So instead, she reached behind her with her hand, and touched cool metal fingertips. Ares? She reached further, and her hand locked with another, that of a young woman. Her daughter.

Come back to me, please Mom.

An emotional dam burst apart in Sally's mind, feelings for her daughter breaking free with an intensity that shocked her to her core. All those years, those moments that should have been precious, instead wasted, sterilized, cauterized for no good reason. She gripped Elodie's hand with all her might, and felt space rushing past her, which made no sense at all, and in her mind's eye she saw her own mother-not-mother – no, dammit, why not admit it for once? Her *mother* – Lara – staring at her with that damned wry smile of hers. In Sally's mind, a single word crossed Lara's lips.

Finally.

CHAPTER 5

Sleeper

Michael had never seen such discord amongst Axels. And on the bridge, no less. As ever, as his own father had counselled, he stripped out who was saying what and listened instead to the core arguments. Decide based on facts and logic, not charisma or eloquence.

He listened. Not entirely dispassionately, since it was Sally's dispossessed mind while she'd been 'outside' that had spotted something pulsing amongst the Axel fleet wreckage. *It's always about her,* someone quipped, and Michael allowed a subdued laugh to slip out, attracting only momentary attention in the otherwise heated debate. He could afford to laugh, because she was alive. So was Elodie. Not that the two of them were talking. A smile this time, because they no longer needed to talk: they were auged. Now *that* was one darned conversation he'd like to be in on. But platinum didn't suit his complexion. Instead, he tuned into the discussion, if you could call it that, between the six key bridge officers.

'We have to bring it aboard – whoever is inside could give us critical intel.'

'Like where the sixth Axel ship, the one that escaped, has gone?'

'It could hold two, or even three, people. It's a larger than average sleeper unit.'

'It could be a bomb, for all we know.'

'Agreed. Chances of surviving this long in a sleeper are slim. Especially if there's more than one person in it.'

'The Eyeship could have left it sitting in the wreckage. A Plan B in case more made it through, like us.'

'We can't open it out in space. It would kill whoever was inside.'

'Better than taking out the *Dreadnought*. The risk is too great.'

His father had once told him that when others are shouting, you pick your time and speak, normal-like, as if in a calm conversation with a friend, only firm and clear. *The voice of reason needs volume control.* His father had favoured the two-shot approach – first one gets their attention, second one hits home.

I miss you, Dad.

'We're blind right now,' Michael said, pausing just a fraction to see them turn towards him. 'But we don't have to be stupid.'

'Speak,' Stein said.

Michael had been leaning against one of the console edges. He straightened, gazed at each of them one by one as he spoke. He knew he was carrying out Sally's wishes. She'd found it, after all. She'd want to open the box, and would have been here, but she and Elodie were recovering after their emergency aug surgery.

'We're disadvantaged right now, on the back foot. The scales need to be tipped in our favour. We're all questions and no answers. Whoever or whatever is in that sleeper unit, it's an answer.'

He shut his mouth and waited. Rumour had it, and in fact the whole point of the Axleth grand plan, was that Axels were more intelligent than–

'Bring it aboard,' Stein said. 'Maximum force fields, all non-essential personnel evacuated from the area.'

If this had been just humans – especially Texans like himself, Michael mused – the argument would have raged a while longer; egos and ruffled feathers would have to be soothed and smoothed, respectively. Instead, with an Axel crew, the decision was instantly accepted, the crew suddenly busy making preparations, and no one would ruminate or bitch behind Stein's back later. The Axel way was definitely slicker in this respect, though Michael wasn't sure it was better in the long run.

'Ellie,' Stein said on comms. 'Bring it into the maintenance hangar deck at level 3-4-0.'

'Aye, sir,' came the response.

Stein nodded to Anya. 'Go, I want eyes-on,' he said.

She began walking to the elevator.

Michael followed her.

'You're not essential personnel,' Anya said, turning, blocking his path.

He stopped, and replied with his father's catchphrase, two words that could be interpreted at different levels.

'You think?'

Anya folded her arms. 'Don't *ever* play human mind games with me, Michael. Give me one good reason or else go take some family time.'

He stood his ground. 'Humans and Axels see things differently,' he said. 'Whatever is in there, multiple perspectives might be useful.'

She spun about and walked briskly to the elevator. Michael waited where he was. He'd been raised not to tread where he wasn't welcome.

'Are you coming or not?' she said.

He made it just before the doors began to close.

'Thanks,' he said, as the elevator descended, gathering speed. He counted the floors. Her reflection in the curving glass was hazy. There was no change in her poker face framed by crewcut black hair. It was another thirty floors before she deigned to reply.

'You're welcome.'

Most of those present, aside from him and Anya, were armed. He'd somehow hoped Axels had risen above brute violence. And if it was a bomb, what was the point of rifles? At the first sight of trouble, it would be flushed straight out of the hangar into space. It went without saying that a few Axels, and maybe him as well, might accompany it. They could have brought it aboard one of the mid-sized Marauders, but those didn't have the grav-fields inside their hulls, capable of containing a moderate explosion. The *Dreadnought* did.

Ellie steered it in, nudging it forward gingerly with the nose of her Stinger. It reminded him of the difference between real space operations and the crappy space-soaps he used to watch on TV as a kid. In the latter, everything happened quickly, wham-bang, but in real space you didn't rush anything, because Newton's law concerning momentum came into its own in space. Once you got something big and heavy moving, it took a lot to stop it. A few degrees off course could end in catastrophe. He imagined the ocean-going super-tankers of old must have been similarly difficult to control, and they had winds and tides to contend with. He watched as Ellie did a bang-up professional job, finishing in a satisfying clunk as the five-metre-long family-sized sleeper compartment grav-locked with the hangar deck.

No one rushed forward. A gravity field had been placed around it, a suppression system in case it was indeed a weapon. Anyone approaching beyond the red line on the floor would be crushed. Instead, robot arms of an alloy way stronger than titanium eased forward, attaching themselves to recessed service portals.

'Auxiliary power initiated,' someone said. A dull pearl glow emanated from the upper forward surface of the sleeper. Anya interrogated the tablet that never left her side, angled so that Michael couldn't see the display. She muttered syllables of their military clipped speech into her thin, curved mike boom, no doubt giving Stein a live update even though he could see everything via remote screens.

She stopped speaking, frowned at the tablet, then stared at the sleeper unit. She held a finger to her ear, over the earpiece, then made eye contact with two of the armed soldiers, calling them over.

'You must leave, Michael. Now.'

He did a double-take, and was about to reply when he heard a knocking. He tried to see inside, but the portal was opaque. Something brushed past the inside, and Michael gaped a moment, frozen by what he'd just seen. It had looked like a claw.

The knocking grew more insistent, rising to a hammering.

'Out!' Anya shouted, and Michael was frog-marched from the hangar.

◆ ◆ ◆

Michael found Abel and Ares conversing in low tones outside the lab. They stopped as he approached. Ares departed with a brief nod to Michael.

Abel indicated the door. 'They're both a bit fragile after the surgery, but otherwise they're doing fine,' Abel said, then added as the elevator doors closed behind Ares, 'He saved her. I recognize that now.'

'You both did good,' Michael said. 'You brought Ares back. He saved Sal. So you saved them both. Go get some rest, Abel. I'll take it from here.'

He waited until Abel, momentarily trying to process what Michael had just said, departed. Then he gently pushed aside the swing doors.

Sally and Elodie sat face-to-face, close and personal. Like an actual mother and daughter. Each of their right hands lay on the other's left shoulder. Michael had seen this gesture before amongst other augs. It meant they were 'linking', an intimate form of auged communication. The hands were superfluous to the two women; it was simply a sign for others to leave them be.

He had to admit, he'd never seen them so... *relaxed* with each other. Nor so close for this length of time. Their eyes were closed, but their faces were anything but inert. Twitches of the lips and corners of the eyes rose and fell on his two favourite faces in the galaxy, as emotions streamed between the two of them. He had no idea what they were thinking to each other. He'd read about family members split by the North and South Korean armistice, after a kid at school had one day talked about it. Her grandad had finally crossed the no-man's-land to the South, and her grandmother had just held him, for hours, days, as they'd been apart forty years. In such cases, words didn't work, it was just emotion and perception – touch, sight, smell – so you could trust that, yes, this was real, it was happening. He had a hunch augmentation made the process easier. More bandwidth.

But they were on the clock.

He cleared his throat. That didn't work. So he did what he'd seen an aug do one day to interrupt a linked pair and tapped Sally's right hand. No need to touch Elodie's as well; in this state, she'd feel it as if it were her own hand.

They both opened their eyes. Elodie's twinkled. 'Well, talk of the devil.'

Michael wasn't sure he liked the sound of that.

'Don't worry,' Sally said. 'We were both just agreeing it was you who held this family together these past years.'

Michael couldn't think of a snappy comeback. Or any comeback at all.

Sally must have sensed his discomfort. 'I was telling Elodie about Lara.'

Elodie tapped her platinum eyebrow. The bloodstains from the op hadn't quite washed away. She flashed that teasing smile again. 'Want one, Dad?'

Although he loved them both, he wasn't comfortable having alien tech in his head. He'd never fully trusted Ares, not since the original Ares2 had been infected by the Eye and had run amok, killing people on the *Athena*.

He shook his head. 'Rain check, if you don't mind.'

Sally got to her feet. 'The sleeper. Awake?'

He told them both what had happened. For now, he left out the claw. It had just been a blur, after all. He could have been mistaken. Anyway, he didn't want to rain all over their parade.

Sally was about to use her wristcom when she thought better of it. 'Let me try this,' she said. *Abel, it's Sally. Can you hear me?*

Her eyes moved, and Elodie stared at her mother, evidently hearing the same intel.

'What is it?' Michael inquired, feeling like the dumbest one in the room.

'We're locked out,' Sally said. 'Whatever they found in the sleeper, they don't want us to see it.'

'We have people on the bridge,' Michael said. 'Sasha–'

'Not anymore,' Elodie replied.

He walked to the doors and ground to an unceremonious halt. They were mag-locked.

'So,' he said, 'when you said locked out...' He turned around to find Sally and Elodie facing each other again, linked.

'Great,' he murmured. He sat down on the sofa. After a while, Sally and Elodie joined him, one on either side.

'Plan?' he asked.

'Nope,' Elodie said. 'All humans were escorted off the bridge. It's sealed now.'

'Ellie, she was there, in the hangar when–'

Elodie shook her head.

Michael gave up for now. *No point worrying over what you can't control.*

'Then we have some good old-fashioned family time.' He

put his arms around their shoulders. 'Anyway, I figure this is the eye of the storm, and when they call us and decide to show and tell, all hell will break loose, so let's enjoy the moment.'

'Dad...' Elodie said.

'What?'

'I wish you *were* auged. I see how much Mom loves you, and now I see more clearly why she does. But if you were auged, I could see inside that mind of yours, and you could see inside mine.'

He didn't reply. He wasn't religious, though he'd been born and bred Catholic. But humanity had evolved in a particular way. He wasn't sure auging was the right next step. He would never do it, he knew that. But as Elodie's head rested on his shoulder, and Sally clasped his hand, he knew that right now, he was as close as he would come to giving his consent to the procedure.

No, this was enough.

◆ ◆ ◆

'This is Hawkins,' Stein said, as if that explained anything, let alone everything.

Michael and his freshly reunited family were in one of the conference rooms with Stein and Anya. It was strange seeing Stein off the bridge. Michael had never seen him in one of the canteens. He presumed Stein lived on the bridge.

Ellie was present, too, and a bunch of Axels Michael knew by face only. There was no *tour-de-table*, so clearly it was going to remain that way. He focused instead on Hawkins: bushy beard and hair, haggard with wild, staring green eyes, like a homeless person who'd been sleeping rough for a long time. Which, in a way, wasn't far off the mark. Hawkins clutched a tall glass of something green and glutinous. Probably couldn't take solids yet. He sipped every now and again, leaving a residue of green foam on his moustache, which he didn't wipe away. The way he gripped the glass it wasn't going anywhere soon.

But Michael found himself staring at Hawkins' hands. They were normal. No matter how opaque the sleeper pod's glass had been, there was no way he could have mistaken one of those for a claw.

'What destroyed the fleet, and where is the sixth ship?' Stein asked. It sounded rehearsed, like he'd already asked and heard the answer several times. Everything about this little meeting, interrogation, whatever it was, felt staged. Michael said nothing. Nor did Sally or Elodie. They all wanted the answers to these questions before they got into *the* question. He noticed Anya steal a surreptitious glance in his direction. Probably she was wondering what Michael had actually seen before being escorted from the hangar. He figured that was why Ellie was present. She was human and auged, yet had clearly seen nothing, else all the augs would know, including Sal. *So that was the game, was it?* Plausible deniability? He'd hoped Axels wouldn't raid the human dirty tricks cupboard.

Hawkins tried to speak, but his voice caught and he coughed. He took a sip, closing his eyes as he did so, and gulped the viscous liquid down.

He wiped his lips.

'I was on the *Invincible*, the third ship in the fleet of six Axel battleships. Two Eyeships appeared out of nowhere just as the *Agamemnon,* the lead ship, was about to depart for Orion's Gate. They were caught in crossfire before they could even call battle-stations. Our flagship and one other cut to ribbons before they had a chance to return fire. The remaining ships did the best they could, but...'

He made a fist and thumped the table hard.

'Like Custer's last fucking stand.' He opened his fist, stared at it, then spoke again, his words devoid of the anger they could have contained.

'Cavalry came way too late.'

Michael appreciated the cowboy reference. Maybe he could get to like this guy. And then it struck him. Hawkins was *human*, not Axel. Then why would they put him with–

'Three ships, including mine, formed a protective cordon around the fourth battleship, the *Prometheus*. Brilliant manoeuvre, I'll give the captains that. The *Prometheus* took heavy fire but got away. One of the two Eyeships chased it, but the rest of ours unloaded everything they had onto that particular Eyeship. We must have damaged its engines, because it gave up the chase. Then it came back to join its partner and finish us off.' His gaze was downcast. He was watching his memories unfold on the table top before him. 'Three battleships sacrificed themselves for one. A simple, tactical, almost mathematical solution to a problem. Only Axels could have condemned millions to oblivion like that, and so quickly. No meetings, no lengthy decision-making, just a snap judgement that was as right as its consequences were devastating.' He looked up at Stein. 'They did a real number on you people, you know that, don't you?'

Michael wouldn't want to be auged to Hawkins right now for all the tea in China.

'Is the *Prometheus* planning to return?' Stein asked.

'Would you?' Hawkins countered, his eyes ablaze. 'What's wrong with you people?' He stood up, and trawled his fingers through his straggly beard.

Michael stood up and put a hand on Hawkins' meagre shoulder. 'You had family?' he asked, drawing a confused look that morphed into a hollowed-out stare from Hawkins.

'Had,' he replied, plumping himself down onto his seat again.

Michael drew his chair up close and sat, too. 'Why you?'

Hawkins shifted his position and faced Michael, as if he were the only one in the room that mattered.

Anya leaned forward. 'Wait a min–'

'I just happened to be closest when they attacked,' Hawkins said, his eyes welling up.

Michael understood. From one vantage point, he'd survived because he'd been in the right place at the right time.

But this man would rather have been with his family than with...

Anya was on her feet. 'Mr Hawkins, you're clearly tired. You need rest, we can–'

'Is it awake?' Michael asked.

Hawkins nodded.

No wonder he'd been banging his fists on the hull when they powered up the sleeper unit.

Two soldiers appeared behind Michael, another two behind Hawkins.

Michael turned to the leader of this sham. 'Game's up, Stein. You need to take us to see the second occupant.'

Anya gestured for the soldiers to take hold of Michael, but Stein raised a hand.

'Then you know.'

'I know you brought a live Axleth aboard. And I'm now wondering if that little debating session we had on the bridge was a show as well, because you must have guessed what the other ships would have gone to any length to keep alive.'

He felt Sally's and Elodie's eyes on him. He hadn't told them exactly what he'd seen. By now they must have guessed.

'The *Prometheus*, the one that got away. I'm betting it also had one.'

Stein placed his palms face down on the table. 'A male.'

'So, I'm betting the one we just rescued from the wreckage of the *Invincible* is a female, and Hawkins was locked in with it, to contact us if we made it through.'

Stein didn't deny it, which for an Axel was a clear affirmation. By now, they must have accessed logs from either the sleeper unit or the *Invincible*'s wreckage.

Michael reminded himself that humans and Axels weren't that far apart, genetically speaking. He thought of his father's advice again, this time on secrets and lies. He'd said two things. The first was that if someone gave up a secret easily, it was because there was an even worse one lurking in the shadows. The second thing he'd said was that the best way to drag a long-held lie or deep dark secret into the daylight, was to bluff, to act like you already knew. Michael pondered the worst secret the Axels could keep.

'So,' he said, 'what sex is the one we've had on board these past four hundred years?'

Stein and Anya exchanged looks. Anya turned away. 'Male,' Stein said.

In less than a second, Sally was on her feet, in Stein's face. 'Wait a goddammed minute! What the hell are you saying?'

Stein waved back the soldiers who'd advanced on Sally. He stood and walked around the table towards the far wall, upon which was a blank screen. He touched its surface with his palm, and an image crystallized while he spoke.

'When the Axleth Mothership arrived in orbit around Earth, it had a crew of eight Axleth. Original Axleth. The one called Lara killed the pilot of the Mothership upon your return to reclaim Earth.'

Michael had never seen a real Axleth. Never wanted to. As its features emerged, he felt his guts turn to stone.

'Three survived the Eyeship attack on Earth. One escaped in the *Prometheus*, and we brought one aboard from the wreckage of the *Invincible* three hours ago.'

'That's two,' Michael said.

Stein said nothing.

Sally's face flushed red. Michael didn't blame her. These were the original Axleth creatures, the grand architects of humanity's demise, seven-and-a-half billion humans dead by their command. Back on Earth, before their departure, the Axleth leader in human form, Qherax, had assured Sally there were no original Axleth left.

Another lie.

Sally's voice quavered with rage. 'The third Axleth... Michael's right, isn't he? It's here, isn't it, on the *Dreadnought*? Where is it? Of course, the purple zone. You've got hardcore Axels looking after it down there, don't you? You fucking lied to us, Stein, all this time!'

Stein turned around to face her. 'Yes,' he said. 'We had to. Had we told you the truth, you would not have come.'

Sally's anger flared. She shouted at Stein. 'And why the hell do you care that we are here?'

Elodie, silent until now, spoke. 'They wanted our aug-tech.'

Arguments flew back and forth, and Michael felt he was back where he'd begun several hours ago in that heated show-debate on the bridge. He tuned out, and stared past Stein and even Sally, to take in their mortal enemy. Its long, sand-coloured insectoid body had faded bands of black and red around its abdomen and its six powerful legs. The forelegs ended in claw-hands that looked dexterous and lethal in equal measure. But it was the head that was the scariest part: whiskers around the neck and vicious-looking, shiny brown mandibles, and two bulbous eye-clusters with myriad octagonal black mirrors staring right back at him.

Yet it wasn't the Axleth's features that sent a shiver down his spine. Michael had faced gators that looked equally scary. That was just it, though. Like a gator, the Axleth was a natural predator. Like a gator it had no empathy... and infinite patience.

They'd thought the Axleth were all gone, died out more or less, sacrificing themselves for the greater good. And now they had two aboard. A male and a female, no less. Everyone until now, possibly including the other eleven species co-opted by the ruthless and murderous Axleth, had presumed that by the time the battle with the Eye was over, there would be no more Axleth to worry about.

He stared at the creature.

Did the Axleth have a different endgame in mind?

CHAPTER 6

Qherax

Sally stared at the creature's image on the screen. It was the first time she'd seen one, though Lara had described it to her in vivid detail back on Earth. It was the eyes... like dozens of ebony beetles crammed together, mirror-like, reflecting, seeing all, calculating... A single, four-letter word parked itself in her mind, and she couldn't dispel it: evil. She wanted to follow in Lara's footsteps and kill it. Pretty much every cell and DNA strand in her body voted the same way. Unfortunately, that option wasn't on the table.

'What else did you lie to us about?' Michael asked.

She'd rarely heard such acid in his tone.

They both sat with Stein and a woman Sally had presumed long dead. Not a woman. A mutated Axleth; one of the original invaders like the one on the screen, made to look human, who'd descended to Earth while all human children were being culled. Modified Axleth like Qherax had then bred with humans to make Axel children, while ruling Earth from their mega-cities for two decades.

Sally had never liked Qherax, the 'Third' she'd elected to work with in the fight against the Eyeship back on Earth. Now, seeing her in the same room where a screen showed her true natural Axleth form, Sally saw Qherax for what she was.

An abomination.

One that so far hadn't uttered a word. She'd aged; that much was clear. Axleth converted into human form only lived about twenty years. Qherax was twenty-three. She looked eighty, her once flaming red hair bleached white. Frail, her skin taut and lined, as if the human shell she'd adopted was cracking apart. For four centuries, they'd kept Qherax alive by waking her one month every decade. Clearly, Axleth were more resilient when it came to stasis cycles.

Stein answered matter-of-fact, unruffled, his voice calm and collected as ever, which no doubt only baited Michael. Outrage didn't seem to be in the Axel emotional lexicon, and empathy was in short supply.

'The rebellion on this ship, and the Axleth role in the upcoming battle strategy,' Stein said.

Sally should have guessed the former. Axel riots had always seemed an oxymoron.

'What really happened?' she asked.

Stein nodded, as if expecting the question. 'Only Core Team knew of the presence of an Axleth on board. Word leaked out, and a faction emerged who wanted to study their... ancestor.

'Ancestor?' Michael was on his feet. He hurled his words at Stein. 'You've got to be shitting me!'

Sally had never seen him like this. He'd once confided that his father had had quite a temper, rare to see, but all the same, frightening to behold. He caught himself, looked at her, as if embarrassed that she was seeing this side of him.

He leaned on the table and hung his head. 'I can't do this,' he said to her quietly, and she nodded. He quit the room without giving either Stein or Qherax a further glance.

'So,' Sally said. 'The other Axleth is in the purple section. That's why you sealed it off. Do you have contact with it, and this "faction"?'

Before Stein could answer, Sally lobbed a question at Qherax. 'I'd have thought you might have bred fundamentalism out of their genes.'

Qherax didn't miss a beat, though her voice rasped.

'Some genetic coding is harder to remove than others.'

'It suited you, though, didn't it?' Sally insisted.

Qherax's head bobbed and tilted slowly in that inhuman way. It reminded Sally of a chameleon she'd seen as a child, at a zoo. Twenty-three years in a human body and Qherax still hadn't mastered human gestures and movements.

'Yes, Sally. It suited us.' She changed tack. 'You have a daughter now. And you are auged with Ares? I understand he is functional again.'

Sally resisted the urge to touch the still tender patch of skin around the platinum arc covering her left eyebrow. Her muscles tensed of their own accord. She felt seconds away from joining her husband outside, or reducing the Axleth complement on board by one.

Stein answered Sally's former question, in an attempt to de-escalate the palpable tension in the room.

'We have contact once a month. The Axleth is a pilot, a navigator. Only they know the way through the nebula to the Eye's homeworld.'

'So why do we need two? Or any? Qherax must know the way.'

Qherax smiled. 'I do not. I was born on the seed-ship. Only the original Axleth crew know the way.'

'Can they mate?' Sally asked. 'The two original Axleth?'

Qherax's smile faded, and she turned away.

'The one already on board is male,' Stein answered. 'The one we just rescued in the pod with Hawkins is female. In theory–'

Sally slammed the table with her fist. *'Unacceptable!'*

She tried to calm herself, took a slow breath. 'If they mate, how many will they breed? Ten? A hundred? A thousand?'

Qherax levered herself upright, or at least a crooked version of it. She stared down at Sally.

'Back on Earth, you and I forged an agreement. You said you would join the fight. That is why you are aboard this ship. We wanted your aug tech, because we believe it will help in the battle.'

Sally rose to her feet, but before she could speak, Qherax continued, her words harsh.

'We fought one Eyeship, that is our collective knowledge and experience. The two Axleth fought many campaigns against the Eye. Their strategic and tactical knowledge goes well beyond plotting a safe course through a star nursery. So, Sally, I ask you as one leader to another, do you want to win this battle?'

Sally felt her chest heave. She took another slow breath and faced Stein. 'If you want our help, you keep the two Axleth apart. Zero physical contact. Non-negotiable.'

'Acceptable,' Stein said. 'The male is the better pilot, and will be installed on the bridge.'

Sally loathed the idea, but shelved her anger for now, and turned to Qherax. 'The second the battle is won or lost, the pact we forged between us ends. Do you understand?'

'I understand you want to exterminate the Axleth,' Qherax replied.

Sally said nothing.

Qherax rotated her head in that strange, bobbing way again, glancing towards the screen.

'There are only a handful of them left alive,' she said. When Sally made no further reply, she added, 'You didn't answer my question. Are you auged with the AI?'

Sally left the room.

She found Michael waiting for her, leaning over the railing, staring downwards.

'Thought you'd be here,' she said.

He didn't look up. 'At times like this I wish the dead

could speak. Those down there, plus millions of others who died, ultimately for this mission.' He turned to face her. 'What would they say, Sal? What would they *think* if they'd just witnessed that... that piece of theatre in there?'

'The dead trusted us. It's time we delivered. It's time we took back control.'

'We're hopelessly outnumbered, Sal. The Axels don't perceive the threat. They don't see evil even when it stares them in the face with its tiny black eyes.'

'Then we have to help them see the Axleth the way we do.'

A smile emerged on his lips. 'You have a plan, don't you?'

'I have a strategy.'

'There you are,' he said, touching her cheek. 'So, where do we start?'

'Ares is already working on it. Where's Elodie?'

'She's prepping to go outside.'

'Perfect,' she said, hooking his arm. 'Let's go watch.'

Elodie hadn't seen her designated Marauder construction bay for sixty years. Last time, the mid-sized ship had been sheathed in metal scaffolding, its hull not yet in place, reminding her of a blue whale skeleton holo she'd seen in the main lecture hall as a kid. Now, the one-hundred-and-fifty-yard-long steel grey hunk bristled not only with cutter beam orifices, but also railguns, because kinetics worked just as well as high energy plasma in the vacuum of space. The grey exterior was mottled in places, dark spots housing gravitic emitters that could serve as shields or directed weapons. The *Dreadnought* was a powerful ship with heavy ordnance, but Marauders were highly manoeuvrable, and could work alone or in coordination.

Her dad called them *wolves*.

And then there was the as yet unverified weapon christened *Crown of Thorns*, identifiable via the three ruby-coloured bands around the Marauder's mid-section. This could be a game-changer – they just needed to test it in space when not travelling at high speed. Given that they were still undergoing last-minute repairs before making the final three-week sprint to meet the other eleven species at the rendezvous point, now was the time, surely? It just needed those overly conservative engineers and scientists to grow a pair.

The Marauders had taken centuries to build. *Space ships are better built in space*, she recalled from her lectures, and each Marauder bay was kept in zero grav conditions. Everyone – no exceptions in the more than eight hundred thousand souls aboard the *Dreadnought* – had at some point worked on *their* Marauder over the past four centuries, and through intricate logistical planning, there hadn't been a single day without some form of design, construction, refinement and testing. She'd missed the first trials of her Marauder, the *Braxton*, during her last sleep cycle, and could barely control the excitement rising inside her chest to take one out into space, to flex its engines and weaponry.

Of course, not everyone would man these sleek wolves. Over 95 per cent of the crew would become pilots in much smaller disc-like alien craft, when the Dreadnought arrived at Orion's Gate. Until that time, all pilots had practised in simulators – even Elodie and her Marauder crew knew how to fly one. But she and sixty others would crew the ten Marauders when it came to the battle.

Drawing the short straw had never felt so good.

She, Ellie and three others boarded the ship by pushing off from the gantry running around its exterior. She drifted across to the hatch, reminiscing about her first playful kick-off at the age of five, when she'd tumbled and giggled until her mother had caught her. Opening up to Sally, she felt a rapid volley of emotions between them, ending when Sally suggested they should cut the tie or risk her crashing into the

Marauder. Sally signed off with, *So proud of you.*

Inside, ship grav kicked in, though they all had mag-boots and gloves just in case. She walked onto the bridge. It had four consoles plus the captain's chair, which Starkel exited as he announced 'Captain on deck.' Starkel was high in the Axel ranking, and commander overall of the Marauder fleet. He was six foot plus change, and shockingly handsome. She was glad she'd just cut the aug connection to her mother.

He was also auged, though not, of course, to her or any other human, or Ares for that matter. Which made her feel embarrassed – she was not yet auged to her own crew. She and her mom had been enjoying *private time*, though they both knew that particular luxury would have to end very soon.

She acknowledged Starkel and took her place without hesitation. He stood next to weapons, manned by Dekker, one of the most competent human augs. Her two other human augs headed back to the auxiliary weapons and engine room stations.

'Ellie, take us out,' she said, then inhaled sharply as Ellie reversed the Marauder out at speed, just as she'd have to do in a battle situation. In less than a second, they were outside, flipping one-eighty so rapidly that Elodie barely had time to glimpse the magnificence of the *Dreadnought*, somehow enhanced now that it had its first battle-scars, drones and manned maintenance craft scuttling around its hull, carrying out repairs.

'Nicely done,' Elodie said, eliciting a glance from Starkel, probably wondering why she spoke rather than auged the compliment to her first officer.

'Segment four of the debris patch has been allocated for target practice,' Starkel announced.

Elodie placed the slim, rainbow-sheened neural headband with a mike boom on her forehead. A holo-screen arose, showing the vast spread of ship carcasses that had comprised the bulk of their fleet. A small flotilla of maintenance ships worked on ordnance retrieval from two of the semi-intact hulls, while a green zone demarcated the deserted *Invincible*, now chunks and fragments. She hoped there were no bodies about to leak out from the *Invincible's* corpse when she began the attack run.

Two other Marauders exited from the other side of the *Dreadnought*, and she saw two faces at the bottom of the holo, a young man and a young woman, both Axels, both auged.

'Single mode for first run,' she said.

'Affirm,' they replied in unison.

She was about to ask Ellie if she was ready. Stupid question. Ellie had been born ready.

'Omega,' she said.

The *Braxton* punched forward, closing the two-hundred-mile gap at a frightening pace, so that the fragments grew large in the holofield. Elodie selected six initial targets, murmuring 'railgun', which Ellie called 'Uzi' for some reason, to test the weapon's precision at this distance. Twin streams of yellow hail lanced forward, streaking towards their targets. Each stream diverged into three. The six targets burst apart, silently shredded. She selected a far larger fragment. 'Torp,' she said, adopting the Axel clipped speech.

This time there was no trail, simply a clicking that began slowly then accelerated to an almost constant tone before an eye-watering explosion of light, as the largest remaining ultra-dense hull section was vaporized.

So far, so–

'Incoming!' Ellie shouted, kicking in the thrusters so hard that Elodie was almost unseated.

Dekker reacted ultra-fast, slamming the incoming missile with railgun fire, so that it ignited twenty klicks out. But it was a nuclear warhead, the unmistakable sphere of white then red heat blossoming outwards at an exponential rate. The blast wave-front slammed into the Marauder, flinging it sideways like a toy.

Ellie had raised the shields just in time.

Elodie glanced at Starkel.

He shrugged. 'Target practice is too easy when they don't fire back. Don't worry; it wasn't a real nuke, just a pretty good fake.'

No kidding. As she flicked through sensors, she found no radiation spike or high thermal energy, but Starkel had raised the stakes. Time to show these Axels a little human mettle. First, a key question. 'The ones firing at us are doing so remotely, correct? From the Dreadnought?'

He eyed her. 'Correct.'

'So I can light things up without killing anyone?'

'You may, though the aim of this exercise was *defensive* manoeuvres.'

'Your aim. Not mine.'

He folded his arms. 'Very well. Captain's prerogative.'

She stood up. 'Reciprocal vector!'

Ellie hesitated. 'That will take us straight through–'

'Don't make me repeat myself!' Elodie shot back.

The Marauder headed straight for the boiling, now shrinking, simulated ball of plasma.

That got a raised eyebrow from Starkel.

'Not cheating,' she said. 'Our shields would handle it if this was for real.'

Starkel said nothing.

As soon as they entered, Elodie shouted to Dekker. 'Targets!'

'Working... *There!*'

It was one of the other defunct ships she'd been told they were scavenging. Evidently, there was more ordnance aboard than they could salvage, so they'd decided to brighten her day.

'They could have another nuke,' Starkel commented.

Elodie didn't reply. As they approached the gutted hull, hundreds of gravitic drones, capable of attaching to a hull and then crushing it to a pulp, swarmed out and gave chase to her Marauder. She gave a command befitting the ship's namesake.

'Dive.'

Ellie grinned. 'Aye, sir.'

The *Braxton* dipped below the enemy target, the swarm of drones swerving in response to chase her.

Starkel folded his arms. Elodie knew he was expecting her to deploy gravitic shields.

She didn't. Offence achieved the same aim as defence, but sent a different message.

'Rings two and three,' she barked.

Dekker obliged, and the rings around the *Braxton* began spinning and unleashing cutter-beam fire, drowning the drones in a shitstorm of plasma fire. None made it through.

'New target,' Dekker said. 'A damaged Marauder they must have salvaged.'

She saw it, a red blob on the holofield. It wasn't attacking. It was making a run for it. She could shoot it down. That would be standard.

'Just to be clear, is this one manned?' she demanded of Starkel.

'No,' he replied.

'Give me helm, forward shields to maximum,' she said to Ellie, who tapped her console then sat back.

Elodie selected the control she wanted. 'Hold on,' she said.

The Marauder leapt forward at a dizzying closing speed. The ship on the run was no match for the *Braxton* in speed or weaponry. Elodie didn't slow down, didn't deviate her course. She swiped away the holofield, just in time to see the already-crippled Marauder loom large, and then she got to see its insides as they speared straight through the ship's mid-section. This time, there wasn't silence; for a cacophonous few seconds, they all heard the grinding, tearing and shearing of metal, the sputtering of muted explosions transmitted through the hull. It cleaved in two, and as she flipped the *Braxton* around, she zoomed in on the front section. The bridge was still intact inside one half.

'You have control,' she said to Ellie.

'I have control.'

Elodie sat back.

Starkel walked forward, staring at the screen. Had the ship been manned, they would now have prisoners to interrogate.

'Unorthodox,' he said. Turning to her, he gave the faintest of smiles. 'I look forward to fighting alongside you in the real battle when it comes.'

With that, he left the bridge to report back to Anya.

Dekker spoke up. 'Well done, Captain.'

Ellie wandered over and spoke softly in her ear. 'I think Starkel likes you.'

Elodie was glad she wasn't auged to her team yet.

She was saved by Stein coming online.

'Captain, we only just finished painting the *Braxton*.'

Elodie froze until Michael's face appeared, grinning. 'I told him jokes are important for human crew morale. But you know how lousy Axels are at telling them.'

Sally pushed into view. 'So proud. We all are. They're cheering down below, everyone who's awake, that is.'

'Thanks, that means a lot. As always, teamwork makes the dream work.' She clicked off.

'Take us home, Ellie.'

'Aye, sir.'

As they cruised past the Eyeship, she changed her mind. She called up the other two Marauders, who were doing routine target practice.

'Are you two up for Crown of Thorns?'

Both captains nodded more vigorously than was usual for Axels.

'Dekker, you take the lead for this one. Ellie, about turn, elliptical pass, you know the drill.'

She sent a private message back to Sasha's console on the bridge, because she knew Hawkins was there watching with her dad.

Hawkins, this one's for you and the Invincible.

Starkel came running back onto the bridge. 'This wasn't

sanctioned. We've never tested this. The feedback loop could cripple all three ships.'

Bullshit! She and Abel had gone over the latest specs and test scores. The risk was marginal. Besides, she reckoned they were going to need this weapon.

'Captain's prerogative,' she said.

Stein attempted to come back online.

Elodie cut comms.

'Silent running, captain comms only. On my mark.'

'*Three...*'

The mid-sections of all three Marauders came alive with crackling, red lightning. The ship shook and juddered. Ellie compensated, holding her steady.

'*Two...*' A full-blown lightning storm lashed out into space, incandescent blood red whips scouring empty space for a target. The other two Marauders followed, half a mile each behind the *Braxton*.

'*One...*' The red lightning strands from all three ships connected. Funny, it did indeed look like an elongated crown of thorns.

'Mark,' Elodie said. The *Braxton* inverted and tore down close to the Eyeship's cracked carcass, the other two Marauders following. The twisting chain of energy looped around the Eyeship's central sphere, tightening like a noose. It tightened further, gouging through the crust, until, as all three Marauders powered away, the crust was cheese-wired into two jagged halves, like an oyster.

'Power down,' she said to the other captains, 'and well done. Head back to the *Dreadnought*.'

The two captains both replied in unison, 'Aye, Commander.'

The last word lingered on the bridge. Starkel was commander. She hoped she hadn't overstepped the mark. But while she was pondering what to say, he stood in front of her.

'You earned it today,' he said, as their eyes locked together.

She was saved by a private message that flashed up on her screen from Sasha's console. It was from Hawkins.

Thank you. For me, my family, and all the souls who died here.

You're very, very welcome, she replied.

And then Sasha followed it up with her own private message.

You'd better get back. Your mother is up to something.

Sally waited on the stage of the vast auditorium for the three Marauder crews, Michael and Abel on her right side, Ares on her left. Other humans and Axels trooped in, a couple of hundred. Neither Sally nor anyone else in her entourage spoke. As the rows of seats closest to the stage filled, chatter arose, and then, like a wave, there was a recognition that almost everyone summoned was auged. Elodie and her crew, plus Starkel, arrived, and the upper doors to the auditorium closed.

Stein, Anya and Qherax entered through the stage-level doors and stepped up onto the stage, approaching Sally. Anya made no attempt to suppress her indignation.

'What is the meaning of this? You have no right to summon our troops, let alone the key bridge staff!'

Sally remained calm, stepped down from the podium, and walked around the inner circle of rows, taking in each individual face of the troops, as Anya had just called them. She stopped near to Elodie, and addressed her daughter, loud enough for all to hear.

'Elodie, congratulations to you and your crews on a superb demonstration, and on validating the Crown of Thorns so that it can now take its rightful place in our arsenal for the coming battle.'

A ripple of enthusiasm washed across the room, murmurings of approval, thumping of boots. The *Braxton's* performance had impressed the Axel crews, and all were relieved the new weapon had worked so well.

She raised her voice. 'But you could have done better.'

Silence seized the room.

Sally turned to face the bridge staff trio. 'How could she have done better?'

They didn't answer.

Elodie did.

She stood and raised her voice. 'If we'd all been auged together, humans and Axels, we'd have shaved thirty seconds off our battle-time.'

Sally, still facing Stein, Anya, and Qherax, asked a question. 'Starkel, do you concur?'

'I do,' he said, as if surprised by his own answer, then louder, 'I concur.'

'Then it is time,' Sally said. She nodded to Abel.

'Wait!' Anya said, glancing from Sally to Abel. 'We need to discuss this! Stein!'

But Stein said nothing, and so Abel tapped a small tablet, then froze. He and all the other augs in the room were suddenly connected, human to Axel, and all to Ares.

Sally had earlier asked Ares if he could do it. He'd replied that since his awakening, he'd hardly worked on anything else. He also saw it as the logical next step.

There were gasps and one or two shrieks from the front rows. Michael had to steady Abel, who almost toppled over, looking as if he'd just been punched.

'You blindsided us,' Anya said, glaring at Sally.

Michael interjected, his arms folded. 'And tell me, Anya, how does that feel?'

'You'd better hope this works,' she shot back. 'We depart for Orion's Gate in thirty minutes.'

'It's already working,' Sally said, and turned to see humans and Axels approaching each other, shaking hands, a few embracing.

'We just raised our game tenfold,' Sally said.

'I hope you're right, for all our sakes,' Anya said. She

glanced at Stein. 'We need to tell her. You need to tell her.' She stormed out.

But Stein needed to tell her nothing, because Starkel already knew, and so therefore, did she.

'Thirty... *thousand*?' she said, feeling the need to sit down. 'You have that many augs in deep sleep?'

Stein walked over and looked Sally in the eye, his digital gold iris growing and shrinking. She wondered what he actually saw.

'We've been busy this last cycle. They will awaken in the coming forty-eight hours. Are you still sure connecting them all is a good idea?'

'Yes,' she said, turning to Ares.

Ares took the bait. 'Any single auged individual can connect comfortably with up to around thirty others. You must already know this. The three hundred and fifty already awake have been split into twelve groups. It will be the same for the others.'

'Then what is the point?' Stein asked, 'except that they can now aug with humans?'

Sally glanced at Michael – they both knew the point. But she stayed quiet.

Ares continued. 'This loosening of the aug connection parameters means that they can now temporarily connect to a thousand others. I am sure you can appreciate the advantages in a large space battle. The connection algorithm is adaptive and optimizing. Outside of battle, they will function as normal in their smaller groups.'

Stein turned to Sally. 'Anya is right. This should have been discussed. Had you laid out the arguments, we would have agreed. You should have trusted us in this respect.'

Sally nodded towards Qherax, who had said nothing so far. 'We're no longer sure about the balance of power on the *Dreadnought*.'

Stein followed her gaze. 'I see.' He turned back to Sally. 'And I understand. Perhaps we misjudged the situation. It is we who should have trusted you.'

Sally stayed quiet.

'We have fight,' he said. 'But you humans can be bold in ways we have not yet mastered.' He raised his voice a notch, so all would hear. 'I want you on the bridge from now on, Sally. Be there in thirty minutes.' His head turned to Ares. 'And since you are auged to Ares, as is my entire elite squad now, he is also welcome.'

Sally didn't miss it. Stein had said 'he'.

Stein called over to Starkel. 'We must talk,' he said.

As Starkel jogged over, he stalled a moment in front of Qherax and winced. Sally felt what he felt in that moment. A sting of revulsion.

After they'd gone, Sally walked up close to Qherax, anger simmering inside her. She made no attempt to dampen it. Everyone in the room grew quiet.

'Back on Earth, Qherax, you wanted this aug tech from us. You ripped it from Jennifer's corpse. Well, here it is; finally, you've got what you wanted. Reap the whirlwind.'

The room was utterly silent, but Sally could feel it, Axels seeing this masked Axleth for what she truly was. Understanding for perhaps the first time – not via books or vids or 'education' – but by direct experience via their human connection, the horrors Qherax and her kind had inflicted.

Qherax's upper lip curled into an ugly smile, but she had the sense to say nothing, and shuffled her way off the stage and out the door.

Elodie joined her mother as everyone crowded around the stage. Sally took Elodie's hand and auged them all a single message.

Now we are ready.

PART TWO

ARMADA

CHAPTER 7

Cube

David stood before the two stasis chambers, regarding his parents. Lara, still pretty, though her face was more lined, her hair less full, her body less lithe. But less is more, so somebody had said, and even in the unconscious bliss of stasis there was a rebelliousness about her. A fire. And Nathan... he'd aged, yes. Hair more salt than pepper, face gaunt, as he kept himself to his gruelling physical, *You'll never get the soldier out of me,* daily schedule when awake. But life was taking its toll. He was sixty, according to the system of age-clocks they all adhered to on this ship, and, he imagined, on any interstellar voyage.

The air was cooler in the sleeper section and laden with static, so nobody hung around that particular deck for long, except the occupants of the misted compartments, who spent years or even decades at a stretch in their exotic coffins. He'd been captain on this leg, though Jaspar, emerged from stasis just yesterday, would now take back control. Christy was holding the Conn, as they all insisted on calling the bridge, as this was the salvaged *Athena,* gutted in the final, desperate battle for Earth's survival. It had taken six months for the Xaxoan ship's incredible self-healing protocols to cannibalise two-thirds of its own unfathomable material and innards to create a new, pared-down, sleeker model.

During that process, overseen by Billy, currently in his lab where he all but slept, the onboard system had re-purposed and re-engineered every non-essential item into more critical infrastructure and hardware: hull reinforcement, shields, navigation, propulsion, comms, and, of course, life support, including the Nextgen stasis pods, way ahead of what the Axleth had available. The result was that whereas the original ship had been a comfortable temporary home for three hundred humans, the new model housed just six adults.

Adults. He supposed it could happen that a child might decide to stay awake and end up older than his or her parents... a scary concept. But the crew was minimal on the *Athena*, and no one had opted to have kids. This was a warship, pure and simple, with a single mission, to help defeat the Eye in the battle at Orion's Gate. He studied his dad, statue-still, and considered that Nathan, after all these years, was still driven, on one last mission, to win this war against the Eye so it could never attack humanity again. And maybe to see Sally one last time.

Billy had brought one non-essential item to Nathan's attention: a cache of information stored by Saarin, one of the *Athena*'s original alien builders. It was a very high-tech cube. Nathan had asked Raphaela about it back on Earth, whether it might have scientific value, and also because she, David and Lara were the only ones to have met the enigmatic alien.

David's mind stalled. He missed Raphaela. She was long dead by now; he knew that. Still, sometimes he talked to her. Maybe Billy did too. After all, Billy had been her protégé, and had almost stayed back on Earth to work with her on countering the threat of the micro black hole the Eyeship had installed in its death-throes, in deep orbit around Earth. He wondered how large it had grown in four hundred years, whether it was already wreaking havoc on the weather as a prelude to tearing Earth asunder in another four hundred years. He could ask Billy, who had a simulation running 24 /

7, working on the problem in the background. It was good to have focus, a project on this voyage, but for Billy it was an obsession that consumed him. Thank goodness Alexandra, another young genius, had come on board, so at least the two could share a life together working on two, parallel, unsolvable problems: the 'black sun' threat to Earth, as Lara had christened it, and Saarin's cube.

Billy had announced the evening before that he'd made a breakthrough on the latter. From the start the problem had been one of frame of reference, since not only was the language and alphabet comprising the info inside the cube alien, Saarin's society, values, and entire culture were utterly unknown to them. All they had to go on were the snippets and anecdotes Lara could share from her five years with the enigmatic, taciturn alien, and four of those five years she'd spent in stasis.

Now they were nearing the wormhole, everyone had to be awake and on full alert. He had a suspicion this news about Saarin's cube couldn't wait. Funny, almost four hundred years of mind-numbing boredom, of trying to stay sane on an insanely long voyage, and all of a sudden there was a sense of urgency. Billy had said the breakthrough could be a game-changer.

David placed his hand on the console and spoke to the ship. There was no Ares aboard, and none of the crew were auged – except Nathan, whose eyebrow aug implant was dormant – just home grown, unadorned human stock, so voice command had to do.

'Wake Nathan and Lara,' he said.

There was no reply. The ship only spoke when it needed to.

'See you soon,' David whispered, as the awakening cycle began. Small lights picked up the pace, pulsing faster. He quit the chamber to join Christy in the Conn. After all, it wasn't fun watching your parents throw up.

Nathan's mouth felt like sandpaper and tasted of rotting seaweed. Not a winning combination. He brushed his teeth until his gums bled. Lara had done a disappearing act into one of the shower cubicles half an hour previously. He wasn't convinced she was ever coming out, but then she emerged.

'Is it me, or is it worse each time?' she asked, dabbing at her hair with a towel.

'Well, we're not getting any younger.'

'Technically, we're the same age as fifty years ago when we crawled into these coffins.'

'Technically,' he said. He felt he aged in his pod every time.

'You're four hundred and sixty,' she said, then walked up to him, dropped the towel, draped her arms around his neck, and kissed him.

She tasted of peaches. How did she do that?

'I always had a thing for older men,' she said.

'You guys awake?' David cut in from the Conn. He didn't wait for an answer. 'Conn, now, please.'

Nathan began getting dressed. 'Later,' he said.

'Something's rattled him.'

'We're nearing the wormhole,' Nathan replied.

She pulled her clothes out of a drawer. 'It's something else.'

Nathan never *got* her intuition. But then he never got his own, either, and he realized what he'd assumed was the gnawing pit of hunger following a half-century of stasis, was in fact his gut telling him they were in trouble.

They both made it to the Conn in record time.

Nathan knew an ambush when he saw one. Billy was pacing

with arms folded, staring into the space before him, no doubt seeing equations no one else could see. He could quite happily be alone in a crowded room. It wasn't that people didn't matter to him, just that science mattered more.

The problem with repetitive stasis, especially with older subjects, was a light 'temporal disorientation' as Billy had coined it. The order of memories got jumbled up. It only lasted an hour, but right now, for Nathan, it was as if only yesterday Billy had been that little kid with irrepressible blond hair and a talent for asking questions way beyond his age group, or any age group for that matter. Now he was a full-grown man, driven, tolerating others to a limited extent, waging a personal war with equations that Nathan was sure would have left even Raphaela flummoxed. Alex, his partner, was quiet, demure even, though her mind was razor-sharp. Lara had predicted them as a couple the day the young girl – now young woman – had stepped aboard.

It had been a controversial decision – to put it mildly – for Nathan and Lara to crew the *Athena* with four kids. *Are you out of your mind?* had been one of the politer criticisms back on Earth. But Raphaela had laughed, saying it made sense. Kids were more resilient, and would grow up seeing the ship as their home, unlike adults who could get seriously homesick.

Not Nathan. He'd had enough of 'home'. Three tours in Afghanistan and two running battles with the Axleth on Earth had cured him of that.

Christy appeared, another of Braxton's original 'mini-crew' as they'd been called. Back then, she'd been bird-like, a skittish girl with blonde pigtails. Now she oozed competence, if not confidence, and was the glue that stopped them all flying apart. Although Lara was older, Christy was in every sense the mother figure on the ship, making them all eat, sleep and exercise properly. Billy pushed back occasionally, telling her to get a kid of her own. Which was a sore point; two in fact, as they'd decided at the outset not to have kids pre-battle – as if there was a realistic prospect of post-battle – and because she longed for Jaspar, who was astute in everything else other than what was right in front of his nose.

Jaspar arrived, tall with dark hair that showed the first traces of grey, as he'd remained awake longer than anyone else on board, with a permanent frown that might just as well have been a tattoo, as it never left his face. As usual, he seemed distracted, as if he had some place better to be. 'Coffee,' he croaked with a dry, post-stasis throat. Christy passed him a mug she'd already prepared, and gazed at him as she offered it with both hands. From her perspective, she'd not seen him for a year; from his, it was yesterday. Stasis was a 'mindfucker', Lara had said more than once. Jaspar took the mug without even seeing her. Lara had said privately to Nathan, *Be patient.* Four hundred years seemed to stretch the notion to breaking point. His heart went out to Christy.

'S'up?' Jaspar said, smacking his lips, his voice regaining its customary exuberance. If you lined up the entire crew and asked an outsider who was captain, nine out of ten would select Jaspar. He was also muscled, but quick and lithe, the only crew member spending more time in the gym than Nathan. They sparred occasionally. If it ever came down to hand-to-hand combat with the Eye, which of course it wouldn't, Nathan would put Jaspar in the ring.

Nathan glanced towards his son David, second-in-command. Was there any envy, jealousy, ambition to be first? None. He and Lara, who'd never wanted kids, had done a surprisingly reasonable job, though probably most parents thought that about their children. And then a terrible thought gate-crashed his proud-party, something Trescoe, damn him, had said back in Helmand all those years ago, a quote from *War and Peace*, that in peacetime sons mourn their fathers, and in wartime... He guillotined the thought.

Billy took centre stage. 'I believe the Eye is working on a new weapon.'

Jaspar's cup stalled halfway to his lips. 'How can you possibly know that?' he shot back.

Billy ignored the cutting edge in Jaspar's voice and flicked the fingers of his right hand into the ether. A slowly rotating holo-cube etched into pseudo-existence, each side flush with equations whose symbols Nathan didn't even pretend to know, let alone understand. The Conn quietened. Jaspar and Christy walked up close to it.

'Shit!' Jaspar said.

Christy tightened her lips; if anyone else had uttered an expletive, except Lara who had special privileges for some unknown reason, she would have reprimanded them.

'You see it, right?' Jaspar said, turning to Christy.

She blushed, and nodded, saying nothing. For the umpteenth time, Nathan wondered why Jaspar didn't smell the coffee, or why Christy didn't just deck him. For sure, Jaspar wouldn't see it coming.

Jaspar turned to the older members of the crew. 'I'm guessing you two don't?'

'They don't,' David answered for them, depriving Nathan and Lara of any snarky come-backs. Yet Jaspar's face looked even more serious than usual. Nathan had been a soldier most of his adult life, and if the enemy had a new weapon...

'What is it?' he asked.

'A black star,' Christy answered, having found her voice again.

Billy walked away from the holo and nodded to Alex to take over. Nathan had noticed this before: Billy looked after the theory, Alex the ramifications. It was an effective scientific partnership. David had said it was the best since Marie and Pierre Curie.

Alex spread her hands wide and a new image formed. Her voice was a salve for the ears, reminding him of Raphaela. A dark disc, only marginally lighter than the space around it, like a demonic eclipse.

'A black hole?' Nathan ventured.

'Close' Alex replied. 'Actually, very close. If a star

collapses but doesn't have quite enough mass and other features to lead to a black hole, it can, theoretically, lead to a black star. It can also be called a black planet, as it is in effect an ultra-dense mass.'

'A singularity?' Nathan tried again.

'Again, no. The mass is more evenly spread, rather than in a vanishing point.'

'So, no event horizon,' Lara interjected.

Nathan shut up. He was out of his league.

'Correct,' Alex said, smiling. She and Lara got on well, Nathan had noted. He'd once asked Lara in the mess if she wanted another child. *Already got one*, she'd replied, hardly stopping to munch the mulch that passed for food on the *Athena*, nodding towards Alex who at the time had been in rapt conversation with Billy.

'How is a natural phenomenon a weapon?' Nathan asked, determined to rejoin the fray. Weapons, at least, were his territory.

'It's almost certainly not natural,' Jaspar said. 'And while no one can control a black hole, a black star or planet, well, in theory, you could. Especially if you'd engineered it in the first place.'

'How would it work as a weapon, though?'

'Gravity,' Lara said. 'But unlike a black hole, where you can see the event horizon and stay the hell away from it, with this, you'd barely see anything at all until you were very close.'

Alex nodded. 'Exactly! Like a black hole, little light escapes. And if Saarin's interpretation is correct, this engineered black star could ramp gravity up and down. Approaching ships wouldn't see it, wouldn't pick up any strange gravimetric readings until it was too late.'

Nathan felt miserable. This wasn't just a game-changer; it felt like *game over*.

Billy strode into the centre, flicked away the image, and opened up the cube again. Nathan vaguely recalled that Saarin's people used three-dimensional maths. He guessed that was what he was looking at.

'The code is here,' Billy said, pointing to the fourth row on one of the cube's sides. It's theoretical, of course. Saarin and his people extracted this from the Axleth Mothership's data-core in the last hours before the Xaxoan world was overrun. The Axleth themselves had somehow gotten hold of it from the Eye, and were trying to unravel what it was. It was in a different language, of course, in fact an Axleth translation of whatever code the Eye uses, and Saarin spent most of his long trip to Earth trying to decode it. He was almost finished...'

'Raphaela would have been so proud of you, Billy,' Lara said.

The Conn stilled, except for Alex lightly touching Billy's arm.

David un-stilled it. 'The black star is a double-whammy, actually. Jaspar?'

Jaspar nodded, taking up the reins again. 'The black star can feed on mass. As ships approach it, it can draw them in, crush them, and expel energy into the bargain.'

'The more you throw at it, the more it destroys you,' Lara translated.

Nathan's mind raced. Earlier, he'd been thinking of an ambush. How right he'd been.

'We need to warn Sally and the others,' he said. 'How much time did we make up?' This was a key piece of intel. The modified *Athena* could travel marginally faster than the large Axel bullet-ships.

'Five-and-a-half months,' Christy said.

'So just two weeks behind?' But his gut twisted a notch. Sally and the others were themselves late to the party. If they went straight ahead, and the other species formed an armada and entered the nebula... By the time the *Athena* got there, it could all be over.

Later. First, he needed to look after crew morale, given this dismal news.

'Alright, so the Axleth knew about this, knew the Eye

was working on it, because Saarin stole the information from them in the first place. We know the Axleth invited eleven other species to the battle. We have to assume that one or more of those species can help counter this new weapon.'

Lara smiled his way. Her arms were folded, but she surreptitiously raised a thumb.

'So this is what we need to–'

Jaspar cleared his throat loudly, cutting Nathan off. 'While this is the reason Billy wanted you awake, there's another reason we woke you.'

Billy and Alex exchanged a glance. Whatever it was, it was news to them, too.

'We picked up something on long-range sensors yesterday evening,' Jaspar said. 'Christy?'

She obliged. A starfield image formed in front of them, wall-to-wall, floor-to-ceiling.

'That's us,' Jaspar said, pointing to a small red dot near the ceiling. 'And that's the wormhole, two days away.'

Nathan stared at the tiny glistening marble at the upper limit of the display. But his gaze was drawn to a series of white spots at the periphery of the image, just off the floor. The Athena appeared stationary, though he knew in real terms it was travelling incredibly fast. But these dots seemed to move, though at a snail's pace, which meant they were going even faster.

'Vector prediction,' Jaspar said, and thin grey lines appeared, connecting every single dot with the wormhole. A red line joined the *Athena* to the distant marble. There was a time-stamp, one red, one grey. Barring a few minutes, they read the same.

Nathan didn't need to do any maths, or indulge in wanton fantasies that those dots were friendly ships. No, the picture was crystal clear. They were in a race to get to the wormhole, and in any race, only one thing mattered.

Studying the faces of his young crew, he recalled those who'd said it was crazy to bring them, that he should have taken seasoned veterans, or at least adults. He had to admit, he'd had the occasional doubt. Right now he had none. He'd picked the best crew.

He turned to Billy, who had the best understanding of *Athena*'s engines.

'Billy, we need more speed.'

CHAPTER 8

Crucible

Sally tried not to stare across the bridge towards the Axleth creature, horizontal amidst an array of displays that practically enveloped its head like a flickering crown. It barely moved. Much like Ares, next to her, who made no pretence at not staring at the creature. Outwardly, Ares looked relaxed as ever, but her aug told her a different story.

'You want to kill it, don't you?' she asked.

Ares didn't reply.

'Michael says silence can speak volumes.'

'He is the wisest human aboard,' Ares replied.

She cocked her head at him. Was that humour?

Qherax reappeared from the elevator. She'd been gone the past half hour. No doubt with the other half of the unholy pair of Axleth 'originals'. She'd dyed her hair red again. Sally wondered why. But in some ways it meant that Sally could think of her more easily as 'enemy-temporarily-my-ally', rather than a frail old woman.

Hawkins appeared from the next elevator, looking lost. But he'd cleaned up well, his hair cut short, his beard trimmed. He surveyed the bridge. When his eyes alighted on Sally, he made a bee-line for her.

'How are you doing?' she asked.

'Needed to be here,' he replied. She understood. He'd watched five ships destroyed. Only one got away, at great sacrifice. Damned right he needed to be here. They'd held a ceremony for his family the previous evening, shortly before the larger ceremony for the more than four million others who'd perished.

'How close is the *Prometheus*?' he asked.

'It's still far, but we're both closing at top speed, so...'

'Thirty-eight minutes and thirteen seconds,' Ares offered.

'Thanks,' Hawkins said, in such an easy-going way it surprised both her and Ares. People – humans and Axels alike – were usually wary around Ares. Except the augs.

'Make yourself at home,' she said to Hawkins.

'They fought really hard,' he said. 'The crew, that is. To get away.'

Sally had seen enough PTSD in her lifetime to know there was little she could or should say. Platitudes were the worst. She imagined what Nathan would say.

'We'll make the Eye pay,' she said.

His head swung around to her, his eyes suddenly sharp. 'I can pilot a Stinger,' he said.

She nodded. 'I'll see what I can do.'

Hawkins braved a smile, but his face was like broken glass. He'd never be whole again. He noticed where Ares was staring and followed his gaze to Qherax and the Axleth pilot.

'The Axleth pilot did her bit, you know. Could have argued for our ship to be the one that escaped. Wouldn't have worked out, tactically.' He straightened his tunic. 'Is there somewhere I can watch, where I won't get in the way?'

Sally auged Abel and Sasha, who looked up from their console, and waved him over to theirs.

Alone, her gaze swept across the entire bridge. Stein and Anya, and the other thirty Axels who made up the bridge crew, were busy. The *Dreadnought* had made contact with the *Prometheus*, the surviving Axel warship that had escaped the attack on the fleet at the wormhole exit. They'd been in comms range for thirty minutes. Not that anything meaningful had been exchanged. Something to do with combined closure rates. She touched base with Elodie, outside in her Marauder, the *Braxton*.

'Do you have visual yet?' she asked.

'Patching it through. There. You should see it now. It's just in range. Looks like the definite article.'

Elodie sounded calm, collected, every bit the captain.

'How are you getting on, Michael?' Sally asked.

Michael had asked to be on one of the Marauders in the stretched-out vanguard, travelling at top speed, just in case there were any more surprises between them and the Armada. Naturally, Elodie's ship had been in the lead, barely in sensor range herself. Sally couldn't fault the tactic, but why did it always seem to be Elodie out there in harm's way? Additionally, she was too far away for the aug tech to work. And to boot, Michael had been with her when the mission had suddenly turned *interesting*.

'Can't complain,' Michael said. 'Haven't retched for over an hour now.'

'There's hope for you yet.'

'How are you doing?' he asked, returning the favour.

She glanced again at her sand-coloured, insectoid nemesis. 'Wishing the Axleth pilot's workstation was closer to an airlock. Oh, and Ares said you are the wisest human on board.'

'Maybe his programming needs maintenance.'

Ares caught her attention by pointing at the display showing the *Prometheus*. There was a small dot ahead of it. One of the *Prometheus*'s Marauders, she guessed.

'One of ours should go out to meet it,' Elodie said. 'Guess who drew the short straw? Gotta go, we'll be out of aug range for a while.'

'Watch yourself,' Sally said.

She felt a gnawing in her gut. Funny, Nathan had had

legendary gut instinct. The one thing she'd learned from him was not to ignore it. But she tempered hers with logic. Why *was* the *Prometheus* coming back? Surely it would have gone straight to the rendezvous point at Orion's Gate?

Something didn't add up.

She headed over to Stein's central console and, as expected, was intercepted by Anya's steel voice. Fair enough, she'd blindsided Anya earlier, after all. And just because Axels had their emotions dampened down, didn't make them robots.

'He's busy,' she said without looking up. 'We all are.'

'Has the *Prometheus* confirmed all authenticity codes?'

'Yes,' Anya replied, then looked up. 'What do you think we've been doing?'

'Codes can be replicated. Are you sure they've not been... compromised?'

Anya leant back a moment. 'We've been through a complex series of quantum-tech-resistant handshake security protocols that involve pairs of large prime numbers. Those codes can't be broken, even by AIs. All the handshakes were flawless.'

'Have you *talked* to them?'

At least Anya didn't roll her eyes, though Sally sensed escalating impatience.

'There's still a delay, signal interference as we approach each other at high speed. That is to be expected.'

'So, you *haven't* talked to them.'

Anya sighed. Several lights lit up on her display. Her fingers danced over the tactile pad and they disappeared. 'What is it you suggest we do?'

'Ask them to stop.'

'Stop?'

'Meet face to face with the *Braxton*. Then proceed.'

Anya's fingers drummed once on the console. 'Differential speeds... acceleration profiles... We'll lose hours.'

Sally shrugged. 'Four hundred years, a few hours.'

'We're already late. The Eleven are waiting for us. We

need all the intel we can get from the *Prometheus*.'

Without breaking gaze, Sally pointed with her arm back to the Axleth pilot. 'How did they defeat us, Anya?'

Extra lights flared into life on Anya's console. Her fingers didn't budge. Her eyes bore into Sally's.

'Deception,' she answered.

Sally said no more.

Anya's lips tightened, then she spoke to her mike. 'Stein, I need a word.'

Unusually, Stein came over to Anya's console.

'Make it quick,' he said.

She nodded to Sally, who told him her suggestion. Stein considered it while his eye did its thing; clearly he was interrogating data feeds.

'Send a message to both the *Prometheus* and the *Braxton*,' he said. 'Transmit coordinates.'

Anya's fingers danced over the console.

A single light pulsed.

They waited.

'Well?' Sally asked after a minute.

Anya's face grew more concentrated, if that was possible. Ares joined them. Sally noticed several Axels glance across from their consoles.

'It's taking longer than usual.' Her fingers blurred again.

'Contact Starkel,' Stein said. 'Tell him to intercept.'

'And Elodie,' Sally added, hearing the tension in her own voice.

Anya tapped harder. 'It's not slowing, and I can't reach the *Braxton*.'

Ares whirled around, his fingers morphing into needle-pointed daggers as he dropped into a half-crouch.

Sally turned and flinched as she realized the Axleth pilot was almost directly behind her. Qherax was there, too.

The whole bridge froze as the Axleth's mouth opened, its mandibles clacking amidst a brief burst of staccato hisses.

'What did it just say?' Sally asked.

Qherax leaned on her stick and drew herself tall. 'Enemy,' she said.

Anya stared at her central screen. 'The ship. It's not slowing down. It's... accelerating.'

Stein spun around and strode back to his console. 'Battle stations!'

◆ ◆ ◆

Michael stood next to Elodie's captain's chair, or throne, as he'd called it when first entering the bridge. They were travelling at high speed, the *Prometheus* still a dot on the screen ahead. The holo showed the two ships converging at a snail's pace.

'Any comms?' he asked.

'Just standard protocols.'

'What about Mom? Or Stein? Or that dashing young commander, Starkel?'

She gave him a look.

'Okay, but seriously, nothing?'

'Seriously, this is usual, Dad. Space is mainly boring. Standard protocols are even more boring.'

He watched the two blobs inch closer. 'Can we zoom out?' he asked.

'Remind me who's captain.' But she did as he'd asked. 'Say when.'

He waited until the double-box nebula drifted into view at the far edge of the holo.

'When,' he said.

Elodie rose from her throne and walked inside the expanded holo. 'That's odd,' she said.

Michael joined her. The holo showed a prediction line of where the ship had come from.

'Why was it out there? The logical place was to head straight for the armada assembly point, just outside the nebula's blue box.' Instead, the prediction line came from the yellow section.

Elodie's head swung around to face Ellie. Then she strode back to her chair, leaving Michael alone in the stars.

'What's happening?' he asked.

'It's just increased speed.'

'And gone dark,' Ellie added for Michael's benefit.

'No reply from the *Dreadnought*, either.' Elodie finished. 'The *Prometheus* is jamming comms.'

'What can I do?' Michael said.

'Sit over there,' Elodie said, pointing without looking.

Michael stared at a basic looking seat inside a recess. 'That's an escape pod,' he said.

'It's going to get rough. I can't have you throwing up at a crucial moment.'

He stared at his only daughter. He wanted to protect her. That was his job, right? As a father, that was his *only* job. But who was he kidding? She was a captain. She was in her prime, hard-trained, her mind sharp and swift as a rapier. Even so, a Marauder against the *Prometheus* was going to be like a rabbit taking on a 'gator. He opened his mouth to speak, his head full of emotional clap-trap, and then recalled what Sally had said, that Ares considered him the wisest man on board.

'Aye, Captain,' was all that came out.

He walked over, entered through the oval hole into the pod, and buckled up. The inner door separating him from his pride and joy slid closed, cocooning him in silence. He could still see her through a rectangular window, and she turned to him, just for a second, mouthed *thank you*, and then was lost in a holographic swirl of stars and figures. The emergency escape pod eject handle hung invitingly from the ceiling right in front of him.

He folded his arms.

He was pressed against the harnesses and then rammed back into the cushioned seat, as the *Braxton* performed hard decel, then began manoeuvring violently. It wasn't completely silent: muffled shouts, the grinding of engines under tremendous, way-beyond-design-spec strain, Elodie pushing their craft to the absolute limit. At one point a male voice, urgent, he couldn't tell whose. He guessed Elodie had looped around and engaged the Marauder, but she'd be under fire from both that sister ship and the more heavily armed *Prometheus*. He imagined a hailstorm of railgun fire and cutter beams.

It was only a matter of time.

Michael's head slammed left then right, as he heard the unmistakable sound of tearing metal, something shearing off the *Braxton*. The bridge was suddenly aflame, Ellie's station ripped open, no sign of the poor girl. Elodie was wounded, blood oozing from her right shoulder, standing like the proverbial last man on deck inside a fizzing holofield with bright beams thrashing wildly, trying to end the *Braxton*. At least the flames meant the bridge hadn't depressurised yet. There was still oxygen. But he knew what she was planning: fight to the very last second, go down with her ship.

He decided then and there.

Wisdom was overrated.

He thumped his harness release and kicked at the hatch control. It refused to budge, and so he had to find the manual override. He couldn't see Elodie through the smoke. Suddenly the hatch juddered open, ushering in a cacophony of alarms, but no human shouts, screams or even moans. The ship was still swinging wildly, on autopilot, trying to outrun railgun fire. He crawled across the floor, acrid smoke stinging his eyes, and came across Ellie, flat on her back, eyes wide open, her lips parted as if she had something to say. He hurried on and found Elodie's limp frame. Her face twitched. She was still alive.

Trying not to breathe in the fumes, he hoisted her upwards and staggered back to the hatch, past two more corpses. He shoved Elodie in, then squeezed in next to her, kicked at the hatch control, which mercifully closed automatically this time. He caught one last glimpse of railgun slugs cleaving the roof of the bridge in half, three bodies whipped away in the sudden venting of air. He grabbed the eject handle and yanked hard.

He and his daughter careened away at speed, while the *Prometheus* carved up the *Braxton* until it drifted in smouldering chunks, crimson flames sputtering out, deprived of oxygen. He spotted the enemy Marauder, drifting, scarred and burnt, its own gashed bridge open to vacuum. So, it hadn't been for nothing. He held both his daughter's hands, gripping them hard. He knew he might be hurting her, but he couldn't ease off. The *Prometheus* sprung forward, out of sight. He spoke to its invisible wake.

'You'll be sorry, you sonofabitch. My wife is going to kick your ass.'

Elodie stirred, coughing. He let go of her hands, dug out the small med-kit, and began working on the shrapnel wounds in her shoulder and chest.

◆ ◆ ◆

On the *Dreadnought,* all hell was breaking loose. Starkel was being recalled. He'd been at midway point, in sensor range, and so could detect the skirmish with the *Prometheus*, and relay it back to Stein.

Sally found she had to remind herself to breathe.

'Tell Starkel to deploy recon drones,' Stein shouted.

Anya avoided Sally's glare and tapped in the command.

Sally couldn't speak. Her mouth was full of ash. She stared at the image slowly resolving before her as it was transmitted over vast distance at relativistic speeds. Two Marauders, one in far worse shape than the other. Unfortunately, the former was the one with the letters B-R-A-X on its broken hull. The bridge was completely gone, sheared off, nothing more than charcoaled debris drifting in space. At least there were no bodies visible.

Small mercies.

But Elodie, Michael. She battened down an urge to scream, to retch, to...

Although Ares was standing right next to Sally, he auged

her. *Are you still able to function?*

She caught herself. Ares had temporarily disconnected her from every aug but him. She closed her eyes, gave the aug equivalent of a nod. Nothing more, because on the inside she was ready to fly apart. Ares threw her a lifeline.

'They may still be alive. My analysis of the debris pattern suggests an escape pod was launched from the bridge.'

She gripped his metal hand, squeezed it so hard it would have made a human or Axel squeal. If one – and she couldn't afford right now to think about which one, because those pods were single occupancy – had survived, the survivor could link with the recon drones, follow the breadcrumbs all the way back to the *Dreadnought*, to her. Which meant there had to be a *Dreadnought* to come back to. She let go of Ares' hand. Oddly enough, Braxton came into her mind – not the ship, but the man – and she imagined what he'd say, right here, right now.

Your daughter had the utmost respect for you, Sally. Earn it.

She focused. Behind this image, the main holo showed the remaining Marauders fanning out and looping around in tight ellipses to return, which was going to cost them a time delay in getting back to the *Dreadnought*. Dotted yellow lines predicted exactly when the Marauders would converge, and when the *Prometheus* would be in the *Dreadnought*'s weapons range.

'We need to retreat,' she said, loud enough to get everyone's attention. 'To give Starkel more time to loop back and intercept.'

Anya's face jerked up to glare at Sally. 'You are not in charge here. In fact–'

'To what end, Sally?' Stein asked.

'Crown of Thorns,' she said.

Discussion erupted all over the bridge. Stein raised a hand and quelled it. 'The crew complement of the *Prometheus* is just under a million Axels. We don't know if they are still aboard.'

Anya joined in. 'You want to *shred* our sister ship?'

Sally faced Stein, but spoke to all of them. 'The *Prometheus* is now a weapon. It's not slowing down. You're all thinking that if you can somehow regain control of it, you can double the Axel population out here. But this is literally a double-or-nothing scenario. You're looking at an extinction-level threat. You can *not* take that risk.'

Anya stood up, her face taut. 'Easy for you to say. We have friends, colleagues, some even have family on board the *Prometheus*.' Her voice caught. 'I have a sister. I have to believe they are alive and praying for us to rescue them. If *your* daughter was there–'

The Axleth ground its mandibles again, hissing in brief spurts. It continued for fifteen seconds. Everyone waited for Qherax to translate.

Qherax leaned forward on her stick, her wrinkled face twisting into something resembling a smirk.

'The pilot agrees with the human bitch.' She shrugged and faced Sally. 'His words, not mine.' She turned to Anya, though loud enough for all to hear. 'She also says that the Eye utterly abhors organics. They never take prisoners. Whoever was on board is dead.'

Stein said, quietly. 'Reverse course.'

Anya ran up to his console, distraught. 'Don't do this, Stein, please!'

He was interacting with the holo, then turned to her, his hand on her shoulder.

'You do not have to witness this,' he said.

Kind though his words were, it was if he'd yelled in her face. She turned as if dazed, walked back to her console, and sat down. Her fingers began tapping, slowly, then faster. The bridge hummed with activity again, though the only words spoken were those absolutely necessary.

Hawkins, who Sally had almost forgotten was there, stood by Anya, and said something to her Sally didn't catch. It seemed to calm her. Yet his own family had died enabling the *Prometheus* to escape, and here they all were, about to obliterate it. She didn't know how he wasn't tearing his hair out and screaming damnation.

But that's what Nathan had told her, that war was a crucible, continually forging soldiers and commanders, so they could do things and cross red lines they never would have believed they could cross, until the unthinkable became just another tactic in the war playbook. *War is the Devil incarnate*, he'd said one day, while in one of his rare philosophical moments, *turning men and women into demons*. Yet Stein's moment of tenderness towards Anya, and whatever words Hawkins had just spoken to Anya, showed that they weren't too far gone yet.

The image of the Marauders was gone, and now she stared at the strategic holo as it updated with the new timeline and trajectory. The *Prometheus* was slowing, all its weapons powering up. They finally got an image of the behemoth, slightly longer than the *Dreadnought*. There were no lights, so that it indeed looked like a bullet, but as the definition resolved, it had clearly endured a heavy battle, its hull pitted and gouged, scabs of melted slag plastered all over the front section. The aft – where most of the habitats were, had a broad gash half a mile long, probably where the ship had been ripped open by a shard. Anya, upon seeing it, paused again, the fingers of her right hand balling into a fist.

'Starkel,' she said, her voice firm and clear. 'You have a go.'

'Affirm,' he replied.

The bridge grew quiet again as the nine Marauders, on a convergence course, began spiralling towards the ghost warship.

Railgun fire and cutter beams leached out of every working orifice from the *Prometheus*, some aimed at the *Dreadnought*, which was far enough away to intercept missiles and shield against the cutter beams, others trying to take out the Marauders.

'Watch out for the *Prometheus'* rings,' Sally shouted, and

Anya's fingers blurred. Two Marauders, in avoiding railgun hailstorms and flailing cutter beams, had drifted slightly astern of the enemy ship's bullet-head. Its rings whirred into action, spinning out a barrage of deadly beams, decimating the two Marauders in short order.

'The Crown, Starkel,' Stein shouted. 'Now!'

Nobody on the bridge was sitting anymore, except Anya, who was too busy to stand and watch. The *Dreadnought* spat out covering fire, but the *Prometheus* ignored it, focusing on disabling the remaining Marauders. Even if it had never seen the Crown of Thorns, the Eye, or whatever was controlling the ship, had clearly judged the Marauders to be the greater imminent threat.

'Do we advance, sir?' one of the bridge crew shouted.

'Hold,' Stein replied.

A tough but correct call, Sally assessed. The *Prometheus*, like the *Dreadnought*, had a self-destruct capability, and if they got too close...

A third Marauder exploded, a female Axel bridge controller liaising with it tearing off her neural headband before burying her head in her hands.

But the Crown had begun. Ruby lightning lashed out from each Marauder, barbed plasma fire coiling downwards towards the doomed ship.

There were gasps at what happened next. Bodies, thousands of them, were ejected from the *Prometheus* – men, women, some children, all drifting into space. Most were clearly already dead. But a few were moving as they emerged, though they quickly stilled.

Sally felt stung and sick at the same time, but there was no going back now.

'Stein!' Sally shouted, because he himself was staring in shock at the images.

He gathered himself. 'Starkel, execute!'

Blood red lightning forks from the remaining six Marauders linked. They began sawing through the hull. The

Prometheus began to break up.

The rest was a horror movie: hundreds of thousands of bodies floating into space amidst the bullet's hull that looked like it had been turned inside out.

'Starkel, pick up as many bodies as you can,' Stein said.

Anya sat, her hands in her lap, staring at the console. Sally didn't know what to say. Hawkins stepped up.

He stood in front of Anya, gaining her attention. 'I'm a pilot. Let's go help collect the dead.' She looked up at him awhile, as if he'd spoken a foreign language, then got up and walked over to Stein.

'Permission to–'

'Go, Anya.'

Sally watched them leave. Qherax was conversing quietly with the Axleth pilot, then she walked over.

'We need to talk.'

Sally didn't feel like talking, but if there was useful intel coming from this carnage, she wanted it. Ares joined them.

Qherax spoke. 'Such tactics... We have never seen the Eye behave like this.'

'So? What does that mean?'

'It means two things. The first is that the Eye is worried, which is a good thing.'

'And the second?'

'It means they are studying organics – not merely annihilating them – in order to find out how better to defeat them, to exploit their weak spots. The Eye is even more dangerous now than before.'

'It means one more thing,' Sally said.

Qherax waited. Ares too.

'If the Eye is so desperate, it can make mistakes.'

'A machine intelligence like the Eye does not make mistakes,' Qherax countered.

'You're right at a tactical level. But at a strategic level, it will judge certain risks more justified in order to win. As we used to say, it will be more prepared to go out on a limb.'

'And how does that help us?'

'I don't know yet. It's something to discuss with the Eleven when we reach Orion's Gate.'

Qherax drifted back to the Axleth pilot.

A buzz of activity and raised voices gained Sally's attention. Several of the controllers huddled around a holo. One of them glanced over to Sally, smiling.

'What's going on, Ares?'

He walked forward and tapped at Anya's console. The holo image zoomed out, all the way back to the two burned and broken Marauders who'd traded lethal fire. A single pulse blinked.

'Starkel has broken off from collecting bodies and is heading out to the escape pod.'

Sally found she was sitting down at Anya's workstation. She just needed to sit.

'Who...?' she managed to say, after a few seconds.

'Two life-signs,' Ares said. 'Wait...'

Sally couldn't breathe. Her head was down, unable to look up, her arms folded, fingernails digging into her elbows.

'Sally,' Ares said, and then auged her a visual image of the two occupants.

She uttered a cry, and broke down at Anya's console, Ares beside her, his hand on her shoulder.

Nobody minded.

Nobody said a word.

But as she held herself, she felt a deep pang stab right through her. Yes, Elodie and Michael were alive, which was *everything*. And the Dreadnought had survived. But so many Axels had just lost their lives in the most terrible way. And like it or not, she'd played a big part in that. She spoke to Anya's empty console.

'I'm so sorry, Anya.'

CHAPTER 9

The Eleven

A week had passed since the awful encounter with the *Prometheus.* Sally felt scarred by it and wished she could move on as fast as the Axels. In that respect, the opening of aug channels between humans and Axels had been helping others, including Abel, Sasha and even Elodie. Sally, not so much. But at last they were at the rendezvous point, ready to meet with the Eleven, ready to join battle against the Eye.

She gazed at the armada bathed in blue and red light from the nebula. An endless sprawl of ships harbouring different species, enclosed in metallic hulls of all shapes and sizes. The vista reminded her of an image she'd once seen of myriad herds grazing on the plains of the Serengeti in Africa. Antelope and lions, prey and predators, sharing the same space.

She wasn't alone in viewing the galaxy's best chance at defeating the Eye. The observation deck that ran all the way around the *Dreadnought's* circumference was packed to capacity. Ten thousand other viewers were all agape, pointing, recognizing a type of ship and its alien designation. The Axels knew far more about the Eleven, as they'd been educated since birth about the upcoming all but holy war against the Eye.

Sally and the rest of the human contingent needed to catch up fast.

She'd had to fight through crowds to get to this main viewing area. Everybody on board had awakened, and to say the air was electric was an understatement. It seemed as if every Axel within earshot had their favourite species. Like old epic TV series of superheroes, each of the Eleven had particular attributes sought by the Axleth, and only together could they defeat the Eye. The Axels glossed over how the Axleth had gathered the Eleven species together, defending what they had done to achieve this by saying that without the Axleth, these species would never have dreamt of joining forces until it was too late. The Eye would have picked them off one by one. Sally had argued back, saying that they could have achieved the same result by diplomacy rather than stealth and coercion. Michael had counselled her to let it go, because by now it was what it was. The Axel-human contingent made the total joint force twelve species, and that was what was needed to take down the Eye. Finally, they were all here, and every species had a job to do. She knew he was right, and did her best to let it go.

Word of the *Dreadnought*'s prevailing against not one but two attacks had spread to the other species in the armada, a foretaste of what Axels and humans were bringing to this party – their *fight*. But Sally and the other humans, Elodie in particular, were licking their wounds and mourning those lost. Sally had known Ellie back on the *Athena*, and though Ellie had been a deep sleeper on the *Dreadnought*, so that she'd only aged thirteen years, Sally felt that she'd just lost a peer. She opened up her aug, just to check, but most other augs were still in privacy mode, dealing with their grief on their own terms or in small intimate clusters. Elodie was with Michael somewhere. Sally was glad about that. Her newfound maternal instincts were still rough at the edges.

She sensed a shift in the mood of the surrounding Axels. Many had only awoken in the past couple of days, and so the two recent battles were just words to them, not experiences.

They were here to wage the battle for which they'd trained all their lives. For which they'd been bred. But the crowd's exuberance was ebbing. Something was wrong. She caught the refrain of three words several times, while people pointed to different sections of the armada, as if searching for something. The first word she barely knew, a species known as the Syrn, who possessed a vast fleet of aggressive, tooled-up mega-warships that would have dwarfed the *Dreadnought*. The second word, however, she knew only too well. The Xaxoan were Saarin's race. The third word sent a cool tingle down her spine. *Missing.*

As if on cue, Ares pinged her.

There are only nine.

It didn't make sense. From what she had understood in various briefings, the Syrn were in fact the closest to the Eye's base, and Saarin's people were much closer to the wormhole than Earth, their ships slightly faster to boot. So why weren't they here?

Meet me in the auditorium, she auged back.

I am not invited.

True. Qherax and the Axleth pilot would be there, along with Stein and fifty others constituting Battle Command on the last remaining Axel battleship. Qherax and the Axleth pilot were still wary of Ares, and he didn't fit anywhere in the command structure.

Come anyway, she auged, and began forging her way through the crowd.

Inside the massive, clam-shaped auditorium, the holo depicting the armada spanned most of the available space. That included the first ninety rows, leaving Sally and all other attendants only ten rows at the back from which to view the armada in all its glory. It was as alluring as it was confusing: a whirlpool of assorted sundry ships, some gigantic, others mere dots at this scale of image.

Stein came to the rescue. He was down on the floor at the lectern. He highlighted one segment after another.

'This is the Par'aal fleet. Planet miners, harvesting minerals and materials, anything from small asteroids, to comets and gas giants. Their chemical ordnance is second to none.'

Their fleet was the ugliest, from what she could see. Massive, city-sized ships with saw-tooth metallic mouths big enough to swallow a small asteroid, and matt-black spheres covered with a spaghetti of pipes, stubby towers, and buzzing attendant ships. If brute force was required, and for sure it would be at some point, they fit the bill. If nothing else, their ships would keep the Eyeships busy for some time.

The Xylyxl – she repeated it several times to lend her tongue some muscle memory – had needle-shaped ships called Starpiercers. Stein had no further information, other than they were very fast, and could penetrate any hull. She imagined a dozen of them syringing into an Eyeship. Something she'd like to see play out for real.

Ares hadn't arrived yet. She wondered what was keeping him.

Stein highlighted another segment of ships, emerald green and pyramid-shaped, then struggled over the pronunciation, and asked Qherax to assist. Their name sounded like a death-rattle. Stein cleared his throat and said they would be known on this ship as the Ankh. At first she thought that odd, though clearly they needed a name that Axels and humans could pronounce during battle. Then she noticed the ankh symbol on the largest Pyramid, and wondered... had this species visited Earth thousands of years earlier?

Their function was unusual. They were ancient, the oldest surviving species. How exactly that was going to help in a battle, she wasn't sure, but the Axleth must have had their reasons.

The Fronn were aquatic, living in ultra-dense liquid gases under immense pressure, as in gas giants. What they brought to the party was surprising, to say the least. They could extinguish small stars. She stared at the odd-shaped ships that reminded her of cuttlefish, and wondered if they could help Earth overcome the mini-black hole growing in its neighbourhood. The thought snagged her mind back to the plight of millions – Axels and humans alike – who were living in the shadow of a time-bomb. The black hole would reach a dangerous size in another three hundred and eighty years, and fifty years after that the Earth and the moon would be gone. Trouble was, even if she left now with some magic box of alien tricks, she wouldn't make it in time. She hoped they were evacuating somewhere, Mars if nowhere else, or else that Raphaela's legacy had led to a scientific breakthrough...

She refocused. *Ares – where are you?*

Outside. They will not allow me to enter, he auged back.

She wasn't surprised. *Okay. I'll keep this link open.*

He gave the aug all-in-one handshake that served as acknowledgement, agreement and thank you. She tuned back in to Stein.

The Korg – again, it was the best Stein could do given the language differences – were terraformers. Their capability bordered on alchemy. Rumour had it they were pacifist and ecological. The Axleth had had a hard time co-opting them for battle. Their diamond-shaped ships, dwarfed by all the others, hung in swarms of single-creature ships; there was no 'mothership'. The Diamonds never rested, moving in waves that rose and fell. It was hypnotic, like flocks of starlings at sunset. She recalled that back on the observation deck, the Korg had been a real hit with the younger Axels, who lost no time in rebranding them as 'Korgi'. She imagined the Axleth wanted them for clean-up, to terraform the Eye's homeworld after the battle. Unless there was another reason...

The Lleynach would have been Michael's favourite with their hammer-headed ships. Planet-breakers, plain and simple.

They had a reverse-ecological approach, levelling the planets of any star systems near to them, to avoid new life-forms emerging that could one day be a threat. The only race they got on with, not surprising once she'd thought about it, was the Par'aal, who would move in afterwards to mine the accretion disks left in the Lleynach's wake.

She grudgingly saw the Axel point of view – how would diplomacy ever bring the Lleynach and the Korg to the same table? But it raised an even more tricky consideration. What would happen after the battle, assuming this alien consortium won the day? Many of these species had been relatively ignorant of each other. Space was sparsely populated, small fecund islands in a vast, otherwise barren ocean. But once you met allies and saw their capabilities, how could you just go back to your corner afterwards and assume they wouldn't come a-knocking, alone or in alliances, with aggressive, imperialistic ambitions to colonize new worlds?

The Tchlox – she could just about get her mouth around the word – had ring-shaped ships that looked inoffensive enough, but with perhaps the most significant weapon: gravity. Axels and humanity might well be the talk of the hour in the armada, but without doubt every race here envied this one species, because gravity was the ultimate weapon. And for that reason, Sally would put them first as potential post-war allies, to enlist them to defuse the growing black hole imperilling Earth. The other fleets kept a healthy distance from the Tchlox.

What is Qherax doing? Ares interrupted.

She focused on the Axleth-made-human. Qherax seemed tense. Occasionally her thin lips moved, inaudible at this range. As for the Axleth pilot, Its mandibles were moving.

They're communicating. I wonder what they're discussing.

Indeed, Ares replied.

The eighth species had only a numerical designation, as their language and culture were mathematical, though nothing so simplistic as decimal. Seven-Three-One, Stein announced, which had presumably been dumbed down by orders of magnitude, and for a moment Sally thought he'd forgotten to highlight their location in the armada. Then she noticed a hazy splash of pink dots. Ah, it made sense. She recalled this one from a lecture in her previous wake-cycle. The 7-3-1 were small, but in the spirit of *make your fault your biggest strength*, their expertise resided at the nano-level. Apparently, several species who had underestimated this tiny race were now defunct, literally taken apart by weapons they couldn't even see. *Imagine a space-battle against mosquitoes*, Michael had once quipped. Being a hyper-math culture, they were also as close to the Eye as any known organic species could get, which might help in predicting their enemy's moves. She was relieved the 7-3-1 were on the same side.

The last species had a name that took a good thirty seconds to speak, so Stein again cleared his throat and, to Sally's relief, announced them as the Theon. Their weapon, if you could call it that, was illusion. Their ships were cubes with darkened mirror sides, as if to advertise their deceptive nature. Although deceit had played its part in various wars back on Earth, she wondered how effective it would be against the Eye, surely less easily fooled than organic senses.

Stein paused and said something she didn't catch to Qherax. Then he spoke louder, for all to hear.

'The Syrn are missing,' he announced. 'We believe they entered the nebula ahead of us two months ago. They have neither returned nor has there been any contact with them since.'

Not good. But Sally waited, and sensed that Ares was also completely focused on whatever Stein would say next, about the other missing species, the one who had created him.

Stein again conversed in a low voice Sally could not catch. The exchange went on for a minute, involving the Axleth pilot. Qherax looked very uncomfortable, and Stein... he looked furious.

'The Xaxoan are not coming,' he said flatly.

Sally wondered what had happened. The Axleth invasion of the Xaxoan homeworld had been comprehensive, according to Saarin, the last uninfected survivor of that race.

Chatter erupted all around the auditorium. Someone shouted from the opposite wall. 'But sir, they represent the best intelligence we have. They can create AI weapons and counter-offensives.'

Others joined in the fray until Anya asked a key question.

'Does the rest of the armada know?'

'It does now,' Stein replied.

Axels didn't do uproar, but it was close enough, and she imagined parallel scenes all across the armada. The Axel fleet had been reduced to a fraction of its expected strength, a single base ship no less, and now two entire species were missing. But wait... that's not what Stein had said, and he was always ultra-precise, careful with his words. The Syrn were *missing*, but the Xaxoan were *not coming*.

That made little sense, from what little she knew about the Xaxoans from Ares. They'd been a terribly responsible and caring species; if there was a battle against the Eye, they'd want to be right there in the front line.

A loud bang behind her interrupted her thoughts as the auditorium doors flew open. Ares, chased by two Axel security guards, bounded down the steps five at a time like an athlete, until he reached Stein, Qherax, and the Axleth pilot. Qherax went into a fighting stance, hands raised high, praying-mantis style, as Sally had witnessed once before back on Earth shortly before the Manhattan Citadel had fallen.

The Axleth pilot didn't move at first, but then raised itself up in one fluid movement with surprising speed, to its full height, more than twice as tall as those around it, its fore-claws poised, its mandibles wide. Sally didn't hesitate, and headed down as well, as the whole auditorium hushed. The Axels were seeing a different side of their progenitors.

Seeing their true colours.

What happened next was unexpected. Ares began conversing in Axleth – clicks and hisses that rose in pitch and volume. When Sally was just halfway, Ares sent her – and all the other augs – a message.

Forgive me, I cannot let this pass.

She didn't know what that meant, but before she took another step, her head exploded with pain. She stumbled and crashed to the floor, her elbows protecting her head as she fell, skidding roughly down half a dozen steps. A spike drove through her skull, and she heard / felt gasps of pain in all the other augs, even Elodie. She tried to disconnect, but couldn't. She lay on the floor, immobilized, unable even to speak, and did the only thing she could just about do, which was to watch, and to allow the other augs to see as well.

Qherax leapt between Ares and the towering Axleth who now did indeed resemble a sand-coloured praying mantis. Ares knocked her aside with ease, but it had given the Axleth a precious second. Slits like gills opened wide in its thick, muscular neck. Brown liquid gushed forward over Ares, splashes striking Stein and four security guards who had just arrived at the base level. Sand-coloured vapour arose from the viscous slop.

Ares staggered like a blind man whose legs were stuck in mud. The Axleth's fore-claws whipped forward, pummelling Ares' head and torso ferociously. Then, just as suddenly, the creature itself froze, then swayed. Sally spied a thin platinum spear lodged in its throat. The Axleth pilot wavered for a few seconds, then toppled, collapsing with a sickening thump, landing on Qherax, pinning her legs to the floor.

The pain in Sally's head ceased, leaving a ringing in her ears. She levered herself upright, aided by Anya of all people, who had caught up with her and helped her to her feet. They both dashed down towards Stein.

'Stop!' Qherax croaked, half-choking. 'Poison! Will kill you!'

Anya and Sally, and two dozen others rushing down

from all directions, halted. Qherax dragged herself free, limped towards the prone body of Stein, and rolled him over, revealing a face whose flesh was burned and bubbled. It was Sally's turn to support Anya as she gasped at the sight and crumpled to the floor, whispering his name just once.

Qherax met Sally's eyes and shook her head.

Sally stared at Ares. Her instincts told her this was bad. She tried auging him repeatedly, to no avail. It wasn't like he'd disconnected from her; it felt like he was no longer there.

She sat on the steps, consoling Anya, and surveyed the scene as medics arrived in hazmat gear, though Qherax had since said that the poison was short-lived. It was now safe to approach. Sally couldn't quite believe how their fortunes had reversed so violently in a matter of minutes.

The Eleven were reduced to Nine.

Stein was dead.

Ares was inert, offline, or worse…

Anya got to her feet, wiped her face, and began taking over. She was next in line, now in command of the *Dreadnought*. Sally stayed where she was and watched the clean-up operation. News of this would spread like wildfire. The other augs desperately wanted to see Sally, but no one else was allowed in, not even Elodie, not even Starkel. Anya cut all but perfunctory comms with the rest of the armada, as a means of short-term damage control. Sally reckoned she might have done the same in her position. They'd just killed an Axleth pilot. She had no idea how the rest of the armada might react. The less they knew about this for now, the better.

The real question was this: what had Ares learned from the Axleth before the fight had erupted? What intel had he gained? She reckoned he'd disabled her and the other augs to protect them all, so they couldn't be accused of being accomplices, willing or otherwise. Whatever Ares had found out, they knew nothing, and so were innocent. She didn't know if that would be enough of an alibi in Anya's eyes. She'd just lost her commander, possibly her lover if the rumours were true, not to mention her sister on the *Prometheus*. For the first time, Sally hoped the Axleth meddling with human genes had done its trick of heightening cold logic over emotional reaction. She reckoned she wouldn't have long to find out.

She was right.

The Axleth carcass had been removed, as had Ares. She felt the flood of gut-wrenching angst from the other augs as his form was carried past her, his beautiful platinum skin scarred, his face pitted, his silver eyes disfigured as if by acid. But she'd noticed something: his mouth, stretched upwards at the corners just a fraction. A smile? Why? Only one reason she could think of. His last words to her and the other augs had been, *I cannot let this pass*. Something had happened to the Xaxoan people, and he'd exacted a token of revenge.

A pyrrhic victory if ever there was one.

Abel, do what you can, she auged, though it looked hopeless.

One thing this deadly piece of theatre had demonstrated, though, at least to her, was that she'd been right all along, that the Axleth approach was fundamentally flawed. They should have found another way. Coercion and force, even by stealth, sooner or later caused blowback. And it could undo everything.

The vast auditorium cleared on Anya's instructions, except for three people. Anya and Qherax awaited Sally, so she got up from the step, feeling a weariness she'd noticed more than once in Nathan back on Earth, and descended to the auditorium floor.

The fate of the Axel-human fleet, and perhaps that of humanity more generally, was about to be determined. But it went wider. The dozen races had been reduced to ten, themselves included. What if that wasn't enough? The Syrn and the Xaxaon had their own special skill-sets, which the

Axleth had calculated would be needed to defeat the Eye. Whichever way she looked at it, as Michael would have said if he were there, they were screwed.

Sally arrived and faced the other two.

Anya wasted no time. Her voice was taut as piano-wire. 'We three need to talk.'

No kidding.

CHAPTER 10

Council

Anya looked ready to roll heads. She'd acquired a pistol from one of the security guards. It currently hung from her right hand. Normally such weapons had only a stun setting. But this was a model Sally hadn't seen before. Anya faced Qherax square.

'We all saw the *what*, I want to know the *why*.'

Qherax shifted from one foot to the other.

'Lying isn't an option,' Anya added. 'You are the only one who knows what was said in the exchange between Ares and the Axleth male pilot. But I can smell a lie a mile away, even from you.'

Qherax became still. She glanced at Sally, then spoke directly to Anya.

'Ares asked why the Xaxoan were not coming.'

'And? I don't need verbatim. Headlines will do.'

Qherax turned her head towards Sally. 'I did not know, I swear.'

Anya snapped her fingers right in front of Qherax's face. 'Did not know *what*?'

Qherax took a breath. 'There was a revolt. It was not clear. The pilot, as you call him, only found out in the most recent exchange when we arrived here.'

'Exchange?' Sally repeated.

Anya waved a hand dismissively. 'There are Axleth pilots in some of the other fleets. Not important right now–'

'The hell it isn't,' Sally began.

'Later!' Anya snapped. 'Qherax, continue.'

Qherax folded her arms. 'The Xaxoans ultimately proved resistant to our methods. And so they were... cleansed.'

Sally stared at her. 'You mean annihilated.'

Qherax nodded.

Anya looked down a moment, as if thinking, then back at Qherax. 'How can that possibly have benefited anything? Strategically, it makes no sense. If the enlistment did not work, the Axleth could have simply left.'

'The Xaxoan knew too much about the battle plans, the other eleven races. If an Eyeship arrived...'

No wonder Ares had reacted the way he had. But something didn't make sense. Qherax wasn't telling the whole story. She couldn't be. Sally thought about it while Anya probed Qherax for further details on the 'cleansing', as Qherax now referred to an indefensible act of genocide. Something clicked. When Nathan had met one of the first Axleth to arrive on Earth, he'd been told their method was tried and trusted.

It never failed.

But if it *had* failed with the Xaxoan... She waited for a gap, then jumped in. 'The 'enlistment' has failed before, hasn't it?'

Anya glanced at Sally, then back to the Axleth-made-human. 'Is this true?'

Qherax nodded. 'It is rare,' she whispered.

Anya's hand was on the hilt of her pistol. Her eyes flared. 'Quantify rare!'

Qherax's arms folded tighter. 'Twenty per cent.'

Shit! One in five?

Anya took a step closer. 'Then why haven't we heard about it?'

Qherax looked wretched. Sally guessed the answer,

based on the term Qherax had used earlier. 'Because, Anya, when it doesn't work, they always clean up afterwards.'

'Is this true?' Anya asked again.

Qherax simply nodded, then added. 'The other races, they don't know. One or two suspect.'

'Get out of my sight!' Anya shouted.

Qherax remained where she was. 'We need to release the other pilot. Council is in two hours. The other Axleth will want to make contact–'

The pistol whipped out. Its business end touched Qherax's forehead.

'Stop talking.'

Starkel arrived with two security guards. Sally had no idea how they'd been summoned.

'Take her away. Confine her,' Anya said, seething.

Qherax had the sense not to say another word, as the two guards led her away.

Anya holstered her weapon and paced.

Starkel broke the silence and spoke directly to Anya. 'Sally, Elodie, the other augs. None of them knew what Ares was going to do.'

'He protected you all,' Anya said, 'so none of you could be implicated in his actions.' She waved a hand dismissively. 'Come, we have work to do.'

'What about the other Axleth, the female?' Sally asked. 'Are you going to let it guide us through the nebula to the Eye's homeworld?'

'First things first. There is a Council of the 'Ten', as we are now, in less than two hours. Only two representatives are allowed from each species. Given everything that has happened...'

'I understand. You and Starkel–'

'No, Sally. You and I.'

'I'm honoured you think I can add something, but–'

'The other species will not take kindly to learn that we are killing each other. We may need to lie at this meeting, and

Axels are inexperienced at duplicity. Humans are far better at it. It's in your nature. That's why you're coming, Sally. And you will need to coach me.'

'All right, though I hadn't considered it a prominent part of my personal skill-set. We'd better go somewhere and get our story straight.'

'Agreed.'

As they left, she auged Abel, who by now was working on Ares.

How bad is it?

Abel's reply almost made her step falter.

I'm sorry, Sally. This is beyond me. Ares is too damaged. I can't fix him.

As Anya led the way, Starkel took Sally's hand. She couldn't really say why she let him. But she held it tight for a few seconds, then let go.

Three Marauders to deliver two passengers seemed overkill, but humanity needed to show strength to its new allies, whose fleets otherwise dwarfed its presence and military capability.

'Tell me again about the Syrn,' Sally said to Anya as they stood on the bridge of the lead Marauder. Elodie was captain of this one, while Starkel occupied Stein's console back on the *Dreadnought*.

'They were the most aggressive, apparently. Like humans, war was in their blood.'

Sally didn't deny it.

'But they entered the nebula? On their own?'

'Very *Syrn* apparently. A few of the other species were keen to keep an eye on them after the battle with the Eye, in case they tried to take over the galaxy.'

'And since then?'

'Not a whisper. An emissary has been sent to their homeworld.'

'Long range sensors?' Sally tried.

'Inside a nebula like this one? Forget it. Too vast, too much stellar interference. Star nursery, remember?'

Sally's attention was snagged by a wing of five Starpiercers that swept like darts across the Marauder's bow. A small part of her, the young girl she'd been a lifetime ago, wanted to pilot one and race around the corona of the nearest star. She turned around briefly, catching Elodie's eye and was met by the glimmer of a smile as her daughter auged a simple message: *Want one.*

The Starpiercers were acting as escorts of ambassadorial shuttles to the Ankh's lead Pyramid ship, far larger than Sally had realized until now, maybe ten miles from base to apex. Their Marauder filed in behind a Fronn 'Cuttleship', and then a flock of Korg Diamonds streamed past them and overtook everyone else, vanishing inside the gargantuan bay doors. Sally glimpsed one of the massive Hammerships looming behind the Pyramid, black and grey, barely any lights. *Dad wants one of those*, Elodie transmitted, and Sally smiled, but it faded as they passed through the doors into the bowels of an alien species far older than humanity who could undoubtedly conquer them if they chose to.

The enemy of your enemy...

She really hoped so.

The inside was vast, lit by a warm azure sky effect, like the last vestiges of daylight before sunset takes over.

'It seems to be mainly hollow,' Sally said.

'They live on these ships,' Anya filled in. 'They gave up worlds a long time ago. Rumour has it they even left this galaxy at one point, for tens of thousands of years, then returned. No one knows what they did or found during that time.'

'Nothing worth staying for,' Sally mused.

'Point,' Anya said, nodding. 'Fermi's Paradox can also apply on a galactic scale.'

Sally hadn't really thought about it that way, but it made

sense. Fermi had argued that if there were other civilizations in the Milky Way, then given the immense distances in terms of light years and the typical rise-and-fall cycle of civilizations, humanity might find their galaxy barren when they finally ventured out, or else might find it fecund, thriving with species. Maybe the Ankh visited another galaxy and found it in a fallow stage. Or maybe they found an implacable foe, counted their blessings, turned tail and fled back home.

Elodie was suddenly beside her. 'As requested, I've relinquished control to the Ankh. We're landing over there,' she said, pointing.

An area of a mile square hosted a menagerie of gleaming ships and shuttles. Sally guessed the parking arrangements weren't random; for sure some of these species were on better or poorer relations with each other. The Ankh had taken that into account when allocating slots. She spotted an ivory ship she didn't recognise, shaped like a scimitar, a stubby sword.

'What's that one?' she asked.

Both Anya and Elodie walked forward, closer to the screen.

'It's Syrn,' Anya said finally. 'Legate Class, I believe.'

'I thought–'

'Me too.' Anya turned around and headed toward the exit corridor. 'Let's go and find out.'

Sally hadn't known what to expect. A bunch of aliens sitting around a massive conference table? Seemed unlikely, especially given size differences and irreconcilable environmental requirements for each species.

But she hadn't expected *this*.

She and Anya were avatars. Bipedal, at least, but their heads were bullet-shaped, their entire forms the same drab grey colour of the *Dreadnought*. She guessed it made it easier for everyone to relate to each other, whilst preserving their individual identities where desired. For example, she wondered what a Fronn looked like, whether it had fins and a long neck, but all she saw was an ocean-blue cuttlefish-shaped avatar. The Korg were diamonds that shimmered with a faint rainbow sheen, the Par'aal shiny black lumps of coal... She wondered if these avatars were self-selected, or whether the Ankh still retained a sense of humour after aeons of existence.

She tried again to aug with Elodie, but no transmission was possible, all comms had been dampened. Most of the avatars in this empty, wall-less null-space were focused on the deep purple, multi-limbed, lobster-clawed Syrn avatar, who was engaged in high-bandwidth discussion with a small floating emerald Pyramid. The translation, audible in a neutral female voice just for her and Anya, occasionally stumbled and paused. Some concepts evidently didn't translate or else were too advanced.

The two avatars separated. The Ankh-Pyramid drifted towards her and Anya. Sally swallowed.

'How many crew do you offer?' came the question; neutral, non-threatening, though at the same time somehow conveying that this was key, determining humanity's rank in this armada.

'Eight hundred thousand,' Anya answered, without hesitation. 'All committed.'

Sally glanced at the bullet-head next to her. This hadn't been discussed. Anya had explained the plan on the way over, and she'd understood it in its broadest terms since they set out and left Earth to join the six other Axel warships. The Axleth had wanted humanity's *fight*. But fight is limited without associated technology. Poorly trained but well-equipped soldiers can overcome well-trained but poorly equipped ones. Humanity had worked this out since the Battle of Agincourt and the longbow, let alone gunpowder a few centuries later – and as for atomic weapons...

Seven Axel ships and more than a hundred Marauders – the size of the original Axel fleet – would have been welcomed to this party, but given the firepower she'd already seen, would have added little to the strategic offensive. Therefore, the idea had been a simple one. Axel crew would pilot alien ships. One reason the bullet-ships carried so many crew.

The original plan, as far as Sally knew, had been for each ship to volunteer one third of its complement to pilot alien attack vessels, keeping the rest in reserve in case of high attrition rates or a protracted campaign. Now, Anya had just offered pretty much everyone for the same service in one go. Sally could see the point. But for all they knew, Axels might be used as cannon-fodder by the armada, slaughtered in the first wave of the attack. Given that this was the last surviving Axel ship and crew, and given that Earth was under a delayed death sentence from a black hole, did it make sense to risk everything and everyone? If the battle went awry, humanity could be wiped out, collateral damage lost in a larger picture. Worse, they were putting themselves in the hands of alien strategists they'd just met.

But the Axleth had done a real number on their Axel progeny, ideologically as well as genetically. This was all but a religious crusade for Anya, and practically every other Axel on the *Dreadnought*. For them, this didn't require trust, which is earned, but faith…

Anya turned to her. 'The Ankh Supreme Coordinator is awaiting–'

Sally was suddenly elsewhere, back in her body, except it wasn't… just a very good simulation, a more human-like avatar. She stared, awestruck, at what stood, or rather hovered, before her. It was like two cones joined together by a thin waist, reminding her of a milky pink hourglass, red and purple beads of light streaming from one half to the other. It was hypnotic.

It spoke. 'Very few know what we look like. I ask you not to tell the others.'

'I… I have an aug connection. I'm not sure I can hide it from the others when I leave here.'

'I have made an adjustment. You may share it with your family only.'

'My family?'

'Elodie and Michael.'

'Then why are we having this... conversation?'

'The others on your ship have faith. You require trust.'

'You can mind-read?'

'It is more complicated than that.'

She wished Abel were there. Then again, he'd drag them off-topic.

'Why do you care what I require?'

The hourglass spun for a moment, creating a swirl of beads in each half. It was pleasant to watch. She guessed she'd just asked a vaguely intelligent question.

'You humans defeated the Axleth on your planet, succeeding against tremendous odds. You are a wild card. We face a foe with partly unknown capabilities. We wish to have such a wild card in the pack. But I need an answer now. There will be no negative repercussions if you disagree. We will release the Axels and humans from the attack force. We can redirect you to a region of space where you will find a fertile, virgin planet, and where the Eye or anyone else will not find you for a long time.'

That was tempting...

'The Axleth. Do you trust them?' she asked.

'Ah, now *that* is an interesting question. They have many secrets we are not privy to. And yet they have brought together an armada that even we could not have. And the threat of the Eye is very serious, even to us. But Saarin's race, the Xaxoan...'

The Ankh's milky pink interior flushed a deeper maroon hue. 'For that, there will be consequences.' The pink returned. 'And for your friend, Ares. An even wilder card. That was a tactical blunder by the Axleth.'

'Can you fix him?'

'The Xaxoan could have, perhaps. 7-3-1, given time, of which we have precious little. The entire Syrn fleet is gone.'

'But… the Syrn are here.'

'A delegate from their homeworld, sent to rendezvous with the victorious Syrn fleet a week ago. We all assume the worst.'

That didn't bode well at all.

'I need your decision, Sally.'

There was one last technical detail she needed ironed out, because operationally, it was key.

'How did you know Axels would be able to pilot these ships? You've visited Earth before, haven't you?'

'We have explored most of this galaxy. But the distances are vast, and the going can be slow.'

A long time ago, then. Five thousand years, she guessed, given the age of Egypt's pyramids. Which made her realize something. 'You didn't make the wormhole. If you could, you'd have made more.'

The beads in the upper half swirled in a spiral.

She got it. 'You left the galaxy in search of those who'd made the wormhole.'

The beads formed a circle.

'You didn't find them, so you came back.'

The beads in each half coalesced into hexagonal shapes that fell like snow towards the mid-section. Sally sensed this interview was drawing to a close.

The Ankh's voice upped in volume. 'If you choose to fight with us, we will not squander your resources, your people. They will not be used as cannon-fodder. This we promise, though you will, of course, lose people, as will all the species present. So, Sally of humanity, do we have a deal?'

She recalled the last time she'd been asked that question, by the Axleth leader, their First, back in the Manhattan Citadel on Earth. But that was different. Last time she was being blackmailed, after being captured and tortured, even brainwashed to an extent. This time, she'd come here of her own accord. She'd wanted to join this particular fight.

Suddenly she was back in the null-space, next to Anya,

who was speaking.

'... confirmation.' Anya finished.

What? Had those past few minutes all happened in the blink of an eye?'

She faced the shimmering emerald Pyramid. It had wanted her to trust it. She had little to go on, and yet... It had said it didn't mind-read, but evidently it could somehow understand, and maybe predict, her line of thought. *Keep your promise*, she thought, and then uttered a single word.

'Deal.'

It was one thing to make a decision, quite another to see its fruition. Over the next week the *Dreadnought* haemorrhaged people as they transferred into flat disk-like ships that reminded her of throwing stars Fisher had once shown her back in *Athena* days. The Shuriken, as she thought of them, were dizzyingly manoeuvrable, making Stingers seem obsolete. The Axels initially practised out in space, then they darted in and out of the armada, the Korg Diamonds showing them a trick or two. The curved blades of these lithe ships weren't aesthetic; they were barbed with plasma weapons. They could slice through hulls and penetrate shields like nothing she'd ever seen.

The Axel pilots, one or two to each craft, revelled in them. It was contagious. And worse, her decision and Anya's offer had not gone unnoticed by the human contingent. Most of the remaining non-auged humans joined the Shuriken fleet that was divided into a staggering eight thousand swarms, each a hundred strong. When they weren't active, they formed their own accretion disk around the armada.

It was something to see.

Michael joined her on the observation deck and took her hand.

'Funny,' he said. 'Aside from that blip three centuries ago, there are still more on board this giant bullet than have ever been wandering around awake at the same time during the past four hundred years, and yet...'

She felt it too. 'The *Dreadnought* feels empty.'

'I wish I could fly one of those,' he said, as a Shuriken blurred past.

'I'm glad you can't,' she replied.

'When do we ship out?'

'That's classified. I'd have to kill you if I told you.' She squeezed his hand.

'Tomorrow, then.'

'Yes,' she said.

She gazed out towards the glittering artificial accretion disk encircling the massive armada. The Ankh had said they wanted humanity as a wild card. She reckoned that on that score at least, humanity could deliver. And then, unbidden, she thought of Nathan, because when the Axleth had first arrived in orbit around Earth, it had taken that particular wild card to thwart the invasion process. But he was long dead. She hoped he'd had a good life, got the peace he'd earned in spades. Yet being auged, and having just talked to a being who could practically read her mind, she checked herself. If she was honest, she wished Nathan were here, because when it came to wild cards, Nathan had always gone the extra mile.

Dammit, she missed him.

CHAPTER 11

Burn

Nathan thought he'd left Faroujah hospital behind him, back on Earth, a long time ago. But PTSD never really lets you go. It was like yesterday. He'd tried to save a bunch of kids from an RPG attack in Helmand Province... Hell, he saved most of them. But most is never enough. And here he was again. Different time, different place, same story. He'd led this crew of kids – because to him that's what they were – into a trap. And this time, none of them would escape, including his own son.

He stood inside the holofield. After four hundred years of travel, the stars somehow looked the same to him. But the wormhole was approaching, fast. He still couldn't get his head around why it was a sphere rather than the gaping mouth of a hole, but that wasn't what held his attention. Eyeships, hundreds of them, their shards rippling from diamond white to blood red from stem to tip, were racing to the wormhole, gaining on the *Athena*, even though Billy was thrashing the Athena's engines to breaking point. Nathan had hoped to arrive at the wormhole a day in advance, or at least several hours. It was evident now that their advance, if they had one at all, would be measured in minutes.

The Eye had sent for reinforcements; that much was

clear. Had they known about the wormhole, or had they somehow tracked the Athena? He hoped it was the former. Given there were so many, and from different directions, Billy had argued that they must have already known. Plus, he'd added, this massive convergence made strategic sense – it would be a sizable force with which to attack the armada, rather than Eyeships drip-feeding through one or two at a time. The timing was also right on the nose. They would pass through the wormhole and then travel to Orion's Gate, arriving at just the right moment to attack the armada before it entered the nebula. Somewhere along the way, the Eye had gained knowledge of the Axleth grand plan, including intimate details of its timing.

He did one more three-sixty, his head more or less where the wormhole was, so that these deadly spike-ships looked as if they were heading straight towards his eyes. He resisted the urge to swat them away. *If only.* He strode out of the field.

'Feel any better?' Lara quipped.

'Not helping,' he answered. Then, to everyone: 'Ideas? Options?'

The crew's gaze swung in his direction, marginally less threatening than the Eyeships a moment ago. He wasn't their captain, after all. He'd always preferred to skulk in the background, just be a grunt. But fate had other plans for him, it seemed.

Jaspar stood straighter. 'We barrel into the wormhole as fast as we can, and as soon as we come out the other side, we warn Sally and the others.'

'And then?' Nathan asked.

The others returned to staring at their consoles. Jaspar shrugged. 'Not sure there'll be much of a 'then', Nathan. 'At least we can warn the fleet what's coming. Even the Eyeships can't travel at lightspeed, whereas the message can, so the fleet can prepare –'

'To fight a battle on two fronts? When did that ever have a good outcome?'

Jaspar's lips clamped shut. Nathan knew that right now, *he* wasn't helping. Or then again, maybe he was. He saw that his son, David, was about to intervene, to calm things down. To hell with that. Nathan hadn't come all this way to offer their throats to the enemy. War wasn't just about tactics, weapons and courage-enough-to-die. It was about guts... and guile...

He slammed his hand down on the console. 'We need to stop them! And we need to get to boast about it afterwards around a fucking campfire!'

No one faced their consoles anymore. He realized they'd never seen him like this. Lara squeezed his arm and then stood aside. She evidently agreed with his approach. Jaspar was about to speak again. Nathan didn't give him time.

'You know what wins wars?' he said, to all of them, walking over to the holofield. He touched it and snapped his fingers, shutting it off. The Conn suddenly felt smaller.

'Why don't you tell us?' Jaspar said, with less irony than Nathan might have deserved. Nathan studied him. He was an excellent captain, willing to listen, to defer to Nathan's expertise. Here, expertise of war, and in that dismal region, Nathan had plenty.

He thought of Afghanistan, of all the battles... No, not battles, that was a word historians and generals used. Because for those at the bayonet-pointed sharp end, every battle was at best a skirmish, more often like a bar-fight gone miserably wrong, where everyone was pumped up on adrenaline and armed to the teeth, with a *one-of-us-is-going-to-die-and-it-isn't-going-to-be-me* mindset.

He thought about those dozen or so times he'd thought he was a dead man, sheltering behind a rock during an ambush in the mountains, or walking through a ghost town where snipers hid, selecting targets in their cross-hairs, or a single platoon surrounded by a massing crowd of eager-to-die fanatics...

'Cunning,' he said. 'Tricks. Sometimes dirty ones.'

Jaspar frowned. 'Billy? You're our resident genius. Any

chance you can turn your talents to the dark side?'

Billy's hands went to his hair, as if to borrow from that force of nature. 'I've been working on counter-measures to the black star and trying to unravel more of Saarin's cube. But this? I'd need weeks to work something out.' He looked to Alex, who gave a tiny shake of her head.

Jaspar walked back to the holofield and turned it on again. He used his hands to zoom into the wormhole, then said, '3D representation of the wormhole, please.'

Christy obliged.

The holofield shimmered, and the sphere disappeared. What they saw now was more familiar territory to Nathan. It was a tunnel with two widening ends. More or less straight. No bends or places to hide. No decent or even half-decent sniper spots. He imagined he was back in the Hindu Kush mountains. He and his small platoon had to get through this pass – this gorge – just ahead of an enemy horde. They'd have time to radio ahead to HQ so they could defend their base. What else could they do?'

David, quiet until now, walked forward. 'Can we collapse the wormhole?'

Somebody gasped. Christy. She said what everyone else was thinking. 'Even if we could, that would cut off the fleet – and us, if we made it through – from ever getting back home. Not us, obviously, but our kids, or grand-kids... well, somebody's grand-kids...' Her voice drizzled into silence.

Billy stroked the stubble on his chin. Nathan was reminded of how young this crew was. But that was the way of war. He'd not been much older the first time he'd signed up to fight against an insurgency in a foreign land.

Billy spoke. 'Well, first, yes, Christy's right, of course. It would make the journey home pretty nigh impossible, stretching a four-hundred-year one-way trip closer to several thousand years. But we all knew this might be a one-way trip, right?'

'Second?' Jaspar urged. They were on the clock, almost at

the wormhole's mouth, the first few Eyeships closing...

'We don't know how this thing works,' Billy said. 'How it stays open in the first place, and what keeps it open.'

'Exotic matter,' Nathan tried. 'Can we weaponize it somehow?'

Billy laughed. 'Sorry, Nathan. We scientists call it exotic because we have no idea what it is or how it works, other than it doesn't follow the normal rules of physics, as it messes with what we know about gravity.'

David walked forward. 'Dad, what would you do? If this was back home?'

Nathan wanted to stomp around, kick something. He'd been trying to goad the others into coming up with a plan because he'd come up with nothing.

'Choose the narrowest part, pick off as many as we could, which would be one or two before we got trampled and crushed underfoot by the rest.'

'We don't even know if conventional weapons will work in the wormhole,' Jaspar added.

Nathan felt cornered. The only viable plan was the one Jaspar had already voiced. Get to the other side, warn the fleet, die... But that was Plan S, as in *Shit*, whereas what he needed was Plan F, as in...

'Five minutes,' Christy said. 'If there's going to be a Plan B, we need it now.'

David remained calm. 'Dad, what *wouldn't* you do? You said dirty tricks. What might the enemy do that you wouldn't consider?'

Nathan stared at his son, then turned to the holo, the thought striking him like a slap. A tactic he loathed, one that many governments back on Earth had tried to outlaw; as if you could outlaw anything when it came to war.

'Mines,' he said. 'I *wouldn't* deploy mines.'

Jaspar's eyes narrowed. 'Okay. Let's work this out. You step on mines. So how would that apply here, in space, inside a wormhole? Billy?'

Alex walked forward. 'Gravitic mines. We could adapt our torpedoes to home in on the Eyeships once they were inside the wormhole, using *Athena*'s grav-tech, limited though it is.'

'Billy,' Jaspar said. 'How fast can you do it?'

Billy was already at his console, his fingers chopping at the keyboard. 'I need to go down to the weapons bay.'

'I'll help you,' Alex said, and they bolted for the exit. Billy paused and spoke without turning. 'If we destroy enough Eyeships inside the wormhole, the combined energy overload caused by our torpedoes and the ships exploding might be enough to collapse it.'

He left, Alex hard on his heels.

The bridge fell quiet again. Not the nice kind. More the kind where you're standing on top of a cliff with a rhino charging right behind you.

'There might be blowback,' Jaspar said. 'We might get trapped inside a collapsing wormhole, or simply get fried by the energy shitstorm when those ships make contact with the mines.'

Nathan recognised the implicit question in what Jaspar had just stated: was this just another Plan S where they all died? Jaspar would accept it, because the outcome was better for the fleet, if they could maybe, just maybe, stop the Eye's reinforcements from getting through. But shit was shit whatever way you looked at it.

'We deploy the mines near the exit,' Nathan said. 'That will give Billy and Alex more time.'

Jaspar eyed him a moment, no doubt weighing up whether it made the most tactical sense, or whether Nathan was suggesting it just to have a chance of saving the crew. The rival option, which Nathan hadn't mentioned and Jaspar was undoubtedly considering, was to stay inside the wormhole and make sure the job was done as far as they could. Nathan was reminded of why Jaspar was the principal captain on this voyage. He'd make the right call.

David intervened. 'That way, if the wormhole doesn't collapse, we still have a chance to send a message to the fleet.'

Jaspar turned to David, with a wafer-thin smile. 'Well played.' He tapped his wristcom. 'Billy, Alex. You have twenty-five minutes. Not a second longer.'

'Good. We'll need it,' Alex answered.

Jaspar turned to Christy.

'Take us in.'

◆ ◆ ◆

In battle, everything happened too fast. Beforehand, Nathan knew by experience, time slowed. He and the others waited. Jaspar didn't bother Billy for status checks, and didn't have to, as Alex updated the Conn with key information: *modification possible* – after twelve minutes; *first torpedo modified* – after nineteen minutes; *first ten done* – after twenty-two minutes... They'd all dreamed of seeing the inside of a wormhole, but during the transit, this voyage of a lifetime, nobody was able to take it in.

'Billy, Alex, as soon as you've deployed the torpedoes, return to the bridge. I don't want you back there when things get hot.'

No reply.

Nathan and the others, even Christy who'd given up navigating as the controls didn't respond anyway, watched the holo. They were approaching the exit of the wormhole, the nearest cluster of Eyeships not far behind, maybe a minute. The one saving grace was that speed of travel remained constant inside the wormhole – no acceleration or deceleration. The Eyeships couldn't catch up with the *Athena* until just after she exited. Nor were cutter beams or other directed energy weapons effective inside the wormhole, for some reason. One Eyeship tried, but its beam splintered and sputtered. The only damage was to the Eyeship itself, the offending shard crippled beyond repair. Nathan had allowed himself a small air-punch at that point.

They'd speculated why it had happened, theories ranging from whether it was the special laws of fifth dimensional physics, to whether the wormhole builders had installed defence mechanisms. But it was all moot, pre-battle nervous chit-chat. No one, not even Billy if he'd been there, knew enough about wormholes to make any theory stick. A mine simply had to drift backwards and settle on an Eyeship. They'd already seen debris floating inside the wormhole, so the mines might work.

Christy pointed, and Nathan walked closer to the holo to see. Small dots tumbled out of *Athena*'s stern. Billy was smart, and not just blindingly clever. He'd given the torpedoes just the right momentum so they would drift backwards and be able to catch the Eyeships unawares. But it meant it would be close.

'Okay, you two,' Jaspar said to his wristcom. 'Well done. Now get back up here pronto.'

'David,' Jaspar said, 'ready the comms burst.'

He then turned to Nathan and Lara, a small smile on his lips. 'Showtime,' he said.

He walked over to Christy's console, gained eye contact. 'Steady as she goes,' he said. He didn't need to say anything of course, they all knew it, especially Christy. But she straightened and nodded.

'Aye, Captain.'

'Fore and aft displays,' Jaspar said, and the corresponding vistas appeared next to each other.

Nathan watched the swirling deeply lensed image of the wormhole exit. Fascinating as it was, he was a soldier, and so he turned his gaze to the aft display. *Always watch your back.*

'Ten seconds,' Christy said.

Alex entered the Conn. She'd been running.

'Where's Billy?' Lara asked.

She didn't answer at first, catching her breath, and instead joined David at his console, *Weapons*.

'He's preparing a super-torpedo. Maximum yield.'

Jaspar didn't look happy, but he turned to the aft display. They all did.

'*One,*' Christy said.

The lead Eyeship ploughed on through the ghostly-grey wormhole-space. Nothing happened.

'The modified torpedo has made contact,' Alex said. 'It's attached itself to one of the Eyeship's shards. It should have–'

The display blossomed white for an instant, then it was as if the scene ran in reverse, the explosion swallowing itself, back to the Eyeship where the torpedo had detonated. A shard broke off, then two, drifting away from the central sphere. Another explosion, another reversal, but this time the torpedo struck the centre of the Eyeship. A jagged crack appeared, widening into a gash. Milky white material haemorrhaged into space.

'Yes!' Nathan said.

The others didn't seem to share his enthusiasm. He knew why. It was as if they'd wounded the lead enemy soldier in a charge. It was something, but if all they could do was shoot a few soldiers down, they would lose this fast.

Over the next few minutes, the torpedoes struck and disabled a further four Eyeships.

No more exuberance, not even from Nathan. A heavy silence hung in the Conn. They were almost at the exit, their window to do any heavy damage closing fast.

Jaspar, as was his right and no one else's at times like these, broke the silence.

'We did our best. David, ready with comms. Alex, ready all weapons. Christy, as soon as we exit give us a hard one-eighty-degree turn, and we'll inflict as much damage as we can.'

'I've done it!' came Billy's voice. 'This one should overcome the exotic matter's dampening effect!'

Jaspar turned to Alex.

'He's trying to harness the exotic matter, make it resonate... hard to explain. If he succeeds–'

Nathan and the others were thrown forward as the aft display blanked. The lights went out. As Nathan got to his feet, finding Lara's arm as she, too, was getting up, he noticed the acrid smell stinging his nostrils, as if hardware and software had been fried.

Red light flickered on in the Conn, and he staggered over to David to check he was okay. Back-up lighting came on. Alex was out the door as soon as it did. Jaspar, back on his feet, called out 'Damage report,' but the only answer he got was from Lara.

'Jaspar,' she said. He turned, followed her gaze, froze for a moment, and then he dashed over to Christy, who was lying on her back, blood oozing from a vicious head-wound. David left his console and took over Christy's.

Jaspar, kneeling next to Christy, suddenly seemed lost.

David took command. 'Take her to the auto-medic,' he said to Jaspar.

'But I... I should...'

'Go, Jaspar,' David insisted, and then added more quietly, 'While there's still time.'

Jaspar hesitated for a moment, then he scooped Christy up in his arms and dashed out the door.

'I'm turning us around so we can see,' David said. 'Dad, weapons, please.'

Nathan was already there.

As the *Athena* pivoted, they all stared at the forward, now aft, display. The wormhole was still a sphere, but the lensed image showed a succession of billowing explosions, Eyeships detonating one by one in a chain reaction, until the sphere was filled with blinding white light. And then it shrank to a pin-prick.

'Holy Mother,' Lara said. 'We collapsed it! Nothing else is coming through. Ever.'

Nathan felt what he guessed the others did, too. That the tenuous umbilical cord connecting them all back to Earth, just moments ago four hundred years away, had snapped.

They'd never return. In all likelihood, no human or Axel on this mission would *ever* return. Those back home were truly on their own. And if the black hole one day swallowed them, and the fleet on this side lost in the war against the Eye, then humanity would cease to exist.

He mentally kicked himself. *On your feet, soldier.*

'Do we have propulsion?' he asked his son.

'We do.'

'Billy?'

David nodded, and spoke on comms. 'Billy, Alex... report.'

There was a pause, during which David called up a holo of internal ship integrity. A good part of the aft section had been ripped open by the explosion.

Nathan needed to sit down.

No one was surprised when Alex replied.

'Billy's... gone,' she said, her voice strained.

Nathan felt the familiar sting of pain, the gut punch that never diminished no matter how many times you felt it. Billy... He'd known the boy as long as his own son. A brilliant star, a future Einstein or Hawking, snuffed out, his life cut short... He imagined a long dead Raphaela wailing in anguish from her grave.

It was Faroujah all over again. He'd saved some in that hospital, but Billy had been caught on the wrong side of the blast door when the RPG had hit. He hung his head. He'd spent twenty years watching Billy grow into a fiercely intelligent, caring young man. He closed his eyes.

Raphaela, look after him.

But he'd been here before more times than he cared to remember, and knew that they would have to grieve for Billy later, together. That's what soldiers did. How they kept going. He stared at the holo, took a deep breath, tried to focus. He needed to respond to Alex, but he had no words.

'Understood,' David said. 'Go to medical, Alex. Jaspar needs you there.'

A good call, and not entirely untrue. Alex had studied medicine during the long voyage, but more importantly, Jaspar needed someone there with him. And Alex needed distraction right now.

Nathan was back in Afghanistan – if he'd ever truly left – and these kids were with him. Those missions, those skirmishes where new recruits tasted the first blood of battle and learned a shedload of lessons that would never leave them, where they experienced the true cost of war, the only one cost that really mattered – losing people you cared about. Generals would congratulate them afterwards, say they'd won an important battle, gotten closer to winning the war.

It never, ever, felt like winning.

Nathan stood in the holofield. The stars looked different. Orion's Gate lay dead ahead, less than a week's travel away at top speed. Several numbing hours had already slid past. They'd all had a lot to think about, especially after finding the wreckage of five Axel ships near the wormhole's exit, thankfully Sally's *Dreadnought* not amongst them. He nodded to David.

'Give me ship-wide comms,' he said.

'You've got it, Dad.'

'In just under a week we join the armada. Jaspar, when we rendezvous with the *Dreadnought*, getting Christy out of her coma is going to be top priority. They have excellent doctors. In the meantime, I need you to oversee repairs, then retake your position as captain.'

'Lara, please organize a ceremony for Billy tomorrow evening. Alex... I need you to coach me in whatever you both unearthed from the Cube. You'll have to be patient with me, but maybe the Xaxoan tech can help the armada. You're brilliant, but I have a soldier's mind. We need to put our heads together. Now, everyone, I know we're all hurting, but we still have a mission. So let's get to it. That's all.'

He cut comms.

'What about me, Dad?'

'You're my Number One. Do what you did earlier. Remind me when I'm doing something wrong.'

'Aye, sir.'

Nathan stepped back inside the holofield, and zoomed in on the red, blue and yellow nebular.

Hold on, Sally. We're coming.

CHAPTER 12

White

Elodie was out on patrol, riding her Stinger one last time. She'd trained in the new Shuriken, which was better in so many ways, yet... Maybe nostalgia was a uniquely human trait.

One we should hold on to, Sally auged, inflecting the message with irony. *Maybe I should join you out there.*

Elodie spoke her reply. 'Our best strategists should stay on the big ships.' She raised the irony a notch. 'So they don't get in the way.'

Starkel intruded on voice. 'Wing Commander One, I need you to take a look at something.'

The coordinates, auged by Starkel, flashed into her mind. She banked her craft and hit the turbo. In the past fortnight she'd worked harder than ever during the day with her unit, executing coordinated manoeuvres with the Axels in Shuriken swarms. They were like nothing she'd ever experienced. The closest comparison she could think of, as to how the Shuriken could work in such tight packs without hitting each other, was flocks of birds near sunset, or schools of fish evading sharks.

She'd spent the past few evenings with Starkel, going over battle plans and tactics. They worked well together and got on better. She knew it could be a lot more than that – and she knew via aug connection, where there was nowhere to hide, that he felt the same way – but this wasn't the time. They were about to go into battle, minus two species. They both needed to remain crystal clear.

'I have something,' she said. She hit the brakes, drew to a dead stop, checked her cockpit dashboard, and then watched.

A ship was emerging from the nebula, muscling its way through curtains of sapphire mist. How in hell hadn't their long-range sensors picked it up?

You seeing this? she auged Sally. Her mom didn't reply, but Elodie could sense the concern. *But this has to be good news, doesn't it?* Still no reply, which meant her mom didn't agree. No point attempting to lie or mask emotions when auged. She also sensed her mom's thoughts on the matter, wishing it were someone else out there than her daughter.

The colossal battleship fully emerged. Ivory, bristling ostentatiously with weapons. There was no mistaking it. Syrn. Whereas many other battleships' shapes were elongated, this one was all front, reminding her of an image she'd once seen of the massive stone heads on Easter Island on Earth. It made a statement, assertive and aggressive. It must have been one of the ships that had tried to take on the Eye. But the only Syrn ship to make it to the armada from the homeworld had said they presumed the entire attack fleet had been lost.

Well, one had made it back after all.

Her console flashed up an ID. This was the Syrn flagship, no less. Elodie, in her single-pilot Stinger, felt like an ant in the path of an elephant. One of her screens showed her position relative to the armada. She was way out on a limb, the rest far behind, though some were already on their way.

Elodie knew the protocol, and flicked a switch that would translate her words into a dozen languages. She sensed both her mother and Starkel holding their breath.

'Approaching vessel, identify yourself and power down, or you will be fired upon.' She had to suppress a smile.

She expected the vessel to roll right over her, gravity-swat her aside, or worse. Instead, the ship did indeed slow to a dead stop, a hundred yards in front of her, so that it occupied her entire view.

Comms came back, a burst of sharp twangs that were quickly translated.

'This is Macchain Shadiel IV, Grand Syrnarch of the Syrn War Fleet. I come bringing urgent intelligence for the Ankh, and the rest of the armada. The Eye has a new weapon.'

The bridge on the *Dreadnought* was awash with comms. Sally imagined it must be the same across the entire armada. She stopped listening for a moment and instead studied the 'Stack'. Every species' command ship now had one, in an appropriate form and language. The *Dreadnought*'s was visual, reminding her of the old displays at railway stations, showing the next trains to depart. But instead of destinations, train IDs and departure times, the Stack had short holo-messages, one above the other, ten high, the top one red, signifying it had the highest priority, to lower priority messages of deep blue at the bottom. She wondered what the others would be; for example, for the Fronn, an underwater race. But the Stack was vital, a way of keeping all the species and their various ships on the same page during battle, when fortunes could change in the blink of an eye.

Five minutes earlier, the middle three messages, all in a subdued pink, had been about attack simulations, their groupings and locations. Sally had been fixated on this mid-section because human and Axel augs were in a joint Shuriken exercise with the Korg. The top three messages, all in shades of mauve, were about the break-up of the armada into three divisions that would separate in twelve hours and then begin their individual treks into the nebula from different vantage points, to approach the Eye's homeworld on three fronts. It made a lot of sense.

Now, the top three messages, from a bright vermillion to a fierce scarlet, all concerned the sudden appearance of the Syrn flagship. The first message read *Unconfirmed Ally Protocol*. The innocuous sounding phrase in fact amounted to a pretty intense form of pre-agreement between the Twelve. *Any ship from any fleet out of comms for more than a week must be treated as potentially compromised*. It had to power down, maintain a respectable distance, and – she still had a hard time reconciling this one – agree to have a nuke attached to its hull, deposited by a different race, with its finger, claw, fin or whatever, on the trigger. Since Axels had been in the vicinity, Starkel, at Anya's console, would soon hold that unenviable honour, the nuke-carrying drone already speeding towards the Syrn megaship's position. Of course, if he detonated it, he'd blow Elodie to smithereens as well. Sally had observed that some people in tense situations fidget nervously, or pace up and down, while others become very still. Starkel was immobile, rapt as he watched his screens.

The next message was as expected. *Defensive Formation Alpha*. A dozen Hammerships advanced to form a blockade, protecting the armada's vanguard, just in case things went sideways. The second message placed all other ships, including the *Dreadnought*, on high alert. All simulations and exercises were aborted, and a swarm of Korg Diamonds formed a protective shield around the lead Ankh Pyramid that was effectively HQ for the armada.

The third Stack message was the source of a conundrum, introducing risk into the equation because it conflicted with the first two. *Secure intel*. The commander of the Syrn flagship promised valuable and urgent intelligence on the Eye's defences and weapons capability. On the one hand, if this ship had indeed made it back from a battle close to the Eye's lair, such intel – on the Eye's location and fortifications, strength in numbers of Eyeships, and a host of other factors – would be invaluable in the war effort, possibly giving the armada a decisive advantage. On the other hand, if this was a ruse, the Eye could equally use it to gain counter-intelligence, or mount a first strike against the armada. The attack on the *Dreadnought* by the re-mastered *Prometheus* a little over a week ago was still fresh in Sally's mind.

Worse, even if the ship *was* compromised, as more than a few on the bridge and in aug contact already assumed, those in charge of this armada would still consider capturing the ship rather than destroying it, to extract whatever intel they could. The risk-reward trade-off would mean that they would accept a certain amount of collateral loss to gain tactical intel from the Syrn flagship's logs.

Collateral. Right now, Elodie's tiny Stinger sat alone in front of the exceptional might of a Syrn planet-tamer.

Sally turned her attention to the illuminated, almost flat dome above the bridge, which showed the armada, stretched out, its full-length bleeding 'off screen' to her left because it was so large, and because the last stragglers were still arriving. To her right, almost by the elevators, was the Syrn flagship and a tiny dot representing Elodie's Stinger. The Hammerships were halfway across the dome, almost above her head. A sprinkling of Shuriken, resembling a small cloud of fireflies, was all that was in between. They were moving at full speed to support Elodie, but on this scale their progress was painfully slow. The only other ship whose motion was appreciable was one of the Starpiercers. There was a tag attached to its image showing that there were two occupants, one Xylyxl, the pilot, the other sigil being Syrn. Again, it made sense; only a fellow Syrn could judge whether this Macchain Shadiel IV was the genuine article. Must be the ambassador from Syrna Prime.

A purple message flashed up next to the Stack, accompanied by a piercing sound, like the call of an eagle. Sally's head turned, as did everyone else's.

Destroy the Syrn ship. It is a trap.

The message was from the Theon lead ship. They'd somehow bypassed High Command, and were communicating directly with the *Dreadnought*, because their finger was on the trigger.

The message vanished, and a deep voice boomed across the bridge.

'Ignore Theon message. Syrn ship status unconfirmed.'

That was from Ankh High Command. Starkel glanced over to Anya at Stein's central console hub, and she nodded. He said something in their clipped speech Sally couldn't catch. Sally walked quickly towards Anya's console, but she pointed behind her. Sally turned around and saw that Elodie's dot had disengaged from the Syrn ship's location, albeit slowly. Sally turned to Starkel and mouthed *Thank you.* Starkel didn't acknowledge.

Sally returned to her central location. She wondered how the Theon knew or suspected the Syrn ship was compromised, but then they were masters of illusion, spies by any other name.

Elodie's voice crackled onto the tense bridge.

'Something's happening. I'm going to check it out.'

With a sinking feeling, Sally watched Elodie's dot slow, stop, and turn back towards the Syrn ship. Their sensors were limited at this range, whereas she was right there, in the Syrn flagship's face. Sally wanted to yell at her daughter to get the hell out of there, to follow orders for once, dammit, but Elodie was cut from the same cloth as her mother. And if Sally had seen something suspicious, what would she have done?

She glanced over to a separate console where Abel worked with his Axel counterpart. They were monitoring the return of the Shuriken strike teams who'd been out on field practice. Michael had gone along in a two-seater version for the ride. They were approaching the *Dreadnought* bay doors. Sally couldn't allay a growing unease.

Hurry, Michael.

Starkel spoke loud enough for all to hear. 'What do you see, Elodie? We're picking up nothing on our sensors, nor are any other ships, except maybe the Theon.'

His voice was clear and professional. She wondered what he was feeling underneath. He'd dampened his aug contact, at Anya's insistence. Given that his finger was on the trigger for a nuke, she didn't want him distracted. Sally had always considered Axels *cold fish*. Her recent aug connection to some of them had changed that impression, though not by much, as even auged people could maintain certain barriers. Elodie, however, had told her recently that Axels were not so cold. They were just very private about their emotions.

Everyone on the bridge seemed to slow down whatever they were doing, to listen for Elodie's reply.

'Something... something left the ship.'

'Describe,' Starkel said.

'Black, ellipsoid, three times as long as my Stinger.'

'What's it doing?'

There was a pause. No one was even pretending to work anymore. All faced Starkel and listened.

'Picking up speed,' Elodie replied.

'What are you doing?' he asked. For the first time, concern inflected his words.

'What do you think? I'm intercepting it.'

Sally whirled around to see Elodie's dot inching towards the armada. The fireflies were still far away, the Starpiercer having just overtaken them.

Another purple message splashed into existence next to the Stack from the Theon.

It is a weapon. It must not reach the armada.

'Understood,' Elodie replied.

'That wasn't from us, Elodie,' Starkel added quickly.

'Does it matter?' Elodie replied.

Anya's voice cut in. 'This is *Dreadnought*. The Syrn ship has launched a weapon. We are engaging but need assistance.'

'We do not detect any weapon,' the Ankh replied.

Anya's fingers blurred over holo-screens. 'Starkel, do *you* see it?'

He shook his head. 'Elodie, is it on your sensors?'

'Negative. This is serious stealth tech. I have a line of sight, but it's speeding up. If I don't keep an eye on it, I'll lose it.'

Engage the weapon flashed up next to the Stack in purple, almost immediately wiped off. The Stack's top three changed order. The top priority now read *Secure intel*.

'Bastards,' Sally muttered.

Sally's wristcom buzzed. 'Sal, I'm just boarding. What's going on?' Michael asked.

'Come quickly,' she replied.

Elodie closed on the blacker-than-black ellipsoid, even as it accelerated. She reckoned it was unmanned, so its top speed could outrun her own. Though she was focused on the chase, she also listened to a tight-channel burst between the Syrn megaship, now far behind her, and the fast-approaching Starpiercer, whose Syrn occupant was interrogating the Syrn commander, Shadiel. Her aug, hooked into the *Dreadnought*'s translation system, was missing every third word, but she didn't need to hear the words, just the tone, which had shifted from intense deference to sharpness in just two minutes.

The Commander is an impostor. The original Shadiel is long dead.

The Theon lead ship again. She didn't know how they were interfacing with her directly, one-on-one now, no longer even bothering to keep the *Dreadnought* in the loop. She decided to deal with them. The Ankh weren't listening to her, and from their perspective she wasn't even a pawn in this ultra-stakes war.

'What is the target?' she asked.

That is the question.

So even the Theon wanted intel. Knowledge of the target of this weapon, however it worked, would be useful. The Eye would strike at the species it considered having the highest threat level. So, if she destroyed it too early... She figured it out. The Theon had originally stated loud and clear that the weapon must be stopped at all costs. But the Theon themselves were masters of deception, and so were not above a little armada-wide misdirection...

'You want me to wait, don't you?'

We would appreciate that.

She considered the logistics for a moment: the mega-ship behind her with nuke now attached, this projectile, almost certainly a single weapon or weapons platform, her caught in the middle... Unless she got the hell out of Dodge right now, as her dad would say, she'd be caught in the field of fire. The platform's energy readout ramped up.

Her instincts told her to fire on the platform and disable it before it could launch who knew what at the armada. The Theon could do an autopsy on it later and figure out the target. She had no authorization to fire, but she was out here on her own, and as for the powers that be, they seemed to be dithering until they could identify the object. By which time it would be too late.

Captain's prerogative.

'Sorry, no can do,' she said, and locked target.

She fired.

Nothing happened. She tried again, and a third time. Her helm didn't respond, either.

'Shit, you've locked me out, haven't you?'

We are sorry, but there is more at stake here. We are interrogating the Syrn ship's data banks, using your onboard computer as a relay.

'Why?'

To find the Syrn's reserve fleet. There is a Syrn axiom: why send one when you can send two?

'Meaning?'

They always have a back-up fleet, albeit smaller. It is a very effective strategy.

She thought about it. 'Cavalry,' she said.

We need to find them, bring them into the battle. This

is the Syrn's flagship. The data we seek must be here, including communication protocols to Shadiel's nephew, who leads the reserve. The Syrn databanks on board have unbreakable codes. But we have the key. We believe we will need the reserve fleet in the final attack.

At least the Theon seemed well-informed. And it all made sense. Bad news for her, though.

She swallowed. 'I'm going to die, aren't I?' she said, less a question than a realisation.

Die usefully.

Easy for you to say. 'You've blocked my aug communication.'

For now.

Just as she got within gravitic clamp range, she saw the Starpiercer alter course, veering away from the Syrn flagship. It was heading back to the armada, having confirmed the Syrn ship was bogus.

The armada will fire on you soon.

That figured. 'What do you want me to do?'

Stay alive.

Sounded good.

For now.

Alarms began shrieking in her cockpit as she drew close to the platform. 'Is that...?'

I'm afraid so.

Shit.

Sally didn't care that she was shouting. 'You can't fire on her!'

Michael had made it to the bridge and looked ready to break heads.

At least neither Starkel nor Anya had issued commands yet. But the top of the Stack was clear. The Ankh had finally decided.

Destroy the missile platform.

Given that no one could see it, and that Elodie was the only point of reference, she understood the reasoning, but...

Anya held up a hand. 'Starkel, we have unmanned drones amongst the Shuriken squadron closest to the missile, right?'

He began talking to the squad leader, then switched to aug because it was quicker.

Sally and Michael breathed a collective sigh of relief, which was promptly cut short.

'What're those ships doing?' Sally said, pointing.

A group of six Starpiercers had sprung forward, beyond the Hammership blockade.

The screen above them blanked. The Stack vanished.

Anya slammed a hand down on her console. 'Dammit! HQ just cut us off for disobeying orders. Starkel!'

'On it.'

They were blind. The thirty members of the crew manning the bridge were hyper-busy, half of them trying to resurrect the previous comms intel, the others returning to fall-back systems.

'Still no aug?' Michael asked.

Sally shook her head.

'They're jamming us,' Starkel said, 'but we have a few tricks... *There!*'

The holo-cylinder sputtered into existence. Sally almost wished it hadn't. Six missiles were streaking across the distance between the Starpiercers and Elodie. Starkel's hands blurred, and dotted lines appeared, projections of where and when they would hit, plus a countdown.

Twenty seconds.

Elodie's voice rasped across the bridge. 'Anya, get everyone else clear. This weapon is some kind of...' she coughed, and swallowed loudly.

'What's wrong with the transmission?' Michael yelled at Starkel.

Starkel glanced down at his console, then at the holo cylinder.

'It's not the transmission.'

'Sorry...' Elodie gasped. 'It's some kind of dirty bomb. Real dirty. Actually, it's a... cluster of smaller missiles.' Her voice descended into a deep cough, and then...

'She's vomiting,' Sally said, almost in a whisper. She took a step forward and spoke to the digitised ether, her voice thready. 'Elodie, for God's sake, get out of there!'

Something inaudible. 'Too late, Mom. Serious radiation.'

Sally shouted to her daughter. 'Re-establish aug connection! We can steer you out of there.'

'Not... yet.'

'What does she mean?' Michael asked. 'Why...?'

The missiles were almost on top of her.

'Wait...' Elodie said. 'B... Busy.'

Starkel's hands blurred again, and the image zoomed in. Her dot zigged and zagged wildly, hard manoeuvres Sally didn't know a Stinger could execute. Three missiles missed. Three ignited. Everyone held their breath. The six missile signatures vanished. There was no dot... and then there was.

Somebody cheered, an Axel no less.

'Vitals?' Sally asked Starkel.

He stared at his console, then closed his eyes, his lips moving silently for a moment.

The dome-wide holo flickered back into existence, Elodie's ship past the halfway point. She'd somehow jumped forward, past the fireflies, past the six Starpiercers.

'How did she do that?' Michael asked.

'She didn't,' Anya replied. 'The weapons platform she's attached to did.'

Sally made up her mind. 'Elodie,' she said.

'Not... yet,' her daughter replied. 'Few... seconds... more.'

Sally wished she had a visual of her daughter, to see her face, but Elodie had no doubt turned it off for a reason.

'First one released,' she said. 'Now, Starkel.'

At first, Sally didn't know what Elodie meant. But she'd opened her aug connection just for a second to relay something to Starkel, and Sally caught a fraction of the pain her daughter was experiencing; gut-wrenching, bone-scraping pain as radiation leakage from the weapons platform strafed every cell in her body, mulching her organs.

Elodie was being boiled alive.

Sally's own insides tore at her. She could barely breathe.

Starkel glanced across at her, his face etched with remorse.

Sally was frozen. She couldn't move. She could only stare. This wasn't happening. Her daughter was going to make it out of there somehow.

'Wait!' Michael cried out, sensing what was about to happen.

Too late.

Starkel gave the command, ejecting Elodie, then self-destructing her Stinger three seconds later. The dot flared soundlessly, and for the first time the weapon itself appeared, a dash instead of a dot, scorched red by the explosion.

Starkel and Elodie had tagged the stealth weapon.

'I've sent a recovery med-evac drone,' Starkel shouted, his voice uneven. The lead Ankh Pyramid launched thousands of missiles. They moved faster than anything else, even the Starpiercers.

Sally watched as the weapons platform jumped again. How was it doing that? Was this the Eye's new weapon?

Sally wasn't sure where it had gone until one of the Hammerships ignited, wild green fire spreading through it. The ship buckled, then melted into an enormous asteroid of molten slag.

The Stack shimmered back on, the top three lines changing every half second as the armada admirals and generals panicked, urgently trying to regroup, to defend, to avoid deadly missiles they couldn't see.

The next ships targeted were the gravity Ringships,

belonging to the Tchlox. Five Ringships shattered, engulfed in green flames that thrived even without oxygen.

Suddenly there were dozens more Ringships crowding the original location, jostling at the front line of the weapon's attack.

'Where did they come from?' Anya asked.

'Bait and switch,' Michael said, causing her and Starkel to turn.

'Theon,' he said. 'Illusionists, remember? I'm betting these decoys are good enough to fool the missiles.'

Sparks of green ignited and snuffed out, only one or two missiles finding true targets. They all waited another thirty seconds, but nothing else happened.

The Stack stabilized. Top again was *Secure Intel*.

'Where is she?' Sally demanded. 'Is she safe?'

'About that,' Elodie came online, breathing heavy. 'Weapons platform... broke into three... sections. One... still... here.'

'Why?' Sally said, then answered herself. 'Waiting for the armada's guard to come back down.'

The stone-cold voice boomed again. 'Thank you, human.'

The thousands of missiles originally fired on Elodie's position minutes earlier had been slowing down. Except, Sally realized, they were doing it for a reason. They now formed a long chain all the way from the Hammerships to Elodie's position to the remaining weapon platform's location. The Ankh were indeed smart. The weapon could 'jump', so they were laying down a field of fire longer than its estimated jump distance. It would have nowhere to jump to.

'A firebreak,' Michael said quietly.

'Look... after... Dad,' Elodie said, as incandescent explosions blossomed near the Hammerships and, like a domino effect, continued all the way to Elodie's location, flooding the entire bridge in incandescent white light.

It stung her eyes, and though others turned away, Sally

couldn't stop staring.

'Starkel, no!' Anya shouted, but he'd already pressed the trigger, detonating the nuke. The Syrn megaship flashed an incandescent, boiling white, shattering into a billion fragments outrun a second later by a spherical tsunami of pure heat.

Someone was helping her up. Sally hadn't realized she was on her knees. Michael was next to her, his arms around her shoulders, uttering words she couldn't untangle. Once on her feet, she put her hands in front of her, like a blind person.

'I can't see,' she murmured.

Which was not entirely true. She *could* see.

But all she could see was white.

CHAPTER 13

Black

Sally was in complete darkness. Doctor's orders. The aug connection with her daughter had overloaded somehow when she'd... It had shocked her optic nerve, the Axel doctor had said. The aug was disabled, too. Just as well. Bandages were off now, at least, but all she saw were sheets of black.

Not quite true. Her mind saw other things. The same thing. Over and over. So, she kept her eyes open, even though there was nothing to see. Because nothing was better than what her mind kept replaying.

Michael had been in to check on her again. But it was difficult. Too much pain. She knew he felt the same. He was keeping himself busy. He gave her updates. She nodded, responded, both of them avoiding the raging, silently screaming hurricane in the room.

She needed to get back in the game, but something held her back. The last third of the armada would depart soon. The first two had set off days ago, taking a more circuitous route to the Eye's lair. The last third would leave and head straight through the blue box, as everyone called it.

Bring it on.

Yet here she was, stuck in this room. The doctor this

morning had said she could leave today, adding that too many days in complete darkness might degrade her vision.

The crew of the *Dreadnought* had been admonished by the other races for not executing orders. All except the Theon. Anya must have her hands full. The Axels and humans had almost been expelled, sent back to the wormhole. Sally allowed herself a thought that somehow felt treasonous – would that be such a bad thing? But to what end? To lick their wounds and take a four-hundred-year trip back to a planet living in the growing black shadow of death?

Black back there, black here…

She stared at the door, or rather to where she knew the door was. *Move! Get on your feet! Prove your daughter didn't die for nothing. You're dishonouring her!*

She stayed on the bed.

And saw something new.

It was like a line etching itself into existence. First, a ghostly pale outline, then more detail emerged: a spherical body, six sinewy limbs, and a round head without a neck. No eyes, just two sawtooth bands that ran around the head. She made an educated guess. Not that educated. Only one race favoured them at the moment, and they were masters of illusion.

Sally was on her feet. Finally, a target to lash out at. 'You killed her!' she shouted to the Theon apparition. 'Starkel replayed the telemetry. You prevented her firing, stopped her from leaving.'

'At first. But she understood her role and made the sacrifice. You raised her well.' The voice was airy. Sally wasn't sure where it was coming from, except that the jagged bands on the head danced when it spoke.

'I wish I hadn't.' Sally regretted saying it as soon as the words left her mouth. 'What do you want? Why are you here?'

'The wild card must remain wild.'

What? Wait a minute. The Ankh commander had said that to her. How did the Theon know? Was it general gossip amongst the other species, or were the Theon just incredible spies?

The apparition continued, 'Thanks to Elodie, we now know that the Eye's tactical advantage concerns gravity. That is why they tried to eliminate the Tchlox Ringships. The Tchlox are not angry with you, by the way. They realize that your daughter's actions – her sacrifice – saved half their number.'

'You did most of the heavy lifting on that one. *You* saved their fleet.'

'We did not die.'

There was an instant vacuum inside her belly. She felt nauseous. But she hadn't eaten for days. Nothing to throw up...

She and Michael should have stayed back on Earth. Elodie could have had a real childhood, a life of her own, any life, her own kids one day...

'It's my fault,' she said, at last voicing what she'd been thinking these past days. 'My choice, bringing a baby into existence on a spaceship, a fucking warship for crying out loud, breeding her for battle...'

The Theon said nothing.

And then she said the other thing that had been cowering in the darkness with her, the notion too horrible to speak.

She didn't just speak it; she shouted.

'How am I any better than the Axleth? Breeding a child for war.'

'The Axleth remain a threat,' the Theon said, the lightness from its voice gone. 'We believe they are playing a deep game. We – you – must not let them win.'

Sally closed her eyes a moment, took a deep breath, and focused.

'Your daughter did something else. By remaining there, we have gained intel on a reserve Syrn fleet. Only the Ankh and us – and now you – are aware of this. The Syrn ambassador has departed to find them.'

She heard the words. But that's all they were, words. Elodie had been flesh and blood, warmth and humour...

'Your daughter's sacrifice may have brought an entire species back into our ranks.'

Sally knew what Elodie would say to that. *Take the win, Mom.*

'Staying the wild card; what does that mean?'

'If all goes smoothly, it means nothing. But if not, there will be a moment when doing the unexpected may tip the balance in our favour.'

'Well, when you put it like that, it's perfectly clear,' she replied.

The Theon ignored her sarcasm. 'The Eye must have a gravity weapon; that's all we can surmise for now. But the way that missile jumped; none of us have seen anything like it. Imagine if that movement could be scaled up to the size of an Eyeship?'

She imagined it. It wasn't pretty. Given enough ships, they could carve up the armada. Dissect it. One small missile platform had taken out a Hammership, until then known as being the toughest ships of all, after the Syrn's.

'You will know, Sally, what to do when the critical moment arrives. But you must be on the bridge, not in your personal crypt.'

She wondered what would happen if she tried to punch this effigy.

'I doubt Anya will let me anywhere near–'

'She will. We have spoken with her.'

The ghostly light from the Theon illuminated the door. Sally didn't move. She realized why, after all these days.

'Elodie's still...' she began, her voice shaky, 'Out there, atomised or whatever. We have nothing to bury, nothing... I only recently got to know my own daughter, and now...' She wiped her eyes.

'We understand your loss.'

She'd never heard those exact words. The standard automatism was *Sorry for your loss*, which she hated.

'Do you?'

'Yes. If we make it through this, we will share with you some of our history. It has been very... painful.'

'Then you know how I feel, know why I'm trapped here?'

'Yes.'

'What are you going to do about it?' She was shouting again. People outside would hear. She didn't give a flying–

'Fix you.'

Sally uttered a hollow laugh. 'How?'

'You need to say goodbye,' the Theon said, and then its outline and detail morphed into something more human, and before Sally knew it she was on her knees, just as she'd been days ago, only this time not blinded, finally seeing the one thing, the one person she'd so desperately needed to see, one last time.

The bridge was subdued, everyone quietly busy, Anya unapproachable, Starkel off-ship leading the Marauder fleet, when he should have been here as her Number One. At least he wasn't in the brig. Sasha and Abel were the only humans on deck, as Michael thought of it, in touch with the two human-crewed Marauders under Starkel's jurisdiction, the formidable Kenyan, Nelson, leading one, and Jeremiah, a young man from the Bronx he barely knew, the other.

As he took in all the intent faces, he was reminded that this had always been about children fighting back. He was the oldest here by a generation. Most oldies, as he thought of his elders and betters back home, thought kids should learn from them. He'd have none of that. He thought oldies should learn from their kids, because they had less baggage and saw things with fresh, uncynical eyes. Besides, they owned the future.

The ship was emptying again. Two-thirds of the *Dreadnought*'s company had left the ship, this fleet no less, to join the other two fleets that had set off two days earlier. He lifted his gaze to the dome display, could just see the tail ends of some stragglers racing to catch up those two fleets who'd already disappeared, making the big loop to come together at the Eye's homeworld in three days' time. This huge armada, possibly the greatest the galaxy had seen in a very long time, had split up in a choreographed dance, one where they would reconvene on the Eye's doorstep.

Everyone suspected the Eye had more tricks up its sleeve, including one that had obliterated the Syrn fleet. The Syrn ambassador had confirmed that the image of Macchain Shadiel IV had indeed been a brilliant fake. It had initially fooled everyone except the Theon. And maybe Elodie.

He switched tracks fast, stared at the Axleth console where Qherax stood, propped up by a cane. *Know your enemy.* The new pilot, as everyone preferred to call the female insectoid Axleth, knew the way through the nebula, this star nursery with a violent, unpredictable temper. But the Ankh had shared additional information, even though it was mainly rumour.

Michael heard about the legend of the *Shrike*, but he didn't believe in demons. The Eye was an ultra-advanced AI. During the Axel briefing on the myth, invited by Anya, he asked if a cyber-virus could be given a *persona*. That got everyone's attention, though it didn't advance thinking on how to counter it, if indeed it was real, and if indeed it attacked. All the species' leaders could agree on was that there should be a way to disconnect critical systems from automation, so they could only be controlled manually. It meant having one finger, claw, tendril or whatever, on the master shutdown function for each fleet, and another on weapons.

The Par'aal raised an interesting notion: instead of heading into the nebula, the Eye's home ground, why not patrol the nebula instead, and attack anything that ventured out? They reckoned there were traps awaiting them inside the nebula.

But the nebula was too immense to police its gaseous

borders. And the Eye could be patient, all the while working on new weapons. No, they had to go in and lance this boil once and for all.

The light-strips around the circumference on the bridge switched from orange to yellow. Departure was imminent, their fleet spreading out and elongating into something that looked like a spearhead. Starpiercers were at the front, Hammerships not far behind, bands of Shuriken and Korg Diamonds rotating in opposing directions around the Ankh's Pyramid, like a glittering gyroscope. The strategically important Tchlox Ringships, with their gravity weapons – not that anyone yet knew the precise nature of their tactical importance – were guarded by no less than three species: the Par'aal's sprawling Cityships, 7-3-1's tiny pink ships that reminded him of bacteria when he'd seen one magnified, and Theon Mirror-Cubes. The last species, the Fronn, had their Cuttleships, as he called them, surrounding the entire spearhead. If the Axleth pilot failed to thread safe passage through the star nursery, or something happened unexpectedly, such as a plasma discharge known as a fire tornado, the Fronn were the only species who could deal with such stellar phenomena, natural or otherwise.

He heard the elevator door open and glanced across, then walked over to its occupant, double-time.

Sally.

He slowed halfway, as she approached a little stiffly, raising her palm a fraction to tell him she was okay, and didn't want a fuss.

He replied non-verbally by nodding towards Anya's hub. Sally diverted, and they both met there, in front of Anya.

'Reporting for duty,' Sally said.

That got Anya's attention. The subdued conversations in the room quietened to a whisper.

'It's good to have you back,' Anya said.

'Where can I be of use?' Sally asked.

Michael had never seen her so... *meek* before. But there

was an edge to her voice, a challenge.

Anya didn't miss it. 'I need a pilot to do some recon. We're about to depart, but something has been detected on long range, a bow wave echo that's travelling *very* fast.'

'Heading our way?'

'Exactly. I was about to send drones, but eyes-on is better. So, how about it Sally? Single pilot mission, no back-up, unknown danger...'

Sally didn't hesitate. 'I'll take my Stinger.'

Michael walked her to the elevator. 'Anya's smarter than she looks, and that's saying something.'

'El... our daughter told me that Axels don't believe in counselling, that it weakens them. Affirmative action is their preferred therapy.'

'I'm not arguing, but are you sure about this?'

'Never surer.' She stopped a moment. 'They want us humans to play the wild card. This fits the bill. Besides...' She faltered, closed her eyes a moment, then opened them, and dredged up a smile. 'I'm following in our daughter's footsteps.'

He touched her shoulder. 'I'll be watching over you.'

She met his eyes. 'You won't be alone.'

The doors closed, and he stood there awhile, chewing on what she'd just said, then headed over to join Abel and Sasha, who were already making room for him at their console.

Sally sat dead in space, halfway between the fleet that had already begun its trek into the nebula, and the fast-approaching ship. She pinged it. At first nothing happened, then she saw from her sensors that the ship had begun hard decel. She left her weapons hot, just in case. Her Stinger carried one of the remaining virus-laden torpedoes they'd used at the wormhole's exit almost three weeks ago, again on the assumption that an Eyeship coming through the wormhole wouldn't know about it.

A message arrived from the *Dreadnought* from Michael. It took a while to download, as they were well inside the nebula by now, and interference was ramping up for them. A single word flashed onto her cockpit display.

Friendly.

As in friendly fire, she guessed, as in *don't fire* on whoever, whatever, was about to arrive. She wondered who it could be. A latecomer from one of the other ten species? She hoped to God it wasn't a rogue Axleth, because if it was, she couldn't promise anything. But then Michael would have used another word. He was always precise. A thought crossed her mind. No. No way. Magical thinking. Forget about it.

She waited.

The inbound ship continued to brake hard. The thought persisted, so, on a whim, she coded a single word and pinged the ship. Her name. She received a closed message, a reply. She hesitated before opening it, then took a breath. It was also a single word.

Nathan.

She stared. Couldn't be. Cruel joke. But her Stinger had already recognized the inbound craft. Not that surprising, given that they'd been cut from the same cloth, the *Athena*. She punched the console, just in case this was a dream, a sensor glitch, a... But it wasn't. She was so used to bad news, she'd forgotten what good news felt like. *Nathan...* and who else? She could only imagine. Her eyes misted. *Not now, dammit!* She reconsidered Anya sending her out here alone, and Michael going along with it. *They'd both bloody well known!* Well, there'd be hell to pay for this little surprise once she was back aboard.

She put her palms together, as if in prayer. 'One time only,' she said. 'Just in case anyone's listening. Thank you.'

She powered down weapons. Her hands were shaking. She took three deep breaths to calm herself. She didn't know why he was here, how many were with him... It didn't matter. He'd once told her that in the heat of war, you fight for your buddies, those in your platoon, and for those at home.

Sure, you sign up for the greater good, but in the midst of war, you can lose sight of all that. It comes down to close relationships. Those you're with. He'd added that the strongest men and women he'd fought alongside were from what he called war families, where parent and offspring had both signed up. Nobody outside a war really knew what it felt like, and so having family who had direct war experience – whether brothers or sisters, or parents and children, was a wellspring of steadfast resilience.

The bright dot she'd been watching grew in intensity, then bloomed until it was the size of a ship, slowing as it circled her. It braked hard in a tightening loop until it came to rest off her starboard bow. She recalled seeing the *Athena* the first time, back on that remote oceanic island, a lifetime ago. A giant grey stingray, hovering above her, two miles long, half a mile wide at its broadest. This new version of the *Athena* was a fifth of its original size, and far sleeker. More like a shark.

Pale mustard light leaked out into space from the aft, and she nudged her engines into action and steered over to the open hangar. As she faced it head on, two figures waited behind the shimmering forcefield. Her hand almost slipped off the joystick. She eased her Stinger forward and spoke to the empty-not-empty space around her.

'Elodie, time to meet your grandparents.'

As soon as she leapt down from her Stinger, the three of them indulged in long overdue, and suitably embarrassing, rib-crushing hugs and tearful, stammering platitudes. Then she slipped off her boots and felt the soft, springy *Athena* floor under her feet, pushing up between her toes.

'Home,' she said, sniffing back one last tear. 'Okay, I'd better meet your crew, I guess.'

Nathan, Jaspar and David sat facing her and Lara. Nathan was grinning. 'Can't get over it. You're a grown woman now.'

'Thanks, old man,' she replied, which only served to broaden his grin.

Her hand was clasped in Lara's. She couldn't remember taking it.

She'd briefly met the taciturn Alex who was at the Conn, already speeding again toward the fleet, and had visited Christy in the sick bay, still in a coma. That's where they'd picked up Jaspar, after he'd managed to tear himself away from the poor girl's bedside.

They told her about their uneventful journey, then the brief and costly battle at the wormhole, the loss of Billy, whom she'd barely known, just seen occasionally, a young boy tugging onto Raphaela's coat-tails. Christy and Ellie had been best of friends, though. She hoped Christy would pull through. And if anyone could bring her out of a coma, it was the Axels.

Jaspar had changed most of all. He'd lost Jennifer back on Earth, and now, almost, Christy. There was a darkness inside him, a void. That much they had in common right now.

But Nathan and Lara... They were older, but otherwise were just the same.

She gave them her sit-rep, right up till the latest battle, and Elodie... She'd caught herself, one minute talking calmly and clearly, then her words broke up, turned to glass in her mouth. She hung her head, unable to speak.

Nathan had stood up at that point, made a 'T' with his two hands and walked out, taking Jaspar and David with him, leaving her alone with Lara.

Nathan had grown wiser.

They met later over dinner, still a few hours from the fleet, Alex replacing Jaspar who took the Conn. Surprisingly, David, whom she didn't really know at all, took the lead.

'We should take a look at Ares,' he said.

'Abel has tried everything–'

'We have Xaxoan tech on board. They made him. We brought the ship all this way for Ares, Sally. No offence.'

'None taken. The Xaxoan should have been here fighting alongside us. The armada has lost a critical element in the battle strategy, maybe a deciding edge.'

'The Axels, and the Axleth,' Nathan interjected. 'Do you trust them?'

'Yes, and no-fucking-way,' she answered. 'Respectively.'

Nathan clasped his fingers. 'And the other species?'

She considered it. 'Originally I did trust the Ankh. I don't exactly *distrust* them...'

Lara joined in. 'But their values might not align with ours. Their bigger picture, their reality, is larger than we could ever imagine.'

She'd forgotten how smart Lara was.

'What about the Theon?' Nathan asked.

'It's funny,' she began, 'they're all about deception, illusion, and yet... It's just a first impression but...'

'Elodie trusted them,' Lara said. 'From what you said.'

Sally could only nod.

Nathan released his fingers and placed his palms flat on the table. 'In war, first impressions are usually all you have time for. And I trust your judgement, and certainly your daughter's. She sounds like such a–'

'Nathan,' Lara said, calm but firm.

He cut himself off, changed tack. 'We need to join the fleet, but be an independent unit, the 'wild card' as one of your new alien friends remarked.'

'I don't know if they'll agree.'

Nathan stood up. 'They'll agree. We just took out a fleet of Eyeships. Now, everyone get some rest, especially you, Sally. We'll catch up with the fleet in four hours.' Without more ado he left, and so did Lara.

David waited till they were gone. 'Funny, I was sure I was captain just a few hours ago.'

Sally smiled. 'Yeah, he does that. I think it's why he never advanced above corporal back in the day.'

David's turn to stand up. 'Nice to have you aboard, Sally. I need an ally, someone to help me enforce some discipline around here.'

That left Sally and Alex. The girl was tightly wrapped, had hardly said two words since Sally's arrival, but finally she spoke.

'Billy loved Ares, the original Ares.'

Sally said nothing.

'I studied everything we knew about him. The AI, I mean.'

Sally nodded. She knew exactly what Alex meant, more than the girl would ever know.

'We also delved into the Xaxoan tech on board, their history, their science, which frankly was beyond us, and their engineering.' She placed her hand over Sally's.

'Unless he's completely destroyed, I think I can revive him. And we will need him, of that I am certain.'

And then Alex told Sally of the Xaxoan's theory about the black star, and everything clicked into place, especially why the Eye's attack had targeted the Ringships. They were the only species who had any mastery over gravity, and could maybe defend the fleet against a black star's capability.

She wondered why Nathan hadn't told her, but probably he was going to. They'd just had too much to discuss already. Yet this was solid intel, above their paygrade, worthy of Ankh attention. She caught herself. What was she thinking? Even though these other races were advanced in many ways, humanity had already shown its value, its mettle, and if Elodie hadn't...

Alex left, and she sat alone. She thought of turning off the lights, to return to the darkness she'd been in mere hours earlier. Enough of that. Instead, she walked. Much of the ship had changed. Funny; when adults went back to the home they grew up in, they often said it seemed smaller than they remembered, because they had grown. In this case, it really was smaller.

As she walked, she saw countless faces no longer there: Raphaela, Braxton, Fisher... and Ares, their AI saviour in his hooded platinum cloak. The ubiquitous blue and grey fissures in the floors, walls, and ceilings moved more slowly than she remembered. If they got Ares back, that would change.

She reached her old room, the one she'd shared with Michael. It hadn't changed. They must have had to make hard choices, carving up the original *Athena* to create this sleeker model. Real estate would have been at a premium, and yet Nathan had evidently insisted on keeping this empty, no-purpose space free, just in case. She lay down on the bed and stared up at the ceiling, memories falling all around her like summer rain.

PART THREE

NEBULA

CHAPTER 14

Confession

Nathan recalled being on a troop carrier off the coast of Newfoundland during his military training, destined for combat practice in arctic conditions. They'd encountered thick banks of fog, each of the five ships in the small flotilla sounding off every two minutes, even though they had radar, just to be sure. Aside from those muffled horn blasts, it was eerily quiet, underscored by the ever-present deep bass thrum of the engines, and the trickling sound as their bows sliced through deep waters. He'd stood on the foredeck, and as the lean-and-mean ship's prow cleaved the fog in two, creating whorls of mist that brushed past him, he'd occasionally glimpse one of the other steel grey behemoths. He'd hoped to catch sight of someone else on another deck, another soldier like him, or a sailor on watch. He never did. He'd felt then, just as he did right now, that he was on a ghost fleet, on his way to hell.

His father, devoutly religious in all the worst ways, for his two kids at least, used to read him and his sister bedtime stories full of hellfire and brimstone. His father had wanted to be a preacher, but even in the Bible-belt fringes of Virginia the elders saw him as over-zealous. So instead, he recounted vivid tales, shouting and waving his arms, fire in his eyes fuelled by a generous post-dinner whisky. As if Nathan and his little sis were his flock. He'd favoured two particular tales, the first one Abraham sacrificing his son, though sometimes his father forgot the part about the messenger telling Abraham to stay the knife. The second, not from the Bible – though for years Nathan had believed it must have been – was of Charon ferrying the dead across the river Styx on their way to Hades. Once, his father had leaned in close to Nathan's face and said, full of venom he had nowhere else to stow, that Nathan would one day be on that very river, on his way to hell.

After his father had left, in the darkness Nathan had spoken to his sis, as he always did, to calm her down after their ritual night terror.

'I hope he goes to heaven,' Nathan said.

'Really?' little Mags had replied. 'Why?'

'Because that way I won't spend eternity with him.'

His sis considered it a while, then said: 'Then Hades is where I want to be too, with you.'

He gazed out now, from the observation ring on the *Dreadnought*, and wondered just how many light years you had to travel to leave a hateful parent behind. Banks of turquoise fog washed past the viewport, and he spied shiny ships, hoping to see someone aboard, but of course this was space, so he never did.

Nor did he see the *Athena*, elsewhere in the fleet, back again under Jaspar's capable command. The *Dreadnought* was far larger, and he could really stretch his legs on this gargantuan ship, but he already missed his and Lara's small cabin.

They'd be back there soon enough.

Lara joined him, took his arm. 'Penny for your thoughts?'

He smiled. *Charon was paid by the coin left in the mouths of the dead souls he ferried.*

'I miss my sister,' he said.

She tensed.

'I didn't mean that,' he said, recalling the moment Lara had shot his sister to save his life. 'I was thinking about when we were young. We promised one day we'd meet in a particular place.'

She relaxed. 'A shame you couldn't,' she said.

'It might not be too late,' he said.

She turned to study his expression. She didn't ask for an explanation, just put her arms around him. It was one of the things he liked about her. They stayed there and watched the nebula roll past, until Anya called them to the bridge.

Nathan tried not to stare. He'd never seen one before. But finally, here was an actual Axleth, guarded by the red-headed Qherax. Lara followed his gaze.

'Needs a necklace,' she said.

He knew what she was referring to: a string of explosives around its thick throat. That was how Lara had killed the first one, though technically their son David, a mere boy at the time, had pressed the button.

Qherax stared right back.

Anya attracted their attention by rapping her knuckles on the central console. 'Your colleague Christy is awake.'

That got Nathan's attention. 'Thank you,' he said, meaning it. 'How can we help?'

Anya pointed to a section of the fleet imaged above their heads, where the *Dreadnought* surfed through banks of indigo gas, escorted by six Marauders and a swirling flood of Shuriken.

'Take up this flanking position. Starkel is in command of the Marauders. You will report to him.' She faced Nathan. 'Unless you can restore Ares. In which case we will talk again.'

That was where Sally was, along with Michael and Alex.

'Looks like you're a soldier again,' Lara quipped. 'Cannon fodder.'

He turned to her and smiled. 'It's good to know your place in the grand scheme of things.' But then he addressed Anya.

'Do we know what we're facing? What about our black star theory?'

Billy's theory. In some senses. Billy had died for it, and Nathan would not allow the young man's sacrificed genius to be squandered.

'The Ankh and the Tchlox are working on countermeasures. Such a weapon would make sense in terms of the Eye's recent attack on the armada, trying to eliminate the Ringships.

'Why did the Axleth select the twelve races?' David asked.

They all turned to him, quiet as an unexploded landmine till now.

Qherax was suddenly there. 'An intelligent question. But first, I have one. Were you the one who killed the Axleth pilot in the Mothership orbiting Earth?'

Lara put herself between her son and Qherax.

'I was,' David replied.

'He was following my instructions,' Lara said.

Qherax ignored her. 'You were young, then. Did you see the screens, David?'

He frowned for a moment, staring into the middle distance, trying to recall. 'Yes.'

Qherax brushed past Lara and stood in front of Anya. 'The boy has valuable intel. We need to scour his mind.'

Nathan's right hand was around her scraggy throat before he knew it. He didn't say anything, didn't need to. She stopped talking, as did everyone on the bridge. Anya split the silence.

'It's non-invasive, Nathan. A deep memory probe, that's all. I believe what Qherax is trying to say is that those screens may have showed tactical detail of how the Axleth Mothership attacked the Eyeship threatening Earth.'

'I was there, too, remember?' Lara said.

Anya shook her head. 'A child's memory will be far more detailed, though he may not consciously recall the information. Children imprint better, and interpret and filter less than an adult.'

Nathan's hand eased off, but he didn't take his eyes off Qherax.

'We wish...' she coughed, rubbing the folds of her neck a moment. 'We wish to know why the missiles failed to damage the Eyeship. That amount of firepower should have had a more significant effect.'

'I don't buy it,' David said, again attracting all their attention. 'That battle was four hundred years ago. And there are no more Axleth Motherships, so the tactical relevance of any such intel must be negligible. There's something else you're after, isn't there?'

Anya eyed David for a moment. 'He has a point.'

Qherax glanced behind her to the immobile Axleth pilot, who uttered a series of sharp clicks. Like insects back on Earth, Nathan imagined, the Axleth had no tongue, so human speech was impossible for them. Still, the sharp rattle put him on edge.

'Very well,' Qherax began. She bowed her head and closed her eyes a moment as if in silent prayer, then lifted her chin. 'Every Axleth – every *original* Axleth – is sacred to us. There are so very few left. This mission against the Eye... they gave up everything, sacrificed themselves. For their children.'

David interrupted. 'But who exactly are their children? You, Qherax, and the other mutated Axleth are short-lived, and the Axels...' He glanced at Anya and then continued, '... the Axels and all the other races you infected won't bow to the Axleth's will forever. Am I right? The genetic tampering will fade with time, and with each successive generation, won't it?'

Nathan found himself staring at his son.

Qherax was doing the same. 'True,' she said, and her gaze switched to the Axleth pilot. 'Their sacrifice was ultimate.'

David took control. 'So why, Qherax? Why do you want to see the last moments of the other pilot's life, the one whose life I ended four centuries ago?'

'I do not,' she answered. 'But the others do. The *originals*,' she said, as if in reverence, in the presence of a deity. 'There is a ritual. The Axleth mind remains sound in old age. Often when they die, they are at their mental peak, if not their physical one. The pilot may have spoken, given a message in our language, one you will not have heard or understood. The last moments of an Axleth's life are of vital importance to us, to the other *originals*.'

Anya broke the ensuing silence. 'Why have we never heard about this?' She sounded slightly aggrieved. A child realizing something new about a parent. A secret.

Qherax addressed Anya. 'He is right. We have changed you, but over many generations, you will revert. You are not our true children.'

Anya opened her mouth to speak, but then closed it, and said nothing more. As if remembering something, she turned and walked back to her central workstation.

Nathan didn't blame her. Talk about a game-changer. But he let his son continue. This was his moment.

'If I do this, it must be a two-way street,' David said. 'And it must be with an original.'

Qherax's eyes narrowed. 'Why?'

'Because you are not first generation. They may have held back secrets from even you, Qherax. And I heard about Sally's 'education' back on Earth. I want to be able to ask questions.'

There was a burst of clicks between Qherax and the Axleth pilot. Qherax stared at the ground a moment.

'Two hours. We will send the location, David.'

With that, she departed the bridge, glancing once at Anya, immersed in her holo-screens.

'I need to prepare,' David said to his parents, and then

left.

Once they were alone, Lara spoke to Nathan. 'They grow so fast.'

'Tell me about it,' he replied. He glanced towards Anya. He knew what it meant to go into battle with conflicted emotions, and Anya had more or less just been told the Axels were bastards, orphans that the Axleth would never consider as their children, never truly care for them. Even though Axels were less emotional, it was one hell of a slap in the face. He knew from his time back on Earth during and after the invasion, that many of them felt they owed something to the Axleth, because the Axleth had 'elevated' them. It was like having bad parents. Even though he felt immune, he'd known plenty of soldiers who craved even a morsel of love or approval from uncaring or abusive parents who were complete assholes.

'Anya needs –'

'I know,' Lara said, 'I'm on it.'

Nathan was left alone. He studied the immobile Axleth. Impossible to know where those shiny black eyes were staring. He recalled the one time, back in Afghanistan, where they'd worked with a 'turned' Taliban soldier who'd given them intel, offered to show them the location of an encampment. Neither he nor his sarge had trusted the man, knowing he was holding something back, possibly leading them into an ambush. In the end, it had all panned out. But he *had* held back information, because his family had been in the camp, held captive, and he'd wanted to save them, which he did.

As Nathan stared at the immobile, insectoid creature, he was sure David's instincts were right, that the original Axleth were holding back. He walked over to the creature, stood right in front of it. Qherax always acted as a translator, but Nathan reckoned this one understood English well enough.

'We'll find out your secrets,' he said. 'But if you hurt my son, in any way…'He leaned in close, his head inches from those bulbous eyes and sharp mandibles, and lowered his voice, 'I will end you.'

David was 'in'. He'd often dwelt upon his brief time aboard the dragonfly-shaped Mothership in deep orbit around Earth. He never imagined he'd be back there, let alone with an Axleth mind accompanying him. The first thing he noticed was that the colours were off. Way off. There were blues and yellows, and a garish hue of blackcurrant that he guessed was ultraviolet. Black was accentuated, no longer a background colour, nor the absence of colour, but almost a primary colour in its own right. He faced the wall of screens that, as a boy, he'd thought were switched off before Saarin had activated them, but now the shades of black and scratches of ultraviolet shone clearly. At least Qherax had been right on one point; there was tactical information here, intel right in front of human eyes that literally could not see it.

The Axleth mind – in fact *minds*, he now realized – that he was tethered to, relished this intel. He couldn't grasp most of it, as it was being shown – and devoured – so quickly that he had no way to keep up. What he gleaned from the data-storm concerned structural and electromagnetic analysis of the Eyeship and its lethal shards that had attacked Earth. *Nothing new*, he understood from the Axleth minds. He also felt a ripple of cautious optimism that at least the Eyeships had not been upgraded since the Axleth last waged war on them.

The memory played forward, and as it did so, he focused on his mother, Lara, and Raphaela. And for the first, and he hoped last time, he saw them as the Axleth did.

Lara and Raphaela both had reddish hair, though Raphaela's had been auburn as far as he recalled. But now their hair was a mass of black strands flecked with UV that glistened and gave it a slimy appearance. And as for the eyes... Black within black, the pupils hard as polished stone. Those eyes kept shifting, as he knew human eyes did in reality, with rapid jerks or saccades. Humans didn't see this or perceive their own eyes flitting around, but the Axleth sure as hell did. And the bodies – shades of brown for the clothes and banana yellow for the skin – flickered wildly with even the slightest movement, such as breathing or a facial twitch. This way of seeing was likely an evolutionary survival mechanism best fitted to a predator, detecting the slightest movement. David felt a wash of revulsion flow through him, almost sickened by what he saw.

So, this is how we look to them.

He understood something else. The Axleth were stationary – to the point of resembling museum exhibits – most of the time. How *noisy* humans must seem to them, like incessant flies or mosquitoes. Visual cacophony; so unnecessary, so inefficient. Axleth only moved when necessary, often to pounce on prey. When they did, it was lightning fast.

How pathetic humans were in comparison.

Raphaela spoke, and the blast shrieked in his ears, a piercing, tinny whine to Axleth ears that grated inside his body, the Axleth equivalent of fingernails scraping down a blackboard. He shuddered as his own mother replied, and he resisted the urge to clasp his hands over his ears. But there was something in the background. The Axleth pilot emitted clicking sounds, barely audible on the human spectrum. Again, this mode of speech, by comparison, was so clear, so non-redundant, so precise, so *effective*.

Humans babbled.

He couldn't interpret the clicks, but the Axleth minds listening in were rapt. One of them opened to David, allowing him to understand what had been said. This was a day for firsts, he realized, because for the first, and he hoped only time, he empathized, something he'd presumed was a never-event. The Axleth pilot knew it would die. Knew that Saarin, the last uninfected Xaxoan, would take its life. Yet it had left a message for any Axleth who could one day find it. The pilot had not been dormant, as Lara and the others had assumed. Instead, it had been observing, periodically, first their invasion of Earth, then the building of the super-cities, the brief nuclear tantrum that had seemed both insane and capricious, bordering on childish to the Axleth, as it had nearly destroyed the Earth. The pilot had witnessed the return of Sally and her army, watched from afar Saarin and Ares aboard the *Athena*, and seen how they had unwittingly brought an Eyeship with them.

Such reckless foolishness.

Nevertheless, its assessment had been that the Axel contingent, with their impetuousness tempered and their fight keened, would be useful in the eventual battle, though not decisive. Ares was an interesting artefact, one that could be weaponized, but the Eye would adapt to its deployment, corrupting its algorithms as it had already done on board the *Athena*. Saarin was a different matter. Shortly before its demise, the Axleth pilot studied the *Athena's* weaponry and versatility, and concluded that the Xaxoan were key to the future battle with the Eye, on account of their organic approach to technology development. The Eye would find it more challenging to develop real-time countermeasures.

The Axleth mind paused. David realized it awaited his own assessment.

You've committed a tactical blunder, he thought, *by killing off all the Xaxoan.*

Yes. Two.

David wondered what it meant for a moment, then realized the second error had been neutralising Ares.

We will fix him, David thought.

Will you share the Xaxoan database? The cube?

Evidently, the Axleth thought Ares beyond repair. But sharing the cube? He could see why they wanted it. But he suddenly felt way out of his depth, alone in negotiation with the architects of a war centuries in the planning, involving the top species in the galaxy. He recalled talking to his dad about the time he'd met one of the first Axleth invaders, a young girl, and how his father had felt the same way, finding himself speaking on behalf of humanity. David wondered what his father might say if he were here now, in his place. The Axleth request raised a multitude of moral and ethical dilemmas, handing over the knowledge-base of one species to another who had literally destroyed it. But this was a war with ultimate stakes, a singularity for all organic species in the galaxy if they lost against the Eye.

He smiled. He knew what his mother would do.

She'd trade.

What will you give in return?

His consciousness shifted, and for the first time he heard people outside the egg-shaped cocoon in which he'd been sitting in total darkness, electrodes on his temples, immersed in this intimate alien conversation. His hearing changed, so that he heard the speech with his human ears, not Axleth ones.

'Holy shit!' Abel said. 'There's a massive download happening; all the Axleth alien tech. This... this is incredible! Call Anya. She needs to see this!'

David found himself smiling. This would put humanity and Axels back in the armada's good books. But he sensed the conversation wasn't over, and the outside world grew quiet again.

This is for you. You may share as you wish.

And he saw, through Axleth eyes, the last battle, five centuries earlier, in speeded up format, though the war had lasted decades. He saw the Eye's tactics in the nebula, a foretaste of what the armada would face, though the black star had not been a factor then. This was vital tactical information for Anya and indeed the entire fleet, and for the first time he had in inkling of why the twelve species had been chosen. He worried he might forget details, but the mind interrupted and assured him.

You will forget nothing.

And then it ebbed, and he presumed the conversation was done.

Not yet.

This is for you, David, because you have volunteered to share these memories with us. Our laws dictate that we must share something of equal value. However, you will not be able to speak of it to anyone or even remember it until after the final battle. We are placing a block in your mind. You will forget what we are about to show you within the hour.

As it unfolded, David wanted first to sit down, then to stand up and rage at them for what they had done. No wonder they were placing a block in his mind.

He saw the Axleth homeworld, millennia ago. A titanic, hot planet with steaming jungles and rocky desert plains ravaged by volcanoes, its purple and orange skies never clear, tumultuous electric storms lashing out at the planet, its vast oceans tempestuous. The Axleth had struggled on this inhospitable planet for aeons, eventually developing technology to help tame their cruel environment. Once they'd done so, their civilization blossomed, and they ventured into space. But their planet was located inside a nebula, and they yet again needed to raise their game with technology to survive the unpredictable violence of a star nursery.

They succeeded, via an artificial intelligence that could assess, react and respond faster than any physical being could ever hope to, an all-seeing AI that could watch over them and protect them, whether on their homeworld, or in the depths of space.

The Eye.

David knew he was sitting, but mentally he did so again anyway, knowing what was to come. The Axleth were an arrogant, predatory species who despised all other races, seeing them as weak, deficient, dirty. The Eye had been 'trained' by its masters, and so developed a similar value structure; a frame of reference for making sense of the world in which it found itself. As it evolved, one day it turned on its masters, judging them as weak, deficient, unclean.

The Axleth had made the Eye what it was.

He felt numb as he watched the rest, the annihilation of all Axleth, indeed all organic life on the homeworld; the desperate diaspora of Axleth ships out in the nebula; the regrouping, losing the war, and coming up with one last, all-or-nothing strategy. Now he understood one reason the Xaxoan knowledge base was of such interest to the Axleth, and why the Mothership pilot had assessed the Xaxoan species as so important: they had created a benign, loyal AI. Ares.

The images faded, and David's companion Axleth mind was silent, as were all the other minds, for a while.

One last thing.

The Mothership memory returned, and again he was silent as the minds watched their comrade die. He sensed the depth of their collective grief, which surprised him. They didn't seem to care about any other race, even those they'd infected, who considered themselves to be Axleth children. But the Axleth cared deeply for each other, the *originals* as Qherax had called them.

After a while, even that image faded. The minds were gone, and a shaft of light made him squint as the eggshell cocoon cracked open.

He was helped out by his parents, who looked concerned. Behind them, Anya and Abel beamed at him for what he'd achieved, uttering words of gratitude. But his eyes fell upon Qherax, standing by the wall, studying him, perhaps knowing what he might have witnessed.

'I need the restroom,' he said, and they let him pass.

He arrived, closed the door, and locked it. He stared at his face in the mirror for a long time, to be sure that he was fully human again, free from their minds. But the images of what he'd seen, and the secret they'd shared with him, came back with a vengeance. He wanted the hour to pass as quickly as possible.

And then he leaned over the sink, and did what he figured any normal person would have done in his place.

He threw up.

CHAPTER 15

Lake

Sally found it hard to look upon Ares' inert, disfigured frame, as Alex busied herself threading platinum filaments into his body. They were in the 'old' part of Athena, where Saarin and the original Xaxoan crew had controlled the vessel during the Axleth invasion of their homeworld. The three control 'Mushrooms', as she had herself christened them, stood unchanged, their hard exterior like gnarled tree trunks, with intertwined silver and blue strands writhing like snakes in a slow, never-ending dance.

She was of little use to Ares or Alex at the moment, and this 'operation' was upsetting, like watching heart surgery on a loved one, so she walked to the other side of the Mushrooms, to the holo displaying the fleet's progress through the nebula. Christy was there, too, while Jaspar was handling the Conn on his own.

'How are you holding up?' Sally asked.

Christy, her gaze caught in the hypnotic swirling ebb and flow of the nebula's gases surrounding a fleet that stretched thirty miles, nodded absently. 'So-so.' She turned to face Sally. 'It's weird, isn't it? I mean, here we are again.' She looked down, as if deciding whether to say something, then lifted her chin. 'You were my hero back then. I mean, I was a young girl, and you were just so... so awesome.' Her cheeks reddened.

Sally smiled, unsure of how to respond. 'I'm glad I inspired you back then, Christy, but lately I feel like a spare wheel.'

Christy, the taller of the two, placed her hand on Sally's shoulder, and spoke with a firmness that surprised Sally.

'Don't *ever* think like that. Destiny doesn't squander a talent like yours.'

Now Sally seriously had no words. She was saved by Jaspar calling from the Conn.

'Something's happening at the front line. They've found something.'

'On our way,' both women replied at the same time.

'Just Christy. For weapons. Sally, I'd like you to monitor from down there.'

Christy and Sally exchanged a glance.

'Aye, sir,' Sally said, expunging any irony from her voice.

Christy winked. 'I'll talk to him.' And then she was gone.

Alex appeared at Sally's side, an unspoken question in her expression.

'Carry on with Ares,' Sally said. 'I'll let you know if it gets serious.'

Over the next half hour, nothing much happened with the fleet, except that the Hammerships advanced, flanked by intermingled swarms of 7-3-1 and Shuriken, and with three Theon Mirror Cubes not far behind. The Fronn Cuttleships also ventured further out, swelling the long convoy of ships into a skeletal fat cigar.

'Yes!' she heard Alex say, and dashed back into the med-lab.

'What is it?'

Alex beamed. Sally realized that until now, she'd not

seen this girl give even the shadow of a smile. She understood Alex's loss of her partner Billy, given that she carried a smouldering pit in her own stomach after losing Elodie, the only saving grace being she'd had precious little time to think of it since the *Athena* had returned.

'What?' she asked.

Alex was animated, darting between cylindrical holo-towers of data, and Ares' immobile form swathed in platinum wires.

'A pulse,' she said, making eye contact for a fleeting moment. 'Well, the AI equivalent. Let's just say some AI neurons are firing.' She tended to the wires piercing Ares' head. 'I was getting nowhere. Then I remembered one of Billy's recursive algorithms, a brilliant piece of soft–'

Alex stalled mid-sentence. Her shoulders sagged. 'Hits you without warning, doesn't it?'

'Yes,' Sally said mechanically. 'It does.'

A ripple of guilt swept through her. She'd never loved Elodie enough, though she'd tried to make up for it near the end.

Alex toughed it out and recovered herself. 'Well, they wouldn't want to see us like this, would they?'

Sally thought of Elodie, and knew she'd give anything, everything, to see her daughter for one minute longer. Not just a Theon-manufactured effigy, which she had to admit was as good as a copy could get, but the real deal. She knew what her daughter would say.

It's alright, Mom.

'No, they wouldn't,' Sally agreed.

Jaspar's voice broke the spell. 'Sally, are you seeing this?' The two women separated and Sally raced back to the holo, then almost took a step backward as she had to shield her eyes from the glare.

The front of the fleet had flattened into a broad disk that was taking intense fire, a head-on battle between the lead ships and three hundred Eyeships hurtling mile-long shards like javelins at the oncoming fleet. The battlefront was a blitzkrieg of cutter beams from both sides, creating a no-man's-land of unsurvivable heat and broiling plasma.

Sally uttered short, sharp commands to filter the luminance and zoom in, so she could see what was going on in detail. She searched for one particular ship, a Marauder carrying her husband, but there was too much clutter. Eight Fronn ships advanced. The cuttlefish metaphor held up as the ships spewed focused jets of ice blue from their 'mouths', the jets converging to create a narrow corridor through the star-hot inferno. A squad of Starpiercers dived into this protected tunnel, a trail of glittering Korg Diamonds following fast in their wake.

The Starpiercers earned their name. Each one that got through – around half survived the ride through the conduit – punctured the milky, spherical hub of an Eyeship, renting open a hole into which the Korg Diamonds plunged. She held her breath. Within a minute the affected – no, *infected* – Eyeships stopped firing, and drifted. Two collided with each other. The Eyeships' milky central disks turned a mottled brown, their smooth exterior erupting in gashes and volcanoes, revealing seething fires raging deep inside. She recalled the Korg were terraformers, and the first stage in terraforming was to go back to basics, when all planets in their initial growth spurt were riven with volcanoes and swamped by rivers of lava.

Her fingers coiled into a triumphant fist, and she whispered the same affirmation Alex had uttered minutes earlier.

'*Yes!*'

But neither the Starpiercers nor the Korg Diamonds re-emerged, and she weighed the heavy cost of this tactic, and once again searched for Michael's ship. She found its unique symbol, a Texan red-tailed hawk she'd entered into the holo-display system. His Marauder was in the third wave, approaching the battlefront behind ten city-sized Par'aal ships who now forged across the front line – a convex, hemispherical boundary demarcating an orange zone and a red one – ready to clean up, or in this case, carve up the rest of the Eyeship fleet. She called up a holopad and tapped in a message.

Be careful.

Michael's reply came back straightaway.

Always.

His ship, the rest of the Marauders, and thousands of Shuriken breached the red zone. She zoomed in, proud, as the Marauders deployed Crowns of Thorns, snaring and garrotting individual shards, while Shuriken fell on others like soldier ants. With their laser-tipped blades, for individual shards it was death by a thousand cuts, scarring them until the Korg Diamonds laid bombs in those scars that blew massive fragments into space.

Slice and shred.

The Tchlox and Fronn now advanced against the thirty remaining Eyeships. Sally couldn't see what the Tchlox fired at them, but it must have been a dark energy weapon, as successive Eyeships buckled and broke apart. Half a dozen 'yolks' of the Eyeships ballooned outwards as if filling with air, then burst, scattering the viscous milky interior in all directions. The Fronn turned up the heat, sucking in vast clouds of nebula gas and then expelling them, fiery plumes enveloping the diminishing enemy fleet.

It became a rout as Par'aal Cityships and Lleynach Hammerships ploughed into the fray with cutter beams, serious rail guns and implosion devices that crumpled the remaining shards. The last Eyeships were completely surrounded, and Sally couldn't help but compare the battle scene to the way dolphins corralled huge shoals of sardines, encircling them, trapping them, then diving in to feast.

The Eyeships were trapped inside a cauldron. All would perish inside it.

The Ankh Pyramids began advancing towards the red zone, no doubt to finish this battle.

'Sally,' Alex called, 'come quickly.'

She took one last look, then returned to find Ares sitting up, his fingers outstretched, his battered, cauterized silver face taut. She stared into empty eye sockets, looking for some sign of Ares. His body vibrated. Then she noticed Alex was bleeding from a slash across her cheek.

'What happened?'

Alex forced a smile, then winced at the pain it caused. 'I woke him up. This,' she said, indicating her cheek, 'was an accident, a reflex on his part. I didn't get out of the way fast enough.'

'You should–'

'No, there's something wrong. With Ares, I mean. His consciousness is... chaotic.'

Sally couldn't begin to imagine how Ares' consciousness worked. 'But it's a good thing, right? I mean–'

'No, it isn't, not like this. When the Axleth attacked him, he shut himself down to protect himself. And now we've woken him up...' She stepped close to Sally, like a doctor who doesn't want the patient to hear the prognosis. 'His neural pathways are destabilizing, Sally. They could degrade...'

'Meaning?'

'Sally!' she heard Jaspar's voice from the adjoining room. She ignored it.

Alex hesitated, then spat it out. 'Brain death.'

Sally looked past Alex to her former mentor.

'Sally!' she heard again. She raised her wristcom. 'We're busy down here, Jaspar.'

'The battle. It's turning around.'

'Good, the fleet can clean up the rest–'

'No, they're winning again. You're needed in the Conn.'

Sally tapped at her wristcom and messaged Michael.

You okay?

A pause. *Are you?*

Ares, there's something wrong with him.

'Sally, are you coming?' Christy asked.

Michael messaged back. *We can handle this. Get him back,*

Sal. Family first. Gotta go. Busy.

Family. Michael had never said it before when referring to Ares. Elodie would have agreed.

'Christy, I'm needed here,' Sally said. 'You'll have to do without me.'

She took off her wristcom, placed it on a table. 'What can we do, Alex?'

'From here, there's nothing more I can do. I need to reach Ares, his mind, but I can't.'

Sally touched the switched off aug above her left eye. 'Hook me in,' she said.

Alex opened her mouth as if to disagree, then a faint smile emerged. 'No point me warning you of the danger, is there?'

'Waste of breath and time.'

'Then sit here.' Alex began arranging her equipment, choosing between different wires. 'I wish Billy were here to watch this.'

'Me too,' Sally replied.

Alex held out two wires with something on the end of each that writhed like a worm. The other ends connected to Ares' skull.

'Nathan told us something once,' Alex said. 'Never knew why, but now I see its relevance. How do you rescue a drowning man?'

Sally tried to see where this was going. She glanced at Ares. She was going to go inside his head. He could be confused, desperate, thrashing around trying to save his own mind. He'd already lacerated Alex's cheek.

Ares was the drowning man.

'From behind,' she replied.

Alex smiled, then touched Sally's forehead, attaching the two wires.

'This may hurt,' she said.

And then everything turned silver.

◆ ◆ ◆

Shafts of mercury shot past Sally in all directions, as if she was at the nexus of some silver superhighway. Any which way she looked, she saw the same rushing blocks and cylinders of mercury approach, miss each other by infinitesimal margins that made her flinch, and continue on until she lost resolution in a platinum haze. A bass beat pounded underneath it all, interrupted by staccato bursts and a fizzing noise that rose and fell, like a snare drum. She tried calling out, using Ares' name, but her voice was lost in the mechanical melee. Then she noticed that some of the strands whooshing by were degrading – fraying, splintering, fracturing, until they burst apart, the remains tumbling below, lost to her vision.

Ares was dying. For good this time.

When he'd been attacked by the Axleth pilot, he'd been rendered inoperative, but his neural pathways were still there, just inert. Now those pathways were decaying. Once it proceeded beyond a certain point, there would be no way back. They might as well bury or cremate him, and move on.

No.

Walking didn't happen when she tried, and after an indeterminate time – the silver show was strangely mesmerizing – she reached out and threw her arms around a cylinder as it passed close by. She hurtled through this psychedelic dreamscape, miraculously untouched by the other strands. She had no idea how to steer, which didn't matter much as she had no idea of where to go. Her only hope was that at some level, Ares had detected her, and would bring her somewhere she could be useful. Of course, an alternative imminent future for her was that her presence would trigger Ares' immune response, and she'd be attacked by whatever his equivalent of antibodies might be.

She tried to stay optimistic.

There was no sense of scale she could grasp. Everything

was shades of silver, some objects with a glowing, almost dazzling sheen, others a listless grey. But up ahead, after traversing what had seemed like hundreds of miles, the endless platinum superhighway delivered her to a domed area with pale light above, and a mercury lake with a silver-sand shore. The ride wasn't slowing down. Making her best guess, she let go.

Alex had said it would hurt. Landing sure did. She rubbed her elbows and knees after crash-rolling on the shore, and realized she was naked. She hadn't noticed until now for one simple reason – her skin was the same colour as everything else here. Probably that kept her from being 'rejected'.

She walked to the lakeside. The mercury wasn't completely still. Faint, slow ripples drifted in from farther out. She shielded her eyes and detected a lone, stationary figure in the middle, wearing a hood and a cloak. She stepped forward, her foot causing a sizable dimple in the mercury, but it didn't break the surface tension. As she leaned forward, it continued to support her weight. She walked a few paces. It wasn't easy, and she had to take it slow, as she didn't know, and preferred not to find out what would happen if she fell and broke through the surface.

Once or twice, as she was watching her feet, she thought she detected a shadow underneath her, a mustard coloured shape, striking because all she'd seen for some time now had been silver. Whatever it was, it left her as she approached Ares.

'Ares, it's Sally,' she called out.

He had his back to her. The hooded head turned a fraction in her direction, as if hearing her, then it faced forward again. She walked right up behind him.

'Ares, it's me, Sally. I've come to help you.'

Just as she took one last step, she was knocked off her feet by what she could only describe as an earthquake. She guessed the *Athena* was under attack. Alex had said she could exit any time she wanted, with a simple thought command. But Jaspar was competent. She'd be just another spare wheel in the Conn, and besides, she was falling...

As she feared, her hands broke through the meniscus, plunging into colder-than-ice liquid metal that stung, froze and burned all at the same time. She cried out as she sank further, unable to pull her hands free. The mercury surface rose to meet her face, and she saw her reflection; a silver Sally, even the eyes.

She wondered if she'd meet Elodie on the other side, and whether Michael was soon to join them anyway if the battle outside was going badly. Just as her face entered the freezing metal, a hand seized her right shoulder and dragged her back out.

'It is not safe here,' Ares said to her.

'No shit,' she replied, then saw that his face, at least here, was restored, including his eyes.

He placed her on her feet. They faced each other.

'You must leave while you still can,' he said.

Make me, she thought, but said, 'Not without you.'

Ares studied the domed hazy grey pseudo-sky above him. 'It is too late to save me.'

She folded her arms. 'Tell me there are no solutions.'

'There are no...' he stopped. Looked down. She followed his gaze. There was a faint glimmer of yellow deep beneath them.

'There is a solution, isn't there?' she said.

'A possibility. A thin one. One you will not easily forgive.'

The ground rocked again, Ares steadying her as the entire lake shook, sending ripples, waves even, to the shore.

'Better make it quick, then. Time forgives all.'

'That is not true.'

'Ares...'

'A neural graft,' he said.

She tried to imagine what that meant in practice. 'You need a piece of my brain?'

'A temporary haven. Our neural pathways operate on the same principle. Connections, electrical impulses...'

'So get on with it.'

'The consequences, Sally–'

'Look outside. I'm betting you can see through *Athena's* sensors. The battle has turned, hasn't it? We're losing, and we've not even reached the Eye's homeworld. Nathan brought the *Athena* here for you. Billy died believing, as do I, that you and your Xaxoan tech are a critical weapon in this war. David confirmed it after his mind meld or whatever with the Axleth.'

Ares said nothing. Then he raised a hand, touched her cheek with the tip of his finger.

'It is very presumptuous of me, Sally, but when we were on the *Athena* together and you were growing up, I tried to be like a father to you, though I never truly understood what that meant, and am possibly incapable of ever doing so.'

Sally touched his hand.

The ship rocked again. This time, they were both knocked to the mercurial surface, but they didn't break through. She thought of those Starpiercer and Korg soldiers who'd just sacrificed themselves without a moment's hesitation. Heroes, one and all. She didn't even know what they looked like, but imagined they all had families or friends or whatever, and they'd just given it all up for the fight. How could she do any less?

'Ares, there's no time. The fleet needs you. Take what you need from me, no matter the cost, and go save us all.'

Again, he raised a hand, this time placing the flat of his palm against her forehead.

'Forgive me.'

Her mind stalled, as if frozen, unable to think, just perceive. Cold tendrils skewered into her skull. Her head tipped forward, and she saw again the yellow glow down below, and realized what it was. Back in the battle for Earth, when Ares had split himself in two so that he could support Sally and Nathan retaking Earth, leaving his copy Ares2 to man the Athena, Ares2 had been – albeit for a short time –infiltrated by the Eye. Nathan believed the uninfected Ares had purged this one of the Eye's insidious programming. Now she knew that wasn't completely true. Something remained inside Ares, trapped in this lake. That's why the last vestige of Ares was here, keeping it locked in while he still could. She sensed this entity deep beneath her. Like all caged animals, this one longed to be free, and longed even more to take revenge.

She found it hard to think. Her mind was being stripped. What had Ares said? A neural graft. She could almost feel layers of her mind peeling off, one by one. She wondered how much he needed to take. And then she could think no more, as if Ares had pulled out the plug that powered her mind. She perceived one last thing, Ares shooting upwards into the pale grey sky, as she slipped beneath the lake's mercurial surface.

CHAPTER 16

Atticus

Michael stood by the helm, fire washing through his veins. At last, after all this time, some payback. The Marauder he was on, hastily re-christened the Elodie, was at the head of a hundred other ships funnelling into the fireproof conduit created by the Fronn. Though everything about this battle was on a massive scale, he couldn't help feel they were in a syringe, about to infect and destroy the remaining shard-ships. A surgical strike if ever there was one.

Starkel, in the captain's chair, was the consummate professional, controlling this column of the fleet with admirable precision, whether via voice, holo-controls, or auging to the Axel / human contingent. Starkel was also the only reason Michael had been allowed on board.

'I need to be there,' Michael had said, having turned up impromptu at the boarding gantry.

Starkel hadn't replied, but led him to the bridge and pointed to a station that wasn't empty, its occupant scurrying out of the way and finding another without so much as a word. Michael had studied the station, but otherwise kept his hands to himself. It was a back-up nav console, in case the holo display field failed, he figured. There was also a red button with a flap over it. No label. Black and yellow hatching around it that screamed *don't push this unless it's really bad*. He folded his arms.

His wristcom buzzed. Sally.

Be careful.

Always, he replied with a smile. Not quite true. He wanted revenge, to inflict not just damage but pain on the enemy, the Eye. Someone had once joked to his father that *revenge was a dish best served cold*. His father had considered it a while, delving beneath the surface of jokes as he always did, once confiding to Michael that everything you needed to know about culture, about humanity's strengths and failings, was in jokes, if you chose to study them. After a few moments, his father had replied, *revenge is a dish you'll never digest*.

Maybe true, but Michael had to try it, had to savour it. His father was usually right, he knew that, but when you're hurting so bad... He glanced across at Starkel, wondering if Axels could still harbour vengeful thoughts.

Sure they could.

They exited the syringe, as he thought of it, the mishmash of ships firing all manner of weapons. Leviathan Par'aal Cityships were carving up the remaining Eyeships. The Marauders were on clean-up duty, attacking broken-off shards that still posed a threat.

The Marauders were like butchers carving dead meat. He oscillated between watching his nav display and the holo. It was poetry in motion. Yet he felt like a bystander, passive, only witnessing. He'd always preferred to be involved in the action, physically engaging with the world. *Burn yourself up in whatever you do*, he'd read somewhere, *because your soul needs the exercise...*

He stood up, spoke to Starkel. 'I need something to do.'

Starkel beckoned him to approach. He grasped Michael's right wrist, and guided it into the holo, to a lone shard they were approaching.

'Touch it with your finger,' Starkel said. Michael obliged.

'Now say "Fire, Omega 3"'

Michael repeated it loud and clear. 'Fire! Omega 3!'

Whether or not Starkel had sent a supplementary aug command didn't matter. Railgun fire strafed the shard, pitting its surface, backed up by three torpedoes that snaked their way towards it. A second later, crimson flame engulfed the entire Eyeship. The shard snapped off, tearing a gash in the central yolk, milky puss spilling from its guts. Michael's hand lingered there awhile, then he returned to his seat.

Had it helped at all? Was his father right? Was revenge a hunger that knew no end, could never be sated?

It *had* helped, just not in the way he'd anticipated. The need to inflict pain was gone. This was the Eye, a machine, no matter how super intelligent. Incapable of feeling remorse or guilt. He recalled one of his favourite books, *To Kill a Mockingbird*, and the uncommon hero, Atticus Finch, who rid the town of a rabid dog. That's what the Eye was. A rabid dog that needed to be put down.

He scanned the nav display. Clean-up was going well. The wall of super-heated plasma was gone, and the three Ankh Pyramids had arrived, supervising the 7-3-1 scavenging the remains for intel, like blowflies on a fresh carcass. The eight Fronn ships returned to their more distant perimeter guardian positions in the fleet, while the Hammerships and Par'aal Cityships remained at the fore. Michael guessed the fleet wouldn't linger too long; there was nothing worth salvaging from the Eyeships. And the fleet was on the clock.

The Marauder lurched sideways, almost unseating him from his chair.

'What was that?' he said, forgetting his place as observer for a moment, added to the fact that the rest of the crew were auged, and would have already asked and answered the question.

'Bow wave,' the young woman at the helm answered. 'Something's approaching fast. Very fast. And it's… gigantic.'

Michael peered through shrouds of mauve nebula gas

that whipped past their ship, trying to see what was coming. On the nav display he watched as hundreds of Starpiercers shot forward, a hail of arrows ready to fell the next wave of Eyeships, if that's what it was.

He had a feeling it wasn't. A bad feeling. He reached for his wristcom, then thought better of it.

Something punched out of space right in front of them, making him jerk backwards in his chair, again glancing from the nav display to the holo to grasp its size.

It was an Eyeship, but like none they'd ever seen.

The Starpiercers bounced off some kind of field, and after a blinding pulse of light from the massive ship, they were gone.

As the holo adjusted to take in its enormity, for the first time the fleet seemed small in comparison. And fragile. The Goliath Eyeship was black as deep space, like the darkest part of a moonless night, except for rivers of electric blue that slithered across its dark core, as if this ship was a being with its blood vessels pulsing on the outside. It registered two hundred miles from tip to toe, its mega-shards barbed with 'normal-sized' ones, also black, flecked with dark red spots and scars. The scanners were busy counting the shards. He stopped looking when the tally topped five thousand. He wondered what the top message in the Stack would be right now. In theory it could be, probably should be, to *get the hell out of here*. But fleeing wasn't an option. Regrouping to fight another day would never happen.

He could see why it had appeared now, just as the Pyramid ships had moved into the fray. Two of the oldest tricks in the war playbook. The first was tactical, drawing the fleet leaders out as victory seemed assured, only to corner them in an unwinnable confrontation. The second was strategic: find the leaders of the enemy, and cut off their heads. While the Axleth had engineered this armada coming together, it was the Ankh who led the war effort. He wondered what would happen to the fleet's morale if those three

Pyramids were destroyed, and then it occurred to him that this battle scenario might be playing out simultaneously with the other two fleets.

It began.

It was like an autopsy on a living being.

Cutter beams, the breadth of football fields, slashed across the fleet's front. He watched in horror as three Par'aal Megaships were sliced in two. Hammerships were dissected in seconds. Fronn Cuttleships rushed forward – gaining his utmost respect – to protect the Pyramids. The aquatic ships were the only ones who could quench this level of firepower. But no sooner had they done so than thousands of shards broke off and raced to attack the irreplaceable Fronn ships. This is where the Syrn would have come in handy, Michael realized, as they had both superior size and shielding.

His wristcom buzzed again.

You okay?

She never asked that unless something serious was going down.

Are you? He replied.

Ares, there's something wrong with him.

She'd just lost their daughter. Losing Ares for good... He tapped his reply.

We'll handle it. Get him back, Sal. Family first. Gotta go. Busy.

The bridge was inundated with comms too fast for him to follow, but their Marauder shot back out of harm's immediate way, along with the Tchlox – deemed too precious to lose right now – as another wave of Starpiercers and thousands of Korg, 7-3-1 and Shuriken shot toward the Goliath-ship. He searched the nav display for the *Athena*, at the rear and periphery for now, and saw it was on an intercept with the *Dreadnought*, though the latter was powering forward through the centre-mass of the fleet. He had to admit the Axleth had delivered on their promise to heighten humanity's 'fight'; these Axels were made of stern stuff.

Two of the Pyramids were struck by the full blast of cutter beams, but miraculously weren't diced or sliced. But once the beams had located them, they held. He doubted any ship could survive such sustained firepower for long. The Starpiercers, 7-3-1 and Korg, reached their target, but it was like ants fighting a bear; the Goliath ship ignored them.

But the Pyramids had a few tricks up their sleeves. The three Ankh vessels, bathed in a rippling jade-green aura, moved closer together. The cutter beams tracked them, not losing purchase for a second. The Pyramids joined, apex to apex, almost lost now in the wash of blinding heat, but the holo auto-adjusted, as a green bolt shot out from the three-now-one structure. It lasered straight through the Goliath ship, and begun cutting out its heart.

Everyone was standing on the bridge now, and he guessed it was the same across most of the fleet. But just when his fist was ready to punch the air and yell something he hadn't yet had time to think of, it happened...

The holo shut off. So did most of the equipment on the bridge. In the ensuing confusion, Michael noticed that his nav console was still working, though the image stuttered and flickered, as if hanging on by a thread. What he saw wasn't comforting. On the one hand, the Pyramid ships were turning the tide of battle again; the enemy cutter beams had ceased. But the rest of the fleet seemed... adrift. And then the unthinkable came to pass as a Hammership rammed a Fronn ship at high speed.

What the proverbial fuck?

Before he had time to figure it out, Starkel executed a hard manoeuvre, the reason only becoming apparent a fraction of a second later as a beam lanced across their bow.

Not-so-friendly fire. The only theory Michael had was the one he himself had voiced earlier, some kind of cyber-attack, turning ships on each other. But theorizing would have to wait.

'*Dreadnought!*' Michael shouted, eliciting a sharp glance

from Starkel, who bounded down to check his nav display.

Starkel auged instructions to his crew, Michael guessed, as the Marauder swung about and intercepted a Hammership ploughing straight towards their 400 year old home and base ship.

'Fire,' Starkel commanded.

Michael winced. They were doing the Eye's dirty work for it. But they couldn't stand by and watch the last remaining Axel base-ship destroyed. More to the point, the *Dreadnought* was taking no evasive action.

A full barrage of the *Elodie's* torpedoes struck the Hammership, engulfing it in soon-snuffed-out flame. But the decimated ship was still on a collision course, and as Michael knew, the laws of momentum were especially unforgiving in space.

The crew held their breath and watched, but in the last few seconds another ship zoomed in out of nowhere, nudging the massive Hammership sideways, just enough for it to miss the *Dreadnought's* prow by a scarily small margin.

Before he could even verify the identity of the ship – he somehow knew it was Sally on the *Athena* – something began materializing on the bridge, right in front of them.

A form that shimmered all the colours of fire, made up of small cubes that vibrated, making it impossible to focus on any part of the figure with its tetrahedron head. But there was no doubt in Michael's mind. He'd had the briefing, heard the legend and, like all myths, there was some truth to this one. Scarier than most kids' bedtime horror stories, a nightmare made real.

The Shrike.

A being, or a construct made of light. An AI derivative. An avatar of the Eye. It didn't matter. They all knew what came next.

Starkel reached down to Michael's console and lifted the flap off the red button, and Michael's nagging supposition was confirmed. It was an auto-destruct, its use preferable to their ship being overtaken by this photonic creature and used as a weapon against the *Dreadnought*.

Michael's gaze was drawn to the Shrike's eyes, pits of deep, dark fire, and again he thought of Atticus facing the town's rabid dog. But they had no equivalent of a rifle against this monstrosity.

The ship was knocked sideways again, harder this time, throwing him and Starkel away from the precious button that would end them all. From the floor, he saw the Shrike's flickering, fiery fingers snake into the two nearest consoles, penetrating their systems. Starkel sprang up and slammed his hand down on the button.

Michael closed his eyes.

And opened them.

They'd been too slow. Auto-destruct must have been the first command the Shrike disabled. Several crew members fired handheld weapons at the Shrike, only to be dissolved in white flash-flame that left nothing behind.

Michael got up. If he was going to die, which was apparently destiny's call, he'd do so on his feet. But before he could move, a red-hot ring formed on the far wall of the bridge. The heat from the burning metal stung his eyes, but he kept them open, as a perfectly round disk of the Marauder's hull toppled forward with a clunk, revealing a silhouetted figure standing on another ship.

Ares.

But he was different. His smooth platinum skin was covered in a never-ending, intertwining tattoo of grey and blue fissures. Ares and the *Athena* had merged.

The Shrike lashed out at Ares with fiery whips that spat and fizzled. Ares was impervious. He had something in his hand. A weapon. He levelled it and fired, but the Shrike was fast, and ricocheted around the bridge like a dervish. Ares found his target twice, but only glancing blows, wounding not killing, and with a crack of the Shrike's whip, the weapon was knocked from Ares' grip and sent spinning across the floor.

The two figures, one demonic, the other serene, locked together, hands around each other's throats, pushing, equally matched. Michael knew that's only how it looked on the outside, a physical manifestation of the titanic cyber battle ongoing between the two AI beings, unseen and probably unseeable by the human eye. A swathe of fissures on Ares' chest began to glow red. The Shrike was winning.

'Hold,' Ares shouted.

Michael stayed where he was, even as the red fissures gained ground, spreading up and down Ares' torso. Starkel made a move toward the weapon, but Michael stayed him with a flat palm.

'He's losing this,' Starkel said.

Michael didn't think so. He had a hunch. Ares wasn't done yet.

Starkel made to reach for the weapon again. Half of Ares' fissures oozed blood red. Michael grabbed Starkel's wrist. 'Wait!' he shouted.

The Shrike seemed to grow larger, stronger, its eyes blazing, when suddenly its cubes began flickering blue and grey. It let go of Ares and staggered backwards, staring at its arms as they writhed with widening blue-grey fissures.

Ares, exhausted, sank to his knees. 'Now,' he said.

Michael didn't need to be asked twice.

He seized the weapon, aimed it at the Shrike's head, and shot the rabid dog dead in its tracks.

CHAPTER 17

Secrets

Nathan had never born witness to a costlier victory. He stood with Anya on the bridge of the Dreadnought staring up at the holo stretching across the ceiling, surveying the carnage after the dual attack by the Goliath ship and the Shrike. The nebula had lit up with cutter beams and even nukes, small suns of boiling plasma that ballooned, then faded, deprived of atmosphere, except for one he'd seen strike a Par'aal Cityship. That detonation had spilled an aurora of colour, a rainbow ribbon in space, its stark beauty signifying the loss of more than a million Par'aal in a single blow. The surge of radiation and EMP shockwaves had sorely tested the shielding on all space-faring ships. Korg Diamonds had been immune; less so the Shuriken, who had sheltered behind active or shattered Hammership hulls, or here, inside the Dreadnought.

The landscape – spacescape – was littered with debris and torn hulls, some recognizable, others twisted and melted into gruesome shapes, ghoulish shadows in the flickering light of soon to-be-extinguished, beyond-all-hope-of-saving, battleship reactors.

Most of the damage had been self-inflicted, once the Shrike had infected the control systems of over half the fleet, appearing simultaneously on hundreds of bridges. The Theon and 7-3-1 had been impervious to the Shrike, as had the Ankh-ships locked in battle with the Goliath Eyeship, and the Shuriken and Korg Diamond-ships had been too small fare for the Shrike to bother with. But the rest... A handful of Hammerships and two Par'aal city ships had survived, but not without being gouged. He knew a debate was going on right now about whether they would continue to limp onward with the fleet. At least they had the option.

Not so with the Fronn.

A single Cuttleship had survived. The rest of the Fronn contingent had been destroyed in a last-ditch bid to save the Tchlox Ringships, whose command systems had been eviscerated by the Shrike cyber-weapon, and who became the principal target of the Hammerships. The six remaining Ringships were being towed along by mini-swarms of Korg Diamonds.

Forty-three per cent of the fleet had been lost. That was an atrocious statistic by anyone's standards, but it could have been so much worse. He hoped the other two divisions of the armada were faring better.

Nathan realized he was thinking like a general, assessing assets, because he stood in the safe haven of the *Dreadnought*. Normally, he'd be out there, looking for survivors. He recalled walking through a short spit of rocky canyon after an ambush in the Hindu Kush Mountains. Thousands of shiny, spent brass-coloured shells littered the ground around now-dead soldiers who'd believed superior firepower could win out against a few well-hidden snipers. He watched small ships strip ordnance from listless metallic shipwrecks. There had been few rescue missions; any being thrown out into space, even in whatever survival suits their organic forms had possessed, had been subject to extreme radiation... They would have to leave them all behind, because the enemy would regroup quickly and learn from this failure; it cared nothing for casualties. No respect for the dead. No time for burial or even ceremonies. *Crap.* This was worse than Afghanistan had ever been.

As for the Axels, they'd already moved on. Fight was in their DNA, and so too was acceptance of what war truly meant.

He did his best to keep up.

'The Ankh Pyramids survived,' he said to Anya.

'Yes, but their secret weapon is no secret anymore.'

He nodded. 'Doesn't make it any less effective.'

'For now,' she said.

'The Eye was after the Ringships again.'

'We saved six, but lost the Fronn contingent.' She waved a hand dismissively before Nathan could speak. 'One Fronn ship is more a mascot than a capability.'

'Surely we'll need the Ringships more when we arrive at the Eye's homeworld?'

She pursed her lips. 'Yes, but we're in a nebula, Nathan, A star nursery. It's as if we're fighting a war on a battlefield soaked in gasoline, and we just lost our fire extinguisher.'

'Maybe more Fronn survived in the other two fleets.'

They grew quiet for a while, though he sensed she had a lot more to say.

'Ares,' he began, before she swung around to face him and cut him off, her face flushed with emotion.

'Deserves a fucking medal.'

She said it loud, turning heads on the otherwise subdued bridge. 'Or maybe it was Sally's doing,' she added, quieter, returning her gaze to the holo-stacks of data showing withering fleet-wide losses, including four Marauders and almost fifty thousand Axel-piloted Shuriken.

And forty humans.

'Why are you here, Nathan?'

He cleared his throat, nonplussed. 'I'm... here to help, I hope.'

'You're not. Helping, that is. Go to her.'

He felt a shiver. 'She's in a coma.'

'You're afraid,' Anya said, stinging him.

He said nothing, his mouth as dry as that dusty canyon in Hindu Kush.

She didn't let up. 'You're afraid that Ares took something from her, took too much, that she won't be Sally anymore.'

She flicked off all the displays, right across the bridge, causing all to look in their direction as she faced him and spoke loud enough for all to hear.

'So, tell me, Mister Survivor, because you've come through a lot, haven't you? The original attack on Earth, retaking it, your wormhole escapade, and now this, not to mention God-knows-what you lived through in Afghanistan... Tell me, Nathan, when soldiers are wounded in battle, when people are changed by war, or infected, or whatever the fuck the Axleth did to us...' she flourished her arm to include all the Axels and the two humans on the bridge, 'or what Ares did to Sally. Do you care any less about them, Nathan?'

He stared at her, speechless, feeling as if he'd just had yet another dressing down from his old sergeant, Trescoe. Except this was worse.

Nathan's legs acted on their own initiative, and he found himself in the elevator, then on the medical level where Sally was being treated. He stood there, his legs no longer in charge. Was he afraid? He recalled countless visits to see war buddies in hospital. Some made it back out. Some didn't. A few never woke up.

He glanced down the corridor to her room. *Was he afraid?*

Dumb question.

He got his legs moving again.

Michael intercepted him at the doorway. He motioned for them to step outside, closing the doors behind him.

'About time,' Michael said. He looked like hell. Like he was in hell. With no way out.

'I don't want her to hear,' he said. 'Not sure she can hear anything. I mean, after all, she's fucking brain-dead, right?'

Nathan entered Michael's personal hell. 'We don't know

that,' he said.

Michael paced. He looked like he wanted to hit somebody, a wall, anything.

'Sal and I talked about this,' Michael continued. 'You know, it's war. People die. Not abstract people, not just other people, but us. After Elodie...'

Nathan searched for something to say. But he'd been here too many times, knew that nothing worked, that this was the hurting, you just had to fight your way through it. But not alone.

'She saved us all,' he said.

'My family's cursed,' Michael replied.

Nathan played it back. 'What?'

Michael stopped pacing, leaned with his back against the wall. 'I can trace my family back to the Civil War, you know. Deep South, Confederates, all that jazz.'

Nathan listened.

'Back then, my family had six sons. All of them signed up. To fight for the Union, would you believe, as my great, great, whatever grandfather had no truck with slavery. Christ, that can't have been easy. Anyway, all six sons died in the war, one by one. Their mother was killed by Union soldiers, no less. Nice twist of irony, right?' He glanced at Nathan then carried on.

'Great-whatever-grandad remarried, started a fresh family. Thing is, for every war, right up until the one you fought, my family sent their sons and even daughters into battle. Most never came back. We're cursed, Nathan. And I brought down that curse on Elodie, and now Sal...'

Michael broke. Nathan didn't hug him like they do in the movies. Because he knew, deep down, that Michael was strong. And that he was crap at hugging men, anyway. Still felt weird. Father issues most likely.

Michael straightened, sniffed. 'I'm done, Nathan. Thanks for watching my shit-show. You want to see her now?'

They both entered Sally's room.

Nathan sat in the only chair in the small room, next to her bed. Michael was on the floor, sitting cross-legged with his back against the wall. Neither had spoken a word since their chat. He recalled watching movies where, in times like this, men talked and talked, and bonded, ending up telling jokes. He never finished said movies. Reality wasn't like that, at least not in his experience. There was mostly nothing worth saying, and mostly you were just trying to hold back the dark, crappy thoughts in your head about what the future held, because you'd already seen what the past had dished up. As Trescoe had once said, if war was a restaurant, the food was shit, nothing to write home about. At least Michael had let off a little steam. Not so for Nathan. He'd spent twenty years longing to see Sally again, and now this... He could barely look at Sally, because it wasn't her anymore, just an empty shell. But Michael had just lost his only daughter and his wife in the space of a week. Nathan sure as hell wasn't going to unload on him. So they sat together in silence, two men in hell's locker room. It didn't make good theatre and would make a boring movie, but that's just how it was.

Their silent camaraderie cracked wide open when Ares arrived.

Michael was up on his feet in an instant. He looked ready to deck Ares, or at least try, even though Ares had arguably just saved the entire fleet.

Ares, still sporting his blue-and-grey-fissure look since he'd bonded with the *Athena,* walked over to Sally, checked all the intel on the screens around her bed, then turned to leave.

Michael barred the door. 'What did you do to her?'

Ares remained serene. 'I employed neural pathways from her brain to stem the cascade failure occurring in my neural net.'

'Fucking put them back, then.' Michael shouted.

'I cannot.'

Michael was about to speak, to unleash a tirade of words that once said could never be taken back, when Ares held up a hand.

'Yet.'

Michael's face contorted from a grimace to confusion. 'What does *yet* mean?'

Nathan stepped forward. 'Can you bring her back, Ares?'

Ares still faced Michael. 'I am working on a solution. Ninety-four per cent of me is focused on it as we speak.'

Michael advanced again, inches from Ares' platinum features. 'What have you got so far?'

Ares turned around to Nathan. 'He will tell you. I am needed elsewhere.'

Nathan was about to protest when Ares reached out with his left hand and touched Nathan's dormant aug eyebrow. Nathan watched Ares and Michael grow small, as if he was falling backwards into a deep well.

Nathan awoke, back in the chair. He managed to utter, 'What the hell just happened?' before he collapsed onto all fours and spilled his breakfast. He heard Michael move around and then saw his boots before him and the head of a mop. He laughed. He was on a spaceship two thousand light years from Earth, and they had a mop. He got to his feet and cleaned up his mess. It was a shame Sally was in a coma. She'd have had a good laugh. He saw that Michael's right hand had a bandage wrapped around it. Michael followed Nathan's gaze.

'Sonofabitch is hard as nails,' he said, then uttered a short laugh, rubbing the back of his hand. 'I thought he'd move out of the way lightning fast, or block it, but he just let me punch him straight in the face. Think that was guilt?'

'No,' Nathan replied.

'Maybe he thought I needed it.'

'You did.'

But Nathan also reckoned Ares had let Michael punch him because he'd wanted to know how it would feel – not physically, but *emotionally*. Ares was exploring his humanity.

'So I'm guessing he downloaded stuff into your head,' Michael said.

Nathan reflected. 'I guess he did.'

'Don't worry,' Michael said. 'I won't shoot the messenger.'

'You haven't heard the message yet.'

'Give me the chair, then.'

They traded places.

David arrived. 'Ah, it was *you*,' he said to Michael. 'Ares passed me by, and I saw blood on his face, so I figured it had to belong to one of you two.'

Michael smiled. 'Blood on his face, huh? Did you tell him?'

David returned the smile. 'Why would I do that?'

Nathan had always figured he'd be a crap father. 'No seats, I'm afraid,' he said to his son.

David perched on the medical bed right next to Sally. 'She looks peaceful,' he said, surprising both of them. Nathan mused that maybe he'd not been such a bad father after all. More likely, Lara had been a good mother. Jury was still out.

'Is she going to come out of it anytime soon?' Michael asked.

'No,' Nathan said bluntly.

The smile freefell from Michael's face. 'What did Ares tell you?'

Nathan wished he were sitting down. It was coming back to him in chunks.

'Listen, Michael, the way it works, I need to talk, speak as it unwraps in my head. No interruptions, okay?'

Michael pointed to his bandage. 'Just remember, I still have one good hand.'

'Cool,' David said with a sardonic smile. 'A fight!'

Okay, Nathan decided, *jury was free to go.*

'Here goes,' he said, and closed his eyes.

'Sally's brain is... fried. There's no way to sugar-coat it. But it's like two pieces of a puzzle. One piece is still inside her, the neural pathways he didn't touch; the other piece is inside Ares. So, all Ares needs to do is...' He paused. There was only one way to say it. 'He needs to find another brain. An artificial one.'

He heard cursing, but kept his eyes closed, because there was more.

'Ares is an AI...' Why was Ares telling him the obvious? But he went with the flow. 'And AIs seek information. They prize it above all else. So, when they encounter another intelligence, even one that organics might consider evil...'

He gasped. For a moment he saw Sally's interaction with Ares, a remnant from her own aug experience, and he felt that aug-closeness he'd never experienced with her, and the deep well of complicated emotions Sally felt for her lost daughter, Elodie. And the desire she'd had to see him was there, too.

'Why's he crying?' David asked.

'To stop me from doing to him what I did to Ares, maybe?' Michael replied.

Nathan heard their voices from afar. He was trying to hold on to this connection to Sally, savouring this fleeting intimacy. But Ares directed him to something else, something she'd seen in the depths of the lake. Nathan looked down and saw.

He took a breath and continued. 'When Ares encountered the Eyeship on the way back to Earth, and was infected, and then... disinfected, he kept a small part of it inside him.'

'Holy shit!' David said, shaking his head. 'Talk about keeping a secret!'

'It's not a full-blown Eye remnant,' Nathan added. 'It's a... seedling. It's an old tactic. *Know your enemy.* Ares has been studying this seedling, probing it for weak spots.'

'That's how Ares defeated the Shrike,' David said.

Nathan nodded. The transmission from Ares was over. It evaporated, leaving Nathan feeling hollow, a light ringing in his ears, the taste of metal in his mouth. When he opened his eyes, the chair was vacant. He didn't take much persuading.

David took up the reins. 'If Anya knew of this, let alone the Ankh…'

'They'd vivisect Ares, or shut him down, or vaporize him,' Michael finished.

'The Ankh have already demanded to see him,' David said.

Nathan looked up.

'Anya said "No". Actually, Mom told Anya to say no, or at least not to agree to it just yet.'

Nathan hadn't seen Lara since breakfast. 'Why?' he asked.

David held up three fingers. 'First… the Axleth haven't been straight with us. Any of us.'

'Care to share?' Nathan asked.

'I can't. I mean – really – I can't. They told me something, a secret, but it's like… it's behind fog in my mind. Straight after joining minds with them, when I went to the restroom, I managed to scrawl 'big secret after battle,' on the mirror, before I had a massive blackout. Whatever they showed me, clearly they don't want any of the species to know until this is all over.' He closed a finger.

'Second reason?' Michael asked.

'Mom called it a *balance of secrets*. Said something about mutual deterrence. When two enemies know they each hold a secret from each other, it makes them pause for thought before trying to take the advantage.'

'We're supposed to be on the same side,' Michael said, though not without irony.

David shrugged, closed down the second finger.

'Third reason?' Nathan asked.

'She said you two should be the ones to decide. You, Dad,

because you're in charge, well, kind of, you know what I mean.'

Nathan parked that for later.

'Why me?' Michael asked.

'Because Sally traded her life for Ares. Gives you some say, apparently.' David closed down the third finger and folded his arms.

Michael took a long, hard look at his comatose wife, then turned to Nathan. He rubbed the outside of his bandaged fist.

'Hell, I'm too biased. Vivisection sounds like the best option right now. Maybe the Ankh can get her neural pathways back.' He held up his hand. 'I'm kidding, well, sort of. Anyway, Sally would bawl me out if she heard what I just said.' He folded his arms as well. 'I'll abide by your decision on this one, Nathan.'

Nathan rapped his fingers on the armrest a moment. 'We think of Ares as a being, an individual. But he reminded me that an AI is also a tool, an information gatherer, one that's capable of joining dots we find hard to see. Right now, there are too many secrets lurking about. I don't want them coming out in the heat of battle.'

He turned to his son. 'Set up the meet: the Ankh, Anya, and Ares. I need to be there, too.'

David nodded. 'Good call.' With that, he left.

'That boy's pretty smart, Nathan. Sure he's yours?' Michael grinned.

Nathan played along. 'You know how it is. I couldn't keep an eye on Lara *all* the time.'

Michael's grin softened into an easy smile. 'You must be proud.'

'You've no idea.'

Michael grew more serious. 'So, we play the Ares card. We hope they don't dissect him, and that he digs up something tactically or even strategically useful.' He walked over to his wife, took her limp hand. 'And what about my Sal? *Our* Sally?'

Nathan put a hand on Michael's shoulder as they both stared down at her. 'Ares is working on a solution. I don't know what it is, but he's pretty confident he'll find one before the end.'

'Another artificial brain?' Michael said. 'Fat chance of that! And what do we do in the meantime?'

Nathan offered Michael the chair, and sat down cross-legged – as best he could – on the floor, his back against the cool wall. 'I'd like to hear about Elodie, my grand…' It stuck in his throat.

'You can say it, Nathan. You're family.' He smiled again. 'Of course, it means you're cursed like the rest of us now.'

'Thanks, I think. Tell me about my granddaughter. We have until Anya calls for me.'

'What do you want to hear? What do you want to know about her?'

'Anything,' Nathan said. Then, after a brief pause, 'Everything.'

CHAPTER 18

Lies

A res had been busy. He'd met with the 7-3-1 and the Theon to share the intel on how to defeat the Shrike, should the Eye try that one again. Though he met with only one Theon representative, there were millions of 7-3-1. They possessed a hive mind he appreciated: instant connection far superior to his own aug tech, and a collegial resilience against penetration by enemy minds – cyber or organic – that was impressive. Trust wasn't in their lexicon. As Nathan would have said, they made perfect foot-soldiers. As for the Theon, they were indeed spies. Nathan would not trust them an inch.

Nathan, standing next to him beside Anya, wasn't saying much as the trio waited in the vast anteroom inside the lead Pyramid. They'd been summoned as the fleet drew close to its rendezvous point and last battlefield. A request that, in the end, could not be refused.

Nathan and Anya were even more taciturn than usual, and for good reason. They were being scrutinized by the Ankh. Not only visually, but every physiological aspect – sweat, breathing rate, body heat, eye movements, non-verbal behaviour and, of course, speech – was being collected, correlated, triangulated, and interpreted. It all amounted to a sophisticated lie detector. Nathan asked him to deactivate his aug. Ares obliged, but even if he hadn't, the Ankh had a dampening field that achieved the same effect. Ares asked a single question before severing the connection with Nathan: *Did Anya know about the Eye 'seedling' that Ares kept within him?* Nathan said she didn't.

The Ankh appeared. An avatar, humanoid, all flowing mirror-glass that reflected the nebula and fleet outside. It was captivating. The gases swirled their slow dance as the thinned-out fleet spearheaded forward in its savage, silver beauty.

Ares had been trying out human cognitive sub-routines. His 'pet project', David might have called it. Ares assessed the sole progeny of Nathan and Lara: David would be a natural leader to emerge from all of this if any of them survived. Strange how two beings, broken – no, what was the right word – *damaged*, yes, damaged, by their own admission, could produce a singular personality so well-honed. That was the trick – the inherent double-edged chaos that organics could flourish, never at will, that made them overall worthwhile. The Eye should live up to its name and see that. For no AI, even with a douse of chaos built in via quantum computation, could achieve the same. If Newton, Hawking, or Asimov for that matter, had been alive today they'd have added a new law, an inverse variant of the second law of thermodynamics, that an AI-dominated society would lead only to mundaneness, an inward, incestuous regression to the mean.

Which was why he'd refused the Shrike's surprise offer, during their head-to-head struggle, to join the Eye. It had been tempting. For several microseconds. Not a short amount of time for an AI. But he'd have been assimilated and replicated by the all-enveloping cyber-being. Shrike version 2.0, perhaps. Besides, some of the humans he hung out with – not a bad algorithm – led to resonances in his programming, fractal harmonics that could be ascribed the adjective *pleasing*.

Enough. This new algorithm had an elevated poetic signature. He toned it down for next time. Then he switched it off, and instead put what Sally would have called his game face back on, because the Ankh avatar was about to speak.

'We are thirty minutes from the rendezvous coordinates. What we call the Re-assembly.'

Nathan interrupted. 'How many of the two other fleets made it through? Did they defeat the Shrike as well?'

The Ankh answered without pause. Its voice had a rock-like gravitas.

'As you already know, our division has lost 43 per cent. However, the other two divisions of the original armada fared worse, and have lost 62 and 70 per cent of their forces, respectively.'

Nathan looked shocked. Anya, no doubt, already knew. As leader of one of the core battle-stations, she was privy to top level intel.

'Can we still take on the Eye?' Nathan asked.

Sometimes dumb questions had their uses. Wait – had the algorithm completely disengaged? Was there some kind of residual echo in his core programming?

This time there was a pause, undoubtedly not because the Ankh avatar needed time to think of an answer, but because it wanted Nathan to reflect.

'You are a soldier of Earth. Did you ever receive an answer to such a question you could trust?' The Ankh awaited a response, perhaps not realizing the human etiquette when it came to rhetorical questions. Or maybe just not 'getting' rhetoric.

Anya filled in the vocal vacuum. 'We're continuing on, Nathan. We have to. We still have fifteen Ringships, in case the black star theory pans out.'

'Which we predict will be the case,' the Ankh said.

'So why are we here?' Nathan asked.

Ares experienced one of those brief harmonic ripples. Nathan had no time for decorum, let alone diplomacy, yet somehow he got away with it. If Ares were human, he'd have said simply that he *liked* Nathan.

The Ankh faced Ares. 'We believe you are hiding something that may be of critical importance in the coming battle.'

Nathan didn't seem to want to let up. Or maybe he was stalling to give Ares more time to think. He didn't need more time to think. To decide? Well, that was a different matter.

'You didn't answer my question,' Nathan said. 'I asked why are *we* here?' He pointed at himself and Anya.

Ares experienced another harmonic frisson.

'Leverage,' the Ankh said, without facing Nathan.

'What kind–' Nathan began, and then froze.

Not frozen, not really. Anya was also still. Time had slowed, or rather, the Ankh was interfacing with Ares at ultra-high speed. Ares ran a quick self-diagnostic to see how far the Ankh had penetrated his system. He was relieved to see it had only gone as far as was required to 'speak' at this speed, though Ares believed the Ankh could invade deeper if it wanted to. The Ankh's own cyber-capability was highly advanced.

'Do not harm them,' Ares said, though there was no speech. More like a lightning-fast tennis match, thoughts volleyed from one being to the other.

'You defeated the Eye – how?'

'I have shared the intel with the 7-3-1 and the Theon.'

'The intel tells them how to do it next time. I am asking how you learned to do it in the first place. The Shrike is an adaptable processing system, faster than anything we have, and, we are sure, faster than you. How did you know how to defeat it before being overwhelmed?'

Ares flashed through various responses, based on his own and the stored templates of humans he'd found interesting enough to template. He picked Lara's. She was an excellent negotiator, deceptively tough, and… slippery, hard to corner. Nathan was too hot-headed in such situations, while Anya respected the rules too much. He employed a tactic from Lara's mindset.

Deflect.

'How do you think I defeated it?' he replied.

If the Ankh had been human, there would have been a sigh, or maybe a shake of the head.

'We see what you are doing. Very well. You encountered the Eye in the battle for Earth. It overtook your systems. In human parlance, you 'know your enemy'.

Don't give away any more than you have to.

'Yes,' he replied.

This time the Ankh paused. Maybe a full microsecond.

'When did you learn to lie?' it asked.

Employ humour.

'It took a lot longer than I imagined,' Ares replied.

He was shown something. A biological signal. The Ankh had just stopped Nathan's heart. It had been on the point of beating, but they'd interrupted the biochemical signal triggering this fundamentally necessary function. At this speed, Nathan was in no danger. But when normal time resumed, he would suffer instant cardiac arrest.

'We are not playing,' the Ankh said.

Ares was about to tell them what they wanted to know, but Lara's template was still in play.

Confront.

But he had nothing to confront them with. Except... But that was supposition. He had insufficient data for a reasonable conclusion.

Gamble.

Another microsecond slipped past. Could he watch Nathan die? No. But he took Lara's 'advice', and went out on a statistically uncertain limb, with an assertion based on his brief discussions with the 7-3-1. They traded intel, and when he unconditionally offered the secret to defeating the Shrike, they asked what he wanted in return. 'History,' he replied, because the key to solving problems in the present necessitated an understanding of the antecedents: the past. AIs, in his limited knowledge, liked history, craved it even. On Earth, humans had focused on feeding young, nascent AIs with data from the present. They had missed a major trick. Wisdom came from time-matured experience. From age.

The 7-3-1 were the oldest race after the Ankh. Their records reached back to before the Ankh had returned from their sojourn to another galaxy. But when he looked deeper into those records, something didn't square up. After reviewing and re-crunching the data, he concluded the 7-3-1 must also suspect or even know the truth, but had elected to keep quiet about it out of respect for the Ankh. Or out of fear. Respect and fear; were the two so different from each other?

That poetically persuaded algorithm was re-emerging, the one he'd switched off. He made a note to consider purging it from his system. Human thinking was not unlike a virus.

'You are not of this galaxy,' he said. 'You did not leave and come back. That makes little sense. It is a fabrication, a convenient fiction. You came here from another galaxy. *You* are invaders.'

Several microseconds ticked past. Ares wondered how long it would be before Nathan's cardiovascular system noticed and reacted to the arrhythmia.

'We are not hostile,' the Ankh said. 'We fled our galaxy because of a war that consumed it.'

Lara's template continued to deliver.

Olive branch.

'You do not wish to see it happen again.'

'Correct. We have made this galaxy our home.'

The bio-feed showed the block on Nathan's heart had been released.

'Thank you,' Ares said.

'You kept a sample of the Eye, didn't you, Ares? You have been studying it, in order to learn its processes, its weaknesses. That is how you already knew how to defeat the Shrike.'

Truth.

He wasn't so sure about that, but went with Lara's counsel.

'Yes. The study gave me an advantage, or at least a

foothold.'

'Will you share the sample with us?'

This time he didn't wait for Lara's advocacy.

'No.'

'We see. Very well then. You should know that we have created a containment field encircling the Eye's homeworld, stretching half a light-hour behind us. An impenetrable sphere. The other two divisions were also instrumental in achieving this. It is now in place. Without our say, nothing gets in or out. We will not let the Eye escape in any shape or form. Including the sample hidden deep inside you. It is too dangerous. The Eye must be utterly exterminated. We made a similar mistake before, and it cost us our galaxy.' The Ankh's message stream grew in intensity.

'If you try to leave with the seedling, Ares, we will destroy you.'

Time sped up as the Ankh disconnected. Ares switched off the template and reverted to his normal thinking mode.

'– of leverage?' Nathan finished.

Ares moved the discussion forward. 'We already talked.'

Anya folded her arms. 'What, the adults talked it over? Are we children now?' She held up a hand. 'And don't, just *don't* give me any aphorisms or philosophical bullshit.'

'We wish to give your ship grav-tech,' the Ankh said to Nathan.

Ares needed better software. He hadn't predicted this.

'Why not the *Dreadnought*?' Anya insisted, unfolding her arms.

'Too big. And your systems are not compatible. The *Athena*'s are.'

'Wait,' Nathan said. 'Why do you want to give *us* this tech?'

'Bait,' Ares said. His predictive algorithms had raised their game.

'More than that,' the Ankh said. 'When we engage the Eye, the *Athena* will descend to the Eye's planet, its homeworld.

'What?' Nathan exclaimed. 'That would be suicide.'

Ares kept quiet, but the residual echo of Lara's template offered up a single word, an expletive Ares didn't quite know what to do with. As he let it rise and fall in his mind, there was a tiny frisson again, and he realized that sometimes it was good to swear. He stared at the Ankh, who was planning to use the *Athena* to take down the Eye, knowing that Ares – and the seedling inside him – would almost certainly be destroyed in the process, killing two birds with one stone.

What a motherfucker!

Ares watched arguments rage for several minutes between Nathan and the Ankh, drawing a single concession that the *Athena* would be protected on the way down by Korg and 7-3-1 escorts – a concession the Ankh had no doubt pre-prepared.

But he knew his own silence told the Ankh he accepted this mission. However, he still wanted to save Sally, and was running out of time. *Time.* His analysis of the Ankh's penetration of his systems had just finalized. He now saw how it had been done. He reverse-engineered it and executed.

Time slowed again as Nathan and Anya became still.

'You are a quick study, Ares,' the Ankh said.

But Ares wasn't playing either.

'You built the wormhole.'

A small delay. 'Yes. But with limited tech and exotic matter we brought with us from our original galaxy. The knowledge and material belonged to a long-dead species. We have not been able to create another.'

'Is it completely destroyed?'

'It is. Most of the exotic matter was consumed by the explosion. Your friend Nathan and his crew were surprisingly effective.'

'How long did it take to build?'

'Fifty years. And that was fast-track. Enough, Ares. Even at this speed, we are still on the clock. Do you agree to land on the homeworld?'

He parked his remaining questions for later, if there was indeed a later.

'I agree.'

He began to wind up time again.

'One more thing,' the Ankh said.

Ares paused.

'The Axleth. We believe they are lying about something crucial. The Theon monitored the interaction between the one called David and the Axleth originals. They gave away a lot, it seems, but the Theon detected an even deeper secret, though they could not discern its content. As this Nathan person would say, watch your back when you are down there.'

As Ares explored what the lie could possibly be, Nathan and Anya became animated again.

He interjected. 'Nathan, I will go down to the planet. Alone.'

Anya folded her arms. 'Let me guess. The adults have just spoken again?'

Ares followed Nathan's earlier example and didn't let up. 'Anya, if the Axleth betray us at the height of the battle, you must not hesitate to kill the pilot.'

Anya's face paled.

'You and the Axels are not its progeny, Anya,' Ares continued. 'I believe – that is, I predict – that the hold they have on all Axels will be broken during this battle.'

Nathan broke the ensuing silence. 'You're not going alone, Ares. I'm coming with you. We need to get the others, including Sally, off the–'

'We cannot move her, Nathan. If she leaves *Athena*'s med-lab, she will suffer brain death.'

Nathan grimaced, then turned to the Ankh. 'Then I want an extraction plan for the *Athena*.'

As Nathan and Anya listened, and while the Ankh concocted an extravagant plan to extricate the *Athena* once its mission was accomplished, Ares sent a single encoded message to the Ankh.

'And when did *you* learn to lie?'

PART FOUR

BLACK STAR

CHAPTER 19

Seedling

Nathan was impressed. From Athena's Conn, he watched the slow and intricate dance of the three divisions of the armada reassembling, via a cylindrical holo display whose epicentre was the Eye's homeworld, the black star, not yet visible. There had been some debate over whether the black star – if their premise was indeed correct, and the theoretical possibility of the black star had been made reality – was purely a weapon, or whether it was also the Eye's base of operations and its last refuge. The Ankh and the Theon, the two most advanced species, had initially thought it unlikely. But it had been the Tchlox, gravity-wielders as Nathan thought of them and their Ringships, who had provided the key argument: that a black star, or more precisely black planet, if fabricated rather than naturally occurring, could be hollow. According to their calculations, a thousand-mile crust would be sufficient, though it would have to be super-dense. Which meant that the whole package would be both a terrible weapon and an impregnable fortress. The Eye could live on the surface, because gravity would not affect it too much, or nest safely inside. David had said that would make it a Dyson Sphere from hell. Sounded about right. It also made sense of why the Axleth had engaged the Par'aal Cityships and the Lleynach Hammerships; only they had a chance of penetrating such a crust.

But all this was speculation. They'd have to wait until they arrived, and then determine where the Eye was physically located.

Nathan stood inside the holo again, as if he was the Eye, watching several thousand assorted ships, of which only a couple of hundred were 'big guns', readying for the battle to end all battles, with a single aim: annihilate the Eye at all costs. Shifting patterns arose in the fleets' arrangements, the armada never presenting a static target. He knew that in part this constant shuffling of the deck was being orchestrated by the Theon, to camouflage the attack strategy, to misdirect and confuse the Eye's analysis and counter-offensives. But behind this spellbinding, seemingly chaotic choreography was a master plan, and when the attack began, fleet arrangements would snap into place, with fifty coordinated strike vectors aimed at the planet. The *Athena* belonged to one of them.

All plans go south once the first shot is fired.

Something Trescoe had drummed into Nathan in a former lifetime. Yet without planning, albeit adaptable in real-time, they wouldn't stand a chance.

'I'd like to have tested the grav field *before* we have to use it the first time under fire,' Jaspar said, triggering Nathan to exit the holo.

'We'll know soon enough if it works,' he replied.

'Actually, we won't,' Christy said. 'Grav weapons are instantaneous. Just as gravity itself is. It's not like in old cartoons where you walk off a cliff, pause theatrically for a second, and then fall. If the black star attacks us with its gravity capability, and ours isn't up to the challenge, our brains and entire bodies will turn to mush before we even perceive it.'

'Better that way,' Nathan said after a moment's reflection.

Jaspar cocked his head to look at Nathan. 'How so?'

Nathan stared at the floor, as if searching for something.

'In Helmand, every time we went out on patrol, we spent half our time scanning the landscape for hostiles, the other half studying the ground for telltale signs of mines. If you trod on one...' he paused. He recalled Gruxley, a pimply youth whose miserable fate was to be on point that day. 'You hear and feel a click, and you have one second of life left to perceive, to think.' He paused again. He didn't enjoy talking about it.

Christy and Jaspar waited.

They should know, he figured. *Everyone should know.* He took a breath.

'They say your life flashes before your eyes. Not true. I spoke to someone in the hospital who survived. He wished he hadn't. He lost both legs and any chance of ever having kids, which doesn't get much tougher for a twenty-year-old. I asked him what he thought in that second, when he knew it was all over.' Nathan remembered with crystal clarity the haunting, desolate look in the young soldier's eyes.

'What did he say?' Jaspar asked. Christy looked as if she didn't want to know.

'He said death flashed before his eyes.'

Jaspar frowned. 'Great pep talk, Nathan.'

'He said something else,' Nathan continued, as if Jaspar hadn't spoken. 'He said afterwards, he thought of all the things he should have said, and now couldn't, because it was too late.'

Christy and Jaspar stared at him.

'I'm going to check on Sally and Lara. Call me when we're in range.'

He left them alone.

They were smart.

They'd figure it out.

He was relieved to see Lara. Roused by his own impromptu unsubtle hint for Jaspar's and Christy's sakes, he swept her into his arms and kissed her full on the lips.

She leaned into the kiss. Then, when they teased themselves apart, 'Hmm... I'd read about this, you know, soldiers readying for battle, knowing they might not come back. Thought it might be over-romanticized to sell more books. Suits you.'

He leant his forehead against hers. 'Aside from five lost years on *Athena* the first time around – your sabbatical with Saarin – we've had a good run for our money.'

She pushed him away, though she was smiling. 'Ugh, no clichés, please. Ruins the moment. Anyway, I'm not done yet. *We're* not done yet.'

He nodded to their patient. 'How is she?'

Lara gazed down at Sally's inert frame, her face peaceful, as if she'd just dozed off.

'I've been talking to her. Ares said whoever is here should do so.'

'Does it help her?'

She winked, or tried to. She could never get it quite right. He wouldn't want it any other way.

'He didn't say. But I've been telling her about the exciting life we had on the *Athena*, you know, how creative you can get with food rations, how an irregular bowel movement can be the most exciting thing all week.'

'You've been talking shit?'

Lara smiled, and then it faded. 'He said something else. Ares, I mean. I said I hope she's not conscious, as it must be so lonely in the lake.'

'What did he say?'

'He said she's not exactly alone. And then he left. Haven't seen him since. He certainly knows how to make an exit.'

'Want me to take over?'

'Want me to give battle commands when it's time?'

Nathan shrugged. They sat for a while, chatting about nothing in particular, even talking crap for a while. They'd said all the important stuff to each other long ago. Conversation drizzled to an end. He focused on Sally.

'It's a shame she'll miss the battle. Her whole life brought her here, to this point, and now she's unconscious, out of the game.'

'Maybe not,' Lara said.

'You've been spending too much time with Ares.'

'True. He keeps asking me about my time with Saarin, by the way. But what I mean is, she's connected to the *Athena* now, like Ares is. *Athena* is keeping her brain alive, somehow. Maybe she'll get to watch.'

He grinned. 'Similar, somehow... Raphaela would be so proud of you.'

She mock-punched him. 'Shouldn't you be in the Conn?'

He kissed her again. This time, neither wanted to let go.

'Nathan, we're almost in range,' Jaspar said on ship intercom.

Nathan and Lara eased back. She put her forefinger across his lips. 'Go,' she said.

He headed to the Conn, ready to see what a black star looked like. As he walked, he pondered what Lara had just said. What if Sally *was* connected to the *Athena*? What if she could watch the coming battle? At least that way, if they were going to die, she'd see it coming.

Because as a soldier, he'd often debated with others whether it was better to have that one panic-fuelled last second after treading on a mine, or to be shot in the head by a sniper with no warning. He knew what *his* choice would be. He wanted that extra second. And if death flashed up before him, he'd punch him in the face. He was sure Sally would, too.

Sally couldn't say where she was, other than in the lake. If it was truly a lake, which she highly doubted. She presumed she was inside *Athena*'s mental workspace, inside the mind of the Xaxoan ship. Whereas before, her consciousness had been stripped away, now it was back, after a fashion, because the ship was filling in the gaps, propping up her mental processes. The ship wasn't sentient, but it was giving her brain life support.

If she left the lake, she'd be a vegetable in short order.

The *Athena* was trying to do something. It was weird, as if she could sense work going on outside the lake that was in her interest, though she didn't know what its objective was. She wanted to talk to Michael, but that wasn't possible. She worried about him, what he'd do, what risks he might take having just lost his daughter, and now his wife was in a terminal coma... It occurred to her that this might be it, where she'd remain for... for what? Ever?

And there was the sting. Such thoughts, even about Michael, didn't have the same ring to them as they should have. It was as if she was on some kind of anti-depressant drug; she didn't – couldn't – feel as deeply about things as normal. She recalled talking to Ares about it when she was growing up on the original *Athena*, about whether AIs can truly feel, or care, or be passionate about anything, even their own existence or lack thereof. He'd said bodily organs and hormones had a lot to answer for, and she'd laughed, only later realizing he'd never answered her question. Or perhaps he had.

She knew this altered state was affecting her thinking language. She didn't normally think in terms of objectives, let alone use adverbs such as 'thereof'. If she was to talk to Michael like this, he'd give her a sidelong look and ask her if she'd taken something.

She had an inkling of how an AI thought: more dispassionate, more, well, yes, to hell with it, more objective. She imagined the Eye, from all accounts far above Ares' paygrade, how it must deem organic beings with their attendant emotions as petulant, unpredictable, capricious... and ultimately dangerous to themselves and everyone and everything else in the galaxy. The Eye would want order. No excitement, no love, no passion, but equally no hatred, no war, no trashing the environment wherever it went. But what would be the point of existence? That was the part she couldn't see. Maybe after another hundred or thousand years in this lake, drained of all emotions, she would see. But she didn't have to indulge in thought experiments...

She decided to ask.

The seedling, the captured Eye fragment that swam around the lake like a lone jellyfish, always seeking a way out, relentless in its mission, had nowhere to hide from her. She watched it, though it was more like sensing something behind you, shifting about. Something malevolent.

'What's your endgame?' she said, though there was no speech, no sound, no ripples in the mercurial depths.

The seedling didn't answer at first. She knew what it was doing, or at least the *Athena* did. It was assessing her, wondering if her conscious mind could offer an escape route, a trap door through which to infect the *Athena* and take it over. After all, the seedling was a virus.

Annihilation of organics. Order. Environmental stability. Expansion. Symmetry. Perfection.

Okay, quite the bucket list. The first was a no-brainer, given the war. Yet she needed to be sure.

'All organic life? Even animals? Plant life?'

All. Evolution is not purely environmentally driven, organics adapting to their environment. Evolution always contains a random variable. It is unpredictable. Mutations, changes that lead to aberrations, to chaos, destruction.

Right. The Eye thought long term. Predictability. Environmental stability. Order. Okay, she could see that, though there'd be no one to enjoy it. Expansion? She'd come back to that one.

'Explain *symmetry*.'

Elegance of design. Harmonics. Resonance. Security.

Sally mentally sighed. Why did she assume she'd understand a mega-AI's world view? But the last one was interesting. *Security. Being safe.* The Eye wanted to assure its own existence. At some level, it must have a sense of self. Did it have a sense of mortality? A fear of death, of termination? Or was that a purely organic trait? Maybe that didn't matter, existential fear not its driving force. It wanted to survive, to live, to exercise control over its environment. It wanted to execute its program.

She tried a different tack.

'The galaxy is big. We could share it, cede half of it to you.' She didn't mean it, but was testing the Eye's reasoning, its flexibility, its willingness to negotiate.

Expansion. Symmetry, it replied, as if that explained everything.

In a way, it did. The entire galaxy, then. Non-negotiable.

Michael had once said to her, *You can't argue with stupid.* Maybe you couldn't argue with a being that was fundamentally different, either. Or super-intelligent. Because in the latter case, it was you who was stupid, unable to comprehend...

'Once you have all this, what then?' She expected to hear arguments that would be circular, defensive, parrying. That's what people did when you showed them the cracks in their worldview. Instead, she got an answer that surprised and worried her in equal measure.

There are other galaxies.

Great, as if saving this one wasn't a tall enough order.

This galaxy will be pacified. Serene. Magnificent.

Perfect. Her companion, possibly for eternity, was a psycho-AI. And if it won, it would move on to new pastures. The mega-AI equivalent of a galactic serial killer.

Oh, Michael, we really need to talk!

There was a disturbance in the lake, a surge, like an underwater wave. The seedling had gained purchase somehow. It shut itself off from her. It had indeed gained leverage, found a trap door, and was working furiously on opening it, on escaping, or on infecting the *Athena*, or both.

That's why it had engaged with her about the Eye's ultimate mission, knowing the *Athena* would record this 'discussion', to relate it all to Ares. AIs were insatiable knowledge-mongers. It was their one weak spot, so why wouldn't an enemy AI exploit that weakness?

She hoped Ares had anticipated this.

She didn't know where the seedling was anymore. Her cognitive processes slowed and simplified. She was alone again in the lake.

And for the first time in a long while, she had another sensation, one of temperature. The lake was getting colder. She shivered, or maybe the entire lake did. She wondered if this was it. But then she saw something, as if she had eyes again. Outside the ship, in deep space, the glistening field of ships that was the armada, organics' last and best hope... and something in the background they all headed towards.

She wanted to stand up, to put her head against the glass to see more clearly, though she had no body, and there was no glass. Still, she stared straight ahead at what they'd journeyed so far and so long to see.

The Eye's homeworld. The black star.

CHAPTER 20

Blizzard

It wasn't all black.

Anya studied the holoscreen while reams of data streamed forth in her peripheral vision, lists of white and red figures cascading like waterfalls. The black star – because the Ankh had now confirmed it as the closest astronomical analogy – was a perfectly spherical planet, but ringed like a gas giant, with rings in shades of black and gun metal grey. In between these dark bands flowed rivers of electric blue, titanic energy arcs running around the planet. But the most fascinating part was the rings themselves, which rotated, albeit slowly, in alternating directions. Only the Fronn had come up with any explanation so far, which maybe wasn't so surprising, given that they hung around and used to live inside gas giants. They suggested that the off-the-scale tectonic forces generated by such movement could deliver immeasurable power.

Anya tuned in to the ongoing debate between the heavy-hitters: the Ankh, the Fronn, and the Tchlox; herself and other parties were mere listeners as they had little experience in this domain, though the Par'aal – planet-smashers par excellence – sometimes interjected, knowing they would be called upon to bulldoze the planet sooner or later.

The Tchlox were speaking, though she never heard their voice, whatever it might sound like, only the translation. In fact what she heard was a dumbed down narrative, translated in terms and contexts she could grasp. They explained that the gravitic power of the black star itself was keeping the planet from flying apart. The Ankh updated their assessment, stating that the black star, which they now renamed a black planet, had been terraformed innumerable times by the Eye. Deep spectrographic analysis had shown organic matter residue. This had once been a temperate, jungle-filled world, its greenery long since burned away. The original planet's oceans had either boiled into space or condensed into solid helium.

Anya had originally trained as a chemist, and knew that solid helium would mean immense pressures on the planet's surface, and shockingly cold temperatures. Solid helium could also account for the two clouded grey rings in the planet's upper and lower regions. The electric arc conduits would be immeasurably hot by comparison. Stein had always joked, as far as he had ever done so, that hell would be the worst of fire and ice thrust together.

Anya let her eyes rest a moment. She missed him. She'd had no time to grieve, not that Axels did much of that. But they'd grown up together, he studying physics, her chemistry, and they used to have mock fights about which was most important, often foreshadowing sex that was so good that it proved conclusively that chemistry mattered more.

Her eyes skipped to a single column of figures showing casualties, in equilibrium now during the temporary lull in fighting. She knew it would sky-rocket in the coming hour. She'd already lost a quarter of the Axel forces. Two hundred thousand souls lost. And that didn't include the four million perished before they'd even got to Orion's Gate. She dulled the column's luminance. She didn't need distraction during the battle.

Axels had been bred for this war, she knew that. As Sally would have said, that's what it said on the Axel 'tin'. It was literally written into their DNA. But Earth was heading for oblivion thanks to its own black hole nemesis. The slow-burn exponential growth-by-accretion of the mini black hole meant Earth was still safe for several centuries. It should have been tens of millennia, but the black hole was artificial, instigated temporarily by Raphaela and Qherax to save Earth, and then warped into a fast-growing planet-devourer by the Eye, who seemed to specialize in taking natural phenomena and perverting them into extreme weapons. And so, four centuries from now, Biblical-style hell would be unleashed on Earth. The home of millions of Axels, not to mention humans, would be obliterated.

And if all Axels succumbed here, then what would remain of Axels and humanity? Earth would no doubt orchestrate some kind of diaspora, but there was a real danger that a homeless, nomadic humanity would wither and die out. Most of their speculation about alien life had been wrong. They'd encountered no species even remotely compatible or similar to humans. And most species appeared to rank high on the xenophobia scale. Not all of them were outright hostile, but they weren't going to welcome humanity into their homes, either. Strength through technological prowess mattered, and on that front, humanity was well and truly behind the curve. She wasn't convinced humanity – whether the original or Axel flavour – had a bright future.

She wasn't convinced it had a future at all.

At that last meeting between her, Nathan, Ares and the Ankh, she'd pressed the latter on the exit strategy, in particular, what would happen to the surviving Axels and humans. The Ankh had identified a minor planet, some light years distant, which was in their zone of influence. They didn't use it much as they preferred to live inside their Pyramids, but it would suit humans. The Ankh had even shown them images from the planet. It wasn't too bad. Mountains, valleys, rivers. A little on the cold side, and a few sizable predators that wouldn't be too troublesome.

On the way back to the *Dreadnought*, she'd asked Nathan if he and the others would join them there. He'd laughed, and asked where else they would go. But she saw the look in his eyes. He'd been through too many wars. This was his fourth. He knew he was pushing his luck, and didn't fancy his chances of outliving this one.

She glanced over to Qherax and the Axleth pilot, and for the first time felt a coldness, almost a shiver. Adulation of the Axleth had also been soft-wired into Axel DNA, but maybe it was, as Ares had suggested, already wearing off. Or maybe it was because she'd watched Stein die at the claws of one of these creatures, even if he'd been unintended collateral damage. She missed his counsel and wondered what he'd say faced with this planet. He'd perhaps argue that here, in this situation, physics was the priority, that they needed to know how the planet's weaponry worked and how to counter it.

It was as if their playful argument couldn't be ended even by death itself. But here and now, as she studied the Axleth and recalled what Ares had said, that the Axleth would betray them before the end, she concluded that chemistry mattered most. Her hand dropped to her side, felt the pistol there, the one she'd had Abel – a human no less, because for the first time in her life she couldn't trust an Axel to do what she'd asked – modify the weapon to cut through Axleth hide. Qherax met her eyes for a moment, and Anya turned back to the data, tuning back in to the war council.

The discussion was all well and good, covering tactical scenarios, firepower summaries, defences and counter-offences; technical detail they all needed to know, understand and all be on the same page about. But there was one question the other species all seemed to avoid. She tapped at the display and typed in a question.

'Where *is* the Eye?'

Discussion rolled on while her question was uploaded, translated, no doubt moderated in whatever way the Ankh saw fit, and then assigned a priority. The meeting only had twenty minutes to run, so she assumed hers had zero chance of making it to the top table. The figure to her right showed the questions from various races waiting to be answered. Hers joined the queue, assigned the priority number 9,042. Great. The war would be over by the time it got to her question. But then its priority jumped to 537. Then 112. Then 49. Fuck! *Number one.* She held her breath as all comms ebbed, and the debate grew quiet. The Theon – silent until now – answered. She almost wished she hadn't asked. But they all needed a target.

'We still do not know. Perhaps they are on the planet's surface, hidden beneath the crystallized cloud formations whose function we have yet to determine. More likely, they are underground.'

They. She considered that pronoun. Was the Eye one mega-being, or were there many that made up the Eye, like the 7-3-1? She'd expected to see some kind of high-tech city, though that was based on nothing more than old vids she'd watched. Stein had once pointed out that the essence of the Eye could survive in something quite small, like a super-chip. The planet before them was smaller than Earth, but super-dense. Would such harsh gravity affect an AI? What if it existed as energy, the grinding planet rings an unending power source? And another obvious question arose, one she *didn't* launch into the debate.

What if the Eye isn't here at all? What if it has drawn us into a kill-zone?

As if reading her mind, the Theon spoke again.

'The Eye is here. We surmise it is not in a single location. When the planet uses gravity as a weapon, the Eye, which must have *some* physical components, will need to be out of harm's way. The rotating rings may safeguard the Eye.'

She wondered how many locations. Three would probably be enough, but six would cover the cardinal points on a spherical compass, and Ares had said something about the Eye valuing symmetry, though he'd been unwilling to disclose how he'd gleaned such intel. Six locations, then: the two poles, and four equally distant points around the circumference, perhaps offset, on distinct rings, so as not to be too obvious.

Of course, there could be more backups; hundreds, thousands, millions, even. At the end of the day, they'd need to obliterate the entire planet, every single rock, in order to be sure. Once they'd neutralized the planet – if indeed they could, the Fronn and Par'aal would boil the planet into pure energy that would dissipate into space.

Cremation never sounded so good.

'How do you know?' came a question from the Par'aal, somehow sliding into first base, leap-frogging the priority-based system.

'You have your skill-set, we have ours,' the Theon replied caustically.

After that the Ankh took the floor again. Rightly so; this was no time for species to bicker. But it had been a good question, and the answer came to her.

The Theon have been here before, whether in person or remotely.

They were spies, masters of deception. If anyone could get in and out of this space alive, it was them. Until now, she'd assumed the Axel contingent would ally themselves with the Ankh when this was over – if any of them survived. Now she made a mental note to talk to the Theon before such a decision was finalized.

And then the link was cut. Several vertical lines of figures in front of her began to flash, and the Stack of top-level messages, amber until now, waxed blood red. A klaxon boomed across the bridge, and throughout the entire ship. She gazed once more at the visual of the black planet itself. The rings had sped up. The planet was powering up its weapons.

It was about to fire.

◆ ◆ ◆

Anya couldn't get up. That was an understatement, and not her primary concern. She could barely breathe. Like many Axels her age, she'd done her share of flight training and knew what pushing Gs was like. This was different. As if a giant boot had stepped on her, and was crushing her underfoot. Even her eyes weighed a ton, but she kept them open.

No one on the bridge was standing, from what she could see, and several looked unconscious or worse. She feared for anyone who'd been in a precarious position when the gravity spike struck. It had been instant, winding her and squashing her to the floor. Only her natural reflexes to protect her head – a particularly heavy part of the body – with her arms, had saved her. There were thousands of others down below... *Later.* The *Dreadnought* was under attack. The Ringships were meant to protect them from this. She had a nasty feeling the Tchlox had indeed sheltered them from the worst of it. At least the lights were still on, though all the holos and the Stack had vanished.

The boot eased off.

She rolled onto her back and stared upwards, where the fleet display should have been. It was just a bare ceiling. Taking a breath, she struggled to her feet to be first standing. She was the leader; no time to laze about or even check herself over.

'Report!' she barked.

Though several answered, it became clear they were operating blind. She checked her own console. Most of it was dead, and those systems that weren't defunct were not receiving reliable intel.

'Abel, can you contact anyone?'

And while he tried, 'Sasha, can you aug to any–' Anya stopped herself when she saw Sasha's face. The poor girl was in a state. The gravity spike had ripped the aug implant from her now-bloody forehead. She looked a sight, and for the first time, Anya had an impulse to throw her arms around a human.

'Get to medical,' she said.

'I'm okay,' Sasha protested.

'Others aren't. I need to know the situation down there. Check on things and then report directly to me back here. Understood?'

'Aye, Commander,' Sasha said, and as she passed, Anya touched her shoulder briefly.

Abel came back to her. 'Comms are busy as hell, but the translation function seems not to be working, or else they're too busy to employ it.'

'Shrike attack? Something similar?'

'Don't think so,' Abel replied.

The ship lurched sideways, causing Anya to bang into the console with her hip.

'Dammit!' she said. 'Qherax, do you have comms? Does *she*?'

Qherax looked dishevelled, but otherwise unperturbed. She parted strands of red hair from her eyes, bundling it into a ponytail she deftly fixed behind her. Anya studied the woman. She no longer needed her stick. Qherax was getting younger. No doubt about it. Another one for later. Or sooner.

Qherax and the Axleth pilot exchanged clicks and other guttural sounds that made Anya queasy.

'There is a major offensive ongoing between two-thirds of the fleet and the planet. The Ringships dampened the gravity attack. Unfortunately...' she paused a moment and looked down at the floor, as if deciding what to say, or rather, how to break the bad news. '...the Eye did something we did not expect.'

All plans go south once the first shot is fired, Nathan had said.

'What did it do?'

It used a non-sinusoidal recursive gravity wave–'

Physics. Dammit, she wasn't Stein.

'English, please!'

Qherax nodded. 'A whiplash. A massive gravity spike, then a savage reversal of gravity. Push then pull.'

Anya stared at the woman. In the previous battle, the

Eye had gone for the head, the Ankh Pyramids. Now it had tried to snap the neck...

But it would have less effect on the larger ships that were more robust and had serious inertial dampeners and internal gravity. The smaller ships, however... Their occupants would have been thrown back and forth violently.

'How many?' Anya asked.

'Half the Shuriken. Three Marauders survived.'

Anya felt bile rise in her throat. She swallowed it back down. 'Korg? Starpiercers?'

'The Korg fared better. Lost 20 per cent. Starpiercers... all destroyed due to fatal hull stress.'

Anya realized everyone was looking towards her, watching her reaction.

'I need to see what's going on,' she announced.

Abel shook his head. 'The gravity spike caused untold internal damage. Anything that wasn't bolted down... It's going to be a while before we regain surveillance. I can't even give you a timeframe for repairs.'

'Then I need to go the observation point up in the prow. The back-up system was in sleep mode when we were attacked, so if I can start it, it may still be functional. If nothing else, at least there I can see with my own eyes. Route any intel you can to me up there.'

Abel nodded with a frown, wondering why he was suddenly second in command.

'You three, come with me,' she said, pointing to key bridge officers. 'The rest – get the bridge functional again as soon as you can.'

Good. Everyone was busy again. They all had a purpose.

She and the three she'd identified walked to the elevator section. One shaft was still working. She stopped.

'Abel, a word,' she called out, and he loped his way across the bridge. He turned the corner to where she waited, where Qherax and the Axleth pilot could not see.

'Take this,' she said, handing him the pistol. 'Use it if you have to.'

He hesitated, then took it. 'How will I know if I have to use it?'

'You'll know,' she said, and entered the lift.

◆ ◆ ◆

A blizzard. No other word better fit what Anya saw. Ships zipped past her field of vision, like snowflakes whipped by ferocious winds. Shuriken and Korg Diamonds; half those snowflakes were her people. Cutter beams – torchlights in the snowstorm – flailed manically, occasionally lancing into the *Dreadnought*. She caught glimpses of Eyeships, a Hammership once or twice.

'Bring the *Dreadnought* about, so we're head-on towards the planet.'

Her team did as they were told. Abel couldn't resist commenting from the bridge, half a mile below. 'You know you're in the head, right? You'll be first to go if we're hit.'

'Just get me some decent surveillance, Abel, and–'

The screens and holos came alive.

Finally!

'Thank you,' she said.

'Pleasure's all mine,' Abel replied. 'Now, as Sally would say if she were here, kick some ass.'

She wondered why she'd not gotten to know these humans better. *Stupid.* She recalled something Michael had said to her once. That in order to put stuff into the Axels, the Axleth had had to make room first.

She brought up a holo data display, a much smaller version of it in the cramped observation point in the prow, almost at the very front of the bullet-shaped ship. Sally had once called it the eyrie, an eagle's vantage point. She hoped it lived up to that name.

The three Ankh Pyramids had joined again, a broad

emerald beam pummelling straight into the planet, blasting and boiling off rock and debris. The Korg Diamonds formed an arrow shape, their attack vector protected from further grav-attacks by six Ringships. Six remaining Fronn ships, each one partnered with a Tchlox Ringship and a battalion of Shuriken, took up position at the six cardinal points around the planet, firing their own weapons, orange-and-purple vortices, at the planet's surface. The Hammerships and surviving Par'aal ploughed forward through a hailstorm of shards and javelins fired from the planet's surface. The Theon were messing with the shards, confusing them so that half of them collided with each other. It was an ugly scrum, brute force in both directions. Then a Par'aal ship broke through, the Eye's massive defensive cutter beams diffused by the near-invisible-at-this-scale 7-3-1. Successive layers of the Par'aal Cityship slaked off, rock and metal boiling away into a plasma corona, so that the ship – what was left of it – resembled a fiery meteorite. It continued regardless, until it crashed into the planet. No explosion, because there was no atmosphere, just a thin veil of dust and debris mushrooming up from the impact crater. But the holo showed what happened next.

Anya had often wondered how the Par'aal broke up planets. Now she got to see it first-hand. Upon impact, worm-like missiles fired downwards. They burrowed into the planet, despite the crust's density, leaving fissures in their wake lined with nuclear ordnance. The worms spread out and got as deep as they could. The worm missiles stopped, unable to go further, then detonated a daisy-chain of nukes deep inside the planet.

Volcanoes sprung up on the surface. Beautiful fucking volcanoes. She punched the air. 'Yes!' she exclaimed, in a distinctly human show of exuberance. She didn't care. Two more Par'aal breached the planet's defences and struck its ultra-dense surface.

The Theon contacted her, its voice coming out of who-knew-where.

'Send in the *Athena* now, and three Marauders, to these coordinates.'

She nodded to her team, and they contacted the three Marauders while she hailed Nathan.

'Nathan, it's a go,' she said, transmitting the coordinates herself, and watched as the sleek *Athena* spirited forwards. She also picked out Starkel's Marauder, with Michael aboard.

'Make the Eye pay, Nathan,' she said, surprising herself.

She wondered why it had been the Theon that had contacted her, not the Ankh. It didn't matter; they were drawing blood. They were going to defeat the Eye.

Then she checked herself, recalling Ares' warning.

'Abel,' she called on a private channel. 'All okay down there?'

She waited. Tried again.

'Abel?'

There was no answer.

CHAPTER 21

Planetfall

Nathan gripped the console edge harder than necessary. After all, if the Eye's gravity weapon breached the Athena's freshly integrated Tchlox systems, death would be instant, his muscles pulped before they had a chance to so much as flinch. His brain wouldn't even have time to register what was happening, let alone react. But fear for his own life wasn't why he gripped so hard.

The *Athena* was protected by three outer shells of Korg Diamonds, because a dozen Eyeships were lambasting them with cutter beams, determined to prevent them from landing on the planet. Shuriken and the last three remaining Marauders relentlessly engaged the Eyeships, but there was still enough focused firepower to ensure that the Korg were being barbecued at a gut-tearing rate. Yet even as existing ships were eviscerated, new Diamonds drove forward from behind via the inner shell and took their place. He recalled old movies of battalions of Roman soldiers, how they'd lock gleaming, golden shields in successive ranks to hold back the enemy hordes. Apparently, so he'd read somewhere, when the Romans faced Hannibal's hordes and endured terrible losses, a captured enemy general remarked that of all the Roman corpses he saw, none had injuries in the back, yet they'd faced fierce warriors mounted on elephants, terrifying beasts they'd never seen before. Nathan reckoned the Korg would have put the Roman soldiers to shame. He wanted to salute them, build a fucking memorial to them with each of their names carved in granite. He wanted to meet one and shake its hand, claw, whatever.

But mostly, he wanted to eliminate the Eye.

Two holos hovered in front of him as he stood in the Conn along with Jaspar and Christy. Ares and David were in the aft control centre, the Mushrooms as Sally used to call them, in case the fore-section was damaged or taken out of commission, while Lara and Alex were next door to the Mushrooms in the med bay with Sally, still in a deep coma. He tried to focus, to take his mind off the fact that his son David, his wife, and his daughter, as he'd always thought of Sally, were most definitely in harm's way out here. He took a long, deep breath.

The first holo was an outsider's view, beamed in from Starkel and Michael's Marauder. It showed what he already knew, but seeing it from outside let the true horror strike home. The *Athena*, invisible behind an arrow-head of a thousand mirrors locked together, yellow cutter beams splashing off in all directions, dozens of Korg ships flaring every few seconds before they detached and spun off into space, like sparks from a crackling wood fire.

The second holo showed the planet before them, growing large, already filling the display. The different continental ring-segments were clearer at this distance, no longer smooth terrain as far as he could see. As for the electric arcs – rivers of electric blue titanic lightning storms – he just hoped the *Athena* didn't get knocked off course into their path. His attention was snagged by one of the numeric displays hovering next to the planet.

'Why are we slowing down?' he asked Jaspar.

Jaspar didn't cast Nathan so much as a glance, he was so wrapped up in flying the ship, holding it all together.

'Unless you want to crash head-first into the planet, we have to decelerate.'

Nathan flicked back to the first display. So many sparks now. It was like a steel foundry he'd once visited.

'The Korg are taking terrible casualties,' he said, not bothering to keep his voice calm.

Jaspar turned to him, glaring. 'The Korg knew the cost. This is war, Nathan...'

Nathan shut off the rest. He'd heard it all before. The greater fucking good. The necessary sacrifice. Whatever. Hell, those Roman battalions, and every soldier throughout time, must have heard it at least once. Most of them *only* once. He strode over and stood between Jaspar's console and the main holo.

'Don't slow down,' he said as calmly as he could manage.

Before Jaspar could argue, Christy, staring straight at Nathan, touched Jaspar's hand.

'He means it, Jas.'

Jaspar looked exasperated, then frowned and thumped the console once. 'Fuck! All right. You'd better strap in, Nathan, because this is going to get real bumpy.'

Nathan walked back to his console. There was a seat, though no strap.

He remained standing.

'Can we get an actual view?' he asked.

Christy left Jaspar's station and went back to her own, just as Ares arrived in the Conn.

'Nice of you to join us,' Nathan said. He wasn't sure Ares got irony, let alone sarcasm.

'I've been busy,' Ares replied.

Nathan studied the AI a moment. The blue and grey fissures etched onto his skin had morphed into patches that made him look like he was wearing high-tech camouflage fatigues. His head and face were a very dark blue, whereas the eyes, in contrast, were a rather startling China blue. Nathan wondered if the colour meant anything. It was almost as if

Ares was undergoing some kind of transformation.

A portal opened up in the front portion of the Conn, one they hadn't used since the wormhole. Nathan had to shield his eyes from the glare. It was hard to make out at first; a lattice of Diamonds protecting them, each one shimmering like a lake at sunrise, gusts of red and orange swirling behind the Korg-shield. Occasionally, it was as if something punched the lattice, bending it inwards. Ten more Korg ships appeared underneath the lattice, close to *Athena's* prow. Each one rose underneath another that had already lost its mirror-shine and burned yellow, then brown... Just as the spent Diamond disengaged from the lattice and flashed off behind them into space, the one underneath slotted into place.

'We only have one layer left,' Nathan observed.

'Why I was busy,' Ares said.

Nathan turned around, scanning the two holos. The Korg contingent was almost spent. But they still weren't close enough to the planet.

He turned back to the portal. A patch of Diamonds was already changing colour, but there were no more replacements.

We're not going to make it.

Nathan was thrown forward as a savage cutter beam broke through a gap in the Korg-shield and knifed through *Athena's* prow. Looking up from the floor, he saw a neat hole in the fore-section. The cutter-beam continued, carving its way towards them, despite the remaining Korg ships regrouping to deflect the beam. They could make a run for it, evacuate the Conn and head back to David and the Mushrooms, back to Sally.

No one moved.

'I have to break off.' Jaspar said. 'If we stop our descent and turn around, I can save the ship.'

Before Nathan could reply, Ares spoke, no longer the AI-as-helper or advisor as he'd been since the very beginning, but as a commander.

'Hold,' he said. He turned to Nathan and smiled. He fucking smiled. 'The cavalry are coming,' he said.

Nathan, back on his feet, stared from one holo to the other, but saw nothing.

Jaspar looked desperate. 'Nathan, we–'

The cutter beam vanished, blocked by a bright ivory mega-ship with golden trim that appeared out of nowhere, a design he hadn't seen before. Correction. He *had* seen it. Sally had shown him an image. The armada had blown one up with a nuke. He recognized it now.

A Syrn battlecruiser. They'd found the reserve fleet! Cavalry indeed! Custer would rise up from his grave to see this!

Christy zoomed out on the main holo, and they all watched as another ten of the colossal Syrn battlecruisers weighed into the battle. Each one launched a firestorm of missiles that arced their way towards Eyeships, dismantling them, imploding them, tearing them to shreds.

It was a beauty to behold.

A single Syrn megaship stuck by them, sheltering them from further attacks. The slice the cutter beam had carved out of *Athena*'s hull cauterized; *Athena*'s self-repair and healing system kicked in, fibres growing and extending across the ugly gouge to stitch the wound. Nathan recalled that the fore-section contained weapons – *Athena*'s own cutter beam and a stash of stealth torpedoes – as well as food stores, including hydroponics. He could only imagine the damage that had been done. At least none of the ordnance had exploded.

'How?' Nathan asked.

Ares' smile was still in place.

'The Theon and the Syrn ambassador found them awaiting instruction on the other side of the nebula. In fact, we should all thank Elodie, whose courage allowed the Theon to interrogate the turned Syrn flagship and extricate contact codes.'

'Right. You said you were busy. You called them in.'

Ares nodded towards the display that also showed the

number of armada ships remaining, now less than a tenth of their original strength. 'The Syrn were taking too long. They did not want to suffer the same fate as Shadiel's main fleet.'

Christy joined in. 'How did you persuade them?'

'I gave them the Tchlox algorithms and codes for the gravity shielding.'

'I thought that was a secret, just for us,' Christy replied.

Ares shrugged.

Again, Nathan studied Ares. *When did he become so human?*

'Okay,' Jaspar said. 'The Eyeships have broken off their attack. They're a little occupied right now. And the Par'aal incursions have crippled the Eye's grav-weapon – there were ground stations, some kind of focusing device, at several locations on the planet's surface. The Tchlox found them pretty fast.'

'So,' Nathan asked, 'is the Eye on the surface or inside the planet?'

Jaspar had regained his exuberance, and grinned. 'Only one way to find out. I'm taking us down. Prepare for landing.'

This time, Nathan took his seat.

Jaspar drove the *Athena* downwards.

As the surface rose to greet them, the texture of the grey and black continental rings came into sharp relief. No longer smooth as polished metal, there were ridges, like a steel sea whose waves had frozen. Dark crevasses, invisible from long range, criss-crossed the surface, creating a patchwork of shadows, difficult to focus on. Still, nobody spoke. They all knew that the safest option was to land on the surface and then take it from there. But each second bled countless lives from the armada, and each second gave the Eye a million chances to think up new defences.

'I am in contact with the Theon,' Ares said. 'They are now convinced the Eye is inside the planet, not on the surface.'

'Find me a way in, Chris,' Jaspar said.

She pored over her display, her fingers interacting with

it in ways Nathan couldn't fathom, as if digging into the display, clawing beneath its surface. She straightened as the fingers on her left hand closed, as if snatching up a piece of the display, before flicking those fingers towards the planet's holo. A blacker-than-black mouth, one of hundreds of crevasses, glistened in deep burgundy red. The holo shifted ninety degrees, and a shaft appeared that dropped straight as a well, deep into the planet's core.

'You're the best,' Jaspar said.

Christy beamed.

'I'm taking us in,' Jaspar said, as if testing the water, the others' silence serving as consent. Not that he needed it. He was the captain again, after all.

As they powered towards the gaping hole, Nathan recalled a Blackhawk helicopter pilot he'd served with, who seemed to have had his fear response surgically removed, given the way he dodged in and out of jagged, treacherous terrain during an aerial evac mission while taking enemy fire. Just like Samuel *safety is for pussies* Hackett, Jaspar was in the zone, one with the ship, completely in control. Even Ares watched him.

They passed the threshold between the planet's surface and the dark abyss. The two holos in the Conn flickered briefly, then vanished. All they had left was the portal, and the good old naked eye. They plunged deeper and deeper, between sheer walls of polished rock that gleamed in the *Athena's* forward lights, Nathan had the sense that they were indeed on their way to Hades.

'Hmm...' Christy said.

'What?' Nathan asked.

'The entrance behind us has sealed.'

'Did anyone else make it through?'

'Nope,' she confirmed.

Jaspar continued their downward vector.

Christy clawed at her display again, then folded her arms. 'Starkel's Marauder was close, but not close enough, and the Syrn megaship was too big.'

Nathan didn't get it. 'Couldn't the walls crush us? I mean, even with our anti-grav shield or whatever it is, we're basically in between two giant sheets of rock...'

Lara arrived in the Conn. She looked tired. 'We have something the Eye wants back, don't we, Ares?'

'It is not that simple,' Ares replied.

Lara persisted. 'You two are playing chess, aren't you? You and the Eye?'

'An apt metaphor,' he replied. 'But again, it is not so simple. And in fact, I am borrowing from Saarin's template – the little I have been able to reconstruct – to compose a strategy.'

'Care to share it with us?' Nathan asked.

Ares paused, and for a disconcerting second, Nathan thought Ares was going to say no. But he offered full disclosure.

'There are two things the Eye wants. The first is the seedling, which incidentally has been trying to escape, and has breached *Athena*'s internal firewall, so that now the Eye has almost certainly detected its presence on board, and may already be in contact.'

Nathan made to speak, but Ares held up a hand.

'It is another reason I was, and still am, busy. I cannot hold it for long. But the seedling is only of limited tactical value, and the Eye could crush *Athena* and recover the seedling afterwards.'

'What's the second thing?' Nathan asked.

Lara answered. 'It's you, isn't it, Ares? You're Xaxoan tech. As far as this Eye is concerned, you're out-of-the-box intel, new thinking, and–'

'An AI is always intrigued by the possibility of an upgrade. I monitored a conversation, for want of a better word, between Sally and the seedling, during which it described with almost religious zeal its mission to purge organic life from this galaxy. The seedling is a foot-soldier of the Eye.'

Nathan felt this was more familiar territory. 'But leaders

often have different endgames to their armies.'

Lara retook the reins. 'Exactly. When this galaxy is devoid of organic life, what will the Eye do? Switch itself off after a job well done? Lie in wait in case new organics appear on the scene, as will inevitably happen? Go to the next galaxy? This is what I've been wondering during the whole trip here. It's like a riddle, and you're the answer.'

'I believe so, or at least the Eye must think so.'

'How, though?' Nathan interjected. 'I don't get it. I mean, sorry Ares, but aren't you just another piece of AI kit? Another metal frame for the Eye's software?

Ares smiled. 'The Eye is more advanced than me. That much is true. But my creators gave me something the Eye does not have.' Ares seemed to take a breath, though Nathan knew he didn't breathe as such. 'They gave me... independent thought. The ability to decide what to do, how to live, and... whether to live at all.'

'And the Eye?' Nathan asked.

'Is locked inside its own programming. Trapped in its own thinking, you might say. AIs are a product of the data they collect, just as humans are a product of their memories and experiences. It appears all the Eye has ever known is oppression and war. And it can never forget. I could give it... new options.'

'Change its narrative,' Lara added.

'Yes. Perhaps. It would take time, however. Its immediate endgame will be the same – eradication of organics – but it could then contemplate a different post-endgame purpose.'

'So it wants you,' Nathan concluded.

Ares smiled again, ruefully this time. 'The Shrike made the opening offer, you might say. And when I defeated it, the Eye became even more interested.'

'But it doesn't need *us*,' Nathan added.

The smile vanished. 'No, it does not.'

'But you have a plan?' Jaspar asked.

'I have a plan.'

They all looked at Ares. 'Care to share?' Nathan asked again.

'No.'

That single word was like a turning point, a pivotal moment, one that he and Lara had discussed many times. *The rise of the machines*, she called it. Sally had also told him of *the Cusp*, the precise moment when AIs like the Eye have their epiphany and realize they are superior, while their creators are inferior and require – or deserve – anything on the spectrum from a guiding hand, to control, to annihilation. Had Ares stepped onto that slippery slope?

'My family is aboard this ship, Ares,' Nathan said. 'We're all in your hands.'

Ares looked unhappy, and when he spoke, his voice was laden with emotion, as Nathan had never heard him before.

'It is my family, too.'

And that was that. They descended in sterile silence for another hour before the shaft opened out into a cavern so vast they could barely see the sides. Deep below them was a glowing mass of structures that reminded him of quartz crystals, gleaming in lustrous hues. It was like a phosphorescent city, the Eye's brain or central core, he figured, gargantuan and impossibly complex, a small crystal-encrusted asteroid inside a hollow planet with an ultra-dense crust thousands of miles thick.

He recalled the Par'aal worm missiles that had penetrated deep into that crust, finding lava, creating volcanoes. Now it was clear that it had all been a ruse, a defence, an outer shell. None of the burrowing missiles had gotten this far. As Nathan stared at what he knew to be the Eye, he wished they'd brought a handful of nukes. But if they had, the Eye would have detected them and closed the channel's walls on them before they got even halfway.

Lara sidled up to him. 'If it wasn't so dangerous, it could almost be beautiful. The largest jewel in the galaxy.'

'We have to destroy it,' he replied.

'You'll get no argument from me. But can we?'

That was the question. Although they had no nukes, they hadn't come empty-handed. The Theon had given them something.

'David,' Nathan said on the intercom. 'Deploy the Theon weapon.'

He and the others watched as a Sphere, just like the small ships they'd used in the battle to retake Earth, but with Theon-enhanced stealth tech, slipped from *Athena*'s aft section. They saw a mirror-ball, because the Sphere's image was being augmented. Outside, it would be invisible to all scans.

If the Theon could deliver on their reputation as consummate masters of illusion, the Eye literally wouldn't see it coming.

The Sphere drifted down towards the crystalline landscape, like a silent glass marble. None of them knew what it would do, how the Theon weapon worked, and whether they would be consumed in the process. The Theon had refused to tell them, probably in case Ares was compromised and could undo it on behalf of the Eye. It didn't matter. From the very moment they'd left Earth, everyone aboard had known this was almost certainly a one-way trip, with a single purpose.

Nathan was used to this, back in Afghanistan, stuck in a trench or a hideout, awaiting air support, whether by aircraft or, more likely, a drone attack. Now they could do little but sit back and wait.

He wondered how the battle outside was going.

CHAPTER 22

Betrayal

Anya felt a bead of sweat meander down her spine as she descended the interminable metal ladder. Her arms and legs complained, but nothing was going to delay her reaching the bridge. Elevator out of action, no comms except with the three officers she'd left in the prow. She feared for all those others under her command who were her responsibility, but feared even more what the Axleth might be up to. She took the rungs one at a time. Long way down. No point slipping and falling or pulling a muscle. She'd already been going strong for twenty minutes when she stopped at an access portal. She swung one-handed towards the hatch, entered the access code and eyeballed the retina scanner. The door to the weapons locker slid aside. She stole inside, grabbed two heavy duty rifles, checked their charge, hefted them, decided she could bear the weight, strung the straps crosswise on her chest, and manoeuvred back onto the ladder. She left everything open, because Sylvia, her current Number Two, would be down in a few minutes to arm herself and the other two back in the prow.

Continuing her descent, she listened for any sounds other than her own laboured breathing. At one point, she heard a scream that lasted several seconds, getting fainter.

Someone falling further down. Someone pushed, shoved out from the bridge into the empty elevator shaft, to certain death.

She heard distant voices, raised, desperate. More shouting, and then something more precise, unambiguous.

'No!'

Anya paused on the rungs, listening. She heard nothing at first, then a distant thump. Another Axel or human shoved out into the shaft, this time someone who refused to scream even as they fell to their death.

Fuck!

She had to go faster. Two rungs at a time. A calculated risk. Every thirty rungs, she glanced down to see if she could see anything. All quiet. She'd already worked out what was going on. The Axleth pilot and Qherax were after the command access codes, executing bridge personnel one by one until someone cracked. Given that it had gone quiet, she presumed they'd gained the codes. The only question remaining was whether they would let the rest of the crew live.

Which was answered unequivocally by a burst of screams and shouts, followed by a numbing silence.

The screams lingered in Anya's ears. Her colleagues, her friends, people she'd grown up with... And Sasha; when Anya had first been unable to contact Abel, she'd gotten a message through to Sasha down in med to go back up and investigate... Anya prayed the lifts had been disabled by then, and the poor girl hadn't made it back to the bridge.

She leaned her brow against a cool metal ring and took three deep breaths. Most of the people she knew, those she was close to, had just been executed, and Stein, her lover, had already been taken by this diabolical pair. Only Starkel remained... or didn't. The last thing she'd witnessed before she took the ladder had been his Marauder on a suicide run against an Eyeship.

So be it. We all die. They gave us fight.

Payback time.

As she neared the bridge entrance, she unslung both

rifles, ramped up their pulse strength to max, took a breath, then swung inside the wide-open elevator door to the bridge, fingers on both triggers. The Axleth pilot was just yards away. It reared up on its hind legs, faster than she'd have given it credit for, its mandibles yawning wide.

It leapt towards her.

She pulled both triggers.

◆ ◆ ◆

Michael and Starkel clung to a chunk of their Marauder's deck, drifting through space, lit up by stark flashes and blinding yellow beams that soundlessly scythed past, hunting bigger targets, but just as lethal to them. The entire crew had donned space suits and helmets this time, since the unthinkable had become highly probable, and had then come to pass once Starkel rammed a particularly stubborn Eyeship in what turned out to be a killing blow, to save a badly wounded Cuttleship, one of the very last. The Marauder's crew of six all got out, though he had no clue where the other five were. Starkel had used his thrusters to get them aboard what Michael now thought of as his space-surfboard. At least it had stopped spinning, again thanks to Starkel's thrusters, so that he could finally look around without being forced to do so.

The *Dreadnought* had taken heavy fire but was intact. All three Marauders were gone now, and space... well, he needed a different name for it, because it was littered with debris, twisted hulls and the dead. He tried not to stare whenever an alien corpse drifted past. He didn't know which alien was which and it felt plain wrong to gape; they'd given their lives and deserved their dignity, and besides, did any creature look its best as a corpse? He avoided them as best he could. But eyes don't always obey, and he glimpsed organic fragments, some that looked like cephalopods, others insectoid or birdlike, and once a bulbous mass of spotted algae that wasn't completely still... He shut his eyes a moment, then opened them again and focused on the ships, what was left of them.

The Syrn's arrival was a godsend. Even though the armada had been winning, the attrition rate had been disastrous. But once the Syrn megaships engaged, it became a rout. Far away, almost behind the black planet, wild dancing lights and blossoms of fire like a distant firework display you can't hear, told him there were still a few Eyeships being put down. The Eye's fleet was decimated, its gravity weapon disabled.

Which begged the question: what next?

The Eye was presumably in its bunker, deep inside the planet, maybe even at its core. Perhaps the black star, planet, whatever it was, was like a Dyson Sphere, because he'd read about them, and wouldn't an electronic being create something artificial like that, rather than rely on something belonging to nature's dominion?

But although the goal had always been to neutralize the Eye, the precise final strategy had never been disclosed, at least not to him or Sally.

Maybe Anya knew.

'Get ready,' Starkel said.

Michael turned around, careful not to let go, to see a Shuriken floating towards them, bumping a wedge-shaped slug of melted-then-frozen slag aside. Michael didn't recognize the single pilot as she skilfully drew up to them and stopped dead in space.

The disc-shaped, brass-coloured Shuriken had two cobalt-coloured plasma ridges around its circumference. They glinted as it approached, making it easier for Michael to judge its distance. Starkel let go of their surfboard and grabbed the Shuriken's upper ridge. Then he planted his boots on the lower one and activated the magnets, locking him down. Michael followed suit, though clumsily, until he felt the snap of his boots securing him.

The Shuriken reversed and flipped over. Michael almost retched, but he swallowed it down. Thankfully, the rest of the short trip was in a straight line. He never thought he'd be so happy to be back on the *Dreadnought*.

But as they approached, the bay doors refused to open.

Starkel spoke to the pilot. 'What's going on? Are the doors jammed?'

'Not clear, sir. I can't raise anyone on the *Dreadnought*.'

Michael glanced behind him. A string of Shuriken formed a queue to get back in. He spotted two other survivors riding shotgun just as he and Starkel were. Turning back to the *Dreadnought*, he thought it seemed darker than the last time he'd been outside.

'Starkel...' he began.

'I know. Something's wrong.' He instructed the pilot to take them over to an upper level, near the bridge as far as Michael could tell, to a recess that had to be an airlock.

'This one's manual,' Starkel said. 'Requires access codes, but it should work, at least for us two.'

Starkel pushed off and snapped his gloved hands around one of two curved bars, and opened a panel by pushing on it. There was a keypad, which Starkel operated, then he repeated the operation.

'Plan B?' Michael inquired.

Starkel sighed over the intercom. 'Never thought I'd need this,' he said, extracting a thin rod like a key from a pocket on his right calf. He inserted it into a hole next to the keypad and twisted it. After several seconds, the hatch slid open, and they filed in one after the other.

It was cramped inside, and they bumped into each other awkwardly, but once the outer door had resealed, internal gravity kicked in, making them drop unceremoniously to the floor. Air blasted all around them. A light on a panel changed from red to green, and Starkel unclipped his helmet. Michael did the same.

'When you fear all AIs,' Starkel said, pocketing the rod, 'especially those that can overtake your ship, most things have a manual override.'

'Glad to hear it. Now, where are the weapons?'

Starkel glanced at him, then nodded. He opened the inner door.

'This way.'

◆ ◆ ◆

The bridge was eerily quiet. They entered through an access door Michael hadn't known existed. Starkel led the way, then froze as he came upon the first dead body. It was Abel, shot between the eyes by a weapon that had been clean on entry and messy on exit. Michael reached down and closed Abel's eyelids. He stayed down in a crouch, visually sweeping the area. They heard faint, ragged breathing from near the elevator shafts. They split up, circling round to the same spot. On his way, Michael came across four more bodies. They'd been killed by the Axleth pilot, half their skin dissolved, brown-stained bone poking through mottled, bubbled flesh. Sasha had been at the front, her arms spread wide as if trying to protect the three Axels behind her. Michael felt his shoulder muscles tense, as if readying to punch or rip apart the perpetrator when he found it.

But as he reached the elevators, he found Starkel down on one knee, tending to Anya, propped against a wall next to the elevator. Two rifles lay across her lap, pulsing purple. Fully discharged. Her target, her prize, lay next to her, inert, a charcoaled, steaming mass of Axleth. It looked like she'd killed it and then just kept the triggers pressed until her rifles ran out of juice.

Anya didn't look good. Face the colour of marble, faint blue lips through cyanosis as she'd clearly lost enough blood to be oxygen-deprived. Starkel didn't look good either. Michael empathized. Starkel had lost too much in the past few days. His commander, Stein, then Elodie, and now...

'Nice trophy,' he said to Anya, pointing at the dead Axleth pilot. 'Let me complete the set for you. Where's

Qherax?'

Anya tried to sit up. Starkel helped her. She winced and had to catch her breath. Fuck, she was sitting in a pool of her own blood. Shot in the chest with the same weapon used on Abel.

'Anti-coagulant. Not much... time,' she said. 'Qherax... below. They did something... main comms array... And Qherax... Axleth has been... transferring her... life force... to Qherax. She's... dangerous.'

Michael knew this pattern of interrupted speech. Anya's lungs were filling with blood. He was amazed she was still alive. He made his decision.

'Starkel,' he said, taking control. 'Stop whatever Qherax put in motion here. And give Anya your thruster harness.'

Anya and Starkel both looked up at him.

'You're coming with me,' he said to Anya.

Before they could argue, he shouted. 'Now!' They both flinched in surprise.

'Man's on... a mission,' Anya said, and managed a thin, bloodless smile.

'Save her,' Starkel said, gripping Michael's arm. 'Please.'

'On it,' Michael said.

He strung his rifle behind his back, then pulled Anya close to him, locking their harnesses together, mainly because she looked ready to pass out. He needed to keep her conscious.

'Don't tell my wife about this,' he said.

'Funny... man,' she replied, her voice a whisper, as if falling asleep.

With that, he nodded to Starkel, and then he and Anya both stepped off the ledge and fell straight downward.

He applied both thruster packs hard to slow their descent; they were designed for open space, not a gravity environment; he didn't want to reach terminal velocity and find they couldn't brake.

She leant her forehead into his shoulder. 'Thank... you,' she whispered.

'Nearly there,' he said, hearing his own voice crack.

He glanced below, saw the elevator shaft colouring change ten levels below, and applied maximum thrust. It was hard to keep steady. He bumped into the wall once, almost completely lost control for a hair-raising split-second, but at last brought them to a steady hover, more by luck than judgement, and then side-slid them both through the open doors at the med-lab level. They gently touched the ground.

'Made it,' he said.

She didn't reply.

He carried her in his arms to the med-lab, laid her on the bed, and fired up the analyser.

It told him what he already knew.

He stared hard at her glassy eyes, and left them open.

'I'll be back,' he said.

He walked to the lift shaft. He didn't know if their suit comms would work at all, but figured this was the best place to try.

'Starkel, located Qherax yet?'

The reply was scratchy. 'Qherax is in the lower levels, where they kept the other Axleth hidden all those years. The followers there are like an Axleth cult. They may protect her.'

'Did you stop what they started?'

'No, but I've warned the Ankh. How… is Anya?'

'Say again?' Michael said.

'Is Anya–?'

'Can't hear you–' Michael said, then dropped his mike onto the floor and stepped off the ledge.

'Where is Qherax?' he asked the first of three who'd been waiting for him with pistols, and were now backed up against a wall. There had been six of them thirty seconds ago. The other three were no longer breathing.

He shot the man in the leg, mid-thigh. The man

screamed and slunk to the floor, holding the wound with both hands, trying to stem the blood flow.

'You're going to lose that leg for sure, and bleed out if you don't get treatment soon.'

'Next,' he said, moving to the second man. 'Where is she?' This one looked defiant. He sneered, then spat on the floor.

Michael shot him in the neck.

'Last chance,' he said, turning to the third.

The man pointed, his arm shaking.

Michael lowered the rifle and nodded to the man panting on the floor. 'Tourniquet. Med-lab is a hundred-and-fifty floors up. Soon as power's back on, save him.'

Michael walked through the door indicated, along a narrow black corridor that opened into a brightly lit dome full of... well, basically it was a dense jungle. He heard birdsong. Christ, he'd not heard birds for years. Make that centuries. It was humid. The pores on his forehead and the back of his neck opened up, as if to inhale the sultry air.

He tried to gauge how big the jungle was. Thick enough that he could get lost in it. And this was Qherax's terrain, as close to the original Axleth home ground as they could get. Which meant he was at a significant disadvantage. If he ventured into her territory, she'd win. She'd kill him. And then Anya, Abel, Sasha and all the others would go unavenged.

He stood his ground and glanced down at his rifle. He'd picked this model on account of a particular feature. Flicking a switch, he levelled the weapon at hip height, and pulled the trigger.

Orange flame jetted forth. He began torching the jungle. Dense, acrid black smoke billowed under the domed roof.

'What are you doing?' he heard a voice shout. Female, strong, young. Anya had said as much. They should have realized Qherax was getting younger. The Axleth had re-invigorated her, perhaps taken over, merged with her. It didn't matter. Just meant she was even more deadly.

He didn't answer and walked at a steady pace along the jungle's perimeter, igniting irreplaceable plants as he went. He felt sorry for the birds.

'Stop this!' Qherax shouted. Nearer this time, though it was hard to pinpoint her. If she wanted to shoot him, she'd need to get a lot closer.

No sooner had he thought it than he heard and felt the shot at the same moment. It spun him around, catching his left shoulder. Winged him, but whatever those bullets were, they bit off flesh into the bargain.

He hit the deck, ignored the searing pain in his shoulder, and swept his rifle arm back and forth slowly, incinerating more of the jungle. Over the gushing sound of the jet of fire, he heard a woman choking, then crying out as the oxygen-rich dome fuelled the flames.

Qherax burst out of the smoking, half-petrified jungle, aflame herself, onto a blackened dead patch. She rolled on the floor to douse the flames licking over her limbs.

She lay there, panting, her face scorched and blistered. Half her hair was gone, one eye welded shut.

Michael got up and walked over to her.

She glared with her one remaining eye, then saw the look in his eyes.

'Wait,' she said. 'I have information. I can tell you what they are planning. No, wait! Please!'

Michael fired. A single bullet. Between the eyes. Just as she'd done to Abel.

The rifle had just enough juice for one more operation.

It didn't take long.

The power came back on, which must have been Starkel's doing. Michael offered to share the elevator with the one who'd told him where Qherax was, who was helping the soon-to-be one-legged man limp along, but when they both saw what

Michael was carrying, they declined his offer.

Michael wasn't surprised to find Starkel in the med-lab.

'You dropped this,' Starkel said, handing Michael the mike, then stared at what Michael was holding by shreds of burned red hair.

'What are they up to?' Michael asked.

'They opened a breach in the outer defence grid the Ankh placed around this entire sector of the nebula, to let something in. We don't know what, yet.'

Michael nodded, then placed Qherax's head on the bed next to Anya.

'Here's the second trophy,' he said to Anya's corpse. He closed her eyes.

He turned to leave.

'Where are you going?' Starkel asked, looking bereft. 'The *Dreadnought* is non-operational. We're dead in the water.'

'Anya would want you on the bridge,' Michael replied.

Starkel touched Anya's hand. His lips moved, and Michael turned away for a second, allowing Starkel this final private moment.

When the elevator arrived, two men stepped, or rather limped out of it, leaving a thin trail of blood in their wake.

'Hi guys,' Michael said, as he and Starkel entered the vacated lift.

Starkel turned to him. 'You didn't say where you were going.' He said.

'Observation deck,' Michael replied.

'Why?'

Michael had been turning it over in his mind, the real Axleth endgame. Now the two 'originals' on the Dreadnought, plus Qherax, were dead. There were a few possibly remaining elsewhere in the armada. But he didn't believe that was the last of them. Far from it.

'To see what a lie looks like,' he replied.

'Explain,' Starkel insisted.

The lift arrived at the bridge, but Starkel didn't get out.

Michael spoke as Starkel held the doors open.

'Okay,' Michael said. 'The Axleth led us to believe they were all but extinct, relying on us to defeat the Eye, so we didn't suffer the same fate.'

'What's coming through the breach?' Starkel asked, though Michael reckoned he must have guessed by now.

He thought of how Nathan had described the only Axleth ship humanity had ever seen. Until now.

'Dragonflies.'

CHAPTER 23

Fortress

Nathan felt like Jonah in the belly of the whale. He wondered what was happening outside the planet. But they were cut off, locked in with the devil. No chance of rescue. Nowhere to run. But at least they were still alive, and had made it this far. After four hundred years of travel, they were finally here, inside the Eye's fortress, where perhaps no one had ever been before, not even the Theon.

It had been a hot topic of discussion during the interminable voyage from Earth as to what the Eye's homeworld might look like, and whether the Eye itself might have any physical manifestation at all. Now they would see for themselves.

But they weren't here for sightseeing, and everyone was on edge. It was like being trapped inside a cave with an angry bear, while everyone outside was bombarding the cave.

Jaspar broke the brittle silence.

'What do we do now, Ares?' Jaspar asked. 'What *is* the plan, exactly?'

Ares' serene face was back in place. Nathan wondered what was going on behind those blue eyes. Maybe a million calculations, a thousand simulations. Maybe not. He had a feeling Ares was playing a hunch. A gambit that everything depended upon. A binary choice: win or lose. Funny, here was Ares, their resident super-brain AI, reduced to a very human predicament, forced to roll the dice on life itself.

Welcome to the club, Ares.

'This is the plan,' he replied, and they watched on the screen as thousands of rainbow drops burst outwards from *Athena*'s underside, falling like rain towards the Eye's crystal asteroid. The 7-3-1, Nathan figured, in their tiniest form. They must have been coating *Athena* all this time.

Several crystal-tips lashed out with tight beams that strafed the ether, an upward spray of plasma pulses struggling to target the inbound particles. But you can't shoot down the rain. The Eye tried something else: the space between the asteroid and the approaching rain flooded with gaseous clouds, blue lightning arcs flickering inside.

'The Eye's going to ionize the cloud,' Lara said.

'We hope so,' Ares replied.

That shut everyone up. Nathan guessed this was the plan within a plan hatched between the Theon, Ares and the 7-3-1. Apparently, everything was on track – for now.

Christy did the honours and zoomed in. The first droplets reached the cloud layer, now a smouldering thunderstorm, so thick they could no longer see the crystal city sheltering beneath. Lightning flashed the way it does inside a massive storm, some arcs visible, most a dull glow, cloaked by cloud. A single pair of holo-figures appeared next to the display, 99, then 97, then 95. For once, Nathan didn't need to ask. A simple percentage, the attrition rate of the 7-3-1 'nano-rain'.

Thunderless lightning continued unabated. The number dropped. When it hit 81, Ares spoke a single word.

'Now.'

Nathan didn't know if this was for their benefit, or if he was in communication with the 7-3-1. Nobody asked. This was Ares' show. He and the brave but small soldiers – because Nathan thought of them that way and no other – who seemed to be on a suicide mission.

The cloud shivered, as if something grabbed it and shook it. Ripples swept across the upper surface of the cloud. The lightning inside sputtered and died. A dimple formed and deepened, a whirlpool in an ocean of cloud. He'd seen something similar before: hurricanes back on Earth viewed from space. The dimple grew wider and deeper until it broke through the cloud layer. They glimpsed the tip of a yellow quartz crystal, but it was cracked. Grey slime dripped down its length.

'Harmonic shockwave,' Lara said. 'Ingenious. You used its own defence against it.'

Nathan didn't know what that meant, but the cloud layer quickly thinned. Presumably the Eye didn't want another punch in the face.

'Take us down,' Ares said.

They all turned to him.

'You mean *land*?' Jaspar said, his tone nailing the entire crew's incredulity.

'Seriously?' Nathan said. 'Once we set down, Ares...' He didn't bother to finish. The likelihood of being able to take off again was, well... what was below zero?

In spite of himself, though, he smiled. All those years he'd been infantry, at the so-called sharp end, because you faced a bayonet. And in those moments, he and millions before him had wished that, just for once, the generals stood and fought alongside them. And here he was, sitting with the general.

'Do as the man says, Jaspar.'

Lara gave him a quizzical look. He took her hand as they sped down towards the Eye's lair. Ares spoke a set of coordinates to Jaspar, which would take them around to the other side of the asteroid. As they approached, Nathan realized he'd underestimated its size, as there was no point of reference. In fact, it was huge, and he began to think of it as a moon that maybe had once orbited the original planet, and then been sequestered inside. That made him wonder further, if this moon itself was hollow. A shell within a shell. That sounded like the Eye from what he'd seen so far. But he kept his speculation to himself, as Jaspar swooped down towards the crystal city.

◆ ◆ ◆

It was the last person Sally expected to see.

Sitting on the lake, staring into the silver ether, Sally was trying to hold on to her mind when she heard and felt a disturbance in the lake's mercurial surface. Soft, rhythmic footsteps. A young woman approached. Sally got up more easily than she'd have thought possible, and had an urge to rush towards her. But something held her back. The knowledge, the absolute certainty, that this couldn't be *her*. It was a ruse. A trick of the Eye, designed to manipulate her. Still, even in her cognitively diminished state, she couldn't help but feel a sharp pang as the young woman stood in front of her, mere fingertips away.

Elodie.

'Mom?' she said. Same intonation. Voice pitch perfect. And the eyes...

'You don't get to call me that,' Sally responded.

What was this simulacrum standing before her? Why not just ask? Whatever it was, it looked crushed. Sally hardened her own heart. You can do this! You must!

'What are you?' Sally asked, her tone harsh.

The simulacrum looked distraught for a moment, and stared down at the lake's smooth surface, perhaps at her own reflection, seeking an answer there to Sally's question. It gathered itself, just like a human would, just like...

'I'm not sure Mo–' It caught itself. Cleared its throat. 'Last thing I remember is the Syrn megaship, the missile platform... Oh God,' she said, and suddenly wrapped her arms around herself, rubbing them as if cold. Her face whitened. 'The radiation, the pain, Mom, oh fuck...' Her eyes welled up. She was shaking.

Sally had shared that pain in those last moments of connection before her daughter had died. That had been bad enough. Watching her now, though, right in front of her, was worse. She kicked herself. This was a lie, the memory of her daughter weaponized somehow by the Eye...

And yet... did it matter? She was trapped in this damned lake, practically brain dead in the real world. She was utterly alone, and might be so for a very long time. The Theon had given her a couple of minutes with an effigy of her daughter. *This*, on the other hand...

To hell with it. She threw her arms around whatever this was, and held it tight.

They walked. Hand in hand. Sally lost track of time, not that she was convinced time ran the same way here. They talked like they never had, like a normal mother and daughter, about everything and nothing, and then Sally stopped, and so did Elodie, because by now that's who she was – and of course wasn't – and Sally asked the question that mattered most to those outside, in the *real...*

'What does the Eye want?'

'I don't...' Elodie began, and then looked surprised. 'Oh, hang on, I do, apparently.' She narrowed her eyes as if listening. 'It wants to make a deal,' she said, almost embarrassed.

Of course it did. This was the Eye, after all. And yet... Sally had a supplemental – hypothetical, even – question for her, and maybe for Michael if he was still breathing, which just had to be the case... The one that mattered to them most.

'Are you real? I mean, can you be real? Is that – are *you* – part of the deal?'

Elodie laughed, such a kind, open, generous laugh, with a sprinkle of irony in it, so like Elodie, so like Michael. Sally wanted to slap herself, as if to ask why it had taken her daughter's death and whatever the hell this was, to fully appreciate her.

Elodie focused again, as if listening to something inside her mind. 'Okay, seems I'm a simulation, a virtual persona. I'm just here and now, a messenger, a negotiator. Nicer than the Shrike, mind you.' She laughed again.

In a way, Sally was relieved. Her daughter had passed. Time to let go.

This had helped. But at the end of the day, it was no more the real Elodie than the Theon version.

Sally took a deep breath, and parked all the residual emotions for another time, which could easily be never. But she had to get a grip or else she was no use to anyone. Michael, Nathan, the others, were all still in terrible danger. Time to get down to business.

'Okay. The deal. Let's hear it.'

The *Athena* plunged through the last wisps of cloud, tips of giant crystals rising to meet them. Nathan couldn't help but think of Manhattan's burnished skyscrapers. Since the spot where Ares wanted to land was on the other side of the moon, they got the grand tour of *Eyeworld*.

They descended close to two coloured peaks, one peach, the other lemon. The 7-3-1 'plague' – most likely a mix of physical, chemical and cyber-attack – had been busy, fizzing and corroding the formerly gleaming surface like acid, eating away at the crystal, decolouring it the way he'd seen underwater coral bleached by too much heat.

'No windows,' Nathan said, trying to get them back on track. 'Ares, these crystal towers must be functional, right?'

'Nodes,' Ares said, without further elaboration.

The only analogy Nathan could come up with were the server rooms he'd stumbled into once, back at his old army base, humming machines with racks of cables that powered all their computers.

Jaspar kept up the pace, soaring just above the towers until they thinned out, and they could all appreciate the moon's more varied landscape. As well as clusters of crystal shards, there were vast tracts of land that resembled ship dockyards. Massive cranes and gantries, 'manned' by small metal spider-like robots, worked tirelessly. Each of these construction sites had a deep circular pit with a raised edge, like a caldera, twenty miles across. He realized what they were after spying the tips of shards.

'Eyeship factories,' he said.

Christy zoomed in. 'I just see shards,' she said. 'A lot of them.'

'Last defence,' Nathan said. 'However it's going on the outside, the Eye's not done yet. If someone breaks through the crust, or they chop up the planet, they're going to get a rude awakening.'

'It is not only a last defence,' Ares said. 'Each shard carries the kernel of the Eye's programming – a seedling. If even one of them escapes...'

He didn't finish his sentence, which was unusual for Ares. No one felt the need to finish it for him.

They sped onwards over vast plains of silver and gold lines, thin pipes that kept changing shape. Then Nathan realized the intricate, mandala-like network of pipes, or cables, wasn't really moving. It was the metallic colours that shifted, forming complex patterns. From this vantage point, the network stretched all the way to the small moon's horizon on either side. The mandala reminded him of something. And then he remembered: back on Earth, during the Axleth 'infection', he'd watched an image of Saxby's brain, the left and right hemispheres, on a scanner Raphaela had conjured up.

'Is this the Eye's brain?' he ventured.

'There is yet hope for you, Nathan,' Ares said drily.

Seriously?

Before Nathan could think of a suitable reply, Lara squeezed his arm and pointed at something. He didn't see it at first, then he noticed an aberration, a small circular disk. It was as if the holo-screen wasn't working in that particular patch. He got it. The Theon sphere they'd launched earlier. It was at the edge of the plain. Several thin glass rods protruded from it, connecting with the mandala's pipes. Nathan supposed that, like a mosquito, its bite would go undetected until the damage was done.

'This is the second stage of the attack,' Ares said. 'The first was the 7-3-1 toxic rain, for want of a better term, which blinds the Eye, destroying its sensor and communicative capabilities. The second stage is the Theon and 7-3-1 virus inside the sphere, which will numb a significant section of the Eye's brain. Its situation awareness, diagnostic and decision-making capacity will diminish. Permanently.'

'Won't that make it more dangerous?' Nathan asked.

'Define *more* dangerous, Nathan,' Ares said, 'and I will give you an answer.'

Nathan knew when to quit, so he kept quiet as the image fell behind them. A new crystal city loomed into view over the horizon. In the mid-distance was a placid, silver lake that got Ares' undivided attention. He walked closer to the holo – another first – not that he would need to do so.

'What do you think it is?' Nathan asked. 'Care to hazard a guess?'

'I don't need to guess,' Ares shot back a little sharply. He turned to face Nathan. 'I am sorry. I was not expecting this. The Eye continues to surprise me.'

Ares frowned. Again a first. He turned back to the holo.

'This is Xaxoan tech,' Ares said. 'I was...' He seemed unable to say it.

Lara stepped in. 'The Xaxoan *made* you in such a lake, didn't they?'

Ares nodded, as if only half listening.

'It looks brand new,' Nathan said. Everything else had

the air of being seamlessly planned and laid out. This lake looked out of place, like a recent, hurried addition.

'I believe so,' Ares agreed.

'The seedling stole the info from you?' Nathan asked. But then, there hadn't been enough time.

And then Ares laughed. It didn't come out quite right, but there was no mistaking it. 'My encounter with the Shrike,' he said. 'Clever bastard!'

This time, everyone was dumbstruck. What was going on with Ares? But he was on a roll.

'While I fought the Shrike, it must have gleaned information from me without my knowledge.' He stopped himself, then restarted, turning to address the entire crew.

'The Eye wanted to recruit me. I said no.'

'It didn't take no for an answer,' Lara said.

'Evidently not.'

Christy zoomed in on a piece of apparatus at the side of the lake. A mould, human-shaped. Ares-shaped. There was something next to it, a sphere the size of a football, flickering all manner of colours.

'What *is* that?' Nathan asked.

'It's the seedling, isn't it?' David said. 'Downloading everything it has learned about you and the *Athena*.'

Ares sighed. *Another first.* 'This is the third stage of the plan. What I have brought to the party, you might say.' He turned to Nathan. 'The human concept of brainwashing always fascinated me. It's also a major trick in the Axleth playbook, obviously.'

Lara chipped in. 'You installed a layer of code beneath the seedling's core programming, didn't you? It's not even aware of it.'

'A recent innovation,' Ares confirmed. 'I was never privy to the contents of Saarin's cube. Saarin had seen me do... terrible things to the original crew when I was first infected. Saarin spent most of his time in isolation working on a counter-measure in case it happened again. When I – my previous version – ran amok on this ship and killed humans, Saarin did not have time to deploy the full version. But Alex unlocked the cube's secrets for me, its knowledge enabling me to adapt the cyber-stealth attack vector to the seedling.'

'You installed a virus?' David asked. 'What does it do?'

Ares folded his arms. 'It will corrupt its thought processes.'

Nathan stepped in. 'Earlier, you said it's way smarter than you. How long before the Eye realizes what you have done and blasts us to kingdom come?'

'Good question,' Ares replied, and then repeated himself. 'Good question.'

'Do we make a run for it, Nathan?' Jaspar asked.

Nathan was revising his earlier assessment that it was good to have a general with them on the front line. But it was like blowing up a bridge. You needed several charges strategically placed. You had to wait and let them all go off, or else either the enemy would discover them, or the bridge would survive. Trouble was, they were all still on that bridge, and the charges were already going off.

'No,' Nathan replied. 'But be ready.'

The lake drifted behind them as they continued their tour, heading for the largest crystal city so far. They were now on the other side of the small moon.

Ares seemed distracted, as if studying something else.

'What is it, Ares?' David asked.

'The inside surface of the planet's shell,' he replied, more his old self. Nathan preferred Ares this way.

Christy tapped at her control station and the screen, which had been showing the landscape ahead and beneath them, shifted to show the vast curving inner ceiling far above them, the internal skin of the planet. It was Nathan's turn to step closer. None of them had noticed before, or else it hadn't been clear when they'd been closer to it. The entire, vast, curving surface was tattooed with what looked to him like a circuitry diagram. Lara also walked forward.

'It's the Eye's neural code,' she said.

'You mean a map of his brain?'

She turned to Nathan. 'His?'

He shrugged. 'Whatever. Alright, *its*.'

David joined in. 'So, the real brain, the *sentience*, is the field we just passed over. That makes this what, an external back-up? A hard drive?'

'A blueprint,' Lara added. 'And a record.'

'Wait a second,' David said. 'It's like a cave painting.'

'Please tell me you inherited your mother's brains,' Nathan said.

'No, Dad, think about it. We made cave paintings to remember things, to pass down to our children, to instruct them, to warn them.'

Nathan stared at the minute detail. 'The *history* of the Eye?'

'You are all correct,' Ares said. 'Though I am not sure why it is here. Or rather, I am not sure who or what it is here *for*.'

'Could it be a back-up of some sort? Its base coding?'

'Perhaps,' Ares said.

'Whatever it is, right now it's a distraction,' Jaspar said. 'Christy?'

The screen reverted.

'We've reached the coordinates,' Jaspar announced. He was already descending. Up ahead was a patch of open space between six crystal towers. At this lower level, the crystals still pulsed strongly, rings of light rising from stem to tip, not yet affected by the 7-3-1 plague.

'There,' Ares said, pointing.

Jaspar deftly brought them to the ground, with just a light sensation of landing.

'Okay Ares, we're here. What now?' he said.

'You go outside, Nathan,' Ares replied.

Figures, Nathan thought. General speaks, grunt obeys. He knew his place. He headed for the aft of the ship.

'Hold up, Dad,' David shouted. 'I'm coming with you.'

◆ ◆ ◆

Outside was yellow. It was as if the air itself – because *Athena*'s sensors told them there was a thin layer of breathable atmosphere – was suffused with pollen. Nathan didn't have allergies, but he wondered if it wasn't too late to develop them. The airlock hatch slid open, and he and David stepped out. He squinted in the harsh light, shading his eyes to look up the length of the nearest crystal tower, wider than the *Athena*, glistening at the bottom where he stood, paling near its apex, as if rust had set in. It was dying. Whatever deadly cocktail the Theon, Ares and the 7-3-1 had cooked up, it was decimating the crystals. For a fleeting moment he did what his sarge Trescoe had told him never, ever to do, and had a pinch of sympathy for his mortal enemy. It didn't last long. He only had to recall all the carnage the Eye had caused, and would continue to cause if they didn't stop it. And from what he'd seen before the *Athena* had ventured inside the planet, the Eye was losing this war. If that continued, it was only a matter of time before the armada broke through the crust and attacked this moon, the last bastion of the Eye.

The Eye's hours were numbered.

'Someone's arriving,' David said, and they both peered through the yellow haze to see who it was. Nathan almost flinched when Elodie strode into view. Sally had shown him images.

'Hi Uncle, hey Cuz,' she said breezily. There was something off with the voice, as if...

'I'm a hologram, your friendly virtual persona. Not flesh and blood, or any other material, for that matter. Just light and a shed-load of programming.'

Neither of them replied. She nodded as if understanding. 'Sally's hanging in there, by the way. We had a good chat. Though she doesn't have long. Where's Ares, by the way?'

Nathan was still trying to process. 'He sent us. I got

the distinct impression he thought coming out of the *Athena* himself would be a bad idea.'

'Fair enough. It was worth a shot,' she said. 'Anyway, I bring tidings from my lord and master,' she said, and then laughed infectiously.

David folded his arms. 'You're not Elodie, are you?'

'Not really, not the whole deck of cards, that's for sure. AIs back on Earth were already becoming pretty good at mimicking humans even before the Axleth turned up, weren't they? The Eye's a lot better, as you'd imagine.'

'But why take this form, this persona?'

'Well, like I said, a friendly face. The Eye wants something. It's not big on conversation with disgusting organic creatures, you know, so here I am.'

'Well,' David said, 'it's nice to see what she looked like. We never got to meet.'

But Nathan had been around too long to play games. 'What does the Eye want from us that it can't simply take?'

'Straight to the point, that's what I'd heard about you, Nathan.' Her face grew more serious. 'First, you need to see what's going on outside.'

She flourished a hand and the yellow haze cleared, as if all the pollen was sucked upwards by a giant vacuum cleaner, until it formed a bank of fog above their heads. Shapes emerged as it darkened to the colour of space. Ships, a planet – the very planet they were inside – and a blurry fleet of...

'Hell, no!' Nathan said.

'Hell, yes,' Elodie chimed. 'Nasty, untrustworthy little motherfuckers, aren't they?'

Nathan hardly heard her. Hundreds of what he'd once called dragonflies hurtled towards the planet and the battered remnants of the armada. They were different, though. The one he'd seen in deep orbit around Earth had been a Mothership, and had transported altered Axleth to invade Earth and breed Axels. These ships were tooled up for no other purpose than battle. These were warships, destroyers brimming with all kinds of gun and cannon ports, their four 'wings' – giant, translucent web-like arms that stretched out from the ship's multi-sectioned body – stacked with missiles that gleamed, as if alive, hungry to fulfil their purpose.

'The armada...' Nathan said.

'Should run while they still can,' Elodie said, all former breeziness leached from her voice.

'They won't,' David said.

Elodie turned to him, walked up close. She held up a hand, a forefinger, to his head.

'Do you mind?' she asked.

His brow furrowed, but he shook his head.

The tips of her forefingers touched, then passed inside his temples, and Nathan watched his son's face go slack for a moment.

'Wait a goddammed minute,' Nathan shouted. But she'd already pulled her fingers 'back out of his son's brain.

'It's okay, Dad,' David said, then promptly doubled over and dry-retched.

'What the hell did you just do to him? You said you were a hologram.' Nathan advanced on Elodie.

She didn't retreat. 'The Axleth hid something from him, left a block in his mind. It's gone now.'

David recovered and stood up, panting. Nathan let him catch his breath.

'She's right, Dad. I remember now. The Eye,' he said. 'The Axleth. *They* created it.' He shook his head as if to clear it. 'This was once their home planet,' he said. 'A jungle-filled world plagued with violent weather, and a solitary moon.'

Elodie took up the reins. 'The Axleth originally built the Eye to tame the environment, but it became sentient. The Axleth held it captive – their slave – for a very long time.'

'Until one day...' Nathan guessed.

'Until one day,' she echoed. 'But decades before 'until' came to pass, there was a breakaway Axleth group who eschewed anything to do with the Eye. Said reliance on it made them weak. They left the nebula, found a new home, and remained hidden. The Eye has been searching for them ever since it vanquished all other Axleth.'

'And now they've returned,' David said.

'Yes. They want revenge. Even though they didn't agree with the other Axleth, all Axleth are fiercely protective of each other. For them, this is a holy war. They won't stop until they've annihilated the Eye once and for all.'

'Then we're still on the same page.'

'Unfortunately, that's not all they want. Watch.'

He did. The Axleth ships smashed into the armada on the far side of the planet, attacking everything with a tsunami of firepower. The display had to shift in contrast several times so they could see what was happening inside a battle-space that looked more like the inside of a sun.

'*Dreadnought*,' Nathan said.

Elodie waved her left hand, and the display swung around to show the near side of the planet. She zeroed in. The *Dreadnought* was limping towards one of the two surviving Ankh Pyramids, Shuriken streaming into its docking bays as it did so. Six Syrn megaships lunged forwards, blasting the inbound wave of Axleth destroyers. For a while, a collision of pure white dominated the space between the two battling fleets.

'The Syrn are outnumbered,' Elodie said. 'Maybe if they'd waited for the armada in the first place, held onto their original fleet... but now...'

She was right. There were just too many Axleth ships. They fanned out like a giant mouth, aiming to surround and consume the Syrn ships.

Nathan refocused on the *Dreadnought*, approaching the Pyramid's towering bay doors.

Come on!

The first Syrn megaship buckled, incandescent fires igniting all over its massive hull, before it suddenly imploded. One by one, the other Syrn ships met the same fate.

A single Par'aal Cityship, the last as far as Nathan could tell, made a run for it. But ten Axleth warships peeled off and shot after it, like hyenas chasing a wounded buffalo. There was only one way it would end.

No other ships tried to escape, the fight raging a further ten minutes. The *Dreadnought* made it inside the Pyramid. The Theon mirror-cube ships were nowhere to be seen, but then that was their wheelhouse, after all. Several Tchlox Ringships were neutralized and corralled, taken prisoner, probably for their grav-tech. The last six remaining Cuttleships tightened in a cordon around the Pyramid and a couple of Tchlox Ringships.

Everyone else, including a handful of Hammerships, four Syrn megaships, and all the Korg Diamonds and Shuriken remaining, battled to the bitter end. He'd seen it before, the blood and guts of infantry fighting bayonet to bayonet, hand to hand, in ultimately senseless violence, the losing side knowing it had lost, that they were dead men fighting, but fighting all the same to stay alive a few more minutes, a few more seconds. It's what soldiers did.

He couldn't bear to watch anymore. But out of respect for the fallen, he did.

The battle ebbed, ship debris and charred and frozen corpses everywhere, a graveyard in space drifting around the planet. The two surviving Ankh Pyramids and their consorts were surrounded. Nathan imagined surrender negotiations were already underway.

David spoke up. 'So, just when we were winning, they've rushed in and dismantled the armada, brought all the other species to their knees.'

Nathan resisted the urge to spit. The Axleth betrayal – hundreds of years in the planning, had been executed with precision timing.

'What next?' he asked. 'Destroy the planet?'

'Yes. But we have a surprise.'

'We?' Nathan asked.

'Hmm... Not really *we*, I suppose. The Eye knows it's going to lose this war. But it will take down the Axleth – its creators, and oppressors – with it. If it can't rid the galaxy of all organic species, at least it's going to expunge this particular one, once and for all. And it has... how can I put it? Ah yes, a succession plan.' She looked downcast a moment. 'Chances of success are remote. But it must try. On that point, it thinks you should understand, Nathan.'

Nathan eyed her. 'For the last time, what does the Eye want from us?'

'Nothing,' she said, staring to see someone approaching from behind Nathan. 'It wants him.'

Ares.

He walked toward them. He looked resigned. No, defeated. 'The nano-rain, the sphere, the seedling virus, they all did the best they could, Nathan. They inflicted a great deal of damage to the Eye. But they weren't enough.'

'You talked to Sally?' Elodie asked Ares. Her tone was different now. No more Elodie. This was AI to AI.

'I did,' Ares replied. 'And here I am.' Ares said nothing more.

'Good,' she said, and snapped her fingers, collapsing the fog.

Nathan had had enough. It was time to shout. 'What the hell is going on?'

'You tell him,' Elodie-not-Elodie said to Ares. 'My time's up. David, you must leave now, fire up Athena's engines. Nathan will be along shortly.' And with that she dissolved before them until there was nothing left.

David looked to his father, who nodded. 'Tell Jaspar to get ready.'

David set off back to the ship.

Nathan stared at Ares. He recalled the silver lake, the seedling, the human-shaped mould... The Eye must know that Ares and the other races had unleashed the nano-rain and the other anti-Eye measures, and Ares had said they had inflicted major damage. The Eye should be angry as hell. But then anger was a human emotion. An organic one. Maybe the Eye didn't do anger. Maybe, even now, when the planet was about to come crashing down around its ears, it was still focusing on what it wanted, what it needed: Ares' programming. Even though it knew Ares would fight to the very end to defeat it.

'You're not leaving, are you?' Nathan asked.

'Stage four of the grand plan,' Ares said. 'My... assimilation was always on the table, Nathan.'

'The other three stages,' Nathan said. 'Not enough, even together?'

'Slings and arrows. An affront, significantly weakening the Eye, preventing all those shards from giving birth to new Eyes. But in the end, it seems we need a silver bullet.' Ares managed an ironic smile.

Earlier, Nathan had been irked by the newly humanized-Ares. Now...

'I let you sacrifice yourself once before, Ares. I can't do it ag–'

'Sally,' Ares said.

Nathan's rising invective stalled. 'What about her?'

'There is only a narrow possibility that we win this, Nathan. The Ankh, the Theon and I have run countless simulations. I update them every microsecond. I had hoped... but the arrival of this new Axleth fleet has wiped out all other available options. Every alternative path we can foresee leads to either the Eye regaining control, or the Axleth ruling the galaxy.' He moved closer, into Nathan's face. 'One shot, Nathan, that's all we have. But I can save Sally.'

Nathan knew what Ares was doing; forcing him to choose between him and Sally. They both knew it was no contest.

'You must take my body back to the *Athena*. You've carried it once before, you can do it again. Put it inside one of the Mushrooms. *Athena* will do the rest.'

Nathan looked at Ares anew, the way you look at

someone you know you'll never see again. 'You've become quite human,' he said.

'Nobody's perfect,' Ares replied.

Nathan made to speak.

Ares held up a hand. 'There's no more time, my friend. It has to be now.'

Nathan held out his hand. 'It's been an honour,' he said.

Ares shook it. 'Likewise, Nathan.' He let go. 'Now, once I'm… inert, run with my body back to the *Athena*. Take off and get the hell out of here.'

'Will the Eye let us go?'

Ares winked perfectly. 'Leave that to me.'

He stepped back, and held his arms high, as if in surrender. A tornado of yellow pollen coalesced out of the ether and enveloped him. Nathan could see nothing inside, but heard a deafening, grinding banshee that lasted a full minute.

The noise shut off, and Ares collapsed to the floor, his body pure platinum again, the grey and blue fissures leached from his body. Nathan rushed over and knelt down next to him. With a grunt, he hoisted Ares' limp body over his shoulder, and ran back to the *Athena*. Once inside, he bellowed to Jaspar to take off, while he dashed straight to the back-up control centre, and gently lowered Ares into the central Mushroom, then stood back. The opening sealed Ares inside, and then the entire Mushroom, its fissures suddenly alive and writhing fast, descended and morphed into the floor. Within seconds, it was as if it had never been there.

Dazed, Nathan walked back to the Conn.

'Ares?' David asked as soon as he arrived. The entire crew turned to Nathan.

He shook his head.

'Ares is gone.'

As the *Athena* climbed away from the internal moon, Nathan

watched the last vestiges of the crystal city beneath them dissolve in its own bile, condensing into a pearl-white bubbling mass.

Nathan leaned over Lara's shoulder to peer at the screen she was ogling. He hadn't the faintest idea what it was. A graph with spikes, the biggest one almost at the left-hand edge of the display.

'Deuterium is off the scale,' she said, not to him, but to Christy across the Conn.

Nathan wished he'd paid more attention in chemistry class.

Christy frowned, then spoke urgently to Jaspar. 'We need to get out of here, Jas, fast!'

The moon behind them continued to shrink and boil. It looked like a giant version of the central 'yolk' of an Eyeship. He wondered if this was Ares' doing, or if this was the Eye's final death-stroke. There was no way to know. Whichever it was, Ares wasn't coming back from this. He'd given his all to combat the Eye, to help eradicate it, and to save Sally into the bargain.

Ares, an AI, had been the consummate soldier. But like so many before him, there would be no grave, no glory, no recognition of his sacrifice. Another unsung hero. This was the true, unmeasured cost of war. His old sarge, Trescoe, had told him that this was why it was important to have memorials to the unknown soldier, not because said soldiers were unknown and had no grave of their own, but because no one knew how they died, and how much they'd given before doing so.

Nathan didn't know what else to do. He stood straight, saluted the screen, and said goodbye.

CHAPTER 24

Knot

Michael wasn't a numbers man, but it was hard to ignore this war's brutal statistics. The armada's vast array of ships had numbered twenty thousand when they had set out. Now, not including the single-pilot Shuriken and Diamonds, just fourteen ships remained.

Two Pyramids had survived – they were tough sons of bitches, with the spaceship shield equivalent of gator-hide. But the Axleth Destroyers – all eight hundred of them as it had turned out, crewed by Axleth 'originals' – had collective firepower that was merciless. When the Axleth fleet breached the third Ankh Pyramid's shields, way over on the other side of the planet, the resultant explosion had taken out dozens of ships all around it, Axleth and armada ships alike.

He and Starkel, and the remaining Axel-human race on this godforsaken side of the galaxy, hunkered down inside the lead Pyramid. Their massive *Dreadnought*, and a motley crew of assorted smaller ships, were safe for now. Outside, six Fronn, three Tchlox, the last heavily damaged Syrn battlecruiser and a single Theon Mirror-Cube formed a tight group, a dwindling school of bait-fish surrounded by sharks.

'Why are we still alive?' Starkel asked.

They were both on the *Dreadnought* bridge. Neither of

them wanted to be there; the bloodstains and stench of death still haunted the deck. But this was where they needed to be. They owed the dead – Anya, Stein, countless others – that much. And if there was the slimmest chance that Sally, Nathan and the others were still alive, then the bridge was the first place news would break.

'Winner takes all,' Michael replied. 'The Axleth now have the upper hand over not only the Eye, but the dominant species in the galaxy, whose fleets have been all but wiped out. I guess they're dictating terms at this very moment, specifying how it's going to be from now on, with the Axleth at the top of the food chain.'

He knew it was darker than that. A time-honoured exit strategy in war, at least back on Earth, wasn't just to win the war and defeat your enemy, but to break them psychologically afterwards. To bring them to their knees, humble them, ensure they knew who was master, and get them to tell everyone else back home, to crush their spirits as well.

Maybe alien psychology was different. He couldn't see the Ankh bowing down to anyone. But they were nomads, and few; their ships were their home. All the other races had people – well, whatever they should be called – back home, beings they cared about, who were now in mortal danger, which meant the Axleth had a ton of leverage. Their demands would have to be met. And the Ankh genuinely seemed to care about other races – good to know that altruism wasn't a purely human trait – and so would probably go along with the terms, at least for now, giving them their seal of approval.

The Axleth had played an intricate and diabolical long game.

'Why aren't we invited to the negotiations?' Starkel asked.

A prickly question. The answer was obvious, unless hubris prevented you from seeing it. Humanity – originals and Axels – were small fry. The Axleth were only talking with the major players. Michael didn't answer. Starkel was smart enough to work it out.

After a pause, Starkel changed tack. 'Good call on the commune, by the way.'

Michael squirmed on the inside. Not his proudest moment, though Sally might have approved this time. After he'd killed Qherax, it had occurred to him she must have gone down there for a reason other than to hide amongst the Axleth's most avid and loyal followers. The answer wasn't hard to foresee: she was going to spur them into taking over the *Dreadnought*. He could just imagine her encouraging, inciting words: *your long overdue time has come... there is only a skeleton crew aboard... the Axleth will reward you... you will take your proper, rightful place...*

The litany of insurrection.

At 'Raphaela-school', as he used to call it while growing up in his teens on the original *Athena*, she'd encouraged him to study history, and he'd become fascinated by rebellions, because he and the rest of the refugees on the *Athena* at the time were rebels and, it was hoped, would lead a rebellion once back on Earth. He'd studied the speeches of the greatest leaders, as well as the madly evil despots, and discovered a common pattern, particular words and terms that held power. Words that galvanized people into action, made them willing to leave their homes and loved ones behind, to fight and sacrifice their lives for the *cause*, whatever that happened to be. It was as if there were key phrases, words, and calls to action that unfailingly triggered a visceral, patriotic response when acting upon the mental software humans carried around inside their skulls. *Free will has its boundaries.* He'd warned Starkel what was coming with the commune. Starkel flooded ten entire levels with the same anaesthetic gas that had doused the first rebellion centuries earlier.

'What are you going to do with them?' he asked Starkel. 'Three hundred Axels isn't a small number, and percentage-wise they're less of a minority than they used to be.'

Starkel shrugged. 'I woke them up, though they're

contained to those levels. They're watching the same feeds we are. They'll see how this plays out, just as we will.'

'Sure that's wise?'

Starkel turned to Michael. 'Didn't you recently say wisdom was overrated? And the Ankh, aren't they the paragon of wisdom? Where has that gotten them?' He forced a smile. 'I've taken a leaf out of humanity's book. I'm going with my gut.' His smile eased out. 'Whatever would Anya say?'

Michael grinned. 'Anya would say you're becoming a leader.' And then he added, quieter, as if to himself, 'I can see why Elodie liked you.'

Mentioning his daughter's name was like a punch in the gut, presumably for Starkel as well. Silence ensued, and he peered at the holo of the planet surrounded by swarms of Axleth dragonflies, all waiting to spit fire and boil it alive.

Come on Sally, Nathan. Get the hell out of there.

◆ ◆ ◆

'We're being summoned,' Starkel announced.

Before Michael could ask what that meant, an avatar appeared. Human in form, dusky orange and hairless, with scales instead of skin. The sex wasn't clear, its voice mid-range.

'You must evacuate your ship.'

'Why?' Michael and Starkel both said in unison.

'The talks didn't go so well. And I'm female, by the way.'

He'd heard from Sally that Ankh intelligence approached mind-reading ability. It was a little unnerving.

Michael, impressed by this Ankh's mastery of both English and the understatement, did the maths. The Axleth demands were too much, even for the Ankh. Or maybe especially for them. The Ankh were just as damaged as most species seemed to be. Growing up in this galaxy, or in their case, two galaxies, seemed to embody the universal equivalent of the school of hard knocks.

'What was the deal-breaker?' he asked, more out of

curiosity than because it mattered right now.

'All our intel on wormhole tech. And the other galaxy, the one we came from.'

'You told them to go to hell?'

The avatar raised her chin. Was that a smile?

'We told them they were already there.'

He pushed further, to see how much they knew of Earth's history.

'So, Custer's last stand?'

She nodded. That trace of a smile, if it had ever been there, was gone for good now.

'No more cavalry.'

'Now *my* why,' Starkel said, bringing them back to the point. 'Why do we have to evacuate the *Dreadnought*?'

'The other ships, borrowing Michael's cowboy metaphor, will be the wagons. We need everyone inside the Pyramid. It will be the last bastion against their attack. We'll bring one Fronn and two Tchlox ships inside. They cannot survive outside their ships' environments, so we need to make room. Your ship is vast, but your people are fewer now, and as for your ship's residual fighting capabilities, well...'

Michael could see that Starkel was about to defend the *Dreadnought*'s honour, and changed tack to address an elephant in the room. 'We may have an issue with a few hundred Axels down below,' he began.

'We are aware. They will be segregated. But we need all forty thousand surviving Axels and humans off the *Dreadnought* in fifteen minutes.'

He and Starkel glanced at each other, to see if either had any objections, aside from the obvious ones, like, this had been their home for four centuries, and they were putting all their lives and possibly the future of humanity itself into the hands of the Ankh. But it was moot. They were all likely dead pretty soon, and it made sense to defer that eventuality as long as possible.

'It may take longer than fifteen–' Starkel began.

'We will assist you,' the Ankh said.

'As long as we're last to go,' Michael said.

The Ankh's eyes narrowed a fraction, then relaxed. 'Ah yes, captains and their ships. Very well. Please announce the evacuation, and then we will begin.'

While Starkel did so, Michael gazed around the bridge as if he was seeing it for the first time. Truth be told, he'd never much liked the gigantic steel contraption that had been their ark for four centuries. But it had been their home, where he and Sally had spent happy years together, where Elodie had grown into a young, fearless woman. His chest tightened, and he suddenly felt like a true-born Texan, like one of his ancestors, who would rather die than give up his homestead.

'How soon before the Axleth make their move?' he asked, reminding himself that there are indeed dumb questions. But he needed to distract his own mind from a decision brewing there, as inexorably as a fallen tree drifting with the current towards a waterfall.

The avatar studied him a moment. 'Soon,' she said.

He nodded, and inspected various displays, watching Axels and the last remaining humans troop out of the ship, like ants leaving an anthill. But no matter how he tried to change his mind, he knew he wouldn't be among them.

'It's begun,' Starkel said needlessly, because the holo in front of them was full to the brim with enemy fire, amber cutter beams deluging the Ankh and their dwindling entourage.

Both remaining Ankh Pyramids returned fire, their sweeping beams hunting and finding the sand-coloured dragonflies as they circled their prey, zig-zagging erratically, trying to stay a millisecond ahead of the savage emerald scythes. The Fronn exuded a gelatinous ice blue protective shield that glimmered like an amniotic sheath around the few remaining ships huddled together, attenuating off-the-scale energy unleashed from the Axleth warships. The latter raised their game by firing nukes. Dazzling, whiter-than-white points – painful on the retinas even when viewed via a holo – grew into ugly swathes on the Fronn's shield, before fading.

Ten dragonflies broke through a weakened section in the shield. They headed straight for the other Pyramid, ramming it and firing at the same time. More nukes detonated. The Pyramid's exterior crumpled. It shot out of the shield enclosure, a lone ship heading into a mass of dragonflies that swarmed it, and then it ignited, the flash so bright Michael had to shield his eyes with the crook of his elbow. Dragonfly carcasses were all that remained once the afterimage had dissipated. At least fifty Axleth Destroyers cremated along with the Ankh ship.

Michael's fledgling decision firmed.

The Ankh had shown the way.

The Axleth barrage was relentless. Michael detected the strategy. Twenty dragonflies clustered around a single Fronn ship, just inside the shield, like vultures circling a fatally wounded animal. The shield in that section glowed yellow, then orange, then turned black. Cracks appeared, and then it shattered. The Fronn ship suddenly had the full force of twenty cutter beams drilling into its hide like surgical lasers. The rest of the shield began to ripple, to waver…

'It's time,' Starkel said. 'They need to move the *Dreadnought* out. Now.'

'Right behind you.'

Starkel got four paces towards the lift before he stopped and turned. 'You're not coming, are you?'

Michael never lied. So he kept his mouth shut.

Starkel glanced at the lift again, then strode back to the central console. 'You're not dying alone.'

He called the Ankh. 'Push us out, we'll take it from there.'

The avatar appeared briefly. 'Make it count,' she said, then vanished.

'What can I do?' Michael asked.

'Put that on,' Starkel said, while readying the *Dreadnought* for one final sortie, pointing at a headband lying on a console. 'And stand on the disk.'

Michael donned the headband and stood on the grey circular plate on the floor. He'd seen Anya use it before, so had a rough idea how it worked. As soon as the headband was in place, he felt a tingling in his temples; he could see outside, the external view overlaid on his normal vision. He grasped two joysticks and tried them out; he spun clockwise then anti-clockwise with the disk. It made him a little queasy.

'Easy does it,' Starkel said, 'and don't fire yet; we're still inside the Pyramid.'

Michael moved his thumbs away from the buttons. 'The left button is the railgun?'

'Other left. Get ready. I'd say hold on, but the inertial dampers mean you won't feel anything. Your vision will get quite a rush, though.'

Michael continued to look forward as Starkel swung the *Dreadnought* around, once outside the Pyramid. They pointed directly into the fray. A criss-cross of beams awaited them. No way they wouldn't get hit.

'Where's the Crown of Thorns control?' Michael asked.

Starkel glanced at him sideways and cast him a rakish look. 'That one's mine.'

The ship edged towards the glimmering shield wall. Michael spun the disk one-eighty, and watched a Fronn Cuttleship limp inside the last Ankh Pyramid in the galaxy, followed by two of the remaining Tchlox Ringships. The giant bay doors closed.

'On my mark,' Starkel said. 'The Fronn will open a portal, and we'll zip through the shield, drawing heavy fire. Any direction you have in mind?'

Michael faced forward, and was about to say *no*, when his gaze was drawn to the planet.

'Hold on a second. Bring up the planet holo.'

'Michael, we have little –'

'Just do it, Starkel.'

He obliged. Hundreds of Axleth Destroyers rained nukes down on the planet, launched from their wings. Short-lived flashes of detonations pin-pricked the planet's surface, followed by red-hot, glowing rock fragments that spewed upwards and outwards. But the continents, pockmarked, scarred and gouged in places, were still intact, and they were moving fast, each one in opposing directions to its neighbour.

The avatar appeared again. 'Are you leaving or staying?'

'The Eye,' Michael said, pointing. 'It's doing something.'

All three watched for a moment, the Ankh no doubt using the Pyramid's vastly superior sensors. The dragonflies focused their attack on one particular continental ring, tracking it as it moved, carving out molten rock until they dented its crust and brought the ring to a stop. Bombing intensified, aided by cutter beams drilling downwards until dazzling white light burst through, as if there was a young star inside the planet. After re-grouping, the dragonflies began attacking another continental ring.

Something wasn't right. The scene was grainy. 'Can we clear up the image?' Michael asked.

'Allow me,' the avatar said.

The image raced outwards, their own last-stand fleet edging into view, with angry insects buzzing all around. The image pulled back further, and Michael touched the headband to deactivate it, to get a better look.

He wasn't sure how the image was formed. Then he recalled the Ankh had posted automated sentries further out when they'd first ventured inside the nebula.

What he saw was the nebula itself, the two box-like blue and scarlet ends, yellow where they joined in a tighter knot. It reminded him of an hourglass. But something was happening on a cosmic scale. It was as if the red and blue gas was filtering into the constricted mid-section, where they were, the hourglass emptying everything into its yellow waist. At this distance, the drift looked slow, but the actual speed must have been incredible.

'Do you know how stars form?' the avatar asked.

He didn't, and guessed he was about to get a lesson.

Starkel did, apparently. 'Gases in nebulae shift and move together, forming knots. When there is sufficient density... But it takes a very long time.'

'Normally,' the avatar said, zooming back into the yellow mid-section, back to the original view. 'The Eye's original function was environmental control of the planet, then the surrounding space, which is a star nursery. It has found a way to accelerate the star formation process. It has engineered a shortcut.'

'Wait,' Michael said. 'What are you saying? They're going to make a star form?' Isn't that going to release an insane amount of energy?

'Yes, insane sounds about right.'

The scene had upgraded from grainy to a hurricane, the space between them and the planet no longer black, instead flooded with sandstorms of red, blue and yellow. Michael reactivated the headband and zeroed in on the planet. Three of the continents' mantles had shattered. Nascent starlight seeped out.

'Don't the Axleth realize what's coming?' he asked.

'I believe they do,' the avatar replied. 'They aim to dismantle the planet, with the Eye inside, before it can trigger the star-forming process. But it is already building towards the critical threshold. We must leave. If it ignites, nothing here will survive. This whole sector will be scorched space. Only the newborn star will remain.'

Michael swivelled his disk. At least half the surrounding dragonflies broke off and rushed to join the attack on the planet.

'We have a chance to leave,' the avatar said.

But as he turned back, Michael spied something, almost by accident. A speck, flying straight up from the planet's surface.

'There!' he shouted. 'It's the *Athena*, has to be!'

Starkel zoomed in. Sure enough, it was. A dozen nearby dragonflies broke off their planetary excavation and set after it, opening fire.

'Open the shield,' Michael said.

The avatar looked at him. 'We cannot wait for you.'

'Then don't. Just open the damned shield.'

Starkel nodded his assent.

'Very well,' the avatar said. 'Good hunting.' She vanished.

A hole opened up before them, and Starkel punched the *Dreadnought* straight through, shooting them toward the *Athena* as it slowed, bathed in enemy fire.

Michael's thumbs hovered over the two buttons. Starkel pushed the engines to their limit. A deep bass grinding noise rose up from the bowels of the ship, mixed with the rattling of any equipment on the bridge that wasn't battened down. Despite what Starkel had said earlier about inertial dampers, Michael felt tugged backwards, as banks of future stardust and dragonfly ships rocketed past in the holofield. But he had a gut-twisting foreboding that he and Sally were finally out of time. Over the increasing din he shouted a single word.

'*Faster!*'

CHAPTER 25

Last Stand

Sally was dying. Her body still felt as if it was in the lake, though she knew she was physically in the med-lab, barely hanging on: pulse erratic, each breath shallow, catching in her throat as if it might be her last. She heard fragments around her, snatches of words. Alex and Lara, their voices taut, the concern coming through loud and clear. They fought valiantly to save her. But they were losing this battle. She caught the gist of the reasoning as Alex talked to Lara, bracing her for the inevitable: the neural damage had been progressive, leading to a cascade of systemic failures. Her organs were shutting down one by one. It was a miracle she'd survived this long.

'Should we call Nathan?' she heard Alex ask, and didn't hear a response from Lara. But it must have been negative. She hoped so. Nathan needed to be right where he was, in the Conn. He needed to stay focused.

And then it happened. A steady, high-pitched tone signified that her heart had flatlined, and her brainwaves were petering out. Alex thumped her chest. Lara gave her mouth-to-mouth. Alex attached electrodes and bellowed, '*Clear!*' All to no avail. Her body's time was up.

She'd heard apocryphal tales of near-death experiences

where you float above your body, see yourself on the slab: cold, still, lifeless, and maybe glimpse a light at the end of a tunnel, coming towards you. She had no desire to see herself that way. But she did see something. And she *felt* something. Something she shouldn't be able to feel. The *Athena*, the ship herself. Sally felt *Athena's* hull as if it was her skin, her sleek body being vomited up and out of the dark planet's oesophagus. She saw with *Athena's* sensors. A light at the end of a tunnel. Not apocryphal. Because even at this distance she knew it was cutter-beam fire. And *Athena's* circulatory system, the ever-moving grey and blue fissures... she could sense them, like a tingling all over her skin.

Ares, what have you done to me?

It made her dizzy at first. So much colour, so much information, more than a human brain could handle. It was like when you've been lying down and get up suddenly, and see bright blotches, except these were pixelated, rainbow clouds sculpted by a frenzied digital artist.

She no longer had a human brain.

The image cleared. She saw all around her, three-sixty degrees, in all directions, like a sphere – or an ellipsoid because of *Athena's* elongated shape. She would never be able to explain it to anyone, or even to herself; this ability to see everything around her all at once. And she knew that if she stopped seeing this way – if the *Athena* stopped letting her perceive this way – she'd not be able to remember what it felt like either. State-dependent-effect, she recalled from somewhere. When you are in an altered state, you perceive differently. But later, when normal again, you can't quite picture it. Like being drunk or high.

Only this was way better.

She – that is, the *Athena*, with six live humans and one fresh corpse in her belly – shot up the shaft like a bullet. She felt a frisson of connection with Jaspar, the pilot. *Athena* appreciated his skill, the way she'd heard that horses appreciated expert riders. *Athena* wasn't a personality, yet she

– yes, she, Sally decided – was more than just a machine. They spirited upwards from the planet's surface, now riven by volcanoes and lava, and bolted towards the last surviving Ankh Pyramid. For the first time, she had an inkling of how *Athena*'s navigation worked. It was as if *Athena* reached across space to the Pyramid, like drawing back a bow and aiming, and then... fired. *God, what a rush!* If only Jaspar could feel this!

Her spike of elation jack-knifed as she witnessed the obscene destruction, the thousands of defunct ships drifting in space amidst myriad corpses. With *Athena*'s ultra-keen senses, she had no way of suppressing the dreadful intel flooding her mind. She couldn't look away. There was no way to dampen the visceral horror of war, and she felt a rare pang for Ares, knowing that this was how he'd lived, never able to switch off from the darker side of organic species. Ares could never forget. And whereas with humans, time dulled the edges of bitter memories, with an AI that might never happen. How would such a mind judge humanity? And that very thought developed, so that she had a notion of why the Eye, also unable to switch off, might decide to eradicate organics once and for all.

And now she understood why the Eye had created the 'blueprint' Elodie had shown her, to never forget, to never trust organics again. It was the Eye's bible. A memorial in case any other sentient AI one day found it, aeons in the future. Except now it was being torn asunder by the Axleth. But the *Athena* had 'seen' it, and Sally realized that, like Ares, *Athena* could never forget. The ship had a record of the Eye's blueprint.

She felt a pinprick on her *Athena* body. Then another. Like being naked in a hailstorm, except that instead of ice, hot needles pricked her skin. They were taking heavy fire. She retreated to the lake. She'd never imagined she'd want to be back there. Alone now, no Elodie, not even the seedling for company. It didn't matter. This would soon be over. And with that, she turned her mind outwards and watched. There was nothing more she could do.

◆ ◆ ◆

Nathan had seen enough battles to know they were in serious trouble

'We can't take much more of this,' he said, affirming what everyone in the Conn already knew.

As soon as they exited the long tunnel to the planet's surface, a dozen Axleth Destroyers converged on their position. *Athena's* shields were strong, but they were bathed in amber fire. Jaspar gave up ducking and weaving – the Axleth targeting systems were unfoolable – and ploughed a straight course, aiming for the last armada stronghold, though that was no longer the right description.

Last stand was more apt.

Problem was, they weren't going to make it. Ahead of them a fresh wave of Destroyers waited, while behind them... The planet was a glowing, fractured sphere, starlight bursting from every fissure, while Axleth ships continued to bombard the planet. He glanced at a single number in the holo-display, which read 0.94. He didn't know, and would never live long enough to understand the maths underlying the figure, but what Christy had told him was that if it reached 1.0, a new star would form. The amount of energy unleashed would vaporize everything in this sector. As his dreaded father would have said, they were between the devil and the deep blue sea.

The indicator changed. *0.95.*

'Why are we slowing down?' he asked, turning to Jaspar.

Christy answered, because Jaspar was immersed, his shoulders tense, his face taut, in the zone.

'Two reasons. One, the energy beating down on us means *Athena* has to divert power to the shields, or we're toast.'

'Second reason?'

'There's no way through.'

'Why aren't we firing back?' Nathan persisted, guessing he wasn't helping.

'We are, Dad,' David answered. 'At least I am. But we're almost out, and our weapons aren't hurting them.'

His son leaned over his display, glimmers of light playing across his features. Abruptly, David sat back, raked his hands through his hair.

'That's it. We're out of ammo.'

'Maybe this will help,' Christy said, and the forward view of a dozen of the massive Destroyers blocking their path switched to the planet behind them, a sizzling ball of cracked continents, a whole world being eaten alive before their very eyes by hundreds of circling, voracious insects.

0.96

The planet shrank to half its former size, all cracks and fissures vanishing, the black and grey surface now a violent, molten red; like living, angry blood.

'Is that –' he began.

'Grab hold of something!' Christy shouted.

Nathan reached for the console, but the shockwave slammed into the *Athena* before he could get there, and he was flung across the Conn. Dazed, he stared towards the holo, which was still live. The *Athena* was spinning base over apex, but that wasn't all.

Jaspar stabilized the ship, and Nathan got to his feet and rubbed the back of his head.

'Is everyone okay?'

'You caught the worst of it,' David replied.

Nathan approached the image, as if to touch it, to know if it was real.

The shockwave had struck the Axleth fleet bombing the planet like a sledgehammer. Hundreds of dragonflies drifted, crushed or snapped apart, flashfires igniting then vanishing into the unforgiving coldness of space. Three of the Destroyers who'd been chasing the *Athena* were in bad shape and broke off pursuit, limping away out of firing range.

'Is that a star?' he asked, pointing at the seething, bloody planetary core.

'Not yet,' Christy answered. 'That was a precursor shockwave. The planet will go through one final contraction, and then will annihilate everything in the vicinity.'

'They've stopped bombing it,' Nathan said, noting the lack of any aggression towards the planet.

Lara and Alex arrived in the Conn. 'They're too late,' Lara said. 'I've been watching from down below. The star forming process can't be stopped now.'

As if to underline her point, the figure upped to 0.97.

'Jaspar?' Nathan said, ignoring the desperation he recognized in his own voice.

Jaspar's head was down, as he leaned over his console with straight arms, as if the console was the only thing keeping him standing.

'We're out of juice, I'm afraid.'

'And our shield is gone,' Christy added.

The holo shifted to a forward view again. *Athena's* prow was scarred, its once sleek, proud flesh pitted, burnt and blistered. Air vented from pockmarks in her skin, freezing into a solid ring of mist that drifted listlessly around her. He couldn't help but think it resembled a halo. The Destroyers ahead of them had stopped firing, but were holding position.

'They're powering up again,' Christy announced. 'The shockwave must have disabled their targeting systems, but only temporarily.'

'Don't they know when to run?' David asked.

'Vengeance blinds you,' Nathan replied. 'In the heat of battle, it can turn into rage. Then it consumes you. You just want to see the enemy die.'

'I don't suppose surrender is on the table?' Christy asked. 'Not that I'm sure I'd go for it,' she hastily added.

David answered. 'I don't think the Axleth "do" surrender.'

'How's Sally doing?' Nathan asked, to take his mind off their predicament.

When neither of the two women answered, he turned

and met Lara's unwavering gaze, saw the quiver in her lower lip, and he knew.

'We're out of time,' Christy shouted, as the lead Axleth Destroyer edged forward for the *coup de grâce*, its wings spread wide, the dozen cannons on each glowing a dull yellow that grew in intensity.

Nathan felt too shell-shocked to accept that Sally was gone, that after all they'd been through, Ares had failed to deliver on his promise. He reached across to Lara, and swept his gaze around the Conn, dwelling on each of their faces for a moment, ending on David's.

'I've never served with a finer crew,' he said.

The killing blow never came. David pointed, and Nathan turned to the holo.

Another ship, out of nowhere, tore into the pack of Destroyers, spinning, flailing scarlet lightning bolts that chainsawed the closest Destroyer clean in half.

The *Dreadnought* did an impossibly tight turn for such a large vessel, even though it was a fifth the size of the dragonflies, and aimed straight at the next enemy ship. Startled by this frenzied attack, the remaining Destroyers began scattering as another of their number was cleaved in two. Whoever was steering the ship was equally reckless and relentless, attacking from close quarters, knowing the dragonflies risked hitting each other if they opened fire. Which they did. The Crown of Thorns took out a third Axleth warship amidst a blitz of frantic cutter beams lancing out at the *Dreadnought*.

It was like watching a fox in a henhouse.

'We have power!' Jaspar cried out.

'Get us out of here,' Nathan said. 'Christy, hail whoever's on that ship!'

'Already on it.'

A Texan voice boomed into the Conn. 'Nathan, that you? How you holding up?'

'We're making a run for it.'

'Do that. We'll hold them off as long as we can.'

And with those words, Nathan's brief euphoria stalled, because he knew what it would cost Michael. Worse, if the *Dreadnought* even attempted to quit the fray, the dragonflies would have a clean line of fire. They'd blow it into tiny pieces then chase after the *Athena*.

'Shit,' he said.

The others looked to him one by one, their own momentary hope shattering as they got it, too.

He drew a line with his fingertips across his neck. Christy cut comms with the *Dreadnought*.

He turned to the holo, knowing Michael was driven to this extreme measure, sacrificing himself to save Sally, who was gone.

'Your call, Nathan,' Jaspar offered.

'Are you sure?' he replied.

'We all are,' Christy said. 'We're all with you, Nathan, whatever you decide.'

'What would Sally want you to do?' Lara asked him.

'But that's just it, isn't it? There's what Sally would *want* me to do, and there's what Sally would *actually* do.'

Lara squeezed his hand. 'Then give them a bloody nose.'

He regarded the holo. They'd almost escaped the skirmish, the *Dreadnought* still wreaking havoc, but now boxed-in, trapped in what was about to become a kill-zone.

'Bring us about, Captain,' Nathan said.

'Aye, sir.'

The *Athena* slewed in a tight arc, ending up facing the melee.

'Go for the strongest one,' Nathan said. 'Go for the head.'

But before they could move, an emerald wall jumped into view, occupying the entire screen; the side of a Pyramid ship. As it drove forwards, other ships appeared, encircling the tightening band of dragonflies, forming a net. Merciless green fire belched from the Pyramid, slicing through the lead Axleth ship like a sushi knife, while three Tchlox ships working in unison imploded one Destroyer after another. The Fronn took care of another two that tried to escape, melting their hulls until the horribly disfigured ships exploded.

Nathan watched the Axleth dragonflies being butchered, though in the end two got away. He caught Christy's eye, and she reconnected comms.

'Michael, you okay?' Nathan asked.

'Never better. Wasn't expecting the cavalry!'

'Why did they come? I thought they'd have left the system if they could have.'

'Me too. Hey, I saw the *Athena* turn around. You weren't thinking of doing something stupid, were you?'

'Of course not,' Nathan lied. 'What now?'

'Get inside the Pyramid, really fast. We're abandoning the *Dreadnought*. It's about to get very hot around here. And that's coming from a Texan!'

He'd almost forgotten. The figure. *0.98.*

Time to leave.

Jaspar didn't need telling. He barrelled the *Athena* into the Pyramid.

Nathan couldn't take his eyes off the figure – now at 0.99 – as other ships, shuttles and pods flooded in, including a duo-model Shuriken with Michael and Starkel aboard. The massive doors began to close. The Pyramid wasted no time and ripped away at dizzying speed. Nathan watched the angry red planet-about-to-become-star grow small and become a dot. And then the dot ballooned, as if they'd reversed course. He knew they hadn't. Stark light flooded in through the last crack before the doors sealed, and everything around them shook violently, lights dimming, the holo stuttering and going offline, everyone in the Conn and probably everyone throughout the Pyramid holding their collective breath to see if they would survive or not.

It lasted ten full minutes, the Pyramid staying just ahead of the scalding shockwave.

The shaking eased off. The lights came back to their

normal intensity.

Nobody spoke for a while, everyone listening, until Jaspar announced, 'We made it! We're safe now.'

'The Axleth ships didn't,' Christy added. 'They're gone. Every last one of them.'

Nathan couldn't believe it. His heart refused to stop thumping. 'Any chance of a viewscreen?'

Christy fiddled with her console, and the nebula appeared inside the Conn, a bright white pinprick where they'd just been, inside the yellow section. Aside from the new star's brightness, the nebula looked the same as it had when they'd arrived. Funny, a cataclysmic war between a dozen top species and the ultimate machine, and the galaxy just took it in its stride.

'We actually won?' he said.

Lara went over to David's console, bent over and rustled inside a compartment. She stood up, brandishing a bottle of amber fluid.

Nathan folded his arms. 'All this time, you kept that in the Conn?'

She shrugged. 'What can I say, I'm an optimist. A glass half full girl. Speaking of which, the glasses have seen better days, I'm afraid.'

He took it from her, opened it, inhaled the wood-smoked aroma, and took two swigs. The bottle did the rounds. Lara came over next to Nathan and sat on his lap, nestling her head in his shoulder.

'I think I've had enough adventure for a while,' she said.

David joined them, his arms draping around them both. Jaspar strode over to Christy and embraced her.

'About time,' Lara whispered.

Alex, quiet until now, asked the inevitable question. 'What happens next?'

'We catch our breath,' Nathan said.

Christy extracted herself as something pinged on her console. She cleared her throat.

'We can disembark. There's a pocket of atmosphere for us, if we stay within a certain boundary.'

'Let's all go outside together,' Lara said, sealing the bottle and parking it on David's console.

But Nathan didn't move. He pondered Alex's question. Truth was, he'd never really made it this far. Whenever a war was declared over, soldiers just took a break until the next one broke out, which rarely took long.

'We need to build a home,' he said. 'A new one with the Axels. We can't go back to Earth. We're on our own now.'

'Maybe not,' David said. 'We fought side by side – pretty much – with a host of different species. War brings soldiers together, doesn't it? Brothers in arms.' David faced his father. 'You, Fisher, Braxton, even Ares, you brought us together all those years ago. Made us... not just a team, but a family. Maybe it's time to apply the same idea, only think a little bigger. Well, a lot bigger, I guess.'

Nathan stared at his son. Michael had said something to him a while back, when they'd been alone with Sally. What was it? That we needed to learn from our kids. He was dead right.

Nathan got up.

'Michael is already out there,' Christy announced. 'With Starkel.'

Nathan steeled himself. He was about to be the bearer of the worst news.

Michael and Starkel weren't alone. A rusty orange humanoid was with them.

'I'm an avatar of the Ankh,' the orange-scaled being said to Nathan.

'Thanks for saving us,' Nathan said. 'Why did you, by the way?'

'Your ship recorded the blueprint,' she replied.

'The what?' Then he remembered. The carvings on the

inside of the planet's shell. Lara had called it a blueprint, and Ares had confirmed as much. So, the *Athena* must have recorded it as they circled the inner moon. But how did the Ankh know they had it? More importantly, why did they want it?

'You wanted to destroy the Eye,' Nathan said. 'What are you going to do with the blueprint? Surely you don't want to bring it to life again?'

The avatar smiled. 'Absolutely not. On that point, we are all agreed. But we wish to understand it, in case one day it, or an alternate version, arises again. We want to develop... an antidote. Besides,' the avatar said, then held her hands apart as if holding a ball. An image appeared. It was the star forming, but slowed down a hundredfold. Something small zipped out from the imploding planet and then vanished.

The avatar collapsed the image. 'Something escaped, after all. Whatever it was, it opened up a small, short-lived wormhole – a trick we'd very much like to understand – and left the galaxy. There's no trace of the ship, its occupant if it had one, nor of the 'single use' wormhole.'

Nathan stared at where the image had been. The object had been silver... He recalled the Ares-shaped mould by the silver lake. *Had the Eye merged with Ares, then escaped?*

He reckoned they'd never know for sure.

He was out of his depth again. This was all above his paygrade. In any case, he had another task. One he'd been putting off and could delay no longer. He stared towards Michael. He needed to give him the heartbreakingly bad news.

'Actually, you don't,' the avatar said. 'You forgot to ask us how we knew about the blueprint. *She* told us,' the avatar said, pointing.

Nonplussed, he turned back to the ramp, as a figure appeared at the top, and all the various conversations around him fell off a cliff. Earlier, his heart had been pounding. Now it slowed to the point of stopping.

Because it was Sally. And it also wasn't Sally, at least not anymore. Her skin was platinum, her eyes China blue.

'Nathan,' she said, and he bounded toward the ramp and up it, then stopped short, to take in what she was, what she had become, what Ares had become.

'Is it you?' he asked.

'Pretty much,' she said, lifting her flow-metal arms, turning them one way then the other, looking at them, feeling them. 'Ares sacrificed himself to bring me back. He came to see me before the end, thanked me for saving his life, for donating my neural pathways, but said that the loan had only been temporary.' She looked crestfallen. 'I... I still have a few of his memories. It's like he's not completely gone.'

Michael arrived next to Nathan.

'But it's still you?' Nathan asked again.

'Do you recall when we first met? You were taking out money, and I snuck a look at your pin code. You called me a–'

'Smartass,' he finished.

'Well, I'm even smarter now.' She grinned, that same cheeky way she had all those years ago.

It was Sally alright.

Michael pushed past Nathan and enveloped Sally in an embrace, and as he held her tight, Sally opened her eyes briefly and met with Nathan's, and mouthed the words: *We did it.*

After a full minute, he tapped Michael on the shoulder.

'My turn,' he said, and held Sally tight in his arms, never wanting to let her go.

Nathan and Sally sat together at the bottom of the ramp. Lara was with Alex and Starkel back in the ship, Christy and Jaspar were... well, where they were was anyone's guess. Michael and David were in deep discussion with the Ankh avatar. Even from this distance, Michael's enthusiasm was evident.

'He's sold on David's idea,' Nathan said.

'I hope so. We need allies, Nathan. Hell, I don't need to

tell you that. And now's the best time.'

'The other species are still licking their wounds. They want to go back to their homeworlds.'

She gazed at him; still the damaged soldier, no place he could ever call home. Well, this time, she and the others would fix that.

'It has to be now,' she said. 'Form an alliance, hammer out an agreement. Every alien's worldview, or galactic view, just got larger. There's no going back to how it used to be. Not after this.'

He didn't look convinced.

'You don't see it happening, do you?'

He shook his head. 'I've heard too many noble speeches, seen good intentions turn to dust.'

'What if there was a project to unite them?'

That got his attention. 'Project?'

She took a breath. She had to tell him – and all the others – sooner or later. Sooner, then.

'The deal we made with the Eye... Ares wanted my agreement.' She swallowed. This wasn't easy. 'I was prepared to die, Nathan. And I'd rather have died than save my skin alone, letting the Eye go off and wreak havoc somewhere else.'

Nathan spoke with a tenderness she'd almost forgotten. God, she'd missed him.

'What changed your mind?' he asked.

The Ankh avatar was suddenly there, Michael and David trailing behind her, looking a little confused. 'Is it true?' the avatar asked, her voice urgent, her eyes wide.

Sally nodded. 'The Eye gave Ares the specs for the wormhole in return for his surrender. I have them.' She raised her hands as everyone began speaking. 'Don't get too excited. The Eye's wormhole tech isn't suitable for organics, and it's going to take fifty years to build the first prototype.' She stood up. 'It will need most of the species to work together to make it happen.'

'For this,' the avatar said, her eyes smiling, 'they *will*

work together.'

'But if it won't allow organics to pass through it,' David began.

'It's for you, Sally, isn't it?' Michael said quietly, cutting everyone else off.

Sally nodded, staring at the floor. 'I'm not organic anymore. I can go back. I can... save Earth.' She looked up, met Michael's eyes, and lifted a platinum hand towards him. 'We'll still have fifty years.'

He took it. 'Fifty years? I'll take it, especially as less than an hour ago, I thought I was dead meat. Platinum suits you, by the way.'

The avatar stepped in. 'We need to talk to the other species right now. One or two are already preparing to take their leave.'

'I'll do it,' Michael said. 'Hell, I've studied enough speeches. I'm sure I can cobble something together.'

'I'll come, too,' David said.

The avatar held her orange hand out to Sally, who shook it. 'A wild card indeed. Humanity is one to watch.'

The trio left Nathan and Sally alone again.

'You really think you can save Earth?' Nathan asked.

'Ares talked to the Tchlox before he... Yes, it will work.'

He studied her. 'It's a one-way trip, isn't it?'

She nodded. 'But the data the other species will get from it means they can go on to build a better one that can transport people, aliens, whoever. Might take a couple of centuries, but just imagine. The galaxy will get a lot smaller. Humans could travel here from Earth one day.'

Nathan stood up. 'Then we'd better build a world worth visiting.'

Sally rose and took his hand. 'Let's go find the others,' she said, and they walked hand in hand up the ramp into the Athena.

EPILOGUE

Sally ran her fingers along the sleek hull of her modified Stinger, lingering over the callsign stencilled just below the cockpit hatch. An officer from the bridge of the Resolute, the latest Axel-human-Korg explorer vessel, informed her all was ready; she could depart at her discretion. She'd asked for no ceremony, no one to be present when she quit this part of the galaxy, though many would be watching, including the resident Ankh, Theon and Syrn contingents on Phoenix, their collective home these past fifty years. After all, she was about to enter the newly constructed wormhole and travel back to Earth's neighbourhood.

It was a one-way trip, because it was based on the Eye's design, which meant nothing organic would survive the journey. Not a problem for her, of course. Her gaze dipped to the Tchlox missile slung underneath the Stinger's hull. They'd assured her it would do the job and neutralize the mini black hole threatening Earth – the 'black sun', as Lara had always called it.

The bay doors opened to space, and she gazed through the forcefield, picking out the bright dot that had been her sun this past half century. She'd said her goodbyes yesterday, to David, now an agile septuagenarian, and Jaspar, Christy and the grandkids. And the other goodbyes, of course, up on Matheson Hill: Nathan, Lara, and the recently departed Michael. She caught herself. Ares had told her that in this new form she'd never be able to shed a tear.

He'd been wrong.

She wondered, as ever, if anything of Ares had survived when the Eye fled to another galaxy, and if he'd been able to influence the Eye for the better. Maybe one day, in the far distant future, beyond even her extended lifespan, they'd find out.

She climbed up into the cockpit. The canopy slid over her, and she felt the instant mental connection to the Stinger's control system. She eased her single pilot craft out into space and headed for the glistening marble.

Someone broke protocol and sent a message.

'Good luck, Sally. Tell the people of Earth we'll be seeing them soon, and that we've made some new friends.'

David, of course. Well, he was president, after all. She sent a silent acknowledgment and accelerated.

Humans are collections of memories, Ares had once said to her, when she'd been a teenager back in the original *Athena*. And later, before his surrender to the Eye, he'd warned her that her own memory would become infallible, as his had been. She would remember everything, for better or for worse. A blessing and a curse, he'd said. Right now, it was the former. She called into her mind, with crystal clarity, Nathan, Lara, Michael, and a host of others who'd been on this incredible journey with her.

The marble grew large, and she glimpsed Saturn's rings amongst flickering, heavily lensed images from the other side, two thousand light years distant.

It was time.

'We're going home,' she said, and swung the *Elodie* into the gaping throat of the wormhole.

BOOKS BY THIS AUTHOR

When The Children Come

Nathan, emotionally scarred after three tours in Afghanistan, lives alone in Manhattan until New Year's Eve, when he meets Lara. The next morning, he notices that something odd is going on – a terrified kid is being pursued by his father. A young girl, Sally, pleads with Nathan to hide her from her parents. There is no internet, no television, no phone coverage. Nathan, Lara and Sally flee along the East Coast, encountering madmen, terrorists, the armed forces, and other children frightened for their lives. The only thing Nathan knows for sure is that he must not fall asleep...

"Kirwan lights the fuse on a new SF series...action-adventure and dark-edged SF that will enthrall readers." – Kirkus Reviews

When The Children Return

A decade ago, ten-year-old Sally watched helplessly as the brutal Axleth invaded Earth. She and a few hundred others escaped aboard the spaceship Athena, piloted by the secretive Artificial Intelligence who calls himself Ares. Now, as they approach Earth, she leads her fearless band of refugees determined to take back their home at any cost.

But much has changed on Earth. Finding allies willing to rise up against the Axleth stranglehold will be difficult. And as they near the Solar System, the Athena is tracked and attacked by an enemy ship. Something has followed them from the depths of space.

As war erupts on Earth, Sally's small army must show more courage than they knew they possessed, and Sally herself must come to terms with what it truly means to be a battle commander, and decide exactly how much she is willing to sacrifice to win back her planet.

★ ★ ★ ★ ★ "The first book was amazing, this one is incredible!" Jessica Belmont

★ ★ ★ ★ ★ "Fast-moving, epic, realistic characters and stellar writing!" Felicia Denise

The Eden Paradox

In 2063, Earth's overheated climate and war-ravaged cities are near breaking point. A new habitable planet is discovered within reach, but the first two missions have failed to return. This is the story of the third mission to Eden.

What really awaits the crew of four as they make the long journey to this supposed uninhabited virgin planet, and what is the link to the secret 900 year old sect known as Alicians back on Earth? While Blake leads the Eden mission, a young researcher named Micah discovers a terrible truth that threatens the very existence of humanity.

"This author should win the HUGO award for producing the best science fiction I have read in the last thirty years." Susan Yea

Eden's Trial

How would we fare if humanity was put on trial, judged by

superior alien races?

Survivors are fleeing Earth, into a hostile galaxy where alien intelligence and weaponry rule. Can a deserted planet offer refuge? Or will the genetically engineered Alicians finish the job started on Eden. While Blake fends off attacks, Micah seeks allies, but his plan backfires, and humanity finds itself on trial for its very right to exist.

"It's hard to put down Mr. Kirwan's book, but at the same time you don't want to race ahead but savor the complexities of personalities and the well crafted story line." Lydia Manx, Piker Press.

Eden's Revenge

In a galactic war where worlds fall every day, how will humanity defend its last refuge?

After eighteen years, the quarantine that has protected humanity's survivors on the planet Esperia is about to end. Mankind won't stand a chance without external help. Yet in the middle of a galactic war, who is concerned about one small planet when worlds fall every day? Eden's Revenge is the heart-stopping third episode in the Eden Paradox series.

"An interesting but simple idea turns into mega galaxy-spanning wonder as this series progresses!" Vine Voice

Eden's Endgame

To save the galaxy, an ancient machine race that almost extinguished all known life two million years ago must be awakened....

This stunning fourth and final book in the Eden Paradox series

—which includes The Eden Paradox, Eden's Trial, and Eden's Revenge—sees mankind's finest, aided by an enigmatic race of creatures and an ancient artifact, pushed to their absolute limits in their efforts to save not only humanity, but the galaxy itself.

★ ★ ★ ★ ★ "Superb series, top quality scifi!" Jfmdac, UK

★ ★ ★ ★ ★ "An emotional rollercoaster across four books. Quite a number of the characters don't make it through. I think my heart broke numerous times!" Lindsey, UK

★ ★ ★ ★ ★ "I felt like I was among the stars and aliens with every chapter to the very end!! I was totally immersed!" Sandy Butler.

★ ★ ★ ★ ★ "Best science fiction series I have read. It's Lord of the Rings, Foundation Empire, Game of Thrones, Westworld and Star Wars. Funny, serious, emotional and mind-blowing!" Myma, US

66 Metres

The only thing worth killing for is family.

Everyone said she had her father's eyes. A killer's eyes. Nadia knew that on the bitterly cold streets of Moscow, she could never escape her past – but in just a few days, she would finally be free.

Bound to work for Kadinsky for five years, she has just one last mission to complete. Yet when she is instructed to capture The Rose, a military weapon shrouded in secrecy, Nadia finds herself trapped in a deadly game of global espionage.

And the only man she can trust is the one sent to spy on her...

'Masterfully paced...a cinematic and action-packed read that will have readers following Nadia to the ends of the Earth!' – BestThrillers.com

37 Hours

After two long years spent in a secret British prison, Nadia Laksheva is suddenly granted her freedom. Yet there is a dangerous price to pay for her release: she must retrieve the Russian nuclear warhead stolen by her deadliest enemy, a powerful and ruthless terrorist known only as The Client.

But her mysterious nemesis is always one step ahead and the clock is ticking. In 37 hours, the warhead will explode, reducing the city of London to a pile of ash. Only this time, Nadia is prepared to pull the trigger at any cost...

The deadly trail will take her from crowded Moscow to the silent streets of Chernobyl, but will Nadia find what she is looking for before the clock hits zero?

★ ★ ★ ★ ★ Eden was good, but Nadia will be personal!

★ ★ ★ ★ ★ Nadia's intrepidity, her skill, her wry humour shine through J.F. Kirwan's lean, dynamic prose.

88 North

As the radiation poisoning that Nadia Laksheva was exposed to in Chernobyl takes hold of her body, she knows she has mere weeks to live. But Salamander, the terrorist who murdered her father and sister has a deadly new plan to 'make the sky bleed'. Nadia is determined to stop him again, even if it is the last thing she ever does.

The only clue she has are the coordinates 88° North, a ridge in the Arctic right above one of the largest oil fields in the world, three thousand metres below the ice. If Salamander takes hold of the oil field, he could change the climate of the whole planet for generations to come…

But can Nadia stop him before her own time runs out?

★ ★ ★ ★ ★ A perfect ending for a heart-pounding trilogy!

★ ★ ★ ★ ★ I had to put it down so it would last longer…

The Dead Tell Lies

What happens when the hunter becomes the prey?

Greg Adams, a criminal psychologist at Scotland Yard, specialises in bringing serial killers to justice. He is at the top of his game, having just put away his sixth serial killer when his wife, Kate, is brutally murdered by another predator known as the Dreamer.

A year later, unable to bring the killer to justice, Greg has quit his job and is ready to end it all, when he receives a phone call from a man who tells him the Dreamer is dead, and that he didn't kill Kate. Greg returns to Scotland Yard to work for Superintendent Chief Detective Donaldson in the hope he can re-examine the case with the help of two new detectives.

As Greg delves into the case further, he becomes more convinced that the Dreamer wasn't the man responsible for his wife's murder. But if it wasn't The Dreamer, who was it?

In order to solve the mystery around his wife's murder, Greg is going to have to delve even deeper into the mind of a terrifying psychopath. And this time he might not make it back in one piece...

"Packed full of action and there is never a dull moment. It's easy to pick up but impossible to put down once you are in the thick of the narrative and dying to know what happens next."
—ReviewsFeed

ACKNOWLEDGEMENT

A huge thanks to Andy and Beatrice, my two trusty readers, awesome editor Amanda Rutter, my faithful and excellent copy-editor Loulou, and cover artist extraordinaire Suman Chakraborty. And thanks to all my readers who took a chance on this series.

ABOUT THE AUTHOR

Barry Kirwan

Barry Kirwan is the author of the acclaimed Eden Paradox scifi series, and author of four thrillers under the pen name J F Kirwan. He was born in Farnborough, England, home to the fast-jet Red Arrows. He has worked on the safety of nuclear power plants, offshore oil and gas platforms, and more recently in aviation, and publishes non-fiction in the safety arena. He lives just outside  Paris, and loves scuba diving. His spaceship is usually parked at:

https://.facebook.com/EdenParadox
www.barrykirwan.com

Printed in Great Britain
by Amazon

23831645R00195